ASSASSIN'S APPRENTICE

THE BOOK OF BAWB 2

SCOTT BARON

Print Editions:

ISBN 978-1-945996-70-2 Paperback

ISBN 978-1-945996-71-9 Hardcover

Cover by Jeff Brown

"Do any men grow up or do they only come of age?"
~Stephen King~

CHAPTER ONE

Blood was dripping in a steady stream from Bawb's head, flowing off his chin in a crimson waterfall of sorts. He merely gritted his teeth and waited his turn. The few others also waiting were far worse off than he was and needed to be tended to before him. This was not the first time he would bleed, and it would certainly not be the last.

He was sitting quietly just outside the healer's chamber with several of his likewise-injured classmates. No one was safe from injury in the Ghalian training house, and this chamber in particular was one they had all come to know well as they moved up in the ranks from the greenest of the green all the way to where they found themselves now.

Vessels, in Bawb's class's case, each and every one of them. And after much blood and sweat, they were nearly ready to advance to the level of Adept. Soon they would be sent out on missions alone as Wampeh Ghalian, albeit of the lower ranks.

Naturally, they would be directed toward missions fitting their areas of proficiency at first, the early tasks tailored to their individual skills. But as they progressed, and once they each showed a solid grasp of their own unique fighting styles they were now creating, only then would they be allowed out on more dangerous contracts.

They had come far and excelled, but it had been a long, hard, and deadly road.

Of course, being a teenager was tough on any world. Growth spurts, hormones, and the usual drama that teens tended to find themselves ensnared in were all things one could expect at that age. Most teens, however, did not experience what the Vessels were going through, nor could they begin to fathom the difficulties they faced.

Their resilient bones were growing longer and stronger, while their body mass was simultaneously thickening with wiry muscles forged in the fires of hard work. Wampeh were a hardy race to begin with, but the intense Ghalian training molded them into fit and agile works of art.

They still had several years remaining in the Wampeh growth cycle, but their bodies had already taken on the basic form they would possess for the rest of their lives. Some were wiry, others stocky. Some rounder while others lean. But one thing was universal among them. They were all willing and able to carry out their dangerous tasks without fear their bodies might fail them.

Years upon years of training and hard work had earned them as much, and they were tough, possessing ever-growing confidence. They were good. Better than that, they were beginning to truly believe themselves to actually be *skilled*.

But this? This was a disconcerting reminder that, no matter how much they had learned, they still had a *very* long way to go. The day had not begun easily, and it would only get worse.

During breakfast they were summoned by Teacher Griggitz and directed to stand outside a new chamber they had not yet trained in. They were then called in individually. Beyond that, none knew what the teachers wanted of them. They would, as always, find out soon enough.

The Vessels were each gone a fairly long time, eventually exiting in turn. Teacher Griggitz had sent them one by one on their way to the healer, a group of lower-ranked aides helping when needed. Whatever challenge was awaiting them, it was unexpected, as was the norm with their instructors, but this was also clearly not insignificant. It made for an unsettling situation, and as their classmates were hauled out in various states of agony, it only got worse for those still waiting their turn.

Elzina had long been Bawb's de facto nemesis as the two jostled for rank as they grew. She was a fierce girl and had an impressive level of drive that bordered on excessive. She fought hard and never gave up, but just like the others, she was soon carried out on a floating litter, battered and bloody, her left arm jutting out at an angle it was not meant to bend. Her nose was broken, and her face was swollen, her lip split and trickling blood.

She glanced at the others with dazed eyes but said nothing as she was brought into the healer's chambers, just like the others.

"She's one of the best of us," Zota said in shock, notably disquieted despite his training.

"That is the fourth," Usalla added, shaking her head, her tightly woven braids moving slightly though still tucked away and prepared for a fight. "This does not bode well for us."

"Not well at all," Finnia agreed, wondering if her spy training path might afford her any respite from the challenge.

Likely not.

This was a test. A test each of them would have to face, regardless of their particular area of proficiency or class rank. And so far, none had succeeded. Worst of all, those still waiting had no idea what it entailed. All they knew was that one by one they were called, and one by one they returned in varying states of bloodiness.

"Bawb. You are next," Teacher Griggitz said, then turned and walked back into the chamber.

Bawb would follow, of course. They all would.

"See you soon," the boy said, then rose from his seat and left.

Zota shook his head with a hint of concern, something normally unbecoming a Ghalian. "I do not like this."

Usalla nodded somberly. "None of us do. But it is the way."

As they sat wondering what might lie in store for them, Bawb was finding out firsthand.

"In here," Griggitz said, leading him through the new chamber and into a small room. "All you require for this task is present here."

Bawb looked around, taking in the items present. A few he would have expected were notably not present.

"There appear to be no weapons."

"That is correct. You are to infiltrate a tavern in town. A rough, dangerous place, as I am sure you have surmised by now."

"I have."

"Then you also realize the risk you face. You are to blend in, then find Teacher Demelza in the mix and hand her this," he said, giving him a plain wooden token with a basic symbol burned into it. "If you can accomplish that, you will have succeeded in this task."

"Magic?" he asked.

"You may attempt to use your konus to aid in your disguise, but be advised, you are still a Vessel, and your casting has a long way to go yet. You may do more harm than good. But that decision is yours to make. You are no longer a child. I will now leave you to it. All you require to fashion a disguise is here.

When you are ready, head to the Rusty Kettle. You know the location, yes?"

Bawb, like all the other students, had memorized every street, alley, shop, and tavern in the city over the last few years. It was one thing to quickly adapt on the fly in a new situation, but on their home turf, they were expected to excel. To be better than just good.

"I know it," he replied, then immediately turned his attention to the wares spread out before him.

Griggitz nodded and left him to prepare. He would be situated near the tavern to collect him if things went wrong. And by the looks of Elzina and the others as they were carried home, there was a real likelihood that would be the case.

Bawb wasted no time, opting for a simple coloration spell to alter his skin tone to a light brown rather than the Wampeh's natural pale complexion. That was a spell he was actually becoming quite good at. The other disguise spells, however, were still somewhat lacking.

He used practical appliances to further change his appearance, giving his body additional bulk under his clothing and the semblance of a more muscular build. It wouldn't hold up to close inspection, but it might convince an aggressive interloper to just leave him alone.

Or not.

Some people sought out the more challenging adversaries in hopes of making a name for themselves. He just hoped that would not be the case today. He had to get in, find his zaftig teacher, and get out. The fact that the others to go before him were beaten so badly led him to believe this task would not be so simple.

Bawb noted a small bag of coin on the table and pocketed it. Griggitz had said everything was for his use, and he decided that applied to currency as well. The goodwill a round of drinks could purchase could often calm a rowdy crowd. At least, Master Hozark had told him as much, and had demonstrated in person on a few of their outings as well.

Bawb examined himself in the mirror spell. It wasn't perfect, and he was unarmed, but it would have to suffice.

Not bad, his konus said, the magical band on his wrist having developed even more of a personality in the years he had been wearing it. *Maybe you'll even make it out of this unscathed.*

"You think so?"

No, the device scoffed. *You're pretty much screwed and in for it like the rest, I'd wager.*

"We shall see about that, Konus."

Oh, of that I'm certain.

The device, a gift from Master Hozark himself, had a tendency to give him grief just before a challenging task, but Bawb had learned that this was just something it did when he might actually have a chance to level up in a skill. Sowing doubt and making him work harder for it, as the case may be.

But he had leveled up in many areas since he first received the device, and the icon list, visible only to his eyes, had slowly but steadily been unblurring new skills and levels as he progressed. He wasn't a Master, not by a long shot. Not even a Mavin or an Adept. But he was getting there. It would just take time.

Bawb took one last look at himself. "As ready as I'll be."

It was a short walk to the Rusty Kettle, a path he knew well. This explained how the others had been returned to the training house so soon after their failures. The teachers had selected a location close to their healer. Rather than making him worry, this only strengthened Bawb's resolve.

He strode into the tavern, cock-sure and full of confidence, exactly the attitude he would need to project lest he otherwise be perceived as an easy target. A few heads turned to look at him, but most just carried on with their discussions and drinks.

As was the case on this world, all manner of races were present, but not a Wampeh among them. He knew that wasn't actually the case since Demelza was here somewhere. And knowing the Order, they had a few other Ghalian lurking around as well. But they were all Masters, and their disguises, magical or practical, were so expertly applied, he would be unable to discern which was which.

He would have to use more than a simple reveal spell here. He would have to use what he knew of the target.

Teacher Demelza was a sturdily built woman. Curvy and strong. She was also among the best of them at disguises of all sorts. She could appear as male, female, or even another species entirely if she wanted to, but there were a few aspects that she had a somewhat harder time disguising. Her ample bosom was one of them.

Surprisingly, there were a number of people present fitting that description. A large man with yellow-brown skin caught his attention initially. A violet-skinned woman with her cleavage on display was also quite notable, drawing the attention of many in the tavern. All manner of races were present, many that could conceal her true form. This would not be easy.

Bawb ordered a drink and walked the tavern, greeting those who seemed in a cheerful mood, buying them drinks and creating a somewhat safe bubble from which he could move and observe. He was not rushing this. He would have to be absolutely sure which one was her before he made his move. Elzina was as good as he was. Better, if he was being honest about it, and she had still failed at this task. Miserably at that. Bawb needed to think like she thought, then shift course where she went wrong.

If he could figure it out in time, that is.

He spent a short while making rounds of the tavern, taking note of the busty women and burly men of all races who most closely fit Demelza's description.

"That has to be her," he mused, his confidence in one woman in particular being his disguised teacher growing with every glance.

She was ignoring him, of course, paying attention to the two brutish Tslavar mercenaries she was talking to. By the look of them, that was likely how Elzina had taken a beating. She'd interfered with the green-skinned men's advances and reaped the whirlwind.

Bawb walked toward her, planning how he would buy a round for the two men, pretending to know them from some trading excursion while ignoring the woman entirely. If it worked, his lack of interest in her would at least put them somewhat at ease. From there he could casually adjust course and hand her the token, ending the exercise.

He walked closer, a growing confidence in his plan, when a sense of unease tingled through his body, making the fine hair on the back of his neck rise. Something was not right. He looked at the woman closely and felt a twinge in his gut. His peripheral vision caught movement. Movement that just didn't seem right.

Misdirection was one of the Ghalian's favorite tricks, and he was walking right into it. He trusted his gut and threw himself aside, rolling hard into a group of revelers as a powerful kick swished through the air where he had just been standing.

"Watch it!" one of them growled, shoving him into an oncoming punch.

Bawb blocked most of the blow's force but still took a hit, spinning away as best he could as more attacks rained down on him.

Training kicked in without him having to think about it. He blocked and countered, lunging into an attack of his own, landing a solid elbow to the wiry man charging him, stunning him but not quite dropping him.

Some longed for a brawl and were always looking for an excuse. As such, two others joined in, the fight suddenly shifting to a very outnumbered and unbalanced attack.

Bawb blocked and fought, adjusting his style as fast as he could, shifting and flowing around the very different fighting styles being used against him. He recognized them, having trained at least a bit in each, but combined and overlapping, they were just too fast. Too strong.

Bawb saw two of the attackers moving to pin him in an overlapped attack, the nearest throwing a powerful punch.

He feigned a block but instead ran right into the blow, absorbing it with a painful grunt but also using the momentum to pivot his body around the meaty fist, leveraging his forehead into the attacker's nose with a sickening crunch.

The man staggered back, blood pouring out of his nose. Bawb's own head was ringing from the impact, but he carried on, spinning hard, his foot swinging high, the heel catching the other attacker on the jaw. Bawb knew he was going to wind up on the ground, but he was damned if he wasn't going to at least land a few good shots first.

A solid kick caught him in the ribs, sending him sliding into a stool, upending the large man atop it, his mass pinning the boy to the ground momentarily. Bawb was stuck. Defenseless. This was where he lost. He clenched his teeth, waiting for the flurry of blows that never came.

"Not bad, Vessel Bawb," the barrel-chested man with yellow-brown skin and dirty dishwater-colored eyes said, reaching down and offering him a hand.

He looked around. The other attackers had gone back to their places, though the one with the broken nose was busy applying a healing spell to set the bone back in place and stanch the bleeding.

"Teacher Demelza?" he asked, taking the large, dirt-stained hand.

"You performed above your usual abilities," she said, speaking in her own voice but not shedding her disguise.

"Out of necessity."

"Yes, but nevertheless, you adapted and improvised admirably. But tell me, you were about to approach the woman over there. Why did you stop?"

"She looks too much like I would expect you to look if you were in disguise. But that was all wrong. It is what you have taught us since the beginning. Misdirection is a great tool in our arsenal, and naturally, the person who most closely resembled you in form would be a decoy."

Demelza nodded, a grin flashing her yellow-stained teeth. It really was a disgusting disguise, and very effective, he had to admit.

"Well done, Bawb."

"Not well enough, though."

"In what way are you not satisfied with your performance? You did better than the others we have seen thus far."

"There was more to the lesson, and I only realized that too late. The unspoken part. I was to find you, but I had seen the others return bloodied. Clearly there was an adversary here to slow my progress. My mistake was expecting only one. And when I saw two, I adjusted accordingly. But there were three. I should have been more alert."

She nodded her approval of his assessment. "Very astute. Yet, you speak freely of these things. Is that not against our way?"

Bawb looked around at the crowd and shook his head. "As do you," he said with a knowing grin creeping to his lips. "In fact, I would wager every last person here is of our order."

Heads turned, approving nods cast his way before the patrons went back to their performances.

Level up: threat assessment and disguise detection, the konus said. *For once. Not bad, Vessel.*

Demelza put her hand on his shoulder and walked him to the door. "You are but a Vessel, Bawb. Do not be too hard on yourself. The others did not make it as far as you did, and none of them identified that all present are Ghalian. Your magic is still weak, but we will work on that as well as your practical disguise techniques. That is the purpose of this lesson. To drive home what you must learn in a manner you will not forget."

"I will certainly not."

"I would expect no less of you. Do not be down on yourself. You have performed well."

"Thank you, Teacher."

"Now, go clean up. You still have a long day of training ahead of you, though you will have a bit of a break while waiting for the others' injuries to be healed."

He stepped outside, still walking on his own two feet, bloody and beaten, but not badly, much to Griggitz's surprise.

"I am ready to return if you are," Bawb said, holding back his grin.

Griggitz, normally stoic and gruff, let out a rare chuckle. "You are surprising, Bawb. And in good shape, I see."

"Thank you. I—"

"That means you will have your wounds repaired quickly. After, you can run laps while the others are healing up. Come on, now. Back we go."

Bawb followed, not looking forward to the run, but glad he was intact enough to do so. If Demelza's words were true, and they always were, it would be a busy day indeed.

CHAPTER TWO

The battered, beaten, and subsequently healed Vessels jogged as a group to the afternoon's lesson in the largest of the third subterranean level's training chambers. All had made the trek together after having their hurt mended. All but Bawb.

To their surprise, he was already there, sweaty and breathing hard.

"Where have you been?" Albinius asked.

"Laps," he said, nodding to the vast distance around the chamber.

Usalla cocked her head slightly as she assessed her friend's minor injuries. "I did not see you at the healer's, yet you still show signs of bruising. What happened?"

"About that. My visit to the healer was over fast, completed well before you returned from your attempt. I was told to come here and run laps while I waited for the rest of you to recover." He glanced at Elzina, stifling a grin. "I heard that some of you took quite a beating."

"That we did," Usalla replied. "It was a difficult scenario, and none succeeded in the task. You did not, did you?"

"No, but apparently I came close, relatively speaking."

Elzina laughed disdainfully. "Nonsense. There were multiple concealed attackers coming from all sides. If I was unable to defeat them, there is no way you would have been able to."

"I did not say I defeated them," he replied. "Only that I came close to achieving the objective. And that was not to start any fights. It was to identify Teacher Demelza in the crowd and hand her the token Griggitz gave us. Anything beyond that would be extraneous." He paused, a condescending grin tickling the corners of his lips. "You did not actually *intentionally* attempt to fight them all, did you? That would not only be cocky and near impossible for a Vessel, but also incredibly foolish."

Elzina's darkening cheeks spoke as loud as her angry silence. And just this once, he found he enjoyed her displeasure. He wasn't naturally that way. Bawb was a quieter, more subtle sort. But Elzina's shitty attitude had brought it out increasingly over their years of rivalry. He mused on it a moment, considering that he might need to address this issue and work on controlling his emotions better.

"It was quite a beating," Usalla interjected, doing her part to defuse the tension. "I suffered a few broken ribs in the process."

"And my nose was broken," Albinius added. "But you said you left the healer quickly. Were you harmed at all?"

"Oh, yes. But no broken bones, I am pleased to say."

"Ugh. Broken bones. I hate those. The mending really itches," Albinius griped. "And the pain is pretty intense as well."

"As they say, my friend. Such is Ghalian life. Fortunately, we have grown accustomed to such things. Or, at least, as accustomed as one can ever hope to become. Broken bones, cuts, and concussions seem to be regular occurrences, as we all know firsthand. Of course, avoiding them is still better."

Albinius nodded. "I heartily agree with that."

The thing was, it was *all* a part of their world, the pain and suffering. Training their minds to deal with it and carry on in cases where a lesser person would just succumb to the agony and discomfort and give up. But to become a Ghalian was to learn to push through no matter what. To trust their skills. To learn their limitations and still somehow move beyond them.

They did have one advantage on their side. Having an on-site healer was a large part of that, allowing them, in the back of their minds, to know that so long as an injury was not fatal, they could be mended.

Eventually.

Sometimes injuries were so great it took several days for them to rejoin their cohort and resume classes. But those instances were the exception rather than the rule.

"Vessels!" Griggitz bellowed as he entered the chamber with a burly Ghalian they'd not seen before. "Follow me. We have training one level down."

The students fell in and did as they were told, walking close to their teacher and his assistant.

"You said you almost achieved the goal?" Finnia asked as they walked. Being the spy trainee of the group, this sort of thing was where she usually excelled above the others, but she, too, had taken a beating in the tavern, emerging bloodied and unsuccessful.

"Almost, yes. I saw a woman who seemed most likely to be Demelza in disguise and moved to approach her."

"We all did," Zota pointed out. "And we all faced the consequences."

"Yes. But I pulled up short. It wasn't right. I realized it had to be a misdirection. I still had to engage them, in the end, but at least it was less of an outmatched fight."

"Outnumbered and outskilled and you call it fair?" Albinius asked.

"There is no such thing as fair. We do what we must, that is all there is to it," Bawb replied. "I only wish I had detected their deception sooner."

Teacher Griggitz stopped outside the room they had all come to know over the last few years. It was a smaller space, but one filled with practical implements to be used to fashion disguises strewn about the numerous tables.

"You mentioned detecting the deception," Griggitz said to Bawb. "Well, this is where you make the most of today's lesson. I hope it left an impression you can learn from."

"Yeah, a boot print on my ass," Albinius joked.

Griggitz stared at him hard, freezing any levity before it might gain traction. "You think this is funny, *boy*?"

They all felt their stomachs clench. He only called students boy or girl like that when he was truly angry.

"No, Teacher," Albinius backtracked. "I am sorry for my comment."

"You will be. Out. Now. Back to the third-level training room. I want twenty laps. Do not return until you have completed them."

"I understand."

"I did not ask if you understood. I gave a command. Now, go!"

Albinius took off at a run. How a Wampeh with his sense of humor had ever survived this long in the Ghalian training was a mystery, but somehow, despite his personality quirks, he managed to complete his tasks to the level required to advance with the rest of the class. Whether he would ultimately make a proper Ghalian assassin was anyone's guess, but none could say he did not at least possess the skills.

"Now, the rest of you," he said, turning his attention back on the class. "Quite a pathetic showing you made of it today. All except Bawb, but even he failed the one task at hand. So tell me, what did you learn from the experience?"

"That we should be armed at all times," Zota said.

"Wrong. Though we typically are, there will be instances where *any* weapon will be detected, and you will be forced to improvise. That was also part of today's lesson. To adjust your approach based on the parameters you find yourself dealing with. What else?"

Elzina stepped forward. "That we must always be prepared for a fight. Even the seemingly most straightforward of missions could go sideways and require the use of force at any time."

"Not the point of the lesson, but valid nonetheless," Griggitz said with a little nod. "What else?"

Finnia piped up. "That tricks are to be expected, no matter the circumstances."

"Demelza is a tricky one, for sure," Elzina noted.

"What was that?" the burly man at Teacher Griggitz's side asked in a low, rumbling voice. The students looked at him with a sense of unease. He was imposing, sturdy, and his words alone sounded like they could crush a man with ease.

"Uh, I said that Teacher Demelza is a tricky one," Elzina replied louder.

"Tricky, you say?" the man said, his fingers reaching behind his ear, slowly pulling part of his face off, revealing an altogether different one beneath.

"Teacher Demelza?"

A satisfied smile creased Demelza's lips as she watched their dumbfounded stares as layer after layer of her disguise came off until she was back to her normal self.

"There was no magic used here," she said. "The disguise was entirely practical. Made with the very same items you have here available to you in this room." She picked up the facial mold that had made her appear male. "The skin tone is the same, can you see? If you are forced to improvise and use non-magical methods, while shifting race can be effective, in many cases it is far easier to stick with your own coloring. We are all Wampeh, and of the billions spread across the stars, only a handful are Ghalian. None would think to suspect us if we do not give them reason to."

She picked up the outer garments she had been wearing, the shape of them hiding her large bosom by making her appear to be a sturdily built man, her muscular arms completing the illusion without requiring any additional disguising.

"These simple tools allowed me to craft this disguise in the time it took for you to walk from the healer to your meeting point. Simple is often best, and without using magic, there was nothing for a spell to detect, though I doubt any of you even thought to cast one here inside the training house's walls."

It was true, none of them had even the slightest inclination to scan those around them. What would be the purpose?

Clearly, it was to teach them a lesson. And the lesson was one that would stick with them for the rest of their lives. Book learning was one thing, but being shocked in a practical setting tended to make far more of a lasting impression.

Demelza looked at the class and gestured to the tables around them. "There is more than enough for you to work with here. Let us see what you can come up with on your own."

CHAPTER THREE

The Vessels took their lesson to heart and proved why they had been granted that title, absorbing and containing the knowledge Teacher Demelza had imparted upon them, not only by didactic methods, but with her practical, real-world examples as well. To say she had made an impression on them would be an understatement.

She also had a certain way with them. A degree of a sympathetic nature, albeit barely noticeable, that most Ghalian kept locked deep inside. For teenagers going through physical as well as psychological changes, it helped her connect with them and, as a result, better impart her teachings.

Those lessons were now being put to the test as the students were eagerly trying out the various appliances and pigments available to them on the tables, applying disguises, then shedding them to try other variants. It was one of the few classes that could almost be considered fun and even relaxing. That is, if one overlooked the brutal lessons they had all endured to get there.

"This is foul!" Albinius exclaimed as he opened a small jar. "It smells like feces."

"Indeed, it does. Do not only consider visual disguises," Demelza replied. "While you find the smell disgusting, it will also work to make you invisible in a way a shimmer cloak cannot. People will eschew you if you appear to be soiled in this manner. Posing as a street urchin in your youth is easy at this age, but perhaps you could be a vagrant or drunkard who has lost bowel control as you get older. Regardless of circumstance, smells can work wonders for a skilled Ghalian."

"They can also mask our scent from beasts and trackers," Bawb noted. "And depending on the material, it may also block basic magic-detecting spells."

Demelza nodded her agreement. "Yes, Bawb, that is correct. And we all know you had firsthand experience in just such a situation several years ago. A short learning curve, your excursion proved to be."

"Indeed, it was, Teacher."

"And quick thinking for a mere Aspirant. But now you are Vessels, and, if you work hard, soon you will become Adepts. And with that comes greater skill and subtlety employed in your disguises. You have learned the more physical aspects, both practical and magical, but there is also the psychological to consider."

"Psychological?" Usalla mused. "How so?"

"How to fit in."

"Looking as we are supposed to helps a lot," Zota chimed in.

"Yes, Zota, it does. But even a perfect-*looking* disguise may not be enough. You must learn all aspects of the races you would masquerade as. And among them, you must then further refine your behavior to match what is expected of the persona you have created. Take the Ingarians, for example. They have similar physical traits to Wampeh, so your disguise will consist of altering your skin, hair, and eye color, but so long as you are clothed you will not be required to apply any alterations to your body. However, Ingarians, as all races, have a certain set of habits. Things they say and do without thinking about it. It is these subtleties that are giveaways of lesser infiltrators. Any ideas what these might be?"

"The Ingarians lean," Finnia noted.

"Good. Continue."

"The Ingarians do not stand with their weight evenly distributed when at rest as Ghalian do. Culturally, they shift more weight on one foot than the other, and if a wall, table, or anything sturdy is nearby, they tend to lean against them. It is a subconscious habit they are not even aware they have."

"And if you were to disguise yourself as an Ingarian but then stood with your weight firmly balanced between your two feet, what would happen?"

"They would sense something was off," the spy trainee said. "It would likely be a back-of-the-mind sort of thing at first, but it would make them uneasy."

"Exactly. And that would then draw attention. The opposite of what a disguise is meant to do. And other races have similar quirks. The Yortzee, for example, tend to stand with one foot slightly in front of the other, and the Horgus are animated speakers, utilizing their hands as a vital part of speech. There are countless others, a great many of which you will learn during your training. Obviously, we cannot teach them all, but that is where our spy network and their reconnaissance comes in handy. Full-fledged Ghalian will receive a good amount of detailed information before they begin most contracts."

"Those in deep cover setting the stage," Finnia added.

"Yes, Finnia, our spies are the most skilled at disguises, and you will receive much additional training in this area. By the time you head out into the real world, you will be so skilled at incorporating these little traits and quirks that the enemy won't even think twice about you. At least, not on a gut instinct level.

You will still require a robust backstory, of course, and a fitting persona will help as well. And what have you learned about creating false identities thus far?"

"Master Hozark said that a more dramatic persona, such as a very gregarious trader or gambler, is often excellent for avoiding scrutiny by the act of drawing so much attention to themselves that they could not possibly be an assassin. We are perceived as skulking in the shadows, and attracting the gaze of all present is something people believe we would avoid at all costs."

"Master Hozark is a very wise and very skilled man. And he is right. Traders are excellent disguises. As are drunks and braggarts, all of whom can get close to people in a disarmingly cheerful manner, allowing them access to both targets as well as sources of intelligence. Buying a few rounds of drinks can loosen more lips than you would expect. But we typically avoid presenting as aggressive sorts, and we do not display our skills unless we absolutely must."

"Even if we must take a beating to appear weaker than we are?" Bawb asked.

Demelza grinned. "You paid attention today. Yes, that is a fantastic way to not only be taken for less than you are, but also to gain sympathy and even assistance of those who should fear you. But you must take care judging those situations lest you find yourself *truly* harmed. Small injuries are easily healed or ignored until later. More serious ones can jeopardize your mission."

Demelza opened a locked box, removing a rack of stoppered vials.

"Smell each of these, but do not inhale deeply. And do not let the liquid touch your skin."

"What are they?" Usalla asked.

"These are poisons. Among the most readily accessible ones to common folk, and the types you will most likely have to deal with at one point or another. Remember, while poison is just one of the many tools of our trade, they can also be used against you. For that reason, *never* leave your food and drink unattended, especially in a scuffle. And if you must, cast a detection spell to assess them when you return. Remember, not all poisons are employed to kill. Some are used to drug and render you senseless. But this can provide an opportunity in itself. Sometimes, detecting the drug and feigning unconsciousness will gain you access as a prisoner to a place you would have a much harder time entering as an attacker."

"I thought Ghalian did not use poison as a rule," Elzina noted.

"Typically, we avoid them, you are correct. They are easy to detect and easy to trace in many instances. However, some varieties are very hard to spot, even with robust magic. And not all have antidotes. For these reasons, you will learn about these poisons as well as their antidotes—for those that have one. This is because one day, despite all of your hard work and caution, you may still find yourself on the receiving end."

"Will we learn how to slip these into the food and drink of a target?" Bawb asked. "It seems like a somewhat tenuous task if others are around."

"In time, young Vessel. You will be taught diversionary tricks and even muting spells to hide the sound of your actions should the environment be quiet rather than loud. But for now, focus on the preliminaries. You have all come a long way since I first had the pleasure of teaching you, but you still have much to learn."

Bawb felt a pang of frustration at Demelza's response. He had accepted his fate to be a Ghalian, but that had lit a fire within him. He had also decided he was going to become one of the Five someday, and anything he could learn to advance him toward that goal was eagerly devoured and stored away in his ever-increasing mental repository of spells and techniques. But sometimes, no matter how willing he was to learn, he was left no option but to wait.

"I understand. Thank you for all you have done for us, Teacher Demelza," he said respectfully.

"Of course, Bawb. It is what I do. Now, who is ready to try their hand at identifying the first of these vials?"

CHAPTER FOUR

It wasn't in Bawb's nature to do anything half-assed. Even the tasks he was loath to perform, he still took a degree of pride in carrying them out to the best of his abilities, even if the results were less than ideal. But now he had an idea brewing in his head. After so many years training under these teachers and Masters, an understanding of what they would and would not tolerate had been established. A basic set of rules, more or less.

And he was going to game that system.

The plan was quite simple. He was going to sandbag a lesson, completing his task just slow enough that the others would move on without him, leaving him to finish on his own, but without drawing unwanted attention. He would just be told to catch up, as always. That was fine by him. Doing so in a class that was his strong suit would allow him to quickly make up that lost time once they left. The result? He would have a rare bit of truly alone free time to work on something else. Something he wasn't really supposed to be playing with yet.

Bawb had decided he was going to learn to utilize a muting spell.

That is, if he could get it to work. It was far above his current level, but Demelza's words had sunk in. Eventually, they would learn diversion and muting spells, but in his mind, what better time to start than now? He first set his plan in motion in Teacher Warfin's class.

Bawb worked slowly as he crafted his latest device, taking his time, leaving many pieces incomplete on the work bench as the others finished their projects.

"It looks as though Bawb is having trouble," Elzina quipped with a sneer. "I guess he is not as skilled at crafting as his ego allows him to believe."

"I am doing my best, Elzina," he grumbled with false annoyance.

"And your best is clearly not good enough," she shot back, buying his routine hook, line, and sinker. "But not to fear. You would not reach the top of our class anyway. Not so long as you have me to unseat."

"I do not care about taking the top spot," he lied. He actually *had* developed that particular desire, but there was no way he would admit that to her, of all people. He'd also learned that you could finish low in your class and still become a great Master. They had long lives ahead of them after training. All this did was set them on that path.

Teacher Warfin watched the exchange but did not step in. He had come to know these Vessels well since they had first set foot in his classroom. And while Elzina was as cocky a student as he had ever dealt with, she also backed up her overconfidence with quite substantial skills.

But Bawb? He was a bit of a wild card. He had talents, that was for certain, and on some occasions he truly shined. But on others, for whatever reason, he simply slid back into the middle of the pack instead of vying for the lead.

Apparently, today was one of those days.

"Enough," the teacher said loudly. "Those who have not yet

completed their tasks, finish your work. You may then join the rest of us in the seventh lower-level wilderness cavern. The rest of you, come."

Bawb looked around. He was the only one who had not finished his project.

Just as he planned.

"See you down there," Usalla said as she passed. "Do try to hurry. You know how Warfin gets when people fall behind."

"Do not worry, I will see you shortly," he replied with a little grin, then set back to work on his project. The other Vessels filed out, leaving him in silence.

Once the room was his and his alone, he moved quickly, completing the assembly of what had seemed to be a random pile of components in a flash. He had done well, crafting his device then leaving all the constituent parts in just the right state of disarray to avoid his ploy being detected but still allowing him to complete it in no time.

Bawb chuckled to himself, amused with the knowledge that being first was not always the best. Just because you were done before the others did not mean you would be allowed to do as you wished. Most of the time it merely meant the teachers would come up with some other task for you to do while the others caught up.

As they said, work would always be found to fill the time allotted. He just turned that adage on its head, is all.

Bawb's hands ceased their blur of activity. He looked at the results, satisfied, and set the finished project aside to begin preparing himself, running over the words of the muting spell in his mind.

Level up: Deception and subterfuge, the konus informed him.

"I was not trying for that, but thank you."

You are not *welcome. I know what you're doing, and you're being a fool*, his konus chided. *This is way above your level and is destined to fail.*"

"I have no doubt it will not be easy, but you know me by now."

That I do.

"And you know I am not one to give up easily."

The konus sighed, the frustrated affectation of a device that lacked lungs. *Very well. And I know better than to try to talk you out of this.*

"Then quiet down and let me concentrate."

My silence will not stop your failure. But please, go ahead and make my point for me.

He didn't bother replying, but rather, began to speak the words out loud, doing his best to focus his intent as he pulled magic from the konus and attempted to cast the muting spell.

The konus, for all its smart talk and sass, never failed to provide him just the right amount of power for whatever it was he was doing. Regardless of its opinions on his actions, in that one regard, it was always one hundred percent on task.

"*Omnus vallum niktu,*" Bawb said, trying to dial in his intent, picturing the space around him suddenly cut off from the rest of the world. A bubble of silence in the clamor of the galaxy.

He felt nothing. Heard nothing. Of course, the latter was the entire point, but usually when he cast he could sense the energy flowing through him, even if only faintly. But this time? This felt like failure.

He picked up a small piece of metal and threw it against the wall. It bounced off and fell to the floor with a soft clang.

"That did not appear to work," he noted.

No shit, the konus replied. *I told you. This is out of your league.*

"Be that as it may, there is only one way for it to become *in* my league, and that is by practice." Bawb focused harder, truly envisioning what it was he intended to happen. "*Omnus vallum niktu,*" he said again, this time feeling something stir in his chest.

He picked up another piece and tossed it. Again, it clanged to the ground, but to his ears there seemed to perhaps be a slight difference. A thought dawned on him.

"Konus?"

What? it replied in an annoyed tone.

"This spell. It is a muting spell."

Yes, obviously.

"And its purpose is to trap sound from escaping around a person or small area, correct?"

Your grasp of the obvious is most impressive, Vessel. Oh, how your teachers must be proud of you.

"By this logic," he continued, ignoring the sass, "would the sound still appear as normal *inside* the spell's reach?"

The konus was uncharacteristically silent a long moment.

Finally asking the right sort of question. Yes, the sound inside appears normal. For example, if you wanted to have a conversation but didn't want anyone else to hear it.

"So it is not just muting noises of movement, but anything else, yet all while seeming to have no effect on the *inside* of the spell area."

Again, Vessel Bawb, meet the obvious. Obvious, meet Vessel Bawb.

Bawb tried the spell again several more times, each time feeling that same pull from within. It felt as though it was working. At least, he thought it was. The icon on his konus's display was still blurred out, but that didn't mean he wasn't close. For all he knew the spell was nearly fully functional.

Of course, there were likely to be many levels to this skill as he gained proficiency, but his confidence was growing, and the path to mastery was a long race, not a sprint. The key was to make that first bit of progress. From there he could expand and refine as needed.

Bawb gathered up his things and left the chamber to go join the others. The walk passed quickly, his excitement over this new spell filling him with optimism. This just might work, and if it did, he would make quite the leap ahead of Elzina. Not that that was his goal, but if she was knocked down a peg or two in the process of his advancement he would not complain.

He reached the chamber where the others were already preparing for the next lesson but stopped just outside.

"*Omnus vallum niktu*," he cast, then cracked the door open. "I am here, Teacher Warfin," he called out hesitantly, testing the potency of his spell.

"It's about time, Vessel Bawb. Get in here and line up with the others. You are late enough as it is."

"Damn," he muttered. His optimism dwindling, Bawb trudged into the chamber and joined the class, doing his best to ignore Elzina's somewhat hostile stare.

I hate to say I told you so, but I told you so, the konus chuckled in his head.

"You do not hate it," he replied silently. "In fact, I know you rather enjoy it. But one day, soon, perhaps, you will eat those words."

I'm a konus. I don't eat.

"You know what I mean."

"Bawb, are you with me?" Warfin growled.

"Yes, Teacher!"

"Then pay attention. There is much to be done, and as you are late, you will have to receive the abridged instructions."

CHAPTER FIVE

Terrain reading. Scanning one's environment and taking in elements that might slip by the casual observer. That was the gist of the day's lesson. And while Bawb was busy working on his failure of a muting spell, Teacher Warfin had been driving home the finer points of surveying and understanding all aspects of one's surroundings in great detail.

Being late, Bawb was going to receive the very truncated version.

"All right, Vessel Bawb, I will catch you up as best I can in the short time before the exercise begins."

"What exercise, if I may ask."

"You may. The others are already scouting out the chamber from the starting point as best they can, getting the lay of the land, as it were. They will have an advantage."

"I understand, Teacher Warfin. Any handicap I face is entirely my own doing."

"That it most certainly is," the teacher grumbled. "Listen up, I am only going to explain this once. This chamber is one of the largest, deepest caverns in the extensive network the Ghalian have claimed since the earliest days we established our training house on this world. As you can clearly see, it is illuminated by both natural bioluminescence as well as magical enhancements that we can adjust according to our needs. Do you see that up there?" he asked, pointing to a high point some distance away atop a rocky outcropping.

"It appears to be flowing water, if my eyes do not deceive me."

"They do not. There is a spring up there. It surges and occasionally erupts in a geyser, pushing out a great amount of water in an instant. The stream formed by that spring's normal flow is not connected to the other water sources. This chamber is self-reliant in that regard. What water the vegetation and animals living within need all comes from within. Know this, the water brings life, but it can also bring death," he added, cryptically.

"I think I follow. You said there are animals?"

"There are some native species residing here. Not all are dangerous, but many are. They will help guide you through this place. As inhabitants of the cavern, they are intimately familiar with the pitfalls that lie throughout. You would be wise to heed their actions."

"Understood."

"There are seven flags placed throughout this chamber. Your task is to retrieve them. The winner will be the Vessel who has acquired the most. But I must stress that there are dangers not under Ghalian control. You face very real risks and must gauge your movements accordingly. Small creatures as well as large may attack, and the terrain is not your friend."

Teacher Warfin started walking, leading Bawb to a small open area atop a low hill. The others were all there, straining their eyes, searching for any sign of the flags from their vantage point. It was pointless, of course. The teachers would not make it so simple for them. But the urge to try won out regardless.

"Are you all prepared?" Warfin asked as Bawb fell in with the others.

"Yes, Teacher," they replied in unison.

"Then you may begin."

Several of the students took off immediately, descending quickly from the rise and rushing into the brush and boulders immediately surrounding them. The others, however, took their teacher's instruction to heart and spent more time gaining an understanding of the cavern. To run off without truly knowing the layout could mean coming up against a rock face, a river, or worse.

"Are you prepared to lose yet again?" Elzina asked, heading off and jogging down the hill without waiting for Bawb's reply.

"She really does seem to have a problem with you," Albinius noted with a chuckle.

"Elzina is just overly competitive," Usalla countered. "She would be that way with any of us. It just so happens that Bawb is the closest competition she has."

"I do not let her antics concern me," Bawb said. "And neither should you. Elzina is simply being Elzina. And in any case, we have a task at hand."

"That we do," Usalla agreed. "Good luck. See you at the finish."

She took off in a different direction, setting her course for higher ground rather than lower. All the students eventually chose a path, some low, some high, each of them selecting what they thought would lead them to the first of the flags.

The fact of the matter was the teachers could have placed them literally anywhere in the cavern, and there was no point spending too much time trying to intuit where they might have selected. Rather, it was to one's advantage to select a path that would allow them to cover the most terrain in the shortest time, thus increasing the likelihood of coming across either one of the flags or at least traces of the path to them.

Bawb heard the sounds of fighting and some muffled cries of pain to his left. It was downhill, toward the faint sound of flowing water. He shook his head. Someone had selected a direction that would, given what he knew of the place, likely lead to not just an easier path, but also a watering hole where the local animal threats he had been warned of might congregate.

Judging by the noise, it seemed that theory had borne fruit. Fortunately, someone else was having to deal with it. At least for now.

Bawb spun a slow three-sixty and took in everything he could. A higher trail would be more work, but it would also be less likely to put him in the path of the diverging waterways fed by the lone spring high above. If what Teacher Warfin had said was true, the farther one was from the source the more likely they would be to have to deal with a tributary of some sort rather than the main flow.

Much as they had trained to operate in water, this was a cavern, and that meant water behaved differently than on the surface above. Most notably, like any stream or river, it had to flow somewhere, but underground, in an unflooded chamber, that almost always meant a suck-hole of one sort or another. And while the light was decent to maneuver by, that was one obstacle he would very much like to avoid if at all possible.

Bawb made up his mind and headed out, jogging down from the rise then quickly adjusting course back uphill, following a somewhat precarious rock ridge that would bring him close to the stalactites high above. Whether a flag would be hidden up high or not, it would afford him a better view of the entirety of the vast chamber, whereas he currently only had a partial picture of the full expanse.

"Teacher Warfin said it was one of the largest caverns in the entire complex," he mused as he climbed, casting a detection spell for booby traps just in case they had decided to be sneaky, as was their way, as well as being careful to mind his footing on the damp rocks. "By that measure, if there are seven flags spaced out approximately equidistant, one could expect at most two flags located by a single participant."

But? the konus asked as it fed his spell the requisite power needed.

"But we know the teachers are nothing if not unpredictable."

And?

"And that means they would quite likely have placed two or more close together, assuming most would discover the first and move on, not searching further for another in such close proximity."

A reasonable deduction. But what does it mean for you?

"It means I just need to find a flag in what appears to be a difficult location, then search for additional ones. Others would shift their pursuit, leaving the area."

Giving you an advantage.

"Precisely."

Interesting hypothesis. But let's see if it plays out like you think it will.

Bawb ignored the konus, focusing his attention on the task at hand. He would succeed or he would not, and no amount of doubt casting by the device would change that. He pressed on, climbing higher and higher until he could nearly reach out and touch a stalactite. "*Omixnomusocti,*" he said, casting an unusual vision spell. One designed to help sort items into similar piles, used most often when sifting through salvage or large amounts of stolen goods, but now redirected in a novel way.

There was no way he could accurately detect the flags from so high, but if the spell had enough reach, maybe, just maybe, the shift in coloration between a natural substance and one created by a loom and man-made dyes would give him a hint as to the right direction.

He looked down below, scanning the rises and depressions in the rock between the greenery.

"There," he said, spotting a shift in color barely noticeable in a low point not far from his location.

Level up: Novel use of spells, the konus reluctantly informed him.

He didn't care about leveling up. He cared about winning, and that thing down there was almost certainly a flag. It had to be. Not naturally occurring and not a life form, there was little else it could be. Unless, of course, the teachers were playing another trick on them. But he had a good feeling about this one, trusting his instincts as he rushed down from his rocky vantage point to the depression far below.

It would take time to get there, but he forced himself to slow, minding his steps. A fall from this high could be fatal, and that would be the most foolish way to end one's training. Not in battle, but slipping on a rock.

He eventually made it to even ground, shifting into a careful jog, and it was a good thing he did. The ball of fangs and claws that lunged at him from the bushes was only waist-high, but it possessed more than enough energy and speed to cause some serious damage if he'd been taken unaware.

Bawb drew a pair of daggers and crouched low. He had dealt with smaller ones of this species before and learned the hard way they had a slow-acting poison in their claws. The healer had rectified the problem, but not before he had vomited so hard he feared he would break a rib, his head pounding from the effort.

The beast growled and charged, its aggression ramped up to full force.

Bawb sliced at it as he dove aside, his blade eliciting a yelp of pain and surprise as the creature flew past, not managing to strike a blow of its own. It landed and spun, trickling thick blood behind it as it attacked again, fearless and enraged.

Bawb crouched even lower, feigning injury. This time, the animal took the bait.

It jumped high, instinct telling its primitive brain to attack its prey from above. Bawb, however, was counting on that, his daggers flashing upward and out as he again dove aside. The metal sliced deep, opening the creature's belly wide, its contents spilling to the ground as it landed in a heap. It shuddered a moment then fell still, steam rising from its entrails.

Bawb wiped his blades and sheathed them, already on the move at a fast jog downhill to the target location. The flag was hidden by laying it flat against a boulder at the very bottom of the small ravine. Placed as it had been, one would have to be looking directly at it from just the right angle to spot it. That explained why the spell had given him a general location but no specifics. He simply had not been properly aligned.

Movement caught his eye. It was Dillar, one of the other Vessels who almost always ranked lower in the class due to his tunnel vision tendencies. And he was succumbing to them once more, it seemed. The boy had seen the flag from the opposite side and had then spotted Bawb. As a result, he was rushing down to reach it before him. A race was on.

The ground vibrated slightly. A moment later a loud, rumbling whoosh filled the cavern from high above. A spray began to fall from on high, not quite rain, but more substantial than mist.

Bawb looked around, listening as a new sound reached his ears. It was odd, but somehow familiar. He held out his hand and felt the water droplets landing on them. They were warm.

"The geyser," he realized just as Dillar reached the low point. "Dillar! Turn back! You must climb!"

The boy was either too far to hear, too engrossed in the thrill of competition, or simply did not choose to heed his cries, instead charging headlong toward the flag. And as Bawb watched from above, he actually managed to grab it. When the wall of water rushing down the ravine hit him, however, success turned to horror as the flag and the boy were washed away in an instant.

Bawb was already running, trying to get ahead of the flash flood. Dillar was a good swimmer and had cast his air bubble spell just in time, but the force of the flow would be too much for him. He would need help.

Bawb ran as fast as his legs would carry him, leaping over rocks and shrubs with the urgency the situation warranted. Dillar had managed to grab hold of a rock and was momentarily able to fight the water's flow, but it would only be a matter of time before his grip gave way. Up ahead the water hit the far wall, spinning into a swirling, sucking whirlpool, driving down deep below the rock face.

"Hold on!" he yelled, looking desperately for anything to use as a rope or implement to fish his classmate out.

There were plants but no trees down here. No vines to fashion into a makeshift rope. Bawb was frantic. He knew he could not withstand the rushing water if he jumped in, but Dillar could not hold on much longer. Bawb looked high above the whirlpool. There were stalactites up there. If he could force one or two free, maybe they could plug the drain point enough to slow the water and allow Dillar a chance to climb out.

Bawb pulled deep, casting the hardest force spell he knew, directing it far overhead in as focused a spell as he could muster.

The stalactite shook, small bits of it crumbling off and falling, but otherwise remaining solidly in place. He cast again, but once more the results were the same.

Bawb glanced at Dillar just as the boy's grip gave way. He was swept away in an instant, the water's irresistible flow pulling him to his death.

"*Moro Alginus Latzo!*" a voice boomed nearby, the force of the spell making the air tremble. It was Teacher Warfin, his hands held high, his konus glowing from the power the spell required.

A large ball of water lifted free from the rapids with Dillar inside, flying aside with great force, tossing the boy to the shore. He hit the rocks hard with a terrible snap as his legs broke from the impact.

Teacher Warfin meandered down to the injured student at a disturbingly leisurely pace and hoisted him over his shoulder, then began climbing back up to level ground.

"What are you staring at, Vessel Bawb?" he growled angrily, though his look of relief did not match the tone of his voice.

"Will he be okay?"

"That is not your concern. You have a task to complete."

Bawb pushed his emotions down hard. "Yes, of course. I am sorry."

Warfin nodded, but then glanced toward the ground where the boy had landed. The flag, soaked and torn, lay on the rocks.

"You had best get to it, then," he said with the tiniest hint of kindness in his eyes. "The game is still afoot."

With that he headed for the chamber exit, undoubtedly taking the wounded boy straight to the healer. Bawb turned and scrambled down the rocks, careful to mind his footing so close to the water's edge, though the flash flood was already beginning to diminish.

He scooped up the flag and tucked it in his pocket, turning his attention once more to the area around him. There were six more flags out there, and he intended to find as many as he could.

CHAPTER SIX

Teacher Warfin paced slowly back and forth in front of the line of Vessels standing at ease before him, looking at the bumps and bruises they had managed to acquire in the course of the challenge, none of them coming out totally unscathed.

Dillar was back with them, though clearly weak from the painful healing spells that had knitted his broken bones back whole again. Fortunately, there had been no internal damage, or he would have had to spend the entire day recovering, if not longer. Nonetheless, he was paler than usual and looked as though he wanted nothing more than for the day to end so he could go to sleep.

It had been quite the ordeal. Not just for the near-drowned boy but for all of them. The terrain was difficult, and the hazards, be they animal or environmental in nature, all took their toll. At the end, all seven flags had been recovered, but there was no victor. Elzina and Bawb had each managed to recover two apiece, but the remaining three had gone to other classmates. Sharing first place but not winning outright only added to Elzina's usual prickly mood.

Bawb, on the other hand, was simply glad to see Dillar had

made it back in one piece. And the impromptu rescue attempt had not only supplied him with one rather beat-up flag but had also led him to the hiding spot of another just above the whirlpool's location. Of course, there had been no whirlpool when the flag was placed there, but the nature of this cavern's unpredictable natural events had added that obstacle to the task on its own schedule.

Warfin's pacing boots crunched to a halt.

"Several of you did not pay attention today," he said calmly, but the air of irritation behind his words still crept out. "Tunnel vision set you on a dangerous path. And while danger is part of Ghalian life, we do not put ourselves at risk foolishly. Yet some of you learned the hard way that single-minded focus on a goal can have consequences."

He looked at the other three students who were still drying off from their encounters with unexpected water flow then fixed his gaze on Dillar. The boy was dry now, but the ill effects of his experience were still clear to see.

"And there are those among you who nearly paid the ultimate price," he continued. "In nothing more than a simple training exercise, no less." He shook his head and began pacing once more. "You are no longer Nulls. No longer Novices or Aspirants. You are Vessels now, and much time and effort has been spent teaching you. Molding you into worthy bearers of the Ghalian name. You may perish in your training, but you will not throw your lives away by foolishly rushing headlong into situations you could easily avoid."

The students stood perfectly still. Their teacher was annoyed with them, and while Warfin often put on airs of being a tough-as-nails hardass, they knew it was mostly an act. Part of the persona he had created for this aspect of his work. A teacher who needed to drive home lessons into young and often stubborn minds.

But today he seemed to actually be annoyed. Not upset—Ghalian emotions were far too controlled for that—but he was not amused. Not one bit.

"Follow," he said, then walked away toward the steep slope leading to one of the rocky ravines.

The Vessels did as they were told and joined him at the edge.

"Do you see this?" he asked, gesturing at the trickle of water that had been a raging torrent not all that long ago. "Several of you ignored a basic tenet of wilderness survival. You failed to read the terrain. Vessel Elzina, what do we know of ravines such as this?"

She stepped forward to attention, her back rigid. "We know that water flows downhill, Teacher."

"And?"

"And the low point is a dangerous place to be in case of inclement weather."

"As some were reminded the hard way," he replied. "Even when dry and the sky clear, the lowest points in areas like this need to be crossed quickly, and one's attention attuned to any moisture in the breeze. That alone may provide the few seconds needed to get clear of an incoming flash flood."

"But we are in a cavern," Albinius said, still dripping from his own impromptu swim.

"What does that have to do with basic caution, Vessel Albinius?"

"Well, I mean, there is no real weather down here. Not in the form of rain clouds, anyway."

Warfin shook his head. "And did you not pay attention at the beginning of this exercise? When I directed all of your attention to the spring at the highest point in this cavern? That, too, is a source of water, and as an unpredictable geyser, it had the possibility of causing a torrent at any time. You simply saw dry terrain and did not consider what it might become. You must always be ready in unfamiliar environments. And while it is perfectly natural to hope for the best, you must always prepare for the worst. Look at the terrain. You can tell this was carved by water flow over tens of thousands of years. While the timing of its arrival is unpredictable, the terrain will tell you where it will flow when it does. And the stalactites above indicate a degree of moisture in the air over a long period of time, further informing you of the likely presence of water."

"So, the low paths are inherently dangerous," Usalla noted.

"Yes. But also potentially lifesaving. And higher ground can be dangerous as well, exposing you not only to the elements, but also to discovery, should you be attempting to conceal yourself from others."

"Teacher, you said the low points are possibly lifesaving. Can you explain?" Bawb asked.

"I will do better than explain. I will show you. Come."

Teacher Warfin led the students on a winding path that eventually took them down to an area that had not been flooded by the geyser's eruption. The patch of dry ground appeared to have been blocked from the flow by a rock slide sometime prior, leaving this particular low point relatively safe. At least, that was how it appeared to the now-attentive students' eyes.

"If you were dying of thirst, where would you seek water?" the teacher asked.

"I would traverse to the other ravine," Ovixus suggested.

"Wrong. Assume the rest of this cavern is not an option. Here, in this dry place, what would you do?"

The students looked around at the dry dirt. There wasn't even any moss growing on the rocks in this section of the cavern. Warfin gave them a minute then continued.

"Even the most unlikely of places can provide you with lifesaving water. Do you see this area where the rocks form a bend?" Warfin asked. "Do you see any water?"

Ovixus bent close, scooping up some of the dry dirt. "No, it is completely dry."

Warfin knelt down and pulled out a dagger, quickly digging into the soil and tossing handfuls aside. "It is dry at the surface, but you can tell by the geology that this low point was formed by water, and this particular spot is a natural point for any moisture to collect and pool."

"But it is dry."

"Ah, but is it?" the teacher replied, tossing a handful of darker soil aside. "You see, there is often still water below the surface even in seemingly dry environments. Knowing where to find it is how denizens of those locations survive." He dug deeper, scooping out more of the damp dirt until a small trickle of muddy water began to pool at the bottom of the hole. "Here, all of you. Look."

"It is muddy, but I suppose anything will do when you are dying of thirst," Bawb noted.

"But you are presented here with nature's great filter," Warfin replied. "Observe." He dug a little deeper, allowing more water to fill the hole, then began scooping it out with his hands, dumping it out on the dry soil around the hole.

"Why would you waste your water?" Finnia asked.

Warfin kept scooping it out until the hole was nearly dry. "Wait for it."

The students watched patiently. Slowly, a trickle of water began to fill the hole back up, and it was clearer than before.

"The sandy soil will filter the water as it refills. Do this several times over and you will have gone from muddy to relatively clean water in no time. Come, each of you try, then taste the results."

The students each dug a hole as they had seen him do, then splashed the water out, letting it slowly filter and seep back into the hole until the topmost portion was clear enough to see the bottom. They then drank.

The water had an earthy flavor to it but was otherwise perfectly palatable. More than that, it was refreshing given the amount of exercise they had just done. Yes, they were carrying small water bladders, but knowing this skill would allow them to save that for later. A useful trick when out on a mission with limited resources.

"Yes, there it is," Warfin said, pleased with their efforts. "You are all doing quite well. Lock this in your minds. It is a useful technique. It is also only one of many to provide you with water in difficult circumstances. The others I will teach you in the coming weeks and months when time allows as your training progresses. They will not be the main focus of your lessons, though, and for that reason, I would advise you to practice them in your free time. They may save your life one day."

Warfin stood and brushed the dust off his trousers. "Vessels, line up."

The students did as he instructed.

Warfin pulled tightly folded slips of parchment from his pocket, each with one of their names on the outside. "Do not show the contents to anyone else. The information contained therein is for you and you alone. We still have more lessons to complete in this location, but afterward, there is a new task for all of you. One that will last as long as it must. And you will begin when you leave this chamber."

CHAPTER SEVEN

The students had each opened their folded note, read the contents, then carefully hidden it away in a pocket before heading out into the corridor. They all assumed correctly that they had each received a similar set of instructions.

Dillar was still moving a bit slowly after his healing session, but as soon as Albinius stepped out to join the others, he attacked. The Vessels quickly spread out, pressing their backs up against the walls of the corridor, watching with interest.

Albinius was quick to react, blocking the bum-rush from his classmate as best he could, pushing him away and pivoting in a defensive pose. Dillar spun and attacked with a desperate sort of intensity.

He realized he wasn't going to last long given his low energy from his injuries, and thus decided to make the most of his opportunity before it was too late. He threw punches and kicks, elbows and knees, and while his legs were a bit unsteady, his ferocity threw Albinius for a loop. It was a lapse in attention that allowed the boy to wrap his adversary in his arms from behind.

"Get off me!" Albinius shouted, ramming back into the wall hard, trying to shake Dillar from his back.

"*Zapho orack,*" the boy replied, his palm pressed firmly to Albinius's chest while his legs wrapped tightly around his waist.

"Oh no you don't!"

Albinius dove into a forward roll, intending to shake the monkey from his back, or at least stun him from the impact with the ground. He rolled hard, coming up to his knees, but Dillar still clung stubbornly.

"You're not going to—" Albinius started to say when a small flash from Dillar's palm stunned him into submission.

Dillar slowly rose to his feet, breathing hard, a small cut on his cheek from the ground but a little smile on his face. He pulled the parchment from his pocket, unfolded it, and read it again with satisfaction. *Albinius* had been written on it, along with the words to the stun spell and explicit instructions how to use it.

This was to be a contest amongst all of them. One that could take place at any time, at any location. Day or night, there was nowhere out of bounds. The objective was simple. Lay a hand on the target they had been given and speak the words of the spell. The hard part would be maintaining contact for three full seconds in order for the spell to work. There would be no drive-by stunning taking place. No casting from a distance. And just because one person was your target did not mean that you were theirs, though the spell would also work for anyone as a defensive tool if attacked.

It was everyone for themselves until only one remained, but once someone had been stunned, it did not mean they were removed from the contest. They still had a name to target as well, and so it would go for as long as it might take.

"Damn you, Dillar," Albinius griped as his limbs began functioning once more, though not enough to get up yet. "That hurt!"

"Sorry. I was just following the instructions."

"Well, it still sucks."

Dillar was pale from the effort, his healing clearly not fully completed. He wobbled a little, propping himself against the wall with one hand.

"Are you okay?" Usalla asked, rushing to his side and helping him up. "I can fetch Teacher Warfin if you need him."

"No, but thank you. I am just tired from the exertion is all."

"As you would be. That was quite a display, especially so soon after your injuries."

"Thank you. I appreciate your sentiment and concern, but I will be—" A look of resigned realization flashed across his face just before the spell hit him, stunning him to the ground.

"Sneaky," Elzina said with grudging approval. "I did not even hear you cast the spell."

"I can speak quietly when I must," Usalla replied, her back safely pressed to the wall as she waited for Dillar to regain his senses.

The other Vessels looked at one another, not knowing who might be the next assailant, or who their target would be. At least in that regard Dillar and Albinius were at an advantage. Surely the teachers would not have them stunned twice.

Then again, knowing the Ghalian Masters, anything was possible.

"May I suggest a truce so we might eat in peace?" Moralla asked, eyeing the students around her.

"No truces!" Teacher Warfin's voice boomed out from the doorway. He strode out, looking at the fallen students. He flashed Usalla an amused grin. "Taking down an injured classmate?"

"A target is a target," she replied coolly.

"Well said. And a task well performed. As for the rest of you, *no*, there shall be no truces. At least, not as a group. What you discuss individually is your business, but be warned, a Ghalian will say and do whatever is necessary to achieve their goal. Make alliances with great caution. We do not trust lightly." He helped Albinius to his feet, leaning him against the wall while his legs began to function properly again. "There is one more thing," he added. "The last of you standing will win a prize."

"A weapon?" Elzina asked, excitement in her eyes.

"No. Something potentially far more valuable. One of the Masters has offered to give a limited series of private lessons to the winner. One-on-one training with one of the best among us. I tell you now, this is a great opportunity. I would advise you to do your best to claim it as your own."

Warfin turned and walked away, leaving the students to compose themselves and decide what their next course of action would be. Clearly, a mass brawl was out of the question. No one knew who had their name, and if they were engaged with someone else, it would not be difficult for an adversary to take advantage of that situation to lay hands. The three-seconds requirement would be a somewhat difficult hurdle to overcome, but certainly not insurmountable.

"I do not know about the rest of you," Bawb said, pushing off from the wall, "but I am hungry. Attack if you will, but I am getting lunch. Usalla, would you care to join me?"

She eyed him warily, weighing the offer. He knew she was not the one waiting to attack him, but she had no way of knowing if she was the name in his pocket.

"All right," she finally said. "Let's go."

At the very least she would be on guard as they walked and dined, as would he. And given what had just happened, there was a very good likelihood that no one would be making any attempts again so soon. Not when everyone was on high alert, waiting for an attack.

The others seemed to come to the same conclusion, following after them, albeit spaced out and with their heads and eyes in constant motion, monitoring those around them. Only Dillar was truly at ease. He had taken down his target and been eliminated just moments later. For him, the game was over. Classes would go on as usual, but now without having to look over his shoulder.

His classmates were not so lucky.

Their lunch was tense, and the Vessels all took up seats in a spaced-out circular arrangement that allowed them to keep their backs safely out of touch and any potential adversary in sight. The meal, however, went off without a hitch, and not a single attack, subtle or overt, took place. But that didn't mean they were out of the woods. Not by a long shot.

There were several more classes to attend, and just because a lesson was underway was no excuse to let one's guard down. In fact, the teachers encouraged the students to seek out lapses in attention and exploit them. And over the course of the day, several did.

The fights were typically over quickly, the need to hold a hand to the target's body for three seconds was actually easier than landing deadly blows in some ways. It led to messier engagements, undoubtedly, but not all fights would be clean and wrapped up in a bow. Sometimes they would have to improvise. To scrap and get dirty.

This was just one more bit of training in that regard.

By the time dinner rolled around, many more had been eliminated, in some cases both as targets as well as aggressors. And with the dwindling number of active students came a sharpening of focus of those still in the game. It was easier to keep track of possible threats now, and as a result, they made it through dinner without incident.

Showering *after* was another story.

It started innocently enough. A bump in the showers, a loss of footing on the slippery floor. A conveniently placed patch of soap slicking the ground was the catalyst. And Marzis stepped right into the trap.

Bawb shoved his target high, distracting him with his hands while his foot flashed out low, not kicking the boy's leg, which he was ready to block, but rather forcing it to slide away, his stability ruined by the soap. From there it was a matter of leverage.

The two nude students grappled across the chamber, water splashing everywhere while the others watched with interest. It wasn't every day that someone put this sort of technique to use, and they had only recently learned the basics of wet terrain fighting. Of course, that had been clothed and wearing sturdy boots, but the principles were the same.

But despite them both having received the same lessons, one of the boys had an advantage. Bawb had laid this trap, and he knew precisely where his feet would find purchase on the stone floor, whereas his opponent would not.

In a swirling movement he spun low, feigning another leg attack, but then wrapped his arm around Marzis's head, throwing his hip back hard and knocking him off balance, his momentum taking his target right off his feet, over his head, and slamming him hard to the ground.

"*Zapho orack*," Bawb said while still in midair, the spell cast before they landed. His arm was tight around the exposed neck, his hand positioned to press up against the boy's upper chest. Even the impact of their landing did not jar it free. The boy fought hard, but he was pinned, and seconds later the stun spell ended his resistance.

"Thank you for your efforts," Bawb said as he got to his feet, pulling Marzis out of the stream of water and resting him on his left side to recover.

He looked around at the excited faces of his classmates. It had been a quick and efficient demonstration of several things they had practiced of late, and there was good reason to watch with such interest. Also, one of them still had *his* name on a slip of parchment.

Level up: Trap-laying and water combat.

He didn't reply to the konus, quickly drying off and heading for his bunk while the others moved in to bathe. Given what had just happened, he figured he had at least a few minutes to make his sleeping area as safe as he could before turning in for the night.

Bawb was no great spellcaster, but he had learned a few alarm spells, which he cast around his bunk. He also laid several tripwires, just in case someone got the idea to attack him in his sleep. It was not against the rules, and if the shower ploy hadn't worked, he had been planning on doing precisely that later that night.

But he had won that fight and now only had to defend himself when his attacker eventually came for him. He lay back on his bed and closed his eyes, unable to properly sleep, drifting at the edge of consciousness, alert and waiting for the nighttime attack that would not come.

CHAPTER EIGHT

Bawb managed to rest, though he didn't exactly get a good night's sleep. As a Vessel, he was long used to the disruptions in his schedule and while he would have preferred to slumber undisturbed, he was perfectly capable of functioning on reduced, or even entirely lacking sleep.

Nearly all the other students had no such problems, dozing soundly as they had been eliminated from the competition. The few remaining, however, were on alert at all times, ready for the attack that could remove them from contention. With personal training under the watch of one of the Masters on the line, failure was something they all very much wished to avoid.

The Vessels were quiet about their status for the most part, several having been taken out away from the prying—and judging—eyes of their peers. Even so, a general consensus of who was still active was fairly easily ascertained. You could tell just by the lack of tension in someone's shoulders that they were no longer a target, and a relaxed gaze instead of a calculating one showed one was no longer on the hunt.

And hunters were all Bawb had to worry about now. He had

taken out his target. He just had to make it to the end unscathed and the prize was his.

The students went to breakfast, still sitting in a circle despite the majority being out of the game. It just made sense, and they all fell into it without a second thought. When they went to class, however, no such leeway was to be had. They would do as the teachers instructed, and in many cases that meant working side by side with one another.

It wasn't until evening that someone sneakily lay their hand upon a nearby student, stunning them without notice as they focused on the crafting project in their hands. It was the delicate moment of installing a triggering device, and it required all of their attention. A lapse Finnia took full advantage of.

Usalla was the target, and she hit the ground hard, her project falling apart as her hands locked from the stun spell. Their teacher did not even flinch. This was to be expected. Anytime, anywhere, until there was only one left.

Finnia crouched beside her friend. Gradually, Usalla's body regained function. Finnia helped her to her feet, knowing she had already taken out her target and was not a threat to her.

"Well played, Finnia," Usalla said grudgingly, picking up the scattered pieces of her work. "Your timing was impeccable."

"Apologies for your project, but the opening was there."

"I would have done the same."

"I know you would."

The two set back to work, Usalla out of the hunt but at least able to complete her project in peace. Bawb glanced around the room, wondering who might be on the prowl, waiting to jump him when the opportunity arose.

Zota was a mediocre actor, and though he had been tagged out that morning he was still a threat so far as anyone knew. Finnia was still in the game as well, and on the defensive now.

Bawb bundled up his work and sat beside Usalla as the class ended.

"Too bad about your project," he said.

"I will complete it next time. And yours?"

"Done, at last."

She nodded, a faint smile on her lips as she relaxed into the feeling of no longer constantly looking over her shoulder.

"Okay, that is all for today," Warfin announced. "Put away your tools and clean your workspace."

"I will see you at dinner," she said, sweeping her components into their storage bin and heading out before the others. There was no sense trying to put anything together at this point. The class was over.

"Go get cleaned up," Warfin said to the remaining students. "Then you may proceed to the dining hall."

The group did just that, hurrying back to wash up after a relatively easy day by Ghalian standards. The teachers had taken into account the contest underway, and while they still gave them ample work to do, the intensity was dialed down a notch to allow the students to engage one another as opportunities presented themselves.

Bawb took his time heading back, waiting for the others to bathe before stepping into the shower room, enjoying having the entire place to himself for once. He would be a little late to dinner, but it would allow him a few minutes of peace to let his guard down at least a tiny bit.

Clean and refreshed, he walked the corridor to the dining hall. A familiar face was heading toward him, a smudge of dirt on her cheek and her hair ruffled. Elzina had been up to something, it seemed.

"Elzina," he said.

"Hello, Bawb."

"You seem a bit out of sorts."

A big, gloating grin spread across her face. "Maybe, but I just took out Finnia. Oh, it was beautiful. She never saw it coming."

"And yet you do not look as though it was as easy as you say."

She wiped her face and straightened her clothes and hair. "You wouldn't expect her to go down without a fight, would you? She may be on the spy path, but she is still a Ghalian. Regardless, I am one step closer to victory."

"So it seems," he replied as they reached the dining hall doors. "Well, congratulations, Elzina. May the best Vessel win."

She looked around quickly, ensuring no one was sneaking up on her. "Oh, I intend to."

They walked into the dining hall together, taking the last two open seats, Bawb on the left, where Usalla had held a place for him, and Elzina on the right. Normally, they avoided one another when they could, but as the last to arrive, they didn't seem to have much choice in the matter.

"Quite a day," he said, turning to his friend.

Usalla chuckled. "Quite a day, indeed. I took the liberty of preparing you a plate."

"Thank you, it is appreciated," he replied, tucking into his meal with gusto.

The meal went smoothly. Nearly all of the students relaxed as they ate, and the spacing of the remaining competitors gave them all some much-needed breathing room. It was only as he finished his meal, belly full and happy, that Bawb felt something on his right thigh.

He pivoted and jumped up immediately, swiping away Elzina's hand as she attempted to cast the stun spell.

"So, you *were* faking," he said, ready for a fight. "Your acting was impressive. Quite a deception, Elzina."

"Would you expect any less?" she replied, a wicked grin on her lips.

"So, Finnia?"

"Taken out by another."

"And your attacker?"

Zota raised his hand sheepishly. "That was me. I was unsuccessful."

Bawb locked eyes with Elzina, the two circling one another beside the table. This meant that they were the last two. Whoever won this engagement would win the game.

"Shall we?" she said with a confident chuckle.

Bawb looked around, concern in his eyes. There were a lot of people in a small area, and with tables and chairs in the way, this could get ugly.

Teacher Griggitz was standing against the far wall but said nothing. Normally it was a big no-no to fight in the dining hall, but today was one of the rare occasions it was not only allowed but encouraged.

Nevertheless, Bawb glanced toward the door. The way they were seated, there was no way he could make it there first. Elzina sensed his hesitation and attacked.

The two were evenly matched for the most part, and where Elzina was still a little better in her magical combatives, she was unable to use them in this setting. There were too many innocent bystanders, and while they were Ghalian and could handle themselves, the rules were the same. No indiscriminate damage, if it could be avoided.

So, it seemed this would be a test of physical prowess rather than magical.

Adepts and Aspirants crowded in through the door, word of a showdown drawing them to join the Vessels to watch.

Elzina leapt high, aiming a downward elbow at Bawb's head, hoping to daze him with the blow long enough to apply the stun spell. Bawb pivoted and jumped onto a chair, kicking her in the ribs as she descended. It was a glancing blow, but enough to make her fly off course and nearly crash into their table.

They rushed one another, fists flying, open hands parrying and deflecting in a whirlwind of attacks and defenses. Kicks and elbows quickly entered the mix, as did attempted joint locks. But these two trained together, knew one another's moves. To win, someone would need to try something different.

Elzina moved to kick low but shifted her hips, instead driving a powerful knee into Bawb's chest. He slid back into a chair, grimacing from the impact but staying on his feet. Elzina's aggressive nature took over, her attacks increasing in speed and power, forcing Bawb to retreat.

She pressed on, punching hard and fast. A few shots landed, but Bawb managed to block most. Even so, she was clearly winning. Elzina's grin widened. This was where she would overcome his defenses. This was how she would win.

A quick spin and jerk to the wrist pulled her off balance, switching their positions yet again. She did not hesitate, charging forward again, forcing Bawb back into the dining table. Elzina had a plan. She would drive her fist into his chest hard and keep it there long enough to win. The spell required laying a hand on the target, but no one said it had to be an open one.

Bawb swung his hand forward to meet hers, but she realized something was off. He was holding something. It was one of the large metal mugs they drank from at mealtime. Elzina cast a small spell to bolster her fist against the impact then started intoning the words to the stun spell.

"*Zapho orack,*" she cried out, intending to push right through the mug.

The metal broke apart from the impact, her fist driving into his chest. The spell would only require three seconds, and she had the momentum on her side. Bawb pushed against her, reciting the spell as well.

"*Zapho orack,*" he growled, his hand firmly on her.

She didn't care. She had cast first, and that meant hers would activate before his had a chance. Elzina smiled. She would win.

Then she noticed something wrong. Her knuckles were not pressed against soft flesh but rather hard metal. She looked down at the broken mug. It had broken by the look of it. Or rather, it had *appeared* to break. But in reality, it had changed shape, folding around her hand. She was not in contact with his body after all.

Elzina quickly pulled back, Bawb's hand jarred free, breaking the building spell, but now it was his turn to give a little surprise. He twisted the handle of the mug wrapped around her fist, pulling it free, revealing a fine cable built into it. He kicked her knee while pulling her off balance, spinning her around and wrapping both arms tight to her body and cinching the cable tight as she fell to the hard floor.

Elzina landed with a crash, the wind nearly knocked out of her, both arms immobilized and Bawb's weight on top of her. He quickly unreeled more cable, tying her legs in an instant. It would not hold long, but he didn't need much time for what he had in mind.

Casually, with an amused look in his eye, he pressed his palm to her forehead.

"*Zapho orack.*"

Elzina struggled, but it was clear she was done for.

"You were never at a disadvantage," she grumbled. "It was all a ploy."

"You are not the only one who can act," he replied as the stun spell blasted through her.

No longer a threat, Bawb unwrapped her hand and removed the crafted restraint, returning it to the table.

"Thank you, Usalla."

"I wondered why you asked me to bring that particular mug

to dinner for you," she replied with an amused smile. "It seems you had quite the reason."

The crowd gave approving looks but then went back to eating, the Aspirants and Adepts heading back out into the corridor silently. Ghalian could appreciate skill, but they did not cheer.

Griggitz strode over to the table and picked up the mug just as Teacher Warfin walked in.

"You see this?" he asked, tossing it to the new arrival. "Your design?"

Warfin turned it over in his hands, admiring the tool then tossing it back. "No, this is not of my making."

"Vessel Bawb, where did you get this?"

"I crafted it."

"This is *your* design?"

"It is. Teacher Warfin taught us that anything can be a weapon. I thought this would be a useful project, albeit a more defensively oriented one."

"Clearly," Griggitz replied, a tiny, amused grin tickling the corners of his lips as Elzina struggled to sit up. "You employed that lesson to maximum effect. Well done, Bawb."

"Well done, indeed," Warfin agreed. "And now that Elzina is out of the running, I can confirm that you are the last Vessel standing. Congratulations. You have won this game."

Bawb felt a flush of joy well up inside but kept his face neutral.

"Thank you," he replied, eager for his private lessons, but also knowing full well they would almost certainly push him to his limit. Maybe even beyond.

If it helped him to one day become one of the Five, it would all be worth it.

CHAPTER NINE

The following morning the students were called to a small room and told to wait. They all stood quietly at attention, quietly pondering what could possibly follow the prior day's exciting contest. Judging by the way they'd been gathered, whatever was going on, it looked like it was going to be good.

Demelza entered the room and stood silently in front of the assembled youths, surveying them with a critical eye before speaking. Judging them ready, she began.

"It is time for your training to progress to a new degree of difficulty. This will seem novel, but do not lose focus. You will each be given the same amount of coin. Further, each of your konuses will be restricted to the same amount of power. You will wear the clothing on your backs and bring only supplies from the options presented to you."

Demelza looked at the students' faces, gauging their confidence. Some just *looked* ready for this next step. A few seemed a bit trepidatious, but they were all Vessels and had learned long ago that presenting the impression of confidence was often just as important as truly having it.

The instructions were clear. This was to be quest, taking

place on a different world. And it was entirely up to the Vessels how they would get there, how they would complete their task, and how they would return.

There would also be no teachers monitoring them. This was a real-world exercise. And unlike prior outings, they were explicitly informed that this was not a misdirection. They really were on their own.

And they would be timed.

"Is each of our objectives to be the same?" Bawb asked, noting Elzina's piercing stare.

"No. This will be a different mission for each of you, but given your resources, the distances that must be traveled, and the nature of your tasks, there will be adjustments made to even things out."

"What sort of adjustments?" Elzina asked.

"Handicaps are added to account for those who will have shorter or longer travel times. These are not randomly selected tasks. We are very well aware of the length of time they will require, as well as what nature of difficulties each path is likely to encounter, and we have accounted for them all. It is worth noting that while you will be on your own, we *will* know who wins this competition. The Ghalian have eyes everywhere. There are envelopes along with your coin pouches waiting for you on each of your bunks. In them you will find the details of your tasks and departure times. Gather whatever equipment you feel you will need from what has been laid out, and prepare yourselves accordingly. You have traveled to locations out of the compound walls and even off the planet in your time here, so you know what to do. Secure whatever means of transportation you can manage, and good luck to you all."

Bawb and the others hurried to the bunk room and eagerly opened their envelopes, anxious to see just what sort of task they would be facing. They read the contents quickly then scattered, some afforded longer wait times before departure due to closer proximity of their destinations, while others were free to go almost at once.

Ghalian did not waste time, even if they had an excess of it. Any cushion could wind up being of vital importance and was just one more little thing they could take advantage of.

Bawb hurried to the disguise chamber, gathering a few key items to aid in changing his appearance a few times without the use of magic if need be. He had limited magic available to him and feared he would need to save every last bit of it to carry out his task.

He headed to the exit of his preference and sat to wait for his allowed departure time. His konus would let him know when he was free to go. It seemed that while it was his device, the teachers still had some control over it, though none were aware of its more unusual properties.

"I assume none of the others have enough coin for their journeys," he quietly asked the konus as he worked on his disguise's backstory.

I can't really say for certain.

"Cannot, or will not?"

Either way, it doesn't matter. You've got something to do, so just do it.

"I intend to. I was merely curious if the others were facing the same sort of obstacles. But you are correct, it does not matter. We will all have to find a way to reach our destinations regardless of what the others are doing."

Glad you understand that. Oh, and if I were a betting sort of konus, then yes, I would put coin on the others being in the same situation as you.

"But you have no coin."

That doesn't mean I can't ponder a hypothetical.

Bawb took that to be as good a confirmation of his

hypothesis as he would get from the temperamental device and let it go at that. Securing passage was just one more facet of the test, and each would deal with it in their own way.

The time has come, the konus finally announced some time later. *You may depart.*

Bawb headed out for the landing site located more on the outskirts of town, not running but walking, calm and relaxed, just like any other resident of the city. More cargo passed through that one, and given his limited coin, he would have to find a creative way to get to the world he had been given as his destination. His plan was unusual, and a bit risky, but if his acting was up to snuff, he just might pull it off.

At least, this part of his task.

Bawb purchased a crate of produce from a vendor and had it delivered to a temporary holding area before being forwarded to its final destination. He already secured a secondary crate into which he separated much of the cargo, setting it aside as a donation for a local orphanage. The other crate he labeled and sealed, then set to work.

He presented himself as a young trader's assistant tasked with arranging the delivery of some cargo that missed its original transport. He was in trouble and needed to have it delivered as quickly as possible, his employer furious with him for his mistake. Essentially, he set himself up to be taken advantage of, and that was the entire point.

In a rush and willing to pay extra, it did not take long before he found a less than reputable broker willing to help him secure a fast and off-the-books delivery, skipping the usual import and export requirements and keeping him off the manifests.

Bawb accepted, paid the man, and hurried away to supposedly report to his boss. In reality, he set a small fire nearby as a diversion, then climbed into the crate, closing it around himself.

Passenger ships were less frequent to the world he was instructed to reach, but cargo vessels made a lot more stops. They also remained for far shorter durations. Speed of delivery was how they made their money, so they were by their very nature much quicker than the comfy passenger ships. They also cost far less, but they refused to carry people. Especially the grayer ships run by those with flexible morals. And it was not merchants but smugglers who ran on some of the most efficient timetables in the galaxy.

The broker, reputable or not, had made quick work of securing his cargo passage, and just a few hours after he had sealed himself in the crate, Bawb felt the jostling as he was loaded into a ship. Shortly thereafter they lurched into the sky and left atmosphere.

Bawb knew it would be a while before they arrived. The ship would surely be making several stops along the way, but if he was to spend a good deal of time in flight, he might as well see about making himself more comfortable. And as they were underway with their load secure, the crew would surely not be wasting time in the cargo hold.

Bawb carefully cracked open the lid and peered out. It was dark, but that was expected for a cargo hold. More importantly, it was quiet all around. He felt a surge of joy warm his belly. He was a successful stowaway! Carefully, he eased the lid open wider and crept out of its confines, stretching his limbs with relish.

A fist cracked across his chin from his left, a kick hitting his ribs from the right. Bawb leapt into action, defending himself as best he could from his unseen attackers. He fought back hard, using his skills to sense the invisible adversaries' movements despite the darkness, just as the teachers had trained him. He had only taken a single dagger on this mission, the goal not being of a lethal variety, but now found himself wishing he had brought more.

It didn't matter. The blade had been knocked from his hand the moment he reached for it. Whoever he was fighting, even in the dark, they were good. But he was a Ghalian. A Vessel, anyway. And that meant he had a few tricks up his sleeves as well.

Bawb allowed himself to fall into what felt like the larger of the attackers' hands. As soon as he grabbed tight, however, the Ghalian trainee spun, flipping his attacker to the deck, his hands twisted up in the process. He threw a flurry of punches, hoping to eliminate at least one of the threats, when a much smaller pair of hands grabbed him from behind. Grabbed him and threw him clear across the cargo hold.

He hit the wall hard, falling to the deck with a crash as the lights came on.

"Oh, son of a bitch," a familiar voice said. "It's Hozark's, uh, *apprentice*."

"Uzabud?" the boy said, climbing painfully back to his feet.

Bud shook his head and laughed despite the trickle of blood leaking from his nose. "Hey, kid. That's a solid right you've got there."

"Idiot. I could have killed you," Henni grumbled as the small, fierce woman walked over to their unexpected guest and gave him a tight hug. "But it's good to see you. Been a while."

"It has."

She playfully whacked him on the arm, holding back the true force contained in that diminutive package. "And here you are, a stowaway."

"I wasn't expecting anyone in the cargo hold."

"Yeah, we're a bit more cautious than most. Good thing Henni saw who you were. It could have gotten ugly. Things have been a little tense lately."

"Why?"

"Our, uh, *friend*, got herself into some trouble."

"Freaking Nixxa," Henni sighed, shaking her head. "Always something with her."

"Yeah. But never mind that. It's all being dealt with," Bud continued. "What a mess."

"I actually know her. She kind of has it out for me," Bawb noted.

Bud and Henni laughed. "Oh, we heard *all* about that," Bud said. "*Everyone* has. Man, stealing that drookonus right out from under her nose? That was legendary."

Bawb allowed himself a grin as his adrenaline finally dropped back to normal. "I suppose it was. But what are you two doing here?"

Henni cocked her head. "Us? You're the one who stowed away on our ship."

"*Your* ship?"

"Yup."

"Oh."

"Uh-huh. So, you were about to tell us what you're doing here," Bud pressed.

"Well, I hid in a container to gain passage to Zahlar. I paid a broker to get it there as fast as he could."

"Duggix. Yeah, we know him well. He's the one who contracted us to deliver it, along with the rest of our cargo. But why were you hiding in a crate?"

"I lack the funds for a passenger ship."

Henni gave Bud a look. Bud just shrugged, turning his attention back to the boy.

"Well, there's no way you're running away from the Ghalian, so I'd wager they're putting you through some kind of test, am I right?"

Silence.

"Look, kid, we've known your—Hozark a long time. And let me tell you, we've seen a *lot*. You can talk to us."

"Yeah, there's no shame in being taken off guard," Henni added. "Why, even Hozark's been surprised a few times, believe it or not."

"Really?"

She nodded. "Oh yeah, and what a story that is. But that's his to tell. Anyway, what matters now is that you're here, and we're heading to Zahlar regardless of your little stunt. We have some deliveries to make to the local magistrate."

"But I thought you were pirates. Smugglers."

Henni and Bud looked at each other, amusement in their eyes.

Bud ran his hand across his stubble. "Well, we are, kid. But the best way to go unnoticed is to have a legit gig as a cover story. And making these delivery runs from time to time is exactly that. But you know all about deception by now."

"Teacher Demelza especially has been thorough in her instruction."

"Ah, Demelza. Love that gal," Henni said with a grin. The smile faded a moment later. "We'll take you to Zahlar, but we've gotta treat you just like any other stowaway we caught. You know how the Ghalian are. No special treatment, even for you."

"I would not expect any."

Henni gave an approving nod. "Spoken like a true Ghalian."

"I am not one, technically."

"Not yet, maybe. But I'm pretty confident you will be." She glanced at Uzabud. He gave a reluctant shrug. "I know."

"Know what?" Bawb asked.

"For now, I'm afraid we've gotta restrain you until we arrive. We'll hand you over to the authorities when we land, just like anyone else who stowed away."

"I understand."

"Good. Now, if you happen to figure a way out of this mess by then, well, that's all part of the training too, I suppose."

"Thank you."

"Don't thank us. You still have to do it on your own. If you can."

CHAPTER TEN

Bud and Henni bound their unwanted passenger just as thoroughly as they would any other stowaway, then locked him in the storage room adjacent to the cargo hold for the duration of the trip. They liked Bawb and had spent plenty of time with him and Hozark as their friend helped train the boy over the years, but the rules were the rules. Of course, these two were habitual rule benders, if not outright breakers, but they were on their best behavior in this instance. The Ghalian did not take their training lightly.

Bawb would just have to deal with the consequences of his capture like anyone else.

"Almost there," Henni called out when they exited the jump, arriving in orbit above their destination. "Well, I guess this is it. This sucks."

"I know. But we really can't go easy on the kid," Bud said, reading the tone of her voice and feeling the same regret. But they had no choice. He kept on course and approached Zahlar's atmosphere then started their descent to the landing area.

"Maybe just a little—"

"Nope. I mean, c'mon, Henni. For all we know, Hozark could be watching us, and we'd never be the wiser."

"Would he, though? Probably not, but then he is a sneaky son of a bitch, and hands down the best I've ever seen with a shimmer cloak."

Bud nodded his agreement as he feathered the controls, bringing the ship to a smooth landing, hovering just inches above the ground. "I doubt he'd do that to us after all these years, but it doesn't matter. This isn't just some trainee. This is *Bawb* we're talking about here. He'd want us to play by the rules, and so we will."

"Yeah, yeah," she grumbled as the ship powered down. "Well, I guess it's time to go let him know we've arrived."

"I'm sure he knows already," Bud said as he rose from his seat.

The two headed out of the control room and down to the cargo hold, not thrilled about what they had to do but resigned to the task. What they saw when they reached his holding area, however, surprised them.

The cargo hatch was open, the load master already inventorying the crates as she'd done so many times before. That wasn't unusual. What was, was the empty holding area. That, and the restraints lying on the ground in a neat pile.

"How did he get out of those? Henni, you fastened them tight, didn't you?"

"You really need to ask?" she shot back with her usual sass. "We agreed, no special treatment. He was trussed up just like anyone else would have been."

"And yet he is not here."

"I've got eyes, you *ass*," she said, smacking his arm.

"Hey, just saying! But seriously, how the hell did he manage that?"

"He must be more skilled than we gave him credit for. Considering his lineage, I can't say I'm surprised."

"Shh," Bud hissed. "He might still be here somewhere."

"If he already learned to use a shimmer cloak at this age, we'd have a lot more to worry about than that. And besides, if he did, we'd never have caught him in the first place."

"True. Well, I guess let's go see what Bunkus has to say."

The pair strode across the metal deck to the stout woman overseeing the unloading of the crates destined for this stop. She had a list of them pulled up from her specialized konus and was ticking them off one by one despite the device being perfectly capable of doing it for her.

Bunkus was nothing if not a stickler for detail. That, and any errors, whether caused by the konus or not, would be blamed on her, and that was not happening on her watch.

"Hey, Bunkus," Bud called out. "Where'd the kid go?"

"Kid? What kid? You two finally start a family?"

"We just saw you a few months ago," Henni grumbled. "So the answer is no. And Jeez, Bunkus, how short do you think a gestation cycle is, anyway?"

"I dunno. Your kind is a mystery to me. You're a weird one, Henni, and the only one of your sort I've ever seen."

Bud stepped between them before Henni said something she might regret, her famous temper once again putting them both in hot water. "Yeah, she's something special all right," he said, soothing the ire of the diminutive woman at his side. "But no kid came out of the cargo bay?"

"I told ya, I've been here and didn't see anyone. Why's a kid on your ship, anyway?"

"Oh, just helping a friend. You know how it is. Family visits and that sort of thing. Nothing to worry yourself about. I know you're busy."

"You can say that again. Look at all this stuff. And there's three more ships coming in today."

"Well, don't let us slow you down. We'll let you get back to it."

"Appreciated. Hey, you two sticking around this time? Maybe we'll grab a drink later."

Bud shook his head. "We'll see. We're not staying long. Lots of work at the moment, gotta get it while the getting's good."

"Ain't that the truth. Well, I'll let ya know when I'm done here."

"Thanks, Bunkus," Bud replied, leading Henni to the ship's galley.

The two checked all the smugglers' hiding places along the way. Bawb had spent plenty of time aboard their ship in the last few years and knew them all, but there was no trace was to be found.

"Where in the world did he go?" Henni wondered now that they were out of earshot. "It's not like there's anywhere to hide we haven't already looked."

Bud shook his head, a little grin on his lips. "I honestly have no idea. But I wish him the best of luck."

On the outside of town, a fetid wastewater pool of stinking refuse slowly bubbled into the ground, its contents absorbing and dispersing into a subterranean storage cistern. It took time, but the natural geological feature had proven a convenient resource for arriving spaceships.

Once they were finally out of deep space and able to replenish their ship's supply of fresh water on an inhabited planet, inbound craft would engage their waste recycling storage tank spells that emptied them out, sending the contents into the pool located far enough from town to avoid stinking up the place. It was an automatic feature on some ships but not all. Having flown with them in the past Bawb happened to know for a fact that Bud and Henni utilized the automated feature on theirs. One less thing for a crew of two to keep track of.

It was a seemingly pointless bit of insider knowledge that he was now using to his advantage. At least, he hoped so.

The fall wasn't bad, all things considered. The spell emptied the tank right over the pool, as intended, the anchoring spell making a very clear deposit zone for the waste. What he had been uncertain of was if there were any safeguards on the spell to keep it from activating with a living organism in the tank.

His abruptly leaving the pitch-black confines of the ship's waste tank and suddenly flying though bright air until he splashed down in the disgusting sludge pool answered that question.

He had cast the largest bubble spell around his head that he could, and even managed to extend it a little bit onto his shoulders and torso. It wasn't much, but it would afford him at least a few more breaths if he needed them. As it turned out, it was a good thing he had, because while he had indeed been transported well outside the ship's hull, he'd splashed down deep, and reaching the surface of the pool was taking far more effort than he expected.

Bawb struggled against the sucking filth, straining to swim up to the fresh air he knew was not far above. The effort was great, and he was using up his precious air faster than he wanted, but he pushed on hard. This was do or die. If he didn't make it to the surface, no one would ever find his body, and he would be forever lost, buried in a river of shit.

He pulled with his hands, clawing his way through the filth, until, at long last, his hand broke through the surface. He splashed hard, leveraging himself up high enough to release his spell and take a deep breath.

The pungent air hit his face, putrid and foul. But it was air, and right now that was all that mattered. Now that he was on the surface, Bawb was able to swim-crawl through the muck to the edge of the pool. He climbed out, covered in vile filth from head to toe.

A young boy was sitting nearby on a tree stump. When he saw what surely looked like some sort of demonic shit monster lurch out from the muck he jumped to his feet with a shriek, running as fast as his six legs would carry him.

Bawb chuckled as he quickly stripped off his clothes, hurrying to find the nearest source of clean water. What he located was a runoff stream from a farming canal. The water was brown and smelled slightly, but it was far better than what he was covered in.

Bawb jumped in, scrubbing not only his body but also his clothing, washing as best he could given the lack of soap. Fortunately, there was a strong enough current to constantly refresh the water, and soon enough he was clean from head to toe.

He stepped out of the stream and wrung out his clothes. Looking up, he gauged the time of day. He didn't have time to waste. Reluctantly, he cast a minor drying spell, drying his clothes quickly with only a minimal expenditure of magic. It was a spell they'd been taught as Aspirants back when they first started training extensively in cold and wet environments.

"The cold will kill you if you are not careful," their teacher had noted. "And being wet will only amplify the danger."

From that day forward it was a spell he and the others used regularly, and as a result, the intent to cast it was second nature at this point.

Level up: Bubble spell. Adaptation and novel use of magic.

Another icon flashed then became unblurry. This was something new. *Level unlocked: Exploiting enemy magic system.*

"Bud and Henni aren't my enemies," he informed the konus.

Hey, I didn't name the skills, I just keep track of them. And that was actually pretty clever.

"It was, wasn't it? I must remember to further study the possibility of exploiting such forms of cleaning spells further. They could be quite handy one day."

There's more, the konus said. *Level up: Improvisational survival. That could have killed you, you know, but you expanded your bubble spell and did something most would not consider. Congratulations.*

"Thank you," he said, putting his clothes back on and checking the remaining magic level allotted for this mission. "Let's see if all that work pays off."

CHAPTER ELEVEN

Bawb had been fortunate that Bud and Henni hadn't taken his konus or the things in his pockets when they caught him. The former seemed very underpowered to all but Bawb, and the latter was just a seemingly random assortment of items that had little value and were of no threat.

Unfortunately, while many things had made it through his escape intact, the skin dyes he had among them had not survived his unexpected swim. That would make his disguise work far more difficult than he had anticipated.

Bawb counted the coin in his possession. It was hardly anything, and certainly not enough to source replacement items. At least, not on such short notice. And in any case, they would be far too expensive, not to mention a young Wampeh purchasing them would raise eyebrows. He would simply have to improvise.

The walk from the waste pool allowed him a chance to refocus his mind and run through potential options. By the time he made his way back into the town center he had a few ideas that might work. All he needed now was to put one into action.

He walked a roundabout route, scouting the area around his

target's location, noting potential escape routes just in case he found himself needing one on the fly. It wasn't the plan, but plans often went awry. And as this was his first truly solo mission, he was leaving nothing to chance.

Bawb spent a fraction of his coin in the spice market, acquiring several varieties with which he could alter the color of his exposed skin. It wouldn't be perfect by any stretch, but Demelza had taught them how to make simple dyes with what was at hand, and that lesson would now be put to good use.

The important thing here was the deception. Bawb was not showing his face as a Wampeh, and when he completed his task, none would know who to look for.

In addition to changing his skin color, he added the padding of additional layers of clothing from a beggar's trade pile. It would suit his needs just fine. He was not disguising himself by attire, but rather, using the added layers to bulk up his own clothes, the size giving him the appearance of one slightly larger and older than he actually was.

All of this was just setting the stage for his assigned mission and subsequent escape. He had been given a task, and while it was not of the deadly variety, which he would not expect as a mere Vessel, it was nevertheless something of a surprise. Not the usual sort of thing for a Ghalian to do. But this was how Vessels learned the ropes.

The target was a non-magical person. A man. A trader who trafficked in not only the usual wares found in the marketplace, but also something else. Something far less savory that had viscerally upset the Five and motivated the Ghalian to accept the contract on him at no charge.

Had it been a simple assassination that would have been a different discussion, but this was not that sort of mission. The man would pay for what he did, most definitely, but in a different way. One that would allow his competitors to absorb his regular business and keep the trade flowing smoothly.

As for his secret business, it would be shut down for good, but only after all of its tentacles were identified and cut off. To that end Bawb had been tasked with acquiring the names of those supplying the trader and relaying that information to his superiors. For those individuals participating in his illicit trade it was a given the Ghalian would then have a far bloodier response.

Tormix was the man's name, and he seemed unremarkable so far as traders went. Bipedal, of moderate height, a bit overweight from years directing labor rather than participating in it. He had dark yellow skin and deep brown hair running from his head to his shoulders, almost like a cowl.

But the man's genetics were not the issue here. That he was trafficking in children was.

Bawb had not been given details, but the little he had learned in his mission brief was more than enough to spark a smoldering anger. This was not to be an assassination mission, but if they had asked, he would have gladly accepted the challenge despite only being a Vessel.

But the objective at hand was to get Tormix captured, his lackeys arrested alongside him, and if all went to plan, the entire network shut down. Bawb's task was to topple that first domino and set it all in motion.

The building he tracked the man to was a freestanding affair with thick walls and undoubtedly a few muting spells as well. Half a dozen guards clothed as regular civilians came and went, trying to appear like any other civilians on the street, but Bawb knew what they were. He watched and took note of their patterns and identities over several hours, the mission's ticking clock loud in his head but forcing himself to ignore it despite the time crunch.

Some things one did not rush. And knowing what he was getting into, as well as how to get out, was certainly one of them.

By the time night began to fall he had not only identified all of the guards as well as their routines and the time of their comings and goings, but had also come up with a plan. It would be tough to bring attention to someone who had gone to great lengths to go unnoted despite being in a heavily traveled area, but Bawb felt confident he could make it work. That is, if he could just pull off not one but two rather difficult feats.

The first was to acquire a sleeping drug of some sort and get it into Tormix's food. Bawb had studied many plants and how they reacted with different species and was pretty sure he had found one in the marketplace that would do the trick, dropping his target but not affecting his guards as they were a different, more stout variety of races.

Those people would have to be dealt with in a different manner.

And that was the second part of his task that would strain his abilities. The guards had to be taken out of the equation. Not publicly, but quietly, removing their employer's safety net without him even realizing it.

Bawb purchased a sizable quantity of the plant and crushed it in a piece of cloth, squeezing the juice into a container then using a minor spell to condense it, dramatically increasing its potency. It was both coin and magic he didn't want to spend, but there were simply no better options. He would figure out how to adjust for the expenditure after the job was done.

"Pardon me," Bawb said as he stepped into a small café across the street from Tormix's building. "I'm new. Mr. Tormix told me to bring him his usual for dinner, but I don't know what that is. Can you help me?"

The man at the counter chuckled pleasantly. Bawb had seen several of Tormix's men visit this establishment during his surveillance and figured it was a fifty-fifty chance the ploy would work.

"Of course. I'll whip it right up. You can wait over there."

"Thank you," Bawb said, pulling up a seat.

The proprietor came back with a rather large box of food separated into several compartments. "Here ya go," he said, folding it closed. "Just what the boss ordered."

"Can I see?" Bawb asked. "I just don't want to screw up next time. I really need this job."

"Sure thing," the man said, then went through each of the items, describing them in detail.

Bawb grew wide-eyed and made appreciative sounds, licking his lips as if subconsciously. The man noticed and took pity on the poor kid.

"Tell you what. There was some extra left over. Hang on a minute and I'll get you a little box for yourself."

"Really?"

"Sure. You seem like a good kid, and we look after our own around here."

"Thank you so much. I really appreciate it."

"No worries. Just sit tight. I'll be back in a jiff."

The man left Bawb alone. It wouldn't take long to throw some food in a box, so Bawb had to work fast. He leaned forward, as if smelling the food, dripping the plant extract into several of the dishes, watching it soak in almost immediately. He hoped he got the dosage right. If not, he would have to fight the man and render him unconscious by physical means, and that would spoil the plan.

There was no use worrying. All he could do was carry on until fate either let him pass or steered him another direction.

"Here ya go," the cheerful fellow said when he returned just a couple of minutes later.

He handed a small box to Bawb then continued packing up

the larger one. Bawb rose to his feet and dug in his pocket for coin.

"No need, lad. Your boss has a tab with me."

"Oh, I'm sorry. I didn't mean to offend you."

"Offend? Offering me coin will never offend me," he laughed. "Every little bit helps, you know."

Bawb laughed along with him, mirroring the man's movements to further put his mind at ease and make him feel a certain kinship with the boy. It was pretty basic psychology, but it worked, and that was all that mattered.

Bawb picked up the package but hesitated. He turned to the man and dug the coin back from his pocket.

"Let me ask you something. This is my first day, and I have so much to do if I want to make a good impression. Do you think you could hand this off to the guard inside the door? I forget his name."

"Dinkin's working today, I think."

"Yeah, I think that was his name. Thing is, I'm already behind. I can give you this if you'll help me out. I know it's not much, but I can't afford to screw up today, and I have an endless list of tasks I must still complete."

"Keep the coin, lad. I'm happy to help."

Bawb placed it on the counter anyway. "I appreciate it. But my father always said, 'Pay your way, son, and it will come back to you a thousand-fold in the long run.'"

The man pocketed the coin without argument and picked up the box. "Your father sounds like a wise man. I've got this. You get on with your chores. I'm sure I'll be seeing you around."

"Thank you so much!" Bawb chirped, then picked up his to-go box and took off at a jog as if late for one of a dozen more tasks.

He rounded the corner then turned his coat inside out and put a headwrap on before squatting against the wall like a beggar. He stayed like that as he watched the man deliver the food to the man at the door then meander back to his shop. It was all working as planned. The guard knew this man, so the delivery wasn't questioned, thus negating any possible suspicion. That accomplished, all Bawb had to do was move on to the next part of his plan.

Unfortunately, that would entail taking down a half dozen guards without anyone being the wiser.

He had carefully selected the spell to employ before beginning his mission. It was a minor stun spell similar to what they had used so recently on one another in the training house. Only, this did not require three seconds of contact. It did, however, need to be cast at very close proximity.

As it was relatively short-lived he would have to quickly bind and hide the victims just in case they roused from their slumber and regained use of their bodies, so being forced to be so close was almost a blessing in disguise.

Bawb waited a little while, then made his way to the small alleyway on the side of Tormix's building. He took a deep breath and pictured the spell in his mind, locking in the intent and power as firmly as he could. It was go time, and he would have only one shot at this.

CHAPTER TWELVE

Two guards lay unconscious and tightly bound in a small room just off the side entrance to the building Bawb had successfully penetrated. He had followed one inside, taking him by complete surprise, laying him out in a flash. No one expected anyone to have the nerve to try to break into Tormix's place. Not with his good reputation and respected guards on duty.

It made the infiltration all the easier.

Bawb dragged the man into an empty room and trussed him up tight just in case the spell wore off sooner than expected, then moved fast. He would not have much time to spare. The guards walked a circuit, and eventually, their missing friends would be noticed.

Unless they were *all* taken out of the equation before that could happen.

The second fell as easily as the first, and for the young Ghalian, eliminating adult adversaries in a real-world setting was a heady feeling indeed. Two down, four to go. Four, and their boss. But if all had gone to plan and the drug had done its work, that part would already be handled by the time Bawb reached him.

Bawb thought for a moment he might attempt a muting spell to mask his movements but quickly nixed the idea. He didn't have the magic to spare, and he was still having a lot of trouble with that particular spell. It was above his level, and despite practicing whenever he managed to find time to himself, he still could not seem to get it to cast properly.

As a result, he had to risk being spotted by the guards. That would be bad.

He was still a teenager, and fighting a muscular adult would be a serious issue. His Ghalian training gave him more than enough skills in his toolkit to compensate for that handicap, but the tricky part would be keeping them non-lethal. These men were guards, and almost certainly knew at least some of the dirty dealings that went on in the building, but the instructions were clear. No outside influence was to be apparent. And if he applied the stun spells properly, no one would be the wiser. If he had to fight them, however, all bets were off.

Of course, he would still have to stun the guards once more, and more robustly, before he left, then arrange their sleeping forms with a bottle in their hand. Once their boss was in custody, they would certainly rather admit to drinking on duty than being part of what he was involved in. The Ghalian could determine if they should be allowed to live after that, a decision that was not part of Bawb's task.

He crept through the building, using his stealth and smaller size to his advantage, hiding until they came close then taking down one guard after another, the spell working its magic quickly and efficiently, keeping him from a face-to-face altercation.

It was exhausting work, not for the physical aspect but rather the psychological one. It was a *real* mission with *real* consequences if he were to be caught. When the last of the inside guards finally fell, only then did he feel the tension he had been carrying the entire time. But now there was just one left. After that it was on to the main event.

Bawb checked his victims. All were still unconscious and showing no signs of rousing. Good. This afforded him a little more time.

He carefully crept to Tormix's offices. The man was fast asleep in his chair, his half-eaten meal in front of him. To anyone happening upon him it would just appear as though he was taking a long nap, exactly as planned.

Bawb scoured the office, finding a concealed lockbox embedded in the wall and opening it easily. Inside was a ledger of transactions, trading routes, and most importantly, the names of co-conspirators. Bawb smiled to himself. These men and women were as good as dead, and they deserved it.

He tucked the ledger into his clothing and turned his attention to looking for the hidden door that would lead to the cages the abducted youths were held in. A very slight arc in the dust on the floor showed him where one of the seemingly solid walls would pivot open. All he had to do was find the release mechanism. And as Tormix was not a power user, it took him less than a minute to locate it.

"Sloppy," he said to himself, shaking his head as he triggered the release.

The door swung open, the pungent stink of sweat and fear wafting out to greet him. He peered inside long enough to see at least a half dozen children locked up and cowering. Much as he wanted to release them all himself, that was not the plan. Tormix had to go down for this, and his network along with him if all went well.

Bawb closed the door most of the way but left it open more than wide enough for anyone to notice if they entered the room.

"One left," he said, steeling himself for the final guard. The one standing at the front door. He didn't have a route, didn't leave his position to enter or exit. This one, he would have to lure inside, and that made him the trickiest of the lot.

Bawb made his way to the front door and eased back into the space behind it then quietly unlocked it from the inside. The door was thick and required a little tug to get it moving, but in no time it had swung partially open. Now he just had to hope the guard wasn't too focused on what was in front of him to miss what was behind.

"Yarrik, is that you?" the guard said, turning to the open door. "You know the boss don't like it when you play around like that."

No reply.

"I'm serious. I don't want to get in trouble because of your stupid games. Not again."

Once more there was no reply.

"I'm not messing around, Yarrik," the guard said, stepping inside to scold his friend. "This is not a ga—"

The stun spell dropped him in a heap but his feet were still partially out of the door. Bawb grabbed him and pulled hard, sliding him from view and closing the door tight. He propped the man against the wall and slid a half-empty bottle in his hands.

"One last thing to do," he said, preparing for the final piece of the puzzle.

Bawb moved to the storage room beside Tormix's office and started a small fire. It was nothing large enough to threaten the structure, but it was a fire, nonetheless. He then added a little embellishment in the form of some wooden items he had first poured water on. They would create more smoke, and smoke was what he wanted.

He looked around, satisfied with his handiwork. This might just succeed. A carved piece of bone on a stand caught his eye as he was about to leave. Delicate, but something about it felt powerful. He glanced at the sleeping man then figured he wouldn't be needing it. Not in prison.

Bawb slid the carved bone in his pocket and retraced his steps, hitting each guard with a final stun spell to keep them down before untying them, erasing the only sign of his presence. He then made his way back to the front of the building and cracked the front door open, then turned and headed for the rear, exiting without anyone paying any mind.

It was a short walk around a few blocks to circle back to a vantage point from which he could observe the front door. He purchased a snack from a vendor then leaned against the wall to eat it at his leisure, waiting for things to kick off.

"Fire!" someone finally shouted, noticing the smoke pouring out of Tormix's property.

A group of locals hurried to the building, followed by one of the local constabulary. All rushed inside, hurrying to pull out any victims they could. The guards were hauled out one by one, followed by their slumbering boss. Tormix began to rouse when he was unceremoniously dumped on the ground by the constable.

"What's going on?" he demanded, his eyes going wide when he saw the stream of people going into his building.

"Watch him," the constable said to a pair of town guards who had just arrived, a look of pure anger in his eyes. "He's under arrest."

He then turned and hurried back into the smoke-filled building.

Bawb felt a flood of relief wash over him. The ruse had worked. To all present it just seemed there had been a fire and the locals had come to the businessman's aid. Normally, his guards would have handled it before a wisp of smoke had made it outside, but not today. Today, they had been sloppy. Or so it seemed, anyway. And their boss had been caught red-handed, his hidden illicit slave trade laid bare for all to see.

And best of all, no one suspected outside interference, just as planned.

Level up: Deception and Subterfuge. Misdirection enhancement, the konus informed him.

It was a nice bit of news, but what he needed now was to get back to the training house, hopefully before anyone else.

He hurried for the nearest landing site, hopeful he could find a way off this world and at least somewhat closer to home. He was nearly out of coin, and his magic was low, but that would be the same situation for the other Vessels, knowing the Ghalian teachers. He still had a chance.

Bawb walked among the ships, looking at their rates and counting his coin. There wasn't a good spot to try to sneak aboard a ship this time. He would have to pay and get to a world where he could better manipulate the system to his advantage. But where could he go with so little coin?

"Hey, kid," a familiar voice called out.

Bawb turned, unsure if Bud would try to capture him or just say hello. Fortunately, it was the latter. Henni was at his side, as usual, an amused grin on her face.

"Nice job getting off our ship," she said. "Honestly, I did not see that coming. How'd you do it?"

"With great care," Bawb replied cryptically.

"Ha! He sounds like Hozark," Bud said with a laugh. "Always mysterious, never giving away your tricks and secrets."

"Would you?" the boy asked.

"Me? Oh, hell no. I may be a gregarious fool—"

"Amen to that," Henni chimed in.

"Hush, you."

"You gonna make me?"

"Maybe later," he replied, flashing her a mischievous grin

then turning his attention back to the Ghalian youth. "So, where you off to now? If you can say, that is."

"I do not know. I must get back home, but I am short of coin."

"Ooh, that's a tough one. What's your plan?"

"Find a ship that will get me closer and adjust from there."

Bud and Henni shared a look. "You want a ride?" Bud asked. "Not all the way, but we're heading that general direction."

"I cannot. I must do this on my own. You know the rules."

"Yeah, sure we do. But part of your training is fitting in and making friends. And sometimes friends do favors for each other."

"Like giving someone a ride," Henni added.

"Exactly. I mean, we aren't changing our route, so it won't be all the way there, but we can at least get you closer. From there you'll need to secure a ride the last part of the way. Hey, Henni, you think Olo's still holed up on Maringus?"

"Might be. And if he is, I know he'd happily play ferryman for a price. Bawb, you have anything to trade?"

"Just coin," he said. "Oh, wait. I also have this, but I don't know what value it has."

He pulled out the carved bone and handed it to Henni. Her galaxy eyes sparkled brighter than usual as she examined it.

"Oh, this is nice. I won't ask where you got it, but yeah, Olo will definitely take it in trade." She handed it to Bud, who was likewise impressed with the relic.

"Hell, I'd be tempted to take you all the way for this," he said. "But that would be pushing it a little too much. Come on, we'll take you close and hook you up with our good friend Olo. He's a handful, and he'll talk your ear off, but he'll do just about anything for a price. And giving a kid a ride is a walk in the park compared to his usual gigs. Just one thing. You can't tell him your real name, or your final destination, or why you're going there."

"But he's your friend."

"Yeah, he is, but outsiders don't know about the training house."

"But you do."

Bud shrugged and flashed a grin. "Well, let's just say we have a sort of special understanding with the Five."

Bawb's eyes lit up. "Wait. You know *more* of them? More than just Master Hozark?"

"Kid, we know *all* of them. Why? You have some kind of interest in the Five?"

"I want to be one of them one day."

Bud flashed a bright smile. "Train hard, kid, and one day you just may get your wish. But for now, let's see about getting you home."

CHAPTER THIRTEEN

Bud guided the ship up and out of the atmosphere with the smoothness Bawb had come to expect of him. Having flown with the pirates on several occasions, he knew just how skilled the man was when he wasn't trying to appear to be a lesser pilot to those observing their flight.

With only Bawb aboard and no real itinerary for the moment, he was able to slide back into his usual ways, and that meant expert control over his ship and its powerful Drookonus.

Once they were safely out of orbit, he set their course, flying them toward the edge of the system before he would engage the ship's jump. It was a magic-saving maneuver, allowing them to travel a bit farther without tapping into the more robust aspects of their Drookonus. The less planets and moons they had to jump past, the less power they would use, and as this was a freebie for a friend, they were conserving where they could.

Of course, they knew he was on a timetable and were not lollygagging, but this was how any other passenger would likely be treated, and that was exactly how their teachers would have wanted it.

"We should be clear to jump in a little bit," Bud said once he locked their course in and set the nav spells to alert him of any obstacles in their path. "You hungry?"

"He's a kid, Bud. Of course he's hungry," Henni joked. "And I could do with a meal too."

"Okay then, food it is."

The trio headed to the ship's galley, where Bud set about arranging a snacking board of various treats. Being smugglers as well as pirates, they were often paid in unusual ways. One of those was a share of some of the more-difficult-to-come-by food and drink they ferried from place to place.

As a result, the spread was quite impressive and contained a multitude of treats the young Ghalian had never even heard of.

"You like the Marfus cheese?" Henni asked, scraping another helping onto a savory cracker.

"It is quite nice, though a little pungent," Bawb said, washing it down with a pale green cooler in a frosty mug.

"Yeah, it's kind of an acquired taste."

"Henni, come on. Manners," Bud chided.

"Oh, give me a break," she replied, washing her mouthful down. "You talk with your mouth full too. I see it all the time."

"Yeah, when it's just the two of us. But we have company."

"It's Hozark's—it's just Bawb. He's like family."

"Sure. But still."

"Ugh. You're ridiculous."

"You know you love it."

Bawb watched the two bicker and banter, marveling at the way the pair could seem to fight but never maliciously and always with an undercurrent of affection.

"Hey, kid, you like spicy?" Bud asked, watching their guest tuck into the Orlag peppers with gusto.

Bawb nodded enthusiastically. "I rather do."

Henni shook her head. "Don't, Bud."

"What? He said he likes spicy." He turned back to the teen. "Have you ever heard of Nasturian?"

"Teacher Demelza mentioned it once. A potent spice, and magically enhanced from what I understand."

"You wanna try some?"

Henni flashed him a look. "Bud, I'm serious."

"Just a taste. Come on, he's never tried it."

Bawb was actually quite interested in the novel experience. A spice of that potency was something he would be hard pressed to find on his own, but Bud and Henni had some and were willing to share.

"I am not afraid," he said. "I would very much like to see what all the fuss is about."

"I like spicy, so take it from me when I say this is *not* a pleasant kind of hot," Henni informed him. "Trust me."

"I do. But how better to learn than by experience?"

She shrugged and threw up her hands. "Fine. It's your funeral."

Bud grinned wide as he hurried to retrieve the tiny vial of Nasturian. Henni grabbed several towels and a bucket while he did.

"Okay, so this is Nasturian. Spiciest thing you'll ever taste, bar none," Bud said, carefully opening the vial and dipping a needle into the liquid. He then tapped the tip on a cracker with cheese, the Nasturian not even visible to the naked eye.

"Will that be enough?" Bawb asked.

"Oh, trust me, you don't want more than that," Henni said, sliding the bucket closer to him.

Bawb hesitated a moment. Was it really that bad? Or was Henni just messing with him? Knowing her, either was possible. In any case, he had committed, and frankly, he was quite curious just how much it would burn. He popped the entire cracker in his mouth and chewed.

The answer came at once. It was far, *far* worse than he could have possibly imagined.

Bawb spat out his mouthful into the bucket immediately, grabbing his cooler and draining it in a flash. The cold liquid had no effect.

"It burns! The pain," he gasped, sweat breaking out on his brow.

"Can't say I didn't warn ya," Henni said with a shrug.

Bawb tried to focus his mind, using his Ghalian control techniques to calm himself and control his body. None of them worked. The pain was excruciating. He pounded his fist on the table as his stomach knotted up hard.

"I put some ice water in the head," Bud informed him. "It won't help much, but at least you'll stay hydrated."

Bawb lunged from the table and raced to the restroom, shutting the door and promptly vomiting into the toilet, tears streaming from his eyes and snot running freely from his nose. He grabbed the nearest water container and drained it, promptly throwing it up as well.

What was I thinking? he asked himself as he got as comfortable as he could. It was going to be a long time spent leaning over the toilet, he feared.

"That was mean," Henni said, cleaning up the table.

"It's an experience," Bud replied. "You remember the first time you had it?"

"How can I ever forget?"

"Precisely. And we were here for his first taste, which is going to live on in his head forever."

"But is that really such a good thing?"

"Better with friends than enemies."

"I suppose you're right," she agreed. "He does seem to be making a lot of progress. He's growing up fast."

"Did you expect any less?"

"No, of course not. But when we first met him, he was just this scrawny little kid, and now he's almost a man."

"He's still got a few years to go, but yeah, point taken. Hozark's done a good job steering him in the right direction. You know, I honestly think he might be able to become one of the Five one day. Time will tell."

"Yup," she agreed with a little shrug. "Well, we've got some time before he's done in there. Up for a little sparring?"

"I wasn't planning on having my ass kicked today, but sure, why not?"

The two headed off to the cargo bay, now empty and spacious, leaving Bawb to suffer in peace. He spent a solid half hour curled over the toilet before finally making his way out. Amazingly, once the Nasturian had left his system, it was as if it had never been there. The burning, that is. The cramps in his muscles from contracting so hard would linger a while yet.

Level up: Poisons and magic, the konus informed him. *And now you've experienced—and survived—Nasturian.*

"It was horrible," Bawb said, wiping his mouth with the back of his hand. "The pain would not cease no matter what I tried."

Yeah, that's Nasturian for you. Spicy on its own, but what makes it so potent is the magical component amplifying its heat. That's what makes it so hot. It enhances and elevates it to a level that can even kill if ingested in large enough quantities.

"I only had the tiniest amount. I cannot imagine how bad a full dose could be."

Bad. But keep that in mind. One day it may be of use to you. Anyway, most wait many more years before their first experience with Nasturian. It was pretty dumb of you to try, but you got through it in one piece.

"Thank you?" he said, more a question than a statement, then headed out of the head.

Bawb walked the ship, his body feeling more like itself with every step. By the time he found Bud and Henni in the cargo bay all ill effects of the spicy surprise were gone.

"Hey, there he is. How was it?" Bud asked.

Henni slammed him across the face, dropping him to the ground.

"Never let your guard down," she said with a laugh.

Bud pushed himself up from the floor, rubbing his jaw. "Not fair. I was talking to Bawb."

"So? No one said the fight was over."

"You're ridiculous, you know that?"

"You know you love it," she replied with a fiery grin and a look in her eye that could have melted steel.

Bud actually blushed a little.

Henni turned her attention to their guest. "You feeling better?"

"Much. That was quite an experience."

"Yeah, that's one way of putting it. Hey, you feel up to a little sparring? It's been a long time, and I'd like to see what you've learned since last time."

Bawb rolled his shoulders. "That would be fun. I think it could—"

Henni didn't wait, charging at him in a diving spin, her small but hard fists flying right at his face. Bawb reacted immediately, his training kicking in before his brain could even register what was happening. He blocked the attack, pivoting off to the side.

Henni flung herself back at him, a rear elbow driving into his stomach powerfully enough to send him sliding on the metal floor. But Bawb had trained long and hard, and his abs were more than strong enough to take the blow. Still, this was no joke. Henni was playing hard.

"Don't let her bully you," Bud called out, glad it was someone else's turn to deal with the little dynamo of a woman. "You've got this."

Bawb ignored him, already deeply focused on the whirling dervish bombarding him with attack after attack. He parried and blocked, throwing counters hard and fast. He landed a few, hard enough to slow her attack but nowhere near enough to stop her. Henni just grinned at the blows. He knew full well she was far more durable than she appeared. In fact, from what both Bud and Hozark had said, there were few who could stand up to her in single combat if she was enraged.

Fortunately, this was just practice, but even so, her strange fighting style was enough to keep the teen in a defensive posturing nearly the entire time. She fought with such energy and passion, like a barely contained whirlwind of fury. Some of her moves seemed familiar, and now that he was older, Bawb knew why. Hozark had helped her refine her style from an out-of-control beast into a focused killing machine.

It was no wonder she was one of the few the Ghalian master had ever felt comfortable allowing to join on missions. In a supporting role, of course, but it was impressive. She had gained the Ghalian's complete trust, and that was no small thing.

Bawb was dripping in sweat by the time Bud finally called an end to the session.

"Enough. You're gonna wear the poor kid out," he said.

Henni wiped her brow and grinned wide, giving Bawb a squishy hug and pat on the back. "You've gotten a lot better."

"Thank you. I have been working on developing my own style."

"Yeah, I can see some of Hozark and Demelza's influence in there. Good teachers you've got."

"They are exceptional. But you are something else as well. Your technique is quite unique."

"Why thank you very much," she chuckled.

"I mean it. If you were a Wampeh, I think you could easily become a Ghalian, if you possessed the gift."

"The whole drinking blood and stealing magic thing? Yeah, I'll pass on that. Not my cup of tea, or blood for that matter, if you know what I mean."

Bawb let out an amused laugh. "It is definitely an acquired taste. But back to your fighting style. Would you show me a few of your moves?"

"Sure."

"Thank you. They are so unexpected, and so powerful."

"Well, maybe you'll incorporate them into your own style when you finally graduate," she said. "Most of the Ghalian I've sparred with tend to be pretty derivative in their styles. Sure, they're ridiculously good—better than me, no doubt. But the really impressive ones combine things in ways you'd never imagine."

"Like Master Hozark?"

"Oh, he's at the top of the list. But there are others. Demelza, for one. She's got a *lot* of tricks up her sleeve. And who knows? Maybe they'll share a few of their secrets with you one day. But that's for them to decide, not us," she said with a warm grin. "Anyway, that's for another day. For now, let's teach you a few new moves. Once we jump, we'll be meeting with Olo, so let's make the most of the time we've got left."

CHAPTER FOURTEEN

The pirates used their long-range skree to connect with their friend, then jumped across the vastness of space, arriving at a small system not too far from the one Bawb called home. Their course determined, they flew to the location Olo had directed them to. It was on one of the few dry areas of land on the watery planet of Galaloom that Bud finally set down.

"Olo! Good to see you!" he called out, hurrying across the landing area to give his friend a massive hug.

"Not so hard! I ate too much," the blue-skinned man replied with a laugh.

"Drank too much is more like it," Henni quipped as she stepped out of the ship to join them.

"Henni, a pleasure, as always."

"Olo. You've got your racer on hand, I see. What happened to the hauler you were using last time we saw you?"

"I still have it, just tucked away for the time being. Lately, I've been making some more, uh, let's call them *lucrative* runs."

"Which means you need a faster ship."

"Precisely."

"But there's not a lot of room," she noted.

"Who needs room when you've got agility? If you're gonna get into trouble, you want to be nimble."

Henni shook her head. "Or you could, oh, I don't know… just *avoid* the trouble."

Olo laughed. "But where's the fun in that? I didn't get to be the best damn pilot in the galaxy for nothing, you know."

"*Second* best," Bud shot back.

"You still think you can outfly me, old man?"

"Old man? Olo, *you're* the one whose race lives for centuries," he said with an exaggerated sigh.

"Bah! Olo never ages. Olo just gets better! Just look at me!"

"Sure. But even so, we're *not* old, Olo."

The blue man let out a deep belly laugh. "*I'm* not. But you?"

"Ugh. You're ridiculous. You're *both* ridiculous," Henni groaned as she gestured for their passenger to come join them. "Olo, this is the passenger we told you about. Pingo, meet Olosnah," she said, using the false name they'd agreed upon for the trip.

"Just Olo, please."

"Nice to make your acquaintance," the boy replied. "I have heard many good things about you."

"Oh? Have you now?"

"Yes. Why, Bud and Henni were regaling me with tales of your piloting prowess the entire way here," he embellished. "I am indeed fortunate to be able to fly with one so talented and formidable as yourself."

Olo looked at Bud and Henni then back at the teenager before bursting out in laughter. "Did they tell you to say that?"

"No. I just—"

"Bud? Henni?"

Bud shrugged. "The kid says what he wants, Olo."

"I really am looking forward to flying with you, Mr. Olo."

"Seriously, it's just Olo. And damn right you're looking

forward to it. Not every day you get to fly with the best pilot in the galaxy."

It took every ounce of willpower Bud and Henni had to refrain from rolling their eyes. Somehow, they managed, and Olo got to have his moment of bravado.

Bud nudged the teen. "Show him what you've got in payment, Pingo. We know you're on a tight schedule."

Bawb pulled the ornate bone from his pocket and handed it to the pilot. Olo's eyes widened, darting to his friends. He pulled Bud close and whispered in his ear. "Does he know what this is?"

"Likely not. But he stole it anyway, so you'll want to keep that to yourself for a little bit. Don't go using it. Or selling, it for that matter."

"I wouldn't dream of it. At least, not for the moment." Olo pocketed the payment and turned his attention back to the teen. "Okay, we have a deal. You have much stuff?"

"Just what I'm wearing and this satchel."

"Even better. It can get a little cramped in there if you've got luggage. Well, come on. Time's a-wasting, and I'm gonna get you... where was it we're going again?"

"He's going to Hakan," Bud interjected. "Has family there."

"Ah, nice moon, Hakan. And the view of Dorus is magnificent. Best of all, the spaceport is usually pretty clear, so we should be able to get a landing site no problem. Any word of our mutual friend? I know she frequents the area."

"Lalaynia was on Rimpalla, last I heard," Bud noted.

"No, not her. The *other* one."

"Oh, Nixxa. Yeah. She's been all over. Hitting Tslavar slave ships of late."

"She's picking fights with Tslavars now? What's she thinking?"

"You know how she is. There's plenty of coin to be had, but

also a lot of slaves to be freed. Sometimes she gets a little carried away with her sense of justice, but I can't exactly fault her for it."

"No one can. It's the only reason she gets away with as much as she does. Almost like the good and bad cancel each other out."

"Mostly," Henni chimed in.

"Yeah, *mostly*," Olo agreed. "Well, we should be off. Hop on, my boy, you're in for a fun ride."

Bud waved his farewell. "Just don't talk his ear off, Olo. Poor kid's suffered enough."

"Torture?"

"Nah, just a rough go of it, from what we could get from him. He doesn't really talk much," Bud said, locking eyes with Bawb to make sure his point was heard loud and clear.

Olo was a friend, but he was not in *that* particular inner circle. He may have known some of his friends had on occasion run across the Wampeh Ghalian and lived, but he was not a welcome guest at the training house. There were trusted friends, and then there were *trusted* friends, in whose hands you would put your life. While Bud and Henni were the latter, Olo apparently remained the former, and that meant that so far as he knew, it was just a simple ferryman's job.

"Thank you for your help getting me a ride the rest of the way," Bawb said, shaking Bud and Henni's hands, playing up the part. "I cannot tell you how much my family will appreciate what you've done for me."

"Our pleasure, kid. Good luck, and don't be a stranger," Bud replied, then put his arm around his diminutive copilot and headed back to their ship.

Olo led his passenger to his airlock and cast the unlocking spell. With a little bow, he welcomed his guest aboard.

"Behold, my ship. Well, one of them, anyway. She's small but she's fierce. Kind of like Henni in that way, I suppose. C'mon, I'll give you the tour."

Olo walked into the center of the entry compartment and spun a slow circle.

"Okay, over there is the head. It's also the shower, but I prefer to wait until I land to bathe. Saves on water reclamation that way. Over there is storage. That's the galley, though it's really more of a kitchenette. This spot is where the table and bench fold out of the wall, and dishes are stored up in that cabinet. That seat over there is my captain's chair, and the passenger fold-out is accessed in this panel right here." He pushed a panel, and a small, cushioned seat flopped down, locking into place. "That's your spot. Not the comfiest, but it'll get the job done. And it's not a long flight. Not with this ship."

"Why is that?" Bawb asked.

"Because not only is she small and fast, but with her limited mass I can jump this baby just about anywhere with a fraction of the magic required for a larger ship. Great for making quick exits, if you know what I mean."

Bawb looked around at the very compact vessel and had to appreciate the simplicity of it all. It was designed to do a job without any bells and whistles, and from what he could tell, it did just that. And with Bud and Henni vouching for him, Olo was clearly a talented pilot. Perhaps not quite the grandmaster of flying that he made himself out to be, but a formidable talent, nonetheless.

"It is a beautiful craft," the teen said, settling into his seat. "I am very much looking forward to seeing how it handles."

"You'll be getting your wish in just a minute," Olo replied, sliding into his captain's chair. "Drookonus is already engaged and ready to go." He lifted the ship up without hesitation, the craft hurtling through the sky and exiting the atmosphere far faster than Bawb had ever experienced.

It seemed Olo was a bit of a lead foot when it came to flying. In the rush he was in, Bawb was actually rather glad for it.

"How far out into the system do we need to fly before we jump?"

"Oh, we're not playing by those rules," Olo said with a laugh. "Hang on. You're in for a fun ride."

CHAPTER FIFTEEN

A fun ride.

Olo clearly had a different idea of what fun was than any sane person might. He had come with Bud and Henni vouching for his skills, and he was definitely a more than capable pilot, but he flew like a hopped-up teenager in a stolen ride. And for all Bawb knew, the ship very well could have been.

Fly it like it's stolen, was the saying, and aside from lacking the body damage and burned-out Drookonus one usually wound up with in such situations, the rest felt quite similar. But Olo didn't hit a thing, though not for lack of opportunity.

He jumped them out of the system in a hurry, barely making orbit before powering up the Drookonus even higher and flashing them out of existence. They reappeared in a nearby system from which he would adjust their course and send them on their final leg to their destination.

"Gonna come in a bit toward the outer edge of the system when we get there," he informed his passenger. "There's been some Council activity around the inner worlds lately, so it'll save us a headache dealing with them if we seem to be arriving from within the system."

"Why is that?" Bawb asked.

"Increased piracy of late."

"Oh?"

"Yeah. Don't worry, it's nothing that we need to be worried about, especially with me at the helm, but I'd just as soon not have to deal with the Council digging around in my business if I can avoid it."

"Of course. That is a perfectly logical rationale."

Olo laughed. "Yeah, I thought so too. But the best part? We get to have a little fun because of it. I'll need to turn off the gravity spell, though. I fly better without it."

Bawb felt his stomach sink a little. Not from fear or doubt, but because he had already discerned that this pilot was itching to show off his skills. And as a seemingly normal passenger just getting a ride to Hakan, he could do nothing but sit patiently and let him.

On the bright side, Olo did manage to get them to their target solar system much faster than a regular transport would have made the trip, his ship's diminutive size and powerful Drookonus proving to be a very potent combination. Olo's piloting antics once they reached it, however, left Bawb a little green around the gills, as the saying went.

"Hang on," the pilot said. "This'll be fun."

"Is that the Tivalian asteroid field?" the teen asked as they sped toward a vast expanse of floating rocks.

"Hey, you know your landmarks."

"It is well known for the number of ships it has claimed."

"Number of *lesser* ships, you mean. And lesser pilots. Trust me, I've flown them hundreds of times."

"*Hundreds*?"

"Let's just say I've been around longer than I look."

"Yes, Bud did mention your kind is long-lived."

"You could say that. But rather than get all old and wrinkly,

Olo here uses a stasis spell when I take downtime to rejuvenate. Keeps me fresh!"

"I have never heard of one of these spells. Not for a person, that is."

"Heh. It's a pretty neat trick, though if it's miscast it can lock you up frozen like a statue for hundreds of years, if not more. But me? I've worked out all the bugs, so it's perfectly safe."

Given his odd demeanor, Bawb had to wonder if he was telling the entire truth. In any case, even if he did freeze himself for a few years or even decades, Bawb would be a different person when they next met, the boy named Pingo long forgotten.

"And the asteroids? You say you have flown them before."

"Like I said, I know these like the back of my hand. I mean, sure, a few may have moved since last time, but we'll be fine."

"It's such a dangerous route. Can't we just go around?"

Olo laughed gleefully. "Don't sweat it. Me and asteroids? We have an agreement."

He was talking about inanimate objects. Not potentially sentient inanimate objects like his konus. No, these were properly inanimate. Rocks, floating in space. And Olo was taking them into the asteroid field, and fast at that.

The ship bucked and rolled, the artificial gravity spell that had been keeping him firmly in place no longer holding his butt in his seat. As a result, the forces generated by Olo's drastic maneuvers were already beginning to take a toll.

Bawb had a strong stomach—years of training had helped him learn to control his bodily functions and responses to stress. But this? This was a sensation he had not been prepared for. And it was ongoing without respite.

"Ain't this fun?" Olo said with a laugh, diving and rolling around asteroids with undeniable skill, even if it was nauseating.

"Yes, quite an experience," Bawb said, feeling a trickle of hot bile rise in his throat. "How long until we reach Hakan?"

"We'll be there in no time. Just sit back and enjoy the ride."

Bawb swallowed hard. "Yes. Enjoy. Of course."

There was no horizon line to focus on, no gravity against which to press his body, giving him at least something to utilize as a balance point. He was just going to be at the mercy of Olo's ridiculous flying until they finally landed. If they survived.

Survive they did, exiting the field and leveling out far sooner than expected, lining up for their approach to the moon orbiting the beautiful gas giant.

"Oh, the gravity. Almost forgot," Olo said, reactivating the spell.

Bawb's stomach flipped again, but having the familiar force holding his body in place once more immediately helped quell the nausea that had been rising within him. He couldn't help but wonder what ridiculousness Olo might have lined up next.

The rest of the flight, however, was uneventful. The presence of a Council ship in the system was plenty of motivation no matter how distant it was. This wasn't a smuggling operation, and Olo didn't feel like wasting the magic to get in a drag race with Council goons.

"Almost there," he announced as they descended into the moon's atmosphere without a hint of turbulence. "I'll have you on the ground in just a minute."

Bawb gave his pockets a once-over, ensuring nothing had fallen out during the wild ride. All was in place, most importantly the last of his coin. It was a small amount, but it should be just enough to purchase fare on a planet hopper back home. If Olo had insisted on coin instead of his stolen booty, he would have been forced to extend his mission even longer while he arranged transit, and frankly, Bawb just wanted to get home.

They circled a small landing field and set down smoothly

between two other small ships. This was an area more often used for personal craft than commercial ones. Bawb would have to walk to the larger one, but that was not something he needed to tell Olo. For all the pilot knew, this was his final destination.

"Okay, we're here," the man said, opening the airlock spell, allowing the fresh air to waft in. Bawb felt his spirits rise at the first breath.

"Thank you, Olo," he said, rising from his seat. "The ride is greatly appreciated."

"You like the asteroids? They were great, right?"

"Yes, they were, uh, very interesting. And you are quite the skilled pilot."

"Told ya, I'm the best in the galaxy."

Bawb was already stepping outside, lest the gregarious man talk his ear off when he was so close to completing his task.

"Indeed, you really are. Thank you again," he said, then disappeared into the crowd.

Bawb moved fast now that he was on solid ground, his legs a little wobbly still from the flight, but functioning as he demanded of them regardless. He had dealt with weak limbs plenty in his training. This was something he could handle without a second thought.

Hakan wasn't a very large moon, and all space traffic and commerce happened here in the only real city to speak of. As a result, it was a densely crowded environment, but one in which a talented Ghalian trainee could go unnoticed easily.

Unless, that is, he happened to round a corner at just the moment a tall, tan woman, armed to the teeth, with stripes on her skin and fire-red hair was coming the other way.

"Apologies," he said, quickly ducking aside and hurrying into the crowd.

Nixxa stopped in her tracks, her head cocked slightly.

Something about that teenager was familiar. A moment later it clicked.

"Son of a—" she growled, spinning around, scanning the crowd for the pale Wampeh boy.

"What is it, Nixxa?" the thickly muscled ruffian at her side asked.

"It's the damn kid, Borkus."

"Which kid?"

"The Wampeh. The little shit who stole my Drookonus."

Borkus's expression shifted to one of concern. The story was well known, and Nixxa's anger over being taken for a ride, by a kid no less, was as fresh as the day it happened. Possibly worse, as she had now had several years to ruminate on it.

"You sure, Boss?"

"Damn right I'm sure. I never forget a face. Come on!"

She took off at a fast walk, her lackey following close behind, both of them scanning for the telltale pale skin of a Wampeh in the crowd. Bawb, however, was not the same unskilled youth who had stolen from her in the past. He had learned a few things since then and had immediately used the last of his available magic to cast what little disguise he could, then ducked down a smaller side pathway.

On her ship she would have ample wards in place to detect disguise magic, but out here in the open it would rely on the konus she was wearing. And in this setting, she was unlikely to have cast for that. She would have been saving her magic for other, more violent needs, should they arise.

Bawb didn't take that for granted, though, stealing a very colorful scarf from a passerby's bag as he moved, adding to his disguise and draping it over his head as he shifted course yet again.

He had seen Nixxa a few times over the years, but it had always been from a distance. He didn't know at the time if she would remember his face, but there was no sense in taking the risk. Judging by her reaction just now, it was clear she did, in fact, remember him quite well, despite his no longer being a young boy.

"This is not good," he muttered, shifting his course to a somewhat more roundabout way to the landing site. It would add time to his walk, but with Nixxa in the mix, he really had no choice.

He looked around casually as he moved, his leisurely motions the exact opposite of the urgency he felt. But he had to go without being noticed, and Demelza had taught him well. Move as though you belong, and you will be unremarkable. And with the bright wrap around his head, he was actually avoiding attention rather than attracting it. No one on the run would dream of so loud a garment.

It took longer than he wanted, but he reached the distant part of the landing site without further contact with Nixxa. To his delight, a short-hopper was just loading up at the far end of the field. He scanned the flight schedule. This one was going where he needed. It seemed luck was finally going his way.

Easier still, it was not a private vessel but belonged to a conglomerate that ran flights all throughout the system. As such, fare was paid at one location rather than a line forming at the ship's entrance. If he did happen to be spotted, he could shake any followers and make a quick entrance if needed.

He approached the ticket vendor and casually placed his coin on the small stand. "Just a one-way flight."

The man counted the coin, handed him a boarding chit, and that was that. All he had to do now was make it aboard unnoted and he would be in the clear.

Bawb walked a roundabout circuit as he released his disguise magic gradually rather than waiting for it to fail on its own at a more inopportune moment, making sure his approach was unnoted while ensuring Nixxa was nowhere to be seen. She was a pirate of some reputation, and for her to be on Hakan mingling with the regular people was unusual. As he turned toward his ship, he saw why.

There was a very nice personal craft parked not far from his ride. It was lacking the dust and signs of space travel, clearly cleaned for display. A few of her crew were standing near it, but all of them were clothed in respectable attire rather than pirate garb.

"She is selling it," Bawb realized, his tension releasing slightly.

Obviously, if it was Nixxa's people then this was a stolen ship. But for them to be offering it up in the open like this, it must have been stolen from quite far away. And more importantly, they would be disinclined to raise a scene and spoil their possible sale.

Even so, he melted into the crowd, boarding his transport as quickly as he could without drawing attention. He moved to a seat affording him a view of the doorway and settled down. He had timed it well. The ship would be departing in just a few minutes. All he had to do was make it that long without Nixxa or her people poking their heads in.

"Damn," he said as a familiar face appeared in the doorway just before it sealed. She was breathing hard, clearly having run to catch this transport.

Elzina casually looked around, her eyes flashing over Bawb, not even giving him so much as a nod of recognition. But she saw him. He could feel the chill in her demeanor.

She took a seat at the far end from him and settled in. It seemed their missions had overlapped, and neither of them was over just yet. And now their arrival home would be one last challenge. Once they landed, it would be a race. One in their home city. One in which they could not draw attention to themselves, and especially not to their destination.

The flight went without complication, as one would expect, and the passengers all disembarked calmly with the usual jostling but nothing out of the ordinary. Bawb and Elzina took their time, exiting at nearly the same time, both fully aware of what was about to happen.

"Elzina," Bawb said as they stepped outside.

"Bawb."

"Lovely day, is it not?"

"It would seem so. A fantastic day for victory."

A little grin creased his lips. "We shall see. May the best—"

Elzina cast a tripping spell, sending him tumbling to the ground. To all watching he simply appeared to be a clumsy teen. Scrambling to his feet he couldn't help but appreciate the skill with which she had cast it. And truth be told, he had been planning on doing very much the same thing, although not so close to the other passengers.

He saw her walking fast, heading for one of the several nearby streets exiting the landing area. Her decision was made, her route set. He took off for a different one, each of them knowing all the same shortcuts. Once he was out of the landing area he started running, as he was sure she was doing as well.

They were now at the hands of fate. Each of their paths were approximately the same length. It would come down to the luck of the draw as to which of their routes was less populated today.

Bawb ran hard, weaving through the crowd with the ease of one so in tune with his body. He moved fast but did not bump or jostle anyone, and as a teenager, anyone who did happen to observe him would see a grinning boy running, nothing more. It was something teenagers did all the time, and he had long ago perfected the cheerful facial expressions of his chronological peers.

He crossed town quickly, slowing to a walk around the corner from his chosen entry point. Forcing his breathing to slow to normal, he casually strolled to the doorway and stepped inside. Once safely within the training house walls, he took off running again, opening the secret door to their inner reaches and sprinting for the main level meeting area.

He ran hard, his footsteps nevertheless quiet in the stone hallways. Despite his rush, the teachers would not abide a lack of stealth under any circumstances. Fortunately, it was second nature by now.

"Done!" he exclaimed as he charged into the chamber.

Elzina was already there, chest heaving.

"Five seconds too late," she said, breathing hard.

Bawb felt a pang of disappointment but let it go. Second was better than third, and this was so close he may as well have been victorious.

Teacher Warfin and Teacher Demelza were sitting in comfortable chairs, sipping tea, seemingly perfectly aware the two would be arriving at this exact moment.

"Well done, both of you," Warfin said. "An impressive showing."

"And I won!" Elzina exclaimed, her ego already growing from the victory.

Demelza's head shook slightly. "Yes, but also no."

"What do you mean?" Elzina's concern was palpable. "Did someone get back before us?"

"Oh, no. You two were the first to arrive. But while you reached this room first, your entry route through our inner compound was shorter. Bawb's was the longer path."

"So I won."

"Think of what I said," Demelza urged.

Elzina forced her mind to heed her commands, replaying their teacher's words, properly assessing them and their meaning. Her shoulders slumped a moment later. Demelza seemed satisfied.

"I see you understand."

"Yes, Teacher."

"Bawb entered the training house before you did."

"I am aware now."

Warfin stood up, gesturing to them both. "You have each achieved much, and while one entered the training house first, the other reached this room before the other, and by mere seconds at that." He glanced at Demelza. She gave a little nod. "For that reason, we are declaring this competition, however unusual it may be to do so, to be a tie. You both share this victory. Congratulations."

Bawb felt a little flush of relief. He had gone from barely losing to a tie. It wasn't an outright win, but it was a step up, and given the situation, a perfectly logical decision. Elzina, however, was crestfallen, though she hid it well in the presence of their teachers. She would rage about it later, no doubt, declaring herself the true victor, her ego unable to just let it go. And as always, Bawb would brush it off. It simply wasn't worth the drama.

"Why don't you two go and clean up. Perhaps have a meal together. I'm sure you could each learn from the other's experience," Demelza suggested.

"I am not hungry," Elzina declared. "May I?"

"Of course. There are no classes until the others have returned, at which point we will review each of your missions as well as your performance. Your time is your own until then."

Elzina nodded once and walked out.

Bawb, however, waited.

"Yes, Bawb?"

"You were watching the whole time, weren't you? Not you personally, but there were operatives."

Demelza grinned her approval. "You know our ways well, Bawb. Yes, we kept tabs. But those doing so were under strict orders not to intervene. You did this on your own."

"I see."

"Go rest. Eat. Recover. You did well, and you will get to tell the others of your exploits soon enough."

He nodded to the teachers and took his leave, more than ready for a nice hot shower and a meal. It had been an experience the likes of which he would not soon forget, and undoubtedly easy compared to what was to come in his future years of training.

Oddly, he was looking forward to it.

CHAPTER SIXTEEN

Bawb took a long, hot bath in the lower-level spa area to unwind after his successful mission. It was a natural hot spring with just the right mineral content to soothe one's aching body that fed a series of rock tubs deep underground. The stone was glistening with moisture, the entire chamber essentially functioning as a steam room along with the soaking tubs. Despite the depth and humidity of the small cavern, the air was clean and scented with subtle oils.

As for unwanted growths, the walls, floors, and ceiling were protected by a self-replenishing spell that kept any mold or bacteria from growing, and as a result the whole facility felt as fresh and inviting as the day it had been opened all those many years ago.

The carved steps leading into the tubs had been worn down over the centuries, the soft curvature in them formed by countless bare feet that now left the stone feeling as smooth as if it had been polished by hand.

Bawb was pleased to find that Elzina had other plans for her recovery break. That meant, for a while at least, he had the place to himself, and he took full advantage of it.

"Bawb, I hear you tied with Elzina," Usalla said, walking into the chamber a while later.

"Yes, it was an unusual finish to an interesting challenge."

Usalla shed her clothes and slid into the tub with him, reclining against the warm stone with a sigh of relief. "I am sure we all had interesting challenges."

"The teachers do have a proclivity for keeping us on our toes, that is for certain."

"To say the least. I had to replace a document with a false one. Can you believe that? Sneaking into a compound and executing a target is one thing, but this was spy work."

Bawb chuckled. "They say we must master all aspects of Ghalian ways. And that includes the art of infiltration and deception."

"Oh, that part was easy. It was avoiding the advances of the master of the estate that proved troublesome. I had to shift disguises to manage a little free time to complete my task. And that cost me valuable magic."

"Which delayed your return."

"That it did. What about you? Anything interesting in your outing?"

"The usual. Infiltrate a building, stun a half dozen guards to make them appear drunk, drug their boss, start a fire, free the slaves. You know, run-of-the-mill hero stuff."

Usalla splashed him in the face. "You are an ass, Bawb. You realize that?"

"At times," he said with a grin, enjoying one of the few truly relaxing moments of casual friendship and banter that he was afforded in this place.

More than the others, Usalla had been one of his closest friends since he had first arrived, and he valued their open talks more than even he realized.

They soaked and talked for a long time, the aches and pains

of their respective quests melting from their muscles in the soothing water until, finally, it was time to rejoin the others. Most would likely be returned by now, and that meant they would begin their next lesson shortly.

"Food?" Bawb asked as they headed out of the spa chamber.

"Food," she replied with a nod.

The two made their way to the dining hall and ate well, replenishing their energy stores in preparation for whatever the teachers had lined up for them next.

"Water," Teacher Griggitz said several hours later.

He had led the full cohort of Vessels, all of them decked out for training, to a simple pool chamber on the first level. It was nothing interesting, really, just a deep pool of water in which the students had spent many an hour relaxing in their spare time. It was familiar and it was safe. And that was why he had chosen it.

"Water can be your friend," he continued. "It can mask your approach and hide your escape. It can save your life, just as it can take those of others. You will learn to be as comfortable in water as you are on land by the time you become Masters. And that means you will learn to fight in it as well as swim."

"Teacher? We have become proficient with the bubble spell and can cast underwater. What would you have us do?" Elzina asked, eager to show her skills.

"You are going to swim."

"We know how to swim."

"Yes, so you say," he replied with a menacing gleam in his eyes. "All of you, in the water."

They began stripping off their gear.

"No! Leave it all on. You will not always be able to shed what you are wearing."

The students jumped in the deep pool without hesitation, treading water as they awaited his next instruction. It was not coming anytime soon.

Griggitz looked them over, nodding his satisfaction, then walked out of the chamber.

"What is he doing?" Zota asked. "What are we supposed to do?"

"We tread water," Finnia replied. "Until we are told otherwise."

It was easy at first, just floating in place, casually kicking their legs and staying above water. But minutes dragged on, becoming hours, and by the time Griggitz returned the students were feeling the strain of their efforts, as well as the drag of their soaked clothing.

The teacher counted heads. All of them were still there. Good.

"Swim," he commanded. "Do not stop until you are instructed to do so."

The class began doing laps, some faster than others, all using a variety of strokes as they swam the length of the pool, back and forth and back again. Once more, Teacher Griggitz left the chamber, but this time a half dozen Mavins took his place. They were students, like the Vessels were, but these older young men and women were far more advanced in their training and were now just one level below Master. As such, they were often tasked with assisting and even teaching on occasion. Today, however, they were just there to stand by and wait.

One or two would be normal, but a half dozen? It was rather unusual.

The Mavins spread out around the pool and stood quietly, watching the younger students swim. They did this for hours, observing but not moving. So motionless one could almost forget they were there. It was a skill the Ghalian learned and perfected over the course of their training. How to just *be*. Movement caught the eye, but stillness could afford one opportunities that even the best of disguises could not.

Teacher Griggitz finally strode back into the chamber. He watched the exhausted students swimming in their waterlogged clothes, each and every one of them clearly running out of gas. It was as he had planned.

"Students, to the edge of the pool. You may rest."

They gladly complied, getting their first break in longer than any cared to remember. Teacher Griggitz paced in front of them, looking down on the line of students.

"You have done well, I see. All of you managed to persevere despite your exhaustion. That is good. Now the *real* training begins."

No one let out a sound, but if the mental groans from the Vessels had been audible the walls of the chamber would have rumbled from their intensity. Griggitz reached down and hauled Albinius out of the water with ease.

"Bind him."

One of the Mavins stepped forward, quickly securing the boy's hands and feet, then stepped back, not all the way, but closer to the edge of the water.

"How do those feel?" Griggitz asked. "Too tight?"

"A little bit."

"Can you swim in them? Say, to the far end and back?"

"Swim?"

Griggitz didn't wait for more, shoving the boy hard. Albinius flew backward into the water with a splash, sputtering and gasping for air after he struggled his way back to the surface.

"Well? Swim!" the teacher commanded.

Albinius was fortunate, his hands were at least tied in front of him, but he could not kick properly, and his clothing was weighing him down. Nevertheless, he tried, managing an awkward, lurching stroke all the way to the far end of the pool. He made the turn and started back but only made it halfway before slipping beneath the water. He did not come back up.

Griggitz nodded to the nearest Mavin, who dove in, pulling the boy out onto the deck and rolling him on his side. A quick pressure spell expelled the water from his lungs in a gush. Albinius sucked in air, his breath ragged and loud as he lay there, utterly spent. The teacher turned back to the other students.

"Okay. Who is next?"

The rest of them each took a turn, forced to make the same attempt as Albinius. Forewarned was forearmed, at least to an extent, but none of them were fully ready for just how hard their task would be. Several sank to the bottom of the pool, only to be rescued by one of the Mavins they now knew were there as a safety measure for this exercise. It seemed that, while their training was dangerous, the Ghalian were not ready to let them perish if they failed to perform.

That sort of consequence was reserved for the highest levels of students.

Bawb, Usalla, and Elzina managed to complete the swim without needing rescue, but only just. Teacher Griggitz nodded his grudging respect for their efforts.

Then he made them do it again.

Underwater.

They were strong swimmers, capable of holding their breath a long time, but even when he allowed them to cast bubble spells to get a few breaths along the way, the struggle against their bindings was too much, and each had to be fished out before reaching the end.

Griggitz had all of the students line up, unbound but still soaked and exhausted.

"This is drown-proofing," he informed them. "It is not pleasant, but that is the point. Some of you do not seem to understand the basic principle at work here. It is not to succeed; it is to fail. But in failing, you learn not to panic underwater.

How to keep going until you cannot, then dig deep and somehow find a little more within yourselves. This ability, this mindset, could be the difference between survival and failure one day."

He turned back toward the water, watching it ripple gently. It was an almost tranquil scene. And that was about to change.

"All right. We do this again. This time, with your hands tied *behind* your backs."

CHAPTER SEVENTEEN

More than usual the Vessels had slept deeply after their day's training. To be exhausted after an interplanetary training mission with real consequences was one thing. To then spend hours upon hours not relaxing and sharing tales of the adventure, but rather, swimming to stay alive, drowning a bit, being revived, then doing it again, was enough to leave every last one of them utterly drained by the time they were let out of the water.

And then, when respite had to be in sight, the teachers had them spar, switching partners every few minutes to prevent them from sliding into anything resembling a rhythm. This they did for nearly an hour until their arms and legs were barely able to function, let alone excel in the task.

"Go eat," Griggitz finally told them. "And get some sleep."

For once, he didn't follow that up with his usual cryptic, "You'll need it."

They ate well and slept hard, and the following morning they woke and prepared as usual, though with bodies still a bit weak from the prior day's labors. Even as rapidly recovering teenagers in peak fitness, the continuous strain had taken a lasting toll. Fortunately, after devouring a sizable breakfast they learned today was a recovery day of sorts. It was also their first time meeting a new teacher in years.

"Vessels, your attention, please," a spindly man with rather elongated, knobby fingers called out to the students as they finished their repast. "I am Teacher Brindo. I understand you experienced your drown-proofing training yesterday. Your *first* drown-proofing session, anyway. Well done. I see you all survived. Today we will be remaining on dry land, I assure you. However, it will be a long day, so be sure to bring plenty of water for the trek."

"Trek? Where are we going, Teacher?" Zota asked.

"We are taking a journey outside the compound's walls. It will be quite a long walk utilizing the tunnel network, but you will then be spending the day outdoors, and it promises to be warm today. Now, finish your meals, gather your things, and meet at the fourth-level sparring chamber. We depart from there."

With that the man walked out, leaving the students to wonder just what sort of fresh hell they would be experiencing today.

"He said we are going outside," Albinius said. "And to bring water. What do you think he has in store for us?"

"There is no way of telling," Bawb replied with a shrug. "We prepare, we travel, we learn. It is as simple as that."

"Is it, though? What if it's a trick?"

"Silence your babble," Elzina grumbled. "If it is a deception, so be it. We are Ghalian. Do not forget that. This is what we train for."

Albinius moved his mouth as if he wanted to say something but remained silent, thinking better of it. There was no sense in getting on Elzina's bad side today. Or any day, for that matter. She had always had an attitude of superiority, but with her skills, she could back up her trash talk. It was something they had all just come to accept. She was difficult, putting it nicely, but she was the best of them.

Only Bawb even came close to her skills, which annoyed her, as one would expect, but she still topped the class in training more often than not.

The others just ignored her, finishing their food and trickling out of the dining hall to gather their gear for the day. Teacher Brindo had not mentioned combat, so they could likely carry only light weapons, such as the daggers each of them now wore pretty much everywhere out of habit. Beyond that, they would just improvise if another surprise challenge was presented to them. One could never carry *everything* one might need, so it was best to be as prepared as possible and not worry further about it.

As it turned out, daggers were more than adequate for their needs.

The trek through the tunnels had been longer than they expected, but not due to distance. Teacher Brindo would stop regularly to point out different types of moss, lichen, and plant life growing in the chambers they passed through on the way. The fourth-level tunnel was deep, but the path they took regularly rose and fell, coming so close to the surface they could see roots from trees above, to so deep they could almost feel the weight of the ground above them pressing down.

“Vara moss. Edible,” the teacher said, pointing to a faintly iridescent moss growing near a small stream deep in the ground. “Not tasty, but it provides more than enough nourishment in an emergency situation.” He picked a small clump and passed it around the students. “Vessel Bawb, your arm, please.”

Bawb held his arm out without hesitation. The man’s hands flashed far faster than any would expect from his unimpressive appearance, and a small cut opened on the teen’s arm from a blade none had seen him draw. Bawb did not flinch as a small trickle of blood ran from the wound.

"Vessel Usalla, you have the Vara moss. Would you please press it to Vessel Bawb's injury."

Usalla stepped forward and did as she was asked, pushing the moss onto his arm firmly. Smoke rose as the moss sizzled upon contact with the blood. Bawb's jaw twitched, but the pain actually wasn't that bad. In fact, a moment after it started, the pain was gone almost entirely.

"Vessel Bawb, hold that in place with this," Brindo instructed, handing him a strip of cloth.

Bawb quickly wrapped it around his arm as he was told.

"Good. Now, let us continue."

They walked for some time until they came upon a different sort of light than the bioluminescence in the caverns and their illumination spells created. There was sunlight leaking in. That, and a whiff of fresh air. They were near the surface in a cave network of some sort. How far they had traveled, no one could say exactly. The twisting nature of the caves and tunnels made it impossible to gauge distance. But they had been walking for many hours and had undoubtedly covered a great deal of ground.

When the teacher cast his unmasking spell, revealing a hidden door in the stone wall and pushing it open, they realized that was, indeed, the case.

"It is lovely," Bawb said, his eyes taking in the verdant landscape and wildly growing plant life surrounding them.

"Yes, it rather is, isn't it?" their teacher agreed. "Come. We go this way."

He led them from the small rock outcropping that concealed the doorway, closing and hiding it behind them as they walked. A few minutes later they stopped at the edge of a field, the towering trees stretching out on one side, open land on the other.

There was a small stream nearby. They could all hear and smell it. And as a result the ground was particularly dark and fertile.

"Today you learn something new," Teacher Brindo said, filling his lungs with fresh air. "Look around. Go ahead, take a good, long look. What is it you think you will learn in this place?"

The students did as they were told, taking in the details of the location with the trained eyes of the Ghalian.

"Camouflage," Elzina stated confidently.

"A good assumption," Brindo replied. "But wrong. Who else?"

"Game stalking?" Usalla asked.

"No. But also a logical guess."

"Maybe, shelter construction? Or improvised weapons?" Zota wondered.

"No. None of those things are the focus of today's lesson. Bawb, remove the wrap from your arm."

Bawb did as he was told, exposing the moss beneath it.

"Go ahead, pull it off."

He carefully peeled the clump of moss from his skin. The iridescence was gone now, and the moss felt quite dry to the touch. But that wasn't what startled him the most. The wound beneath it was sealed shut, scarred and healing, though by no means fully repaired.

"How did it do that?" he marveled.

"This is the beginning of today's lesson," Brindo said, grasping the teen's arm and holding it up for the others to see. "Vara moss. Something most overlook, as it grows in damp, subterranean settings. But for those willing to look past that, it is a useful tool, especially for Ghalian, as it reacts quite strongly with Wampeh physiology—much more so than most other races. And for that it has been very useful to our kind when magic is low and injuries sustained."

He released Bawb's arm, allowing the students to come look closer at the healed injury. Bawb felt a surge of renewed interest flow through him that had nothing to do with the moss's effect on his injury. This teacher, odd as he seemed at first, possessed what could be some *very* interesting knowledge.

"Are we to learn how to mend wounds with natural substances?" he asked, eager to continue the day's lesson.

Brindo shook his head. "That is but a small part of what you will be learning in our outings. The focus of our classes will be botany. Botany, and farming."

The students looked at one another, a bit disappointed and more than a little confused.

"Farming?" Albinius asked.

"Yes."

"Like, actually growing stuff?"

"As I said. Farming."

"Not just learning what we can eat?"

"I will show you all manner of plants, edible and inedible, and instruct you on their uses. But while that is part of our curriculum, you will also learn the most simple of tasks, the likes of which have been done by commoners for millennia."

"Farming?" Elzina grumbled. "Actual farming? It is a boring task, and beneath a Ghalian."

Brindo gave her a look, the true power of the Ghalian Master flashing behind his eyes for a split second. But he refrained from a sound rebuke, a tranquil look remaining firmly affixed on his face.

"You are quite wrong," he said, watching to gauge her reaction. "Do you know why?"

"I do not see how working in the dirt is of use to us," she

replied, her arrogant reply a bit much, even for her. Apparently, she was still upset about something. Likely having tied with Bawb after an otherwise successful quest the other day. One thing about Elzina, it took time for her to release a grudge.

Teacher Brindo shrugged the girl's attitude off as one might ignore a toddler having a tantrum. "Does anyone else have an idea how farming could be helpful to a Ghalian?"

Bawb raised his hand. "It could be a useful disguise to gain access to a location," he said. "No one expects the commoners to be more than just that. And covered in dirt, it could be even easier to be ignored. But to blend in, we would have to actually know how farmers move. How they work and think."

"Excellent," Brindo said with an approving nod. "All knowledge is useful, even if it might not appear that way at first. Now, hydrate and prepare to get dirty. It will be a long day."

They quickly learned that Teacher Brindo had not been kidding.

They started off easy, walking the fields and woods, Brindo pointing out the edible plants and how to prepare them. Some could be eaten raw, others required soaking in water to remove toxic chemicals. Then there were tose that had parts that were edible but parts that were not, and they would be well served to learn the difference.

Eating as they went, he then walked them to the field and instructed them how farmers would cultivate if they had little or no magic at their disposal, as was often the case for the poorest who worked the land. In most instances, the farmers were allotted konuses with enough magic in them to do a fair amount of their tasks, but some worlds simply lacked the spare power to give. As a result, manual labor was the name of the game.

Albinius wandered a little from the group as they did some independent foraging under Brindo's watchful eye. They had been given a specific area in which to search, but the boy had managed to stray out of the boundary, staring at the ground in search of food.

A slender reed with a few faint violet blossoms and a cluster of velvety closed buds caught his eye. It blended in with the surrounding vegetation so well he almost missed it. Albinius reached his hand out.

A force spell slammed into him, throwing him aside.

"Do not touch that!" Brindo bellowed, the first real show of his inner power they'd been allowed to see. He stormed over to the fallen boy, looming above him. "I was warned of your absentmindedness, Albinius. It would seem the warning was warranted. Do not stray from the area you were given to work within."

"But, I—"

"That is Slipp you nearly touched. A dangerous poison that absorbs through the skin." He put on a glove and picked the reed, careful to ensure it did not touch bare flesh. "Smell it, but do not touch. All of you, come closer and smell."

The students did as he instructed, carefully inhaling but staying well clear of the plant.

"Do you smell it? Sweet, yet sharp? Learn that smell. Commit it to memory, for that knowledge could save your life." He cast a fire spell, charring the plant to oblivion, scorching the fingers of his gloves as well for good measure.

"How can it save our lives if it's poison?" Zota asked.

"Because it is a common poison added to food. We will get to the use of such things later. They are actually a specialty of mine, but this particular plant has taken a great many lives across many worlds, and not always intentionally. If one is not careful gathering food, it can be inadvertently plucked along with a harvest. When eaten, the flavor is tart, yet sweet. The telltale sign is that it makes the sides of your tongue tingle. When the tingle ceases, it will be too late."

Zota looked uneasy. "Too late?"

"Yes. Too late for this." Brindo leaned down and plucked another plant, this one leafy and short, with deep green leaves that had fine hairs growing on the underside, the top of the plant dotted with tiny, pale-yellow buds. "This is Grazz, and it always grows near Slipp, and a good thing it does. It is a universal antidote for Slipp and its cousin species. Do you see the fine hairs under the leaves? They contain a powerful compound that will bind to and destroy the toxin. But you must crush it and hold it under your tongue to absorb as much and as fast as possible. And unlike Slipp, it not only does *not* taste good, it will also burn your mouth in an excruciating manner. But pain is better than death, as you all know full well."

He looked at the faces of the students, all of them listening far more closely than they had during the more boring farming discussion. Teacher Brindo sighed.

"And this leads us to a logical, albeit somewhat premature segue to what will be in our upcoming lessons. You will learn many compounds, all of them made from plants common to many worlds. Some will make people ill; others are fatal. It is a difference you must commit to memory, as not all compounds will have the same effect on different species. One might react strongly while another has no reaction at all."

"Isn't poison seen as a last resort?" Bawb asked.

"It is often used as such, yes, but sometimes, no matter how skilled you may be, you simply cannot reach a target in person. But if you can infiltrate a kitchen, you can still target them, provided the compound you employ only works on their kind. In these situations, we sometimes use multiples combined, one to incapacitate the guards, the other to eliminate the target."

"Why not just use the most deadly to be absolutely sure?" Elzina asked. "It seems far more prudent."

A sour look flashed across Brindo's face for an instant. The man was a master of poisons, but her suggestion elicited a visceral response.

"We do not wield such tools lightly," he replied in a measured tone. "Innocents could perish. Children, staff, those who have no part in our game." He leaned close to her, locking her in his gaze. "Remember, Vessel Elzina, Ghalian are killers, but we do not kill indiscriminately."

CHAPTER EIGHTEEN

For days the students trekked with their new teacher, their instruction taking place out in the glory of nature rather than a classroom. The excessively long walk out and back every morning and night, however, was quickly getting old.

On the fourth night Brindo had them set up a makeshift camp out in the woods, and it was there they would remain for the next few days before finally moving on to their next lessons. They farmed, tilled the soil, and sowed seeds, learning to work the land, boring as it may be.

More interesting were the nature walks where their teacher would show them all the many things they could and could not eat, as well as describing the cousins of those plants that grew on other worlds. Wherever they might find themselves, they would possess the knowledge to survive in the wild. More than that, they could use what they learned to kill as well.

On the final day Brindo sent them on their way back to the training house while he remained in the wild a bit longer. "You have all done quite well," he said as they entered the hidden cavern doorway. "We will have more classes together. Especially when you become Adepts. Oh, the things you will learn then."

"More about poisons?" Elzina asked, a gleam in her eye.

"You will see. But do not let me hold you up. Teacher Demelza is waiting for you back at the training house. It would not be wise to keep her waiting."

The Vessels entered the tunnel system, the door closing and camouflaging itself behind them. As they had only had a morning lesson, they still possessed plenty of energy. That, and while farming was hard labor, it was nothing compared to the rigors of what they were often put through.

"Race?" Usalla asked with a grin.

"Race," Bawb replied.

"I'm in," Zota added.

"Me too," Finnia chimed in.

Elzina simply started running, not speaking a word or waiting a moment longer. The others took off after her, but at a reasonable pace. Yes, it was a race, but this would last a few hours. Sprinting would accomplish nothing. They had many tunnels and caverns to pass through, and the lead would undoubtedly change hands multiple times as they ran.

Ultimately, Usalla came in first, narrowly beating Elzina in the final tunnel. While Usalla was cheerful as they competed, Elzina was taking the race far more seriously than her classmate. So much so that even losing a casual competition among friends wound up leaving her in a foul mood. But for Elzina, that was kind of the norm.

It was an attitude she took with her all the way to their next class.

"You will be training in pairs today," Demelza informed them as the students entered the sparring area, noting their sweaty appearance. "I see you are already warmed up. Good. This gives us more time to spend on training. You will begin at once. Use any method you wish, any style of your choosing. You have many techniques at your disposal, and I expect to see you employ them all. Take this lesson seriously. Fight hard as if in a duel. There is only one rule. Refrain from lethal blows. Injuries we can heal, death we cannot."

Demelza set to work, pairing off the students with one another as she saw fit. Some wound up fighting friend versus friend, while others faced off against classmates they were not particularly close to. They fought in short bursts, their teacher instructing them to switch it up, moving to a new partner, forcing them to adapt to a new style and not get complacent in their combat.

Each of them knew the same techniques, but they were now beginning to create their own styles, and as such, the combinations they used were becoming unique to each of them. They were still Vessels and had a long way to go, but this was the path to becoming a full Ghalian.

Bawb and Martza faced off first. It was a relatively even fight, but Bawb quickly noted her tells and laid her out on her back.

"Switch!" Demelza called to them.

Bawb helped her up then moved to a new partner. Dillar, this time. While they had trained together for a long time, the two had never really bonded as friends. It was just the way of things as a teen. Some people you clicked with, others not so much. Bawb was glad it was the latter in a way. It made defeating his opponent that much easier.

Dillar liked to employ spinning moves, using his speed to surprise his opponents. But Bawb had been practicing a counter to precisely such a style with Usalla just the other week. When Dillar spun, Bawb charged forward rather than back, robbing him of his momentum. He hooked his foot behind Dillar's heel and drove his shoulder into his chest, sending the boy flying. He did this for several minutes in one way or another, frustrating his opponent until it was time to change partners again.

"Switch!"

Bawb squared off with Finnia. He noticed that Usalla and Elzina were facing one another not far away. And Elzina still looked sour about her earlier loss.

His attention was quickly drawn back to the fight at hand as Finnia landed a series of rapid blows. They weren't particularly hard, but they were definitely enough to get his attention.

"Nicely done," Bawb said.

"You need to pay attention, Bawb."

"I am."

He moved fast, blocking the speedy teen's flurry of attacks. Finnia wasn't the strongest of them, but she was quite possibly the fastest, and that made her a force to be reckoned with even if she was on the spy path rather than the assassin one.

Finnia shifted her tactics, deliberately slowing just as he sped up, using his overcompensation to create a gap. She landed a hard kick to his ribs as he attempted to parry punches that never arrived.

"I told you, you need to pay attention," she said with a grin.

"Point taken."

He just started to launch into a combination he had been working on for just this sort of opponent when he saw Usalla crumple out of the corner of his eye. Finnia's fist slammed into his jaw, but he shook it off, his attention focused on his friend.

Finnia stopped too when she saw what had happened.

It was Elzina. Her fight with Usalla was intense. But while Usalla had simply been trying to score points but not really do damage, Elzina's ire had bled through in her fighting. She pulled no punches. She was out for payback.

Usalla was a skilled fighter and blocked and countered the first of her opponent's attacks, but rather than settle into an equal footing, Elzina pushed hard. Far harder than anyone would have expected. While she did not attempt any killing blows, she was out to cause harm, and a lot of it.

It was a stomping kick and elbow combination that left Usalla lurching as her lower leg snapped. The elbow to the head follow-up was what dropped her to the ground. Elzina had won, but she continued to rain down blows until Demelza called for her to stop.

The teacher's demeanor was calm and cool, as it always was, but annoyance was in her eyes. People got hurt in training all the time, and they had a healer for it, but this was overtly personal, and Ghalian could not afford such emotions.

"Switch!" she called out, summoning assistance to take the girl to the healing chamber.

Bawb stepped in front of Elzina, his face a mask of calm. But inside he was raging. Usalla had been hurt, and rather badly, and Elzina had no justification for what she had done. Worse, she seemed to have enjoyed it.

"Begin."

This was a different fight than his previous bouts. For one, Elzina was far more skilled than the others he had faced. But more than that, her actions had triggered something inside of him, and her aggressive moves drove him into action.

He blocked and parried her punches and kicks, replying in kind with his own flurry of counterattacks. Elzina had fought him many, many times in their training, but today something new reared its head. In his anger, Bawb stopped thinking about the techniques he was using. He just let them flow. And flow they did.

Elzina found herself forced back by not only the intensity of his blows but also the unexpected creativity in their application. He was tapping into his knowledge base without hesitation, his body and mind working in unison without effort.

He landed punch after punch, following them with knees

and elbows. Elzina's expression shifted from one of angry cockiness to worry as she realized she was losing. A hard elbow cracked across her jaw, a headbutt snapping her nose in a burst of blood. She fell to her knees, stunned and minorly concussed.

Bawb wound up for a round kick to her head but pulled back at the last moment, his leg hovering in the air beside her temple before slowly lowering to the ground. He looked up to their teacher. Demelza was watching him closely but had not moved to stop him. She gave a slight nod, satisfied with his actions. Angry as he was, which was still apparent no matter how he tried to conceal it, he had not given in to his emotions. At least not completely.

"Stop!" she called out to the class. "That is enough for today. Those who are injured, see the healer. Those who are not, you have the rest of the day to yourselves. Rest, eat, recover. Tomorrow, you will all separate for individual training for a short while."

"What does that mean?" Albinius asked, wiping blood from his nose.

"It means you will be taken off world to study with Masters outside of the Ghalian order."

The students looked at one another, excitement and a bit of shock in their eyes. They were going off world, and it was going to be an adventure.

"What are we to study, Teacher?" Finnia asked.

"You are now entering the phase of your training where you will learn to master the diverse martial styles taught across the galaxy. Those from outside our order. There are many techniques your enemies will utilize, and the best way to defeat an opponent quickly and efficiently is to already know what their next move will be before they ever make it."

"Are we to secure transit on our own?" Zota asked.

"No. You will each be personally taken by a teacher.

Introductions will be made and you will enter the training facility under a false identity. None will know who or what you are. So far as they are aware, you are simply there to learn to fight, just like anyone else. Maintain your cover story at all times, learn all you can, and in this rare instance, have fun. This can be a rewarding experience, so make the most of it that you can."

CHAPTER NINETEEN

The students had been surprised to be getting such a degree of unstructured free time, and it was something all of them took the most advantage of. Even the injured ones made the most of it, once they had finished with the healer, of course.

Some relaxed, while others studied up on other worlds in preparation for traveling to wherever they might be sent. As for Bawb, he spent the time practicing his combative spells along with attempting some far more advanced ones, even occasionally working on the spell for the famed shimmer cloak as well. He was far too young to be able to proficiently cast it, but it was a key tool in the Ghalian arsenal, and he was going to make the most of his time to be sure he was as prepared as possible when the time came.

Usalla joined him for a late dinner, walking just fine, her broken leg mended and sound. Seeing his friend back in one piece took a load off Bawb's mind, allowing that final knot of tension he had been carrying to release.

"I still cannot believe she did that," he said as they dined. "It was uncalled for. Excessive."

Usalla shrugged. "It is Elzina. That is just how she is." She patted his arm warmly. "I understand you made your displeasure known. I appreciate the concern, but do not draw our teacher's ire because of me."

"It is fine. What is done is done. Besides, we have far more to think about now. Training under non-Ghalian masters? And off world? It should be an interesting experience, to say the least."

"I am quite excited for the opportunity," she mused. "To experience another school firsthand will be invigorating."

"And a good exercise in maintaining cover. I wonder exactly how long we will be away."

Usalla shrugged with calm resignation. "I suppose we will find out soon enough."

"I suppose you are right."

The next morning the students headed out of the compound to the ships they had been assigned. Their rides were spread out across the various landing sites around the city. As a group they would draw attention, but no one would think twice about a lone Wampeh teenager boarding a ship.

Bawb walked to the coordinates he had been given by Teacher Demelza that morning, curious which teacher would be his ride.

"Master Hozark?" he blurted, shocked that a Master, and one of the Five at that, was going to be ferrying him to another solar system.

"Hello, Bawb. I hope you are ready for your training."

"I am."

Hozark looked at the teen a moment. "Something is troubling you."

"Not troubling, so much as confusing. They said it would be a teacher taking me."

"Ah, I see. This is simply a matter of convenience. I have

business with an associate in the same system, so this is two tasks accomplished with one trip."

"Oh, I understand."

"And let us not forget, once a teacher, always a teacher. I may be one of the Five, but that does not mean I cannot still carry out other duties as well from time to time. Now come, climb aboard. We have a long flight ahead of us."

Bawb did as he was told. A minute later Hozark's shimmer ship was in the air.

They exited atmosphere with ease, then Hozark slid aside and let Bawb take the controls. It was something he had done from time to time, teaching the boy to fly when they were together. And not just any manner of ship. A Ghalian shimmer ship. It was one more of the little bits of one-on-one training that would prepare him better than any classroom could.

He had learned early on that a shimmer ship was very hard to cloak in space, but the most powerful and talented of Ghalian Masters could do so. In atmosphere it was much easier, but he was still just a mere Vessel, and as such, even that was beyond him. But he knew that with hard work, one day he would master the skill, and then he would be a force to reckon with.

"Time to jump," Hozark said when they were finally well out of atmosphere and flying clear in the dark vacuum of space.

Bawb slid out of the Master's seat and took his usual place. Hozark sat and immediately engaged the Drookonus's jump spell with such ease it looked as simple as breathing. And for him, it truly was. As the upcoming lessons were going to be long and plentiful, he made quick time of the flight, executing several jumps in succession so his passenger could get started sooner rather than later.

In short order they dropped down through the atmosphere at their destination world, heading to a landing site outside the walls of a quaint town on a planet that looked like a swirled marble when viewed from the inky depths of space above.

"The planet Hokkus," Hozark said. "This is the home of Master Turong. A great and skilled fighter, well versed in many styles and techniques. It is he who will be training you for the duration of this outing, Bawb."

"He sounds impressive."

"He is. And he is one of the few who know who I am. What I do. And while he will undoubtedly deduce what you are as well, you are nevertheless not to speak of it to any but he. Is that clear?"

"Yes. But how is it he knows?"

A faint smile tickled the corners of Hozark's lips. "We have a long history, Turong and I. And he owes me favors. *Many* favors."

"I see."

"No, you do not. But ours is a complicated friendship that expands beyond mere debt of service. And you would do well to know that Master Turong has taught others in our fold. Henni, for instance. Unfortunately, Nixxa as well."

"Henni?"

"You know how she fights."

"She is a most formidable combatant. Whenever we spar, I am unable to best her."

"Yes, she is curiously strong for so diminutive a woman. But that works to her advantage. Many have taken her size for granted, and many have paid the price. I taught her much, but Master Turong took the time to help her tame her rather rambunctious ways."

Bawb's head cocked slightly, but he remained silent.

"Very well," Hozark laughed at the sight. "Tamed *some* of her ways."

"And Nixxa?"

"You have met her on occasion, I know. A talented pilot, fierce fighter, and accomplished pirate. Unfortunately, she has a problem with authority figures. Even those attempting to help her, as Turong was. Ultimately, they parted ways, and her and Henni's friendship suffered for it, among other reasons."

"Parted ways?"

"We will just leave it at that. But always know that there will be some adversaries in your life who have trained where you have trained. Learned what you have learned. At least, partially. And that is why we Ghalian craft our own styles. Very few are the outsiders who have done anything remotely similar."

Hozark brought the ship in for a landing, settling it into a hover inches above the ground without a bump or shudder. He rose and headed to the hatch. Bawb followed, casual in his demeanor but taking in everything around them with great interest.

He had learned to use his peripheral vision to great effect in his Ghalian training, and that skill was serving him well now. The town itself was more sprawling than tall, favoring low-rise structures that fit with the area's natural geography rather than forcing spires into the landscape like jutting eyesores found on some other worlds.

Bawb felt the pressure of the spells protecting the large, walled compound as they approached. This was something only the sensitive could detect, but given the sheer force and volume of the magic, he couldn't help but wonder if normal people might sense it as well.

Hozark saw the shift in his demeanor and nodded approvingly. "You feel it."

"It is so powerful."

"The spells will not harm you, Bawb," he said as they approached the thick entry door. "The constant layering of defenses over the years has made this facility one of the safest places to train in the galaxy. At least, from outside threats."

Bawb knew what he meant. This would be hard training, and no quarter would be given just because he was a student of Hozark's. If anything, he might be treated worse because of it, all in the name of making him a better fighter. Diamonds formed under pressure, and so did great warriors.

Hozark placed his hand upon the door. No knocks, no passphrases. Merely his hand. The door vibrated a moment then swung open.

"Come," he said, stepping through into a small courtyard, closing the door behind them. He paused and placed his hand on the door again, his lips barely moving. It took a moment before Bawb realized what he was doing. Master Hozark, one of the Five, was adding yet one more defensive spell to the massive quilt work of spells protecting the compound.

I wonder, how many times has he done this? How many others have done this? Bawb marveled, realizing just how protected this place was.

It was the sort of thing Ghalian did with their facilities. A defensive technique that required great patience and magic. One that the casters placing it hoped would never be needed, but that contained enough power to withstand even the most direct and brutal of magical attacks. Even the Council of Twenty would be hard pressed to break through those defenses. They would, eventually, but at great cost in both magic and manpower.

"Hozark!" a young man a few years older than Bawb called out, hurrying over to greet him.

Hozark, in the most un-Ghalian way Bawb had ever seen him act, embraced the man in a truly welcoming hug. "Happizano, it is so good to see you. I did not know you were training with Master Turong this cycle."

Happizano laughed, completely at ease with the deadly assassin. "Oh, you expect me to believe that?"

"Well, I may have had *some* inkling you would be here," he replied with a wink. "And your father? Is he well?"

"He's great. I'll tell him you say hi."

"Do. I must make time to visit him soon. It has been too long."

The young man glanced at the teenager at Hozark's side. "Fresh meat?"

"Bawb, this is Happizano Jinnik. A dear friend I have known since he was a boy."

"Hey, good to meet ya," Happizano said, shaking Bawb's hand with a surprisingly firm grip. "You can just call me Hap if you want."

"Nice to meet you, Hap."

"You're going to love it here. *If* you have a bit of a masochistic streak, that is."

"I do not know if I would call it that, but I am eager to learn."

"Good answer," he said, glancing at Hozark's approving smile. "I think you're gonna fit in just fine."

An older man exited one of the buildings across the courtyard and walked toward them. The way he carried himself with an air of absolute calm and quiet, but also unspoken power, there was only one person he could be.

"Turong, good to see you."

"Hozark, good to see you as well," he said, clasping his hand. "And this must be Bawb."

"It is my honor to meet you, Master Turong," Bawb said with a little bow.

The master nodded. "Respectful. A good start."

Hozark watched the exchange with a quiet gaze. The introduction had gone smoothly, as he had been confident it would. "Thank you for taking him in, my friend."

"For you? I am glad to be of service."

"And the coin does not hurt."

"Well, one does not turn down coin, but you know I would do this for no charge."

"I do. But you also know I believe in fair payment for services, even from a friend."

"And it is appreciated." He turned to the new arrival, sizing him up in a glance with very skilled eyes. "Yes, I think we can work with this one. You have brought skilled clay ready for molding before. Young Happizano certainly turned out well. Let us hope young Bawb will be as *adept*."

"I am sure he will be a willing *vessel* for your teachings," Hozark replied, relaying the boy's rank and abilities in a way only a Ghalian, or a very, very trusted friend, might decipher.

Turong nodded his understanding. "Very well. Come, Bawb. You are welcome in my training house. Hozark, I will send word when the boy is ready for retrieval."

"Thank you, my friend. I look forward to seeing you again soon."

Hozark watched as Turong led the boy from the courtyard, leaving him and Happizano alone.

"I like him," Hap said. "Not that he said all that much, but he seems cool."

"Cool?"

"You know what I mean. I think he'll fit in fine here."

"And you? How goes your training?"

"It's been fun. Exhausting, but Master Turong has been showing me some of the more, uh, *interesting* techniques."

"With the power you possess, young Jinnik, I am certain he is. As I am confident you will excel. I hope your example will lead Bawb to similar success, though he possesses no power of his own."

"But then, your kind never do, eh?" the boy said with a wink.

"You know we do not speak of that here."

"And I won't. But there's no one here at the moment. Just you and me."

"Of that I am quite aware."

Hap chuckled. "Of course you are. Well, in any case, I like him."

"I am glad."

"You know, he looks like you."

"We are both Wampeh."

"Uh-huh," Hap said with a smile and a nod, but said nothing more. Hozark let it slide without comment.

"I will see you upon my return, young Jinnik. Be well."

Inside the depths of the compound, Bawb had already dropped his limited gear off in the bunkhouse. Master Turong, while warm and inviting upon their first introduction, was not wasting any time starting his training. And the first step of that would be to properly assess the boy's skills firsthand.

He waved over a boy roughly Bawb's age. He was lean and wiry, his deep-red skin tight across defined muscles built from years of hard work. The boy jogged over, giving a slight bow.

"This is Bawb. He is joining us for a short while."

"Understood, Master," he said, stepping into a sparring circle.

"You will fight with Marius," Bawb was informed. "If Hozark brought you here to me, he must have great confidence in your skills. It is not often we see your kind in these walls."

"I do not know about that. I am just a trainee."

Master Turong's brow raised slightly, but he said no more on that matter. "Go. Fight. Let me see what you can do."

Bawb gave a bow as he had seen Marius do then stepped into the circle.

Marius did not wait for niceties, launching immediately into a flurry of attacks, sending Bawb back on his heels as he parried as best he could. The young Ghalian countered, throwing a dizzying combination of punches and elbows, but his opponent slapped them aside with ease.

"Stop!" Turong called out, stepping into the ring. "What are you doing?"

"Sparring, Master," Bawb replied, confused.

"You do not spar. You *fight*. You are holding back. Do not fear causing or receiving injuries here. We have a powerful healer on-site."

"I thought—"

"Do not think. *Fight*."

Turong stepped back, nodding to Marius. The boy again launched into a fierce assault. Bawb took several strong hits but kept to his feet, though he was unable to land any of his own. He was starting to get the hang of this. Of fighting someone outside the order. This Marius seemed a decent sort, but he was an opponent now, and that meant he was to be met with full force and no hesitation.

A loud roar echoed across the chamber, the ground shaking. Smoke and fire flickered from an arched grating at the far end. Flames spurted out as the bars opened. What emerged shocked the boy.

It was a Zomoki. A small one, no more than a juvenile and clearly not capable of space flight yet. But it was a Zomoki nonetheless. What some in another distant galaxy would call a *dragon*, though Bawb was not privy to that information.

Slender golden links held it in place, the magical chain binding it far better than thick restraints could. But it was close, and it was watching the boys fight with great interest.

Marius's elbow slammed across Bawb's face, driving him to the ground.

"Pay attention, Bawb," Turong chided.

"It-it's just, I have never seen a Zomoki before. Not even a lesser one."

"Ignore what does not affect you. Know your surroundings and continue!"

Marius knew what to do, pressing his attack. Bawb tried to defend himself, but the deadly beast so close was distracting him. Punches and kicks landed, staggering him hard. As soon as he thought he was countering his opponent, Marius would slip into a different technique, rendering Bawb's style neutered.

Bawb kept to his feet, mostly, but he took a beating worse than most he received back at the Ghalian training house. After several minutes of the abuse that felt like hours, Master Turong finally called a stop when the newcomer collapsed to the ground, blood leaking from his nose and lips.

"Enough. Marius, show him to the healer." He walked to the fallen teen, looming over him with an assessing gaze. "When you are mended, we begin again."

Bawb climbed to his feet and bowed, then followed Marius down a corridor to be fixed up. It seemed training under Master Turong was going to be very intense indeed.

CHAPTER TWENTY

Bawb's first week with Master Turong was brutal.

It was exciting and fun, in a painful way, the myriad novel fighting styles and training techniques among a completely new group of students a welcome change from his usual fare. But it was taking its toll.

Despite having years of Ghalian conditioning under his belt, Bawb found that Master Turong was certainly no slouch when it came to driving his students hard, extracting the absolute most out of their potential.

It also meant Bawb was already becoming quite familiar with the healer on the premises. With the intensity of the training taking place, she was busy from dusk until dawn, keeping the trainees fit for combat of the most brutal variety.

Interestingly, Bawb's konus had remained silent. He was learning new skills and techniques, but the odd device was not informing him of any leveling up those first days. When it finally did speak to him, however, its usual sass was present in spades.

You're messing up, you know.

"Oh? How is that, Konus? I think I am learning quite a lot. In fact, I was wondering when I would hear from you. I have undoubtedly leveled up in some techniques."

You think so? Maybe. But all those skills? It's not about just learning the moves. Not for a Ghalian. It's about predicting them and countering the enemy before they can even move to strike. You are stuck in a two-dimensional game when you should be playing in three.

Bawb searched for an appropriately snarky reply, but found himself lacking. The damned konus actually had a point.

Ah, now you get it.

"Stop reading my mind."

I don't read minds. At least, not exactly. Just what you make available to me. It's how we talk without others hearing. I thought you figured that out by now.

"Must you always be so cryptic? I know you're not exactly here to help me. But at least don't hinder."

Any hindrance is entirely your own doing. And by the way, me talking to you right now? That is *helping you.*

With that the konus fell silent, and Bawb could tell by the way it did that it would not be talking to him anytime soon. But that was fine. He had learned to take the device's words seriously, no matter how annoying it might be.

"Countering *before* the attack," he mused. It was a novel concept. Not reacting but anticipating based on the subtlest of tells from one's opponent. His skill level was not there yet—he was not so egotistical as to ignore that fact—but the concept was sound. More than sound. It was something he latched onto.

A flush of excitement flooded his body. He was going to create his own technique one day, and *this* element would be a cornerstone of his fighting style.

Of course, he was still going to get his ass handed to him on the regular for years before that point, but all the pain and sweat would be preparation. And when he finally did become a Master, those blows and spells would be negated before they even began.

Master Turong noted the shift in the teen's fighting style immediately. Something, it seemed, had clicked for the boy. He pulled him aside after training in the middle of the third week.

Bawb had been fighting hard, training with students far above his skill level, taking the beating without complaint, and always returning better for it. He was *learning*.

"I see you have embraced the process," the master said to the sweat-soaked youth, fresh from the healer's table. "Your skills are improving quite rapidly."

"Thank you, Master Turong. Your instruction has proven invaluable, and I am grateful for your efforts to help me grow."

"Oh, those efforts are all your doing. I just show the path. It is you who must choose to walk it. I am glad to see you and Happizano have become friends. He has trained here off and on for many years, and he and Hozark are quite close. It is good he will be one of your allies as well. As you both age into men, this relationship will serve each of you well. His family's magic is incredibly strong."

"I have seen it in training. He is so powerful. A good ally indeed."

"As is a Ghalian."

Bawb held his tongue. Master Turong could speak of these things in these walls, but it was not Bawb's place to confirm nor deny, as Hozark had instructed him. Turong noted his silence and gave an approving nod.

As did the shimmer-cloaked Ghalian Master watching the interaction.

Hozark had visited several times during Bawb's training, always in secret, and always under cover of a shimmer cloak.

Only Master Turong knew he was there, as well as the reason why.

"Yes, I know," Turong said, well aware Hozark would also be pleased with the response. "You must not speak of these things. But I have done this a long, long time, and I know many of your kind's ways. Some see the Ghalian as assassins and nothing more, but I know better. Your order's sense of justice, of right and wrong, sets you apart from all others. The Ghalian have done far more good than the people of this galaxy realize. Of course, that is kept silent for a reason. A frightening reputation —and well-earned, I would add—is far more useful than that of a principled benefactor."

"I am just here to train, Master."

"I know you are. And you are doing well. One day you may face an adversary who knows a great many techniques, and it is against this sort of foe that I am focusing your tutelage in particular. As for what you will eventually make into your own style, be it martial, magical, or some combination none has tried before, I feel confident you will be a considerably powerful warrior, regardless of what form it should ultimately take. It is the Ghalian way."

"And Master Hozark? What of his style?"

"Powerful. Powerful and unique. A force to be reckoned with by any unfortunate enough to cross his path."

"He says you two have known each other a long time. Was he always this talented?"

"More than he would admit. One of the toughest and most creative fighters I have ever seen, and an incredible swordsman, especially with a Vespus blade. Samara was the only one I have known to be his equal in that regard."

"Samara? I have never heard of her."

Bawb could have sworn he was seeing things, but it almost looked as though Master Turong's eyes glistened with drops of moisture for an instant. Then, as quickly as they had appeared, they were gone.

"Perhaps one day Master Hozark will tell you of her," he said quietly.

Hidden under his shimmer cloak, Hozark felt a twinge in his gut at the sound of her name. His lover. His partner. His enemy. The boy's mother. He would one day tell Bawb all about her. All of her amazing qualities, along with the flaws that made him care for her even more. But not now. He was too young.

What the two had done was not the Ghalian way. They did not bond. Not ever. But Hozark and Samara had something special. And when she unexpectedly turned against the order, it had flipped his world upside down.

But Bawb deserved to know about her, in time. Just as he would eventually tell the boy his own well-kept secret. Something only a handful of the most trusted in his circle knew. That the traitor Samara was the boy's mother. And he was his father.

Bud and Henni had been there in the aftermath of the discovery, and Demelza was by his side for every step of that excruciatingly difficult time. Hap was traveling with them at that time as well, though he had never been told of Bawb's origins. He was intuitive, yes, though not a reader as Henni was. But he nevertheless had his suspicions.

As for Turong, he did not know for certain, but he knew how close Hozark and Samara were and had long wondered if there might be an offspring at some point. That the boy looked so much like his father only cemented his certainty, even though it was one question he would never ask of his friend. All that mattered was he would treat Bawb as any other student, but he would also look after him as his friend's son.

Hozark stepped away silently, making his way back to his ship to leave the boy to train in peace. He would come for him soon enough, and then it would be back to the same thing he had been doing since the day he learned he had a child. He would do all he could to mentor him, to protect him, and to make him into a man he could be proud of.

For now, however, the boy would simply train on, none the wiser, but loved by the deadliest man in the galaxy all the same.

CHAPTER TWENTY-ONE

Bawb's time with Master Turong continued, the weeks stretching into months, far longer than he had ever thought he would be away from the familiar walls of the training house. And Master Hozark continued to drop in, keeping tabs on the boy, albeit stealthily from a distance.

The teen was performing well, absorbing the various techniques like a hungry sponge. More than just learning the martial forms, however, he was also picking up on the personality traits and accompanying fighting quirks of his fellow students and using them to his advantage. It was something taught to all, but young Bawb was growing proficient far more rapidly than a normal student might.

Master Turong was pleased with the boy's efforts, teaching him techniques well above the level he appeared to be to the others. Deadly, powerful techniques reserved only for the most accomplished of his students.

There was no telling how long it might be until Bawb might return to his tutelage again, so regardless of whether he could apply the techniques properly at this time, he would be leaving with the knowledge, and be as prepared for whatever he might face in the future as Turong could make him.

The thing about Bawb that stood out was he truly seemed to have an aptitude for this. More than simple drive, when he turned off his brain and just let the knowledge flow through him, he fought well above his age and level. And as a Ghalian trainee, some of the tenets of the warrior's life that other students found hard to truly integrate as a part of their psyche, he had already accepted as fact years prior.

This is how he found himself standing atop a platform in a large courtyard, securely blindfolded, engaged in a slow sparring session with not one but two other boys. The three of them were working on sensing attacks before they were launched, and from any direction.

Punches and kicks were thrown, and he parried and countered to his left and right, moving around as he sensed the others doing the same. They were good. *Very* good. In fact, his opponents were not mere visitors to the facility, they were future elite guards in training, at least if their sponsors had their way. And as such, they had more drive than the recreational students.

There weren't many of the latter, though, and the few that were accepted were never shown any of the master's more serious techniques. He didn't take them on for the money, though his services were anything but cheap. He took them on because of who they were related to. Who referred them. Whom they would work for. In this life, who you knew was far more important than what you owned. And he knew a *lot* of people.

It was part of what made his and Hozark's relationship so special. Neither needed the other for favors or leverage. Though being in disparate worlds, their lifestyles had some overlap, and their friendship was one of relatively equal peers.

Of course, Turong knew that as incredibly skilled as he might be, Hozark was... well, he was what he was. But he was a friend, and if Turong ever did happen to be in *real* trouble, the Ghalian would have his back whether he asked for help or not.

Fortunately for Turong, that was highly unlikely to ever become an issue. He had no enemies to threaten his facility. At least, not living.

Bawb's hands flew in a blur, his speed blocking attacks from both of his sparring partners simultaneously. He couldn't see their movements, but he felt the slight shift of energy as they moved. A trick he had picked up after many painful weeks of trial and error.

Mostly error.

The other combatants reacted in kind, blocking his counters and throwing probing kicks and jabs, attempting to gauge the distance and location of their target. More than normal, the three were cautious in their movements rather than fighting at near full force. Not for fear, but out of necessity. A misstep could lead to defeat, and patience was as valuable as aggression. But not all things went as planned, and that was also a key element of their training.

"Faster!" Turong called up to the boys. "I sense hesitation. This is not a dance, and you do not fear your partners. What do we say about training?"

"The more you sweat in training, the less you bleed in battle," the three replied in unison.

"Exactly. Proceed."

His tone was calm. These were instructions, not an admonition. They were to speed their fight regardless of consequences. It was the fastest way to learn, even if it might be the most painful.

Bawb threw elbows, lunging forward toward the boy on his right. His adversary shifted, the attack meeting air. Bawb spun immediately, a back hammer fist landing on the boy's head, knocking him back. His opponent sucked up the blow and kept his footing, remaining on the platform, if only just. Bawb sensed a surge of fear from him, a barely noticeable hint of acrid tang suddenly accenting his sweat, and reacted with a visceral need to attack even harder, grabbing the opportunity and pressing his attack.

A foot caught him in the ribs from his left. The other combatant had sensed his motion and stepped in, also taking advantage of the opportunity.

Bawb staggered, his foot sliding to a stop close to the edge, anger at himself flaring for not sensing the kick coming. It was too late for a mental replay of his error. The fight was very much afoot, and he was possibly inches from defeat.

He didn't know the exact distance to the edge, but he had a good idea of his position. The attack had nearly upended him. Of course, Master Turong would sometimes remove parts of the platforms as they fought, a new element added to an already difficult task that, on occasion, sent them tumbling to the ground.

Bawb felt the adrenaline in his veins and went with it, taking a chance a prudent fighter would not. He grit his teeth and pushed off hard, dive-rolling to the side, rising with a fist driving up toward what he hoped was an opponent. He felt that his target was there. Sensed it. But the boys he was fighting were very good, and that meant they would anticipate most of his moves.

But the roll? It was unconventional. Risky, especially at an elevated position and blind to boot. And it worked.

Bawb didn't see the boy fly off the platform, nor did he see him land, but he heard the thump and gasp for air as he hit the ground.

Unsure where exactly the other fighter was, he switched to a spinning flurry of kneeling attacks, his fists and feet flying in all directions as he rushed about the platform in what must have looked like a demented and violent duck walk.

His fist found a home, landing with a solid *thunk*. But rather than press the attack, he rolled once more, this time to the side. The counterattack directed against him found nothing but air.

Bawb leapt to his feet, putting all of his force into one kick. One kick that he hoped would fly true. It was a guess, but knowing the way these two moved, he felt he had a fifty-fifty chance of landing it.

The jarring impact he felt run through his foot and leg, and the subsequent thump of a body on the dirt below, told him he had guessed correctly.

"Enough," Turong said. "Remove your blindfolds."

The three did as they were told. Bawb hopped down and lined up with the others.

"Bawb, what is the difference between a warrior and one merely engaged in a fight?"

"A warrior has no fear. A warrior commits completely."

"And?"

"And he fights as though he has either already won or is already dead. Hesitation is not an option."

"Very good. Fear and doubt, even momentary, has ended many otherwise great fighters. But a true warrior is in control of not only his body but also his mind."

Motion caught their attention. A man was walking toward them, though none had seen him arrive. Turong grinned.

"Hozark, so good to see you."

"And you, Turong. I see the boys are practicing sense combat."

"Yes," the master replied, knowing full well the Ghalian had almost certainly been watching them from the cover of his shimmer cloak. "Your student is performing quite well. But I take it this is to be the end of his time with us."

"It is. Time to take him home."

"Very well." Turong turned to Bawb. "Gather your things and say your farewells."

"I will, Master. Thank you for all you have taught me."

"It has been a pleasure, Bawb. I look forward to when you next join us."

Bawb gave a little bow, flashed a smile to Hozark, then took off at a jog to gather his things.

Level up: Sense fighting, the konus informed him.

The icon display flashed up in front of him, visible to Bawb and Bawb alone. A few new skill icons were unblurred now, as well as a blinking symbol he had not seen before. It lingered a few moments, then vanished.

"Konus? What was that flashing thing?"

You have leveled up.

"You said. But that was something new."

You have reached a higher overall skill level and as such, more magic has been unlocked for your use.

"Are you saying I can cast more powerful spells?"

That is generally what having more magic would mean. Have you really not been paying attention all this time?

"You know I have. It is just this is something new."

Well, now you know for next time.

"Next time?"

You have far to go, and there is still a lot *of power you can't access. Don't think about it. It'll just frustrate you. Focus on what's in front of you at the moment, not the future. It doesn't do anyone any good to daydream.*

Bawb chuckled to himself and hurried to get his stuff. The konus was a constant source of sarcastic shit-talking in his life, but it had slowly developed at least a modicum of a friendly tone in its time on his wrist.

Hozark watched him disappear into a tunnel with an approving gaze.

"The boy is talented, Hozark. He has true aptitude for this."

"I know."

"Then you also know that he is a bit emotional as well."

"As teenagers can be."

"Yes. But for one of his, uh, *nature,* that can be problematic."

"It can, but I feel confident he will learn to control his feelings."

"The greatest among us may not show it, but they feel deeper than most."

Hozark felt a little twinge of pride and warmth at the thought of his son following in his footsteps and overcoming much the same problems he had as a boy.

"True words, my friend. Thank you for taking him under your wing for so long."

"It has been a pleasure to work with one so eager to learn."

"I am glad to hear it. He has come a long way."

Turong nodded. "And has a long way to go, if I read his aspirations correctly. He wishes to be a *master* of his skills one day."

"And I think he will achieve that end."

"As do I. Come, sit with me and have a beverage while we wait for the boy. He has made many friends in his time here. I know he will be quick retrieving his belongings, but it may take him a bit to say his goodbyes."

Those words warmed Hozark's heart. Bawb's first steps at building what would eventually become his informal network of deadly friends. And from what he'd seen, these would be formidable. One day, that is.

The two of them sat quietly, discussing the goings-on in the system as well as those nearby. There was always news, and Turong had a robust network of contacts relaying information to him. Not as far-reaching as the Ghalian spies, but impressive for one not engaged in spycraft.

"Have you heard about Lalaynia?" Turong asked as Bawb crossed the courtyard to rejoin them.

Hozark nodded, his face grim. "People are looking for her."

"Looking for who?" Bawb asked, finally joining them. "Sorry, it is not my place to ask."

"No, that is all right. You have actually seen her once. A good friend of Bud and Henni."

"I do not remember the name."

"Because it was not mentioned. She is rather notorious in pirating circles. A very tall, very strong woman. Her presence is impossible to miss."

A light clicked in Bawb's head. "Wait, is she the one who picked up Bud like a boy when she hugged him? I remember Henni was laughing at that rather than challenging her to a fight, which seemed a bit out of character."

Hozark chuckled. "Yes, that would be her. A dear friend of theirs for many years. We have seen some *interesting* times together."

"And you are looking for her?"

"A great many people are. You see, someone took her, and that is no easy feat. Bud and Henni are, understandably, quite upset."

"And you?"

"Let us just say that I will be helping in this personally. But come, we have a schedule to keep. Thank you, Turong. Your efforts are appreciated."

"My pleasure, Hozark. And, Bawb, I do look forward to our next visit. For now, travel safe and train hard."

Bawb nodded and fell silent, falling in behind Hozark as they headed out of the magical barrier surrounding the compound. He didn't speak again until they were back at

Hozark's shimmer ship. Turong was a trusted friend of Hozark's, and the compound was free of prying eyes and ears, but he knew there was only so much he could say in public.

Only when they were back aboard the ship did he speak up.

"Master Hozark?"

"Yes, Bawb?"

"How could someone get close enough to take Lalaynia if she is as fierce a woman as you say she is? I've heard the name spoken before, and always with a sort of awe at what she was capable of."

"It is precisely that which we are attempting to ascertain. It is very likely someone she knew is responsible."

"Nixxa?" Bawb asked.

"Why do you think it might be her?"

"Well, she also trained with Master Turong, so she is clearly skilled."

"That she is."

"And her morals seem to be quite flexible, for a price."

"Accurate as well. But do not worry yourself about this, Bawb. You have training to complete. As for this? Trust me when I say I have a deep interest in seeing a resolution. Now, how would you like to take us out of atmosphere?"

"Really?"

Hozark slid from the pilot's seat. "Really. You know how. You just need practice."

Bawb slid into the seat and felt the power of the Drookonus connect with him as he began forming the proper intent for the flying spells.

"Okay," he said, a little nervous but far more excited. "Here goes nothing."

CHAPTER TWENTY-TWO

Bawb arrived back at the training house on his own a short while later, following a nice walk through the familiar streets of his home city after setting down. It felt good to be back. Almost odd after so long away, but comforting all the same.

Hozark had dropped him at the landing site and immediately taken off to follow up on a lead about Lalaynia's possible whereabouts, or at the very least, someone who may have seen something. Lips often stayed shut for normal questions where only fear or coin were involved. But when a Ghalian was thrown into the mix, and an irritated one at that, people had a tendency to be much more willing to speak up.

The dead could not spend their riches, and for those motivated by fear rather than coin, living for even a little longer was far preferable to taking any secrets they may have to the grave.

Bawb pondered the situation as he walked the streets, amazed that someone with a reputation such as Lalaynia's could have been taken prisoner. Was it revenge? A ransom situation? He had no idea. What he did know was it couldn't have been easy.

Even though he was only a Vessel, Bawb found himself wishing he could help in some way. The time training with those outside the order had made him even more eager to step out into the real world and take part in missions. He knew this dream would not become a reality for some time, but it was, nevertheless, something he thought about all the way back to the training house.

Bawb made his way in through one of the many hidden entrances and went to the bunkhouse to drop off his gear. From there he bathed, donned clean clothes, and headed to the dining hall. It was empty.

He had a quick meal, but nothing too heavy, then asked Teacher Warfin where the other Vessels were training today.

"They will be heading to the dungeon shortly," he was informed. "You had best hurry if you wish to join them."

"Thank you. I will," he replied, hurrying off to the entryway to the tunnel leading to the training dungeon course.

"Bawb, you are back," Usalla said, walking over to greet him.

"Indeed I am. I see the rest of you have returned as well. When did you get back?"

"I returned a week ago. Some of the others came home weeks before me."

"Do you mean I am the last to return?"

"You are. We were wondering if perhaps something had happened to you. If you had been injured. Some of the others faced extremely difficult and rigorous training, and more than a few were seriously injured in the process."

"Were you?"

"Nothing the healer could not handle. But what of your time away? How was it? And why are you returning to us so late?"

"He probably needed to stay longer in order to graduate and be released," Elzina said with a snicker. "That is why I came back so early. I mastered what my instructors were teaching quickly and had little more to gain."

She spun in a strange, twisting manner, her foot swinging through the air high even as her fists passed low. It was an unusual style, and one likely to take even the most seasoned of fighters off guard.

It was also one of the many techniques in which Master Turong had trained Bawb. He kept that tidbit to himself.

"Very nice, Elzina. I am sure you are quite the force to be reckoned with," he said instead.

"Was that sarcasm?"

"Was it?"

She looked at the others. They'd all heard it. Bawb had disrespected her. Full of piss, vinegar, and the cockiness that came with learning a new skill, there was only one thing for her to do.

"You. Me. Let us have a go of it. Show me what you learned that took you so long."

She rolled her shoulders then settled into a fighting stance.

"Elzina, we are about to run the training dungeon again. I would prefer to save my energy for that."

"So you are afraid."

"Not hardly. Just being logical."

"Logical and cowardly."

"Your words do not hurt me, Elzina."

"And your fear is palpable, Bawb. You know I will defeat you, and you do not wish to be made to look the fool in front of the others."

"We are all made to look foolish. It is part of our training. And we do not care."

"Then fight me."

"Are you not listening? You need to put your insecurities in check and step back."

Elzina had heard enough, her ire raised sufficiently to act.

She launched into an attack. Bawb had hoped she wouldn't, but he had been prepared just in case. It was as they had been taught, hope for the best but expect the worst, and always be prepared for it.

He parried and blocked, quickly retreating from her barrage, not a single blow landing on its target. Resigned to sparring after all, Bawb pressed his own attack, driving Elzina across the chamber with a flurry of fast, shifting moves, alternating from high to low with no warning.

She found herself back on her heels, forced to defend when she had planned on a more offensive stance. That would not do.

Elzina changed forms, spinning fast, throwing dizzying combinations high and low as she had just been taught. She was actually quite good, and Bawb was hard pressed to block her, but Master Turong had done a good job training him, and he could see her moves almost before she made them. That key element of his own technique was gelling in his mind, the logic of it settling in firmly.

But he was still a Vessel, and it would take years to master the concept, no matter how much it now made sense to him. Bawb took several hard blows as a result. He felt his temper rise with each impact. He did not want to fight her. This was nothing more than a stupid waste of time and precious energy.

He spun and landed a back-fist to her chin, staggering the girl. Elzina responded in kind, throwing everything she had at him. Bawb saw Teacher Griggitz enter the chamber as he blocked and pivoted. Elzina pressed harder, her attacks finally landing and driving Bawb to the ground.

"Enough!" Griggitz bellowed. "You have a long day of training ahead of you. I would advise you to conserve your energy. You will be needing it."

"I was just demonstrating my new skills to my classmate,"

Elzina said, fooling no one.

"Of course you were," her teacher replied, unimpressed. "Go on. Get to the dungeon entrance and prepare."

Elzina opened the secret passage and took off at a fast jog, the rest of the class behind her. Bawb rose to his feet and dusted himself off, no worse for wear.

"So, Elzina bested you," Griggitz said, skeptically.

"It would appear that way."

The teacher stared at him a long moment, his brow twitching upward ever so slightly. "Very well. Be on your way," he finally said.

"Thank you, Teacher Griggitz."

Bawb turned and headed out at a fast jog after the others.

Level up: Deception. Nice bit of sandbagging back there, the konus said.

"I did not wish to fight her."

And when your hand was forced, you withheld much of what you learned in your time with Master Turong. You could have defeated her, you know, but you chose not to.

"It seemed not to be worth the effort."

The konus laughed despite having no lungs. *And as a side benefit, she just happens to be overconfident in her abilities and will underestimate you in the future as a result.*

"A silver lining, I suppose," the teen noted.

That there is. Level up: Threat assessment and subterfuge.

"Really? Not that I am complaining."

Yes, really. There's far more to being a Ghalian than just knowing how to fight and kill. And you, young Bawb, have just displayed an innate knowledge of that fact. Keep going like this and who knows? One day you may even prove me wrong and become a Master.

"Or one of the Five."

Don't push it, buddy. For you to become one of the Five, you'd have to be better than good. You'd have to be exceptional.

CHAPTER TWENTY-THREE

Exceptional.

The konus was right, of course. Even among the most talented of the Ghalian Masters, most could never dream of ascending to the highest rank among them. Bawb would have to not only work hard and develop a fighting skill set unrivaled by any, but he would have to also go beyond that. To be a thinker as well as a fighter. To utilize his brain as a weapon. One that might be even more dangerous than his hands.

He made the trek to the training dungeon in silence, trailing slightly behind the others, not lost in thought, but nevertheless deep in it. His classmates wouldn't think anything of it, assuming he was simply saving his energy for the dungeon course. And they would be right, at least to an extent.

But Bawb was in a different mental place following his training with Master Turong. The time away had given him a shift in perspective. He had been so deep in Ghalian training for so long he had almost developed tunnel vision of a sort. But his eyes were open wide now, and so many new options spread out before him.

He was a Vessel, but he felt like more. And he was eager for further challenges. He would get his wish far sooner than he expected.

"Something feels off," he said when they stepped through the training dungeon's entrance.

They had been running this ever-shifting obstacle dungeon for years, and even though it never steered them down the same path and order of obstacles twice, they had developed muscle memory in regards to its perils.

"What is it, Bawb?" Usalla asked, lingering back while the others raced ahead, eager to come out on top and possibly add a useful prize to their possessions if the teachers were feeling generous.

"I do not know, exactly. But can you sense it? Something is different."

"It is always different, Bawb. That is the point."

"No, I do not mean the alterations to the tunnels and chamber order. There is a shift in the air flow. The pressure. The traces of magic. Even the smell. The teachers changed something, I am sure of it."

Usalla strained her senses, listening, feeling.

"I believe you may be right," she finally said. "We must proceed with caution."

"I agree. No telling what games the teachers are up to."

They headed to different branches of the entrance. If it was new, then anything could be different. But that didn't mean this wasn't still a race. And friendly as they were, when it came to competition they pulled no punches. They would compete, but not-head-to-head today.

Usalla hurried into the entrance to the right. Bawb selected the center one.

"See you at the finish," she said.

"See you at the finish," he replied as she vanished into the dimly lit passageway.

Bawb moved ahead slowly, walking where he would normally have run, casting sensing spells and using his night eyes as best he could where the shadows seemed darker than usual.

"Ah, very clever," he muttered, bending low, examining some stone rubble scattered about.

This was new. A tripwire spell hung at ankle level, and a very faint one at that, placed at a bend the students often took at speed as they jostled for a good position to enter the next chamber. Bawb stepped over it, following the fine strand of power until it disappeared into the rocks above.

It was a rockfall trap. Nothing so large as to seriously harm whoever tripped it, but enough to take them out of the competition. And by the look of it, someone had already fallen victim to it, injured and removed from the route as the trap reset. Things *were* different, and this would be just the beginning.

There was a faint glow, he noted, firmly affixed to the ceiling. It was roughly hand sized, giving off the slightest whiff of power. He felt it, but he couldn't tell exactly what it was. Better to avoid it than risk setting off another trap. He moved ahead.

Bawb cleared the next two chambers in quick order, spotting the new trigger mechanisms and traps with relative ease now that he knew what to look for. It was in the third chamber that something truly challenging presented itself as he walked across a narrow strip of safe ground, balancing on shifting rocks, a decent fall looming on either side.

That part wasn't difficult. They'd done balance work since his first days with the Ghalian, and he could walk a tightrope with the same confidence as a sidewalk. But periodically a swinging log would release from above, cutting an arc right across his path. He had to move fast but cautiously, timing his steps to pass between them lest he be hit, fall, or the unfortunate combination of both.

But even that wasn't the most surprising part.

A low rumble vibrated the air, the scent of burning lingering. Something else was here, and it was not friendly.

Bawb kept his eyes on the path, using his peripheral vision to scan for dangers. The lighting was magically created, as were the shadows. It was meticulously designed patchwork of light and dark, and something was lurking in the latter. The beast lunged forward, constrained only by the golden control collar around its neck keeping it from crossing the path.

It was relatively big. It was certainly deadly. And it would shock the hell out of anyone not prepared for such a frightening surprise. To keep one's senses was imperative. To fall in the one direction would mean grave injury. The other might very well lead to loss of limb, if not life. This was not just some wild beast. It was a smallish Zomoki.

Fortunately, Bawb had some recent experience with the beasts thanks to his time with Master Turong, his nerves steady and his feet sure on the uneven ground. Ground, he noted, that seemed to be splashed with more than a little blood. Possibly enough that whatever had happened before he reached this chamber could have been fatal. Someone clearly had suffered an unpleasant surprise. He felt relieved in the knowledge that at least it wasn't Usalla. She had taken a different route, though who knew what new challenges she faced on her path.

Bawb hurried ahead, a feeling of confidence trying to sink in as he reached the safety of the far end of the chamber. He forced the sensation away. This was no time to let his guard down, and what was once safe could very likely be dangerous as well. There was no rest. Not this time.

He moved down the tunnel toward the next cavern but, yet

again, something was different. A sensation tickled his senses. The dungeon, he realized, was shifting with him in it.

He stepped into the next chamber, a high-ceilinged cavern with stalactites hanging high above and a cozy glow from the bioluminescent moss growing on them like nature's chandeliers, casting even light through the entire environment.

Bubbling-hot streams crisscrossed the uneven stone ground, the springs feeding them spraying at random intervals. That was something they were all used to. An obstacle they crossed without a second thought, barely slowing them down. But Bawb noted two of his cohort were lying on the ground, not injured, but immobilized.

He squinted his eyes, taking in the details. The ground had collapsed under their feet, the water creating sinkholes that, while not person-size, were still large enough to entrap a foot or leg.

More than that, one of them he had seen enter the dungeon via a different entrance. There were no longer three distinct paths. It seemed any chamber could lead to any other chamber, and no one would have an advantage.

The ground seemed different somehow. Besides the sinkholes, that is. Something was off with the texture of the stone, but he couldn't quite tell what. Not at a glance. It took him a full minute to see the subtle shift that was making his warning senses tingle. Fine crystals had formed on some parts. Crystals that could only exist where there was water present. Water seeping up through the rocks above it.

"Clever," he mused, admiring the subtlety of the teachers' new trap.

Bawb hurried along, stepping fast and confident, scanning for other traps and hazards, but sure at least that the ground at his feet would be stable.

He entered the tunnel at the far end and stopped abruptly,

his toe just over a fine line of power. The ground disappeared, a trapdoor opening and closing quickly, leaving no trace of its presence. Bawb forced his feet to hold steady as he scanned for further hazards. From what he could tell, there were several more, all triggered by spells on the floor. The question was, how would he be able to know which spell opened which part of the floor.

He stood there, calculating the most likely routes, but all of them were bad.

"Do not think as others would," he reminded himself. "Think differently."

He shifted his eyes to the walls and ceiling, looking for anything that might be of use. And then he saw them. Small irregularities in the stone that he had always just seen as part of the tunnel's natural structure. But now they were something different. Something useful.

He stepped back, calculating the distance, then ran forward, jumping not ahead but diagonally, his lead foot landing firmly on the wall, pushing off and driving him to the opposite side, where the other foot found purchase. Bawb pushed hard, not allowing his progress to slow, leapfrogging side to side until he reached the far end of the short tunnel.

Not bad, his konus said, more quietly than usual, as if it didn't want to distract him.

"I am not done yet."

No, but you are doing better than the others. Paying attention.

"If you do not mind, I need to focus."

The konus fell silent without another word. That was also new. It tended to chatter whether he wanted it to or not, but now it was almost rooting for him, it seemed.

Or it could be a trick. Knowing that odd device, anything was possible.

Bawb stepped into a familiar chamber. Tall poles of varying

heights leading to the finish. The last chamber changed regularly, but this one he knew all too well. It was the first one he had ever completed when his class had been taken to the training dungeon for the very first time. And as had been the case then, Elzina was there as well.

Bawb started moving, looking for tricks and traps, adjusting his course atop the poles with perfect balance but an uneasy mind. Something was different. It had to be. But he couldn't quite figure out what it was.

Previously, poles had fallen away, dropping them into the darkness below. He tapped his foot on what should have been a falling pole. Nothing happened.

"Well, this should be interesting."

He began his approach, stepping carefully but still unable to see the new perils in the way. Elzina did as well, noting him at once and increasing her pace. The poles converged into a path that brought the various entrance routes together, the safe—or *formerly* safe—poles condensed into a narrow route.

Bawb felt the urge to race but forced himself to slow his pace. Elzina, on the other hand, let her competitive nature push her faster. She elbowed past him in a risky move, jumping diagonally ahead of him to a slightly raised pole.

"Out of the way!"

"You are careless," Bawb replied.

"I am *winning*," she shot back.

Elzina made quick time, racing ahead, the usual path still holding fast and true. Bawb sped up a little, but something still felt off. Different. There was no way the teachers would have made the final chamber easier. Not unless they wanted to teach them a lesson that sometimes things got easier rather than harder, and that would certainly be a first.

Elzina's right foot reached the last row of poles, her leg flexing for the final jump to solid ground.

The pole did not fall, but it did something this time. Something Bawb would have laughed at if he didn't have to traverse the obstacle himself.

Elzina felt the pole move, but it surged upward rather than down, flinging her high in the air before dropping away into the darkness. She cast a cushioning spell as she fell to at least keep herself from breaking her neck. But she had failed. Failed right at the very end.

"Overconfidence," Bawb muttered, looking down into the void below. "Now, how to overcome this?"

He stood still, a lone student atop a pole, mere steps away from victory. It was there, right ahead of him. He could almost taste it. A smile twitched across his lips, an idea in his head. He turned around and stepped back across the poles to the start. He then carefully headed out on the trigger poles. Or, more accurately, the ones that used to be. But now they held firm, taking him on a different path, one that went around the usual route, taking him to a far side at the far edge of safe, solid ground and with it, victory.

He took the final leap without hesitation. If he fell, he fell. But he was almost certain of his choice. And he had committed to it, come what may.

His feet landed on the path without incident. It had worked. He had won.

Bawb walked to the small pedestal to claim his prize. A gleaming golden box hovered atop it, radiating value and power. He reached for it, but something in his mind stopped his hand.

"This is not right." Bawb moved his hand side to side, feeling the traces of power, casting a sensing spell. There was something odd about the magic holding the box aloft. Odd, but strangely familiar. He stood there for several minutes, perplexed. Then it hit him.

He pulled his hand back and headed not for the exit, but back the way he came, leaving the prize behind.

It wasn't until several hours later that he emerged from the dungeon. All of the other students were sitting there waiting, suffering varying degrees of injuries along with bored expressions.

"Took you long enough," Elzina grumbled. "We can't start the next run until everyone is out. What did you do? Just sit on that pole all this time?"

"Not quite," he said, holding up the prize.

"Very good, Bawb," Teacher Griggitz said with a surprised look in his eye. "*Very* good. Few ever complete this task on the first attempt. Or the second or third for that matter."

"Thank you, Teacher."

Griggitz turned to the others. "A lesser prize has been placed at the end. Go and claim it, if you can."

"Wait. Where is Ovixus?" Albinius wondered.

Griggitz's expression flickered a shade darker. "Ovixus was careless and is now in the belly of a Zomoki. I advise you to not make the same mistake."

The students took the shock of the announcement without showing their surprise, but one of their cohort had just perished in a most gruesome way in the very dungeon they were about to re-enter. They would have to put aside any mourning for later. It was more than a little unsettling. But they were Ghalian. They had a job to do no matter what may happen to their classmates, even death. The group moved to the entrance.

"Not you, Bawb. You have earned a respite."

Elzina glared at him as she entered the tunnel. Teacher Griggitz waited until all of them were gone before speaking.

"You figured out a difficult puzzle and an important lesson today. Tell me, how did you come to realize you had to gather the release magic from your first obstacle in order to claim the prize?"

"I nearly did not."

"Yet you hesitated at the very end. Why?"

"The overall theme of the changes to the dungeon was one of patience. To slow our normally rushed pace."

"Good. *And*?"

"And having stopped to scan the area at the beginning, I happened to notice the unusual magic on the ceiling. Only at the end did I feel the same magic coming from the prize."

"And you went all the way back to the beginning to gather it?"

"Yes. Time was not an issue. Only success."

"The Ghalian way."

"Yes. So I backtracked and gathered the magic, then returned to the end, though the course did change on my way back, which was an even greater delay. The dungeon that was so familiar to us was now a different beast entirely."

Griggitz actually smiled. It was something he did not do often.

"Familiarity equals vulnerability, Bawb. A Ghalian must never get complacent. Lazy. It is in those moments that even the most talented of us may pay the ultimate price. But you? You held back, taking the time to treat the familiar with fresh eyes."

"It was an interesting challenge."

"Indeed. And your prize? What do you think of it?"

"I have not yet opened the box."

"You are not curious?"

"I am. But patience is the theme of the day. I will open it back in the bunkhouse when I add whatever it contains to my possessions."

Griggitz nodded his approval. "Well, then. You are done for

now. Return to your chambers and enjoy your prize. You may practice freely until the post-dinner lesson."

"Thank you, Teacher," he said, then turned and jogged away.

Level up: Puzzle solving and trap detection. Nice job, Vessel.

"Thank you, konus. Now, let us see what I have won."

He reached his quarters and sat on his bunk, examining the box in his hands. He opened it expectantly. It was empty.

"Something of a letdown." But there was something odd to the thing. This didn't feel right.

He closed it and turned it over in his hands. It was not terribly large but had a decent weight to it. Too much for its size, he thought. He traced his fingers over the design etched into the metal, feeling the slightest warmth of the stones embedded in the lid.

"Oh," he said. "*Oh.*"

It was a pattern. Subtle. Easy to miss. But it was there. He placed his fingers on four of the stones, his others holding the box by specific runes decorating the metal. He felt a shift in the hint of magic. Cautiously, he opened the box.

"I see," he said with a smile.

It was no longer empty. It contained a fair amount of coin, and he even saw the pommel of a dagger. He pulled the blade free. It was far too long to fit in the small box, yet out it came, intact and substantial. It was also enchanted, he noted.

"A box of holding," he marveled. "Capable of containing far more than a bag of holding."

It was quite a coup, receiving this item. The magic hidden within was immense, as it would need to be to properly contain many times more volume than its outward appearance.

He examined the dagger next. A fine blade with a fair bit of magic within. That, the coin, and the box, it seemed, were the prizes for being the first to complete this new and more difficult dungeon the first time. It was a prize, and a substantial one. And Bawb had been the one who claimed it.

"Things are looking up," he mused, unexpectedly content but also wondering, what fresh new challenges would be coming in his future.

Their lessons were taking a difficult turn, and he had a feeling it would only grow harder. But unlike his early years, Bawb was actually looking forward to it.

CHAPTER TWENTY-FOUR

"*Most* of you performed poorly in yesterday's dungeon challenge," Teacher Warfin said, calmly pacing in front of the assembled Vessels. "One of your classmates even performed so inadequately as to perish. This is not acceptable."

He was not angry. Not upset or emotional. He was a Master Ghalian and such things were beneath him. Though he would adopt those tones on occasion to drive home his point to the students, those days were coming to an end. The students would soon be too old, too experienced for those little subtleties to have an effect. But they were still in transition, and the shift could quite possibly be a deadly one.

"You are no longer Nulls. No longer Novices or Aspirants. And soon you will no longer be Vessels. At this stage in your training, as has just been made abundantly clear, your actions will begin to have far more serious consequences. If you let your attention falter, not all of you will survive."

The students stood still, faces blank masks. But each of them felt it. The little twinge of both fear and excitement. This was it. They were getting to the good stuff. There was higher risk, clearly, but it was also thrilling, and all of them were looking forward to the challenge.

"You will all be taken to another world and deposited in the wilderness. You have been trained in survival. You possess the skills and knowledge. Now you will put them to the test."

"We are to camp out?" Albinius asked. "That actually sounds pleasant."

"Far more than that, Albinius. Your task is to ascertain your location and make your way to a specific place. A town. One frequented by more dangerous sorts. Therein is an item you must retrieve and bring to the retrieval site. It will not be easy, and each of you will be working alone. You will arrive at dusk with no more than the clothing on your backs. You will use what you have learned to survive. Find food, make shelter, craft weapons, for you will arrive with no weapons, no food, and no equipment beyond the konuses on your wrists."

"Are we all being sent to retrieve the same item?" Bawb asked.

"That is for you to figure out. Remember, we work alone. You cannot rely on anyone. If you do, they may also be seeking what you are after. They may betray you. Trust no one." A small group of Masters entered the room. "Go to their ships. You will be ferried to the same starting area. What you do from there is entirely up to you."

Bawb felt a surge of excitement as they filed out of the room, heading to the landing site. A real task on another world. It was a welcome challenge and one he hoped he would win. He felt Elzina's stare without looking at her. He didn't need to. The entire walk to the ships, he simply ignored her. There was enough to think about without adding her to the mix. And once they were at their destination it wouldn't matter.

The students split up to board the ships.

"See you there," Usalla said, peeling off to a ship on the right.

"Good luck," he replied, knowing even between them there would be no niceties once the game was afoot.

He settled into his seat aboard the craft and calmed his mind, preparing for the ordeal to come. Teacher Warfin hadn't given them much information, but then, that was the point. They were old enough to make their own way, figuring things out as they went. Ghalian would not always have the benefit of their spy network to steer them true.

The ship jumped several times, but the last of them was different. He felt the shift immediately. They had arrived in a system with a *very* powerful sun. One whose magic he felt tickling his senses without even trying.

Interesting, he mused, wondering if he could use this to his advantage somehow.

The shimmer ships descended to the surface, activating their shimmer cloaks once in the atmosphere, hiding their arrival from prying eyes. Bawb watched as they flew down to their landing site, the planet green and lush below. It was almost a jungle, so fertile was the soil. And the powerful sun's magic did not hurt either.

"Good luck, Vessels," their pilot said when Bawb and the other passengers disembarked.

The ship vanished from sight moments later, silently flying away to the designated retrieval site where it would wait with the others. Bawb and his cohort were alone. Truly on their own. And he was reveling in the moment.

The sun was setting, giving them no more than a half hour until dark if his estimates were correct. The others noted the same thing, spreading out at once. Elzina immediately snatched up a fallen branch and chipped piece of stone and began fashioning a spear. She was more interested with a weapon than shelter or food.

Of course she was.

Some of the others started foraging, while others fanned out to distance themselves from the group before beginning the construction of their shelter. There was already a chill in the air. The night would definitely be on the cooler side despite the dense plant life. Nature adapted, it seemed, and the strong magic in this system made the vegetation more resistant to cold.

"*Oh*," Bawb muttered, a realization dawning on him, followed by a little grin.

He took off for a small hill, running hard to the top, not worried about the sweat that would cool and freeze to his body from the effort. He had other plans.

From the top he scanned the horizon. The sun was nearly down, but he had established his general location as well as the path of the burning orb traversing the sky. He stood and waited, not hunting, not foraging, but waiting for the sun to set completely. While he did, he gathered some small, barbed vines, stripping the strong skin into lengths, the thorns still firmly attached. He wove them together, securing them into a pair of small pads he could conceal in the palms of his hands.

While others were crafting spears or stone blades, his creation was tiny. So tiny that unless you were looking for it, it was almost unnoticeable.

The sun finally dipped below the horizon, darkness falling quickly in the wilderness. But from his elevated position he saw what he had been hoping to catch sight of. What those building shelters down below would not see from their location. A faint glow in the distance. The first lights of the evening in a nearby town.

His destination.

Bawb took a deep breath and started moving, descending

quietly, careful to avoid his fellow Vessels as he moved away from the hill and toward the distant glow no longer visible from down below. In short order he was well clear of the area they had been setting up their shelters. He was alone.

Now he could run.

Bawb cast a minor night vision spell, scanning the vegetation around him as he moved, searching for specific plants he had committed to memory. Those that naturally absorbed quite a bit of magical potential. They were few and far between, but gradually, he began to fill his pockets with their leaves.

Many of his classmates made melee weapons. He had other ideas.

His stomach grumbled several hours later when he downed a handful of berries he found along his path. The others would be trapping game and foraging their meals right about now, separated and working alone, but following the same routine they had been taught. Food and shelter were vital, especially on a night as cold as this.

Bawb, however, pressed on, increasing his pace, his body warming itself somewhat from the effort. Even so, it was getting quite unpleasant as the chill set in, but he pushed that thought aside, doing what it took no matter the discomfort.

Level up: Drive

"Drive?"

Just shut up and take your level and keep moving, the konus replied. *You'll need your energy.*

Bawb did not argue.

Deep into the night he marched, crushing the leaves he had gathered, funneling their juice into a small gourd he had cracked open with a rock, using a steady trickle of power from his konus to force the water out, leaving behind a condensed syrup of relatively potent magic.

It wasn't a poison he was crafting, but rather a magical surge of sorts. Something he could use to distract and divert focus from himself, making someone else the object of attention with their unexpected magic boost, setting off any wards or detection spells while he snuck by unnoted.

At least he hoped so.

But if he was noticed, he had another trick up his sleeve. Or in the palm of his hand, as the case may be. His other hidden thorns. Bawb had condensed another small gourd of sap, but this was different. He had been forced to stop his trek long enough to use rocks rather than his hands to extract this particular substance. And for good reason.

The condensed syrup was a potent knock-out toxin of sorts. He knew it would work on his kind, which was why he had identified the plant so easily even in the dark. But how well it might function on other races was anyone's guess. He dipped the thorns of his little device and continued on, hoping he would not need to use them.

Bawb hung the drying thorn device from his waistband alongside the other, but this one he wrapped in a protective layer of bark to prevent accidentally giving himself an unexpected nap out in the middle of nowhere. If that happened, he would quite possibly freeze to death, be eaten by a beast, or worse.

Voices caught his attention. Close and getting closer. A *lot* of them. There was something familiar about the way they spoke. Something in their tone and cadence. These weren't hunters. They were bandits.

He quickly stripped the konus from his wrist. There was no way he could take on a dozen armed bandits on his own and unarmed. As soon as they saw him, he began to run.

"Get him!" he heard someone shout.

A moment later he was tackled to the ground, just as he had planned. He used the impact to slide his konus under a shrub before rolling away. He looked up at the gruff men and women looming over him. Bandits, just as he had assumed.

Strong hands hauled him to his feet, holding him firmly in place. A wiry woman with deep green skin and tufts of black hair jutting from the collar of her tunic quickly patted him down.

"Ow!" she exclaimed, jabbing herself with the exposed barb, not even noticing she had just given herself a dose of magic.

Bawb watched her, searching for any reaction. There was none. He had to wonder if perhaps his condensate was not as potent as he had thought. He would just have to refine it further while he walked. If he made it out of this situation in one piece, that is.

She quickly turned his pockets inside out, emptying his remaining leaves onto the ground.

"Just leaves, berries, and lint," she said with disgust.

"Leave the kid alone, Varra," a gruff voice said from the group.

"Fair game is fair game, Orkus."

A much shorter, stout fellow with a bushy orange beard and eyebrows nearly as long, strode forward from the group. "You know the rules. Nixxa will not be pleased if you go messing with a kid."

"But we're supposed to fill the coffers."

"And we do. But look at him." The man gestured to Bawb with a look that almost seemed to be pitying. "He's filthy and alone. Destitute. Probably hungry. You hungry, kid?"

Bawb nodded.

Orkus swung his pack around and pulled out a small parcel wrapped in a thick leaf. "Here, you can have this. Some Allik Cheese and a crust of bread."

"That's your meal, Orkus," the woman protested.

"And he needs it more than I do. Come on, Varra, you know

how this works. We're supposed to *help* this kind. It's the whole reason we're bandits in the first place." He dug in his pocket and pulled out a coin. "Let 'im go."

The firm grip on Bawb's arms released. Orkus stepped close, pressing the coin into the teen's hand. "It's not much, but it'll be enough for you to get something warm to eat when you get to town. You are heading to town, aye?"

Bawb nodded.

"That way. You're on the right path. But in the future, don't go wandering around in the dark. There are far worse things than us out there." Orkus turned to his compatriots. "All right, let's get moving. We're behind schedule as it is."

The bandits filed past Bawb without another word or thought, leaving him to his own devices, unharmed and alone. Bawb stood there quietly as they did, pondering how odd it was that Nixxa and her supporters stole from pretty much anyone with coin, and indiscriminately at that, having stolen from the Ghalian and the Council of Twenty alike, yet left him alone. Her rules were strange. An unconventional code of conduct baked into them. Take from the rich but also give to those in need. She was a most unusual pirate indeed.

Bawb crouched down and retrieved his konus, slipping it back over his wrist, the metal a welcome sensation against his skin. To have it stolen from him would have been worse than the loss of any coin.

"You see that?"

I do not have eyes.

"You know what I mean."

I am inactive when not worn by my user. But I did feel something in my rest state. I assume you managed to escape your encounter unharmed.

"That I did. And can you believe it?" Bawb said, unwrapping the parcel Orkus had handed him. "They gave me food."

Well done. Befriending bandits is a useful skill, even if not one I can level you up in.

"They're Nixxa's people. Fortunately, they don't know about our history. She really does hold a grudge."

Bawb brushed the dirt from his clothes then picked up the remaining leaves and began crushing them, squeezing their juice into the little gourd as he walked. Eventually, the liquid would be more powerful. It would just take some time, it seemed. But time he had in abundance.

He had the whole night ahead of him.

CHAPTER TWENTY-FIVE

Bawb ran straight through the night, chugging along steadily at a far slower pace than what one might normally consider a run, but he had quite a distance to cover. Pacing himself was essential. Nevertheless, his speed remained constant, save the moments he paused to gather edible forage he spotted on his path or to collect dew from leaves before he knew he would be able to drink from the few small streams he came upon.

Food he could do without if it came down to it. Water, he could not. Especially when running and exerting himself for so many hours. He was on the move, a destination in mind, and eventually in sight.

The air shifted from frigid to warm as the sun peeked over the horizon, warming his body and drawing out a light sweat. He had maintained a surprisingly comfortable body temperature despite the cold thanks to his efforts, but now he risked legitimate overheating and dehydration if it got too hot. Being brand-new to this world, he had no idea how hot it might become.

Bawb pushed on, eating berries for a quick boost of blood sugar, but not stopping to hunt something more substantial. He would easily be able to survive on vegetable matter, and there was no time to slow his pace for game. He had gained a head start on the other Vessels, putting in the effort while they were sleeping in their shelters.

At least, so he believed.

But who could say for certain? It was still a possibility any one of them might have had the same idea. But given what he'd seen when they fanned out to make camp, it seemed unlikely.

A sound grabbed his attention. Subtle. Quiet. A rustling that most would ignore, attributing it to the wind. But this resonated even as the breeze fell still. Bawb spun, hands raised.

The creature launched at him from the brush, its limbs powerful and thick, its dense hair impenetrable even if Bawb had been carrying a blade. Long claws flashed through the air, narrowly missing Bawb's face. He dove, rolling aside, his hands scrambling for the thorny bark-wrapped weapon on his hip. If he could land a blow on its underbelly, he might stand a chance. If not and the paralyzing claws made contact, he would be the creature's next meal.

He knew this beast. Or at least its smaller relatives. It was a Zikik, but far larger than the beasts he had fought in his youth. Apparently, those were juveniles. He had no idea they grew this big.

It charged him again.

"You do not want to do this," he said, focused on the creature. Amazingly, it stopped in its tracks, head cocked, confused.

"Did you understand me?" he asked, genuinely surprised. It had felt as though he had gotten through to it somehow. Maybe not in proper language manner, but there was something.

The beast snarled, ignoring the question and resuming its attack.

Bawb threw a handful of dirt in its face, not intending to

harm it but merely distract it. The creature was unfazed, but it did alter its course slightly as the dirt filled its nose. Bawb knew the Zikik's physiology. They hunted by smell and sound, not sight. And he had just disrupted the stronger of the two senses.

He leapt up, driving a hard kick to the Zikik's face, further disorienting its sensitive nose.

The Zikik reared up and swung its claws, but they found no purchase. Bawb circled, throwing kicks as he could, keeping his distance and testing the creature's reactions. There was a pattern to them, just as he hoped. With every impact it would attempt to make itself look bigger by lurching upward. A sound tactic when facing other animals. But against a Ghalian it was a bad, bad choice.

Bawb struck once more, the beast reacting as he had anticipated. He slapped his palm against the thin fur of the Zikik's underbelly, the thorns piercing the more delicate skin. It was the only vulnerable spot on the beast, but his aim was true.

The Zikik did not roar in pain. It did not shudder and shake in agony or rage. It simply took two steps then dropped to the ground.

"Well, at least I know the knock-out formula works," Bawb said, slowing his breathing, his ears scanning for other sounds of danger.

There were none. They were alone.

Bawb dipped the weapon in the condensed sap once more then wrapped it up safely in the bark. He checked his injuries. Nothing serious. Some cuts and bruises from diving across rocky ground and brush, but no wound had been inflicted by the animal. He crouched down next to the Zikik, examining its resting form. It was quite an animal, powerful and resilient. Fortunately for Bawb, the long claws and their toxic numbing poison had failed to land a blow. If they had, it would have been over fast, and not in a way he wanted.

He rose, looking down on the creature. He could kill it easily now if he wanted, but there was no reason to do so. No honor in it. This was simply an animal doing what it did instinctively, nothing more. And though the Ghalian were the deadliest of assassins, that did not mean they were bloodthirsty killers.

"Rest well," he said, then turned back toward his destination, heading out once more at a slow jog.

Shimmer-cloaked eyes watched approvingly, silently wishing him well as he departed. Bawb had no idea Hozark was keeping tabs on him. And for this task, he really should not have been. But this was his son, and even for the most stoic of Ghalian, that was a hard urge to overcome.

Hozark turned and walked away. Bawb was near the town now. What happened next had to be done alone.

His boy grew smaller in the distance, moving fast but cautiously, blending in with the environment as best he could. What was to come next would be a whole other sort of challenge.

Level up: Beast combat, the konus informed its wearer. *Level up: The Code.*

"The Code?"

The Ghalian Way.

"Everything I do adheres to the way."

In training, yes. But when faced with a true opponent, your grasp of The Code shows its true colors. And you, Vessel, have embraced it, the konus said with what almost sounded like respect, which was more surprising than the animal's attack had been.

Bawb mentally pulled up the display spell from his konus. A great many more skills were visible than when he had first received the device, but so many were still blurred out, unreadable to his Vessel eyes.

But he was getting there. Slowly, yes, but some levels were nearly at their maximum. It was a long road to becoming a master, but he was no longer at the starting line. And the farther along he was, the more clearly an eventual finish was in sight.

Bawb grabbed up handfuls of a familiar plant, the lessons of Teacher Brindo springing to mind. He chewed them then spat the wad into his hand, applying it directly to the more pronounced of his injuries. The healing poultice would hopefully stanch his bleeding and reduce the pain. It wasn't anywhere near as powerful as the Vara moss, but that did not grow in this sort of environment, so he had to make do with what he had at hand.

He ran on until the town came into sight. Only then did he allow himself to come to a stop. Now he could see what he was dealing with. Now he needed to slow his roll and plan.

Bawb looked at the buildings and the people milling in the streets. It was as they had been told when they were given their instructions during their flight to this world. A rough, not terribly advanced place. That meant he would need to come up with a strategy that took that into account.

He surveyed his clothing. Torn, dirty, and a bit bloody. It was also all he had. There was simply nothing to do about that. He would have to adapt on the fly. He started walking, a new cover story forming with every step, his lips curving into a smile as his plan came into focus.

He pulled the poultice off his injuries with a wet rip, letting the blood flow freely just before entering the town. His target item was a scroll. Nothing terribly special, but it contained information the Ghalian said they wanted. Valuable information.

In this place, such an item would only be held in one manner. Namely, hidden with magical shielding. Fortunately for Bawb, he knew a little trick to detect the supposedly undetectable.

He pulled a bent twig from his pocket, channeling a tiny

drop of magic into it, altering the spell that would normally steer him toward a large body of water, if one was present. In this case, however, he focused his intent on magic. Shielding magic, in fact. It was a quirk of this one spell that it could be modified like that, and only by a funny fluke that he had stumbled upon this alternative use of it.

The twig tugged his hand, directing him toward the largest building in town. Naturally. What he was seeking was in the possession of whoever ran this place. It seemed his task was going to take some effort. Of course, he expected nothing less.

Bawb moved directly to the building, adding a bit of stagger to his stride. It was clear this was a private residence, but he burst right in, crashing through the door into a large receiving room.

Armed guards leapt to their feet, weapons drawn. They charged him, but Bawb simply collapsed to his knees, as if unable to fight.

"It's just a kid," another said, sheathing his sword, disappointed there would be no bloodshed.

"Get him out of here," a man with a neck so thick it almost didn't exist growled.

"Wait, he's hurt," the largest of their group noted.

"Lathus pays us to stop intruders," the thick-necked man replied.

"And we do," the big man said. "But a hurt kid? C'mon, Fargis. Just look at 'im."

Bawb focused his mind, forcing his pulse to slow and his skin to grow cool despite his sweat. A neat little trick he had been taught by Master Hozark some time ago. One that was now coming in handy in the most unexpected of circumstances, as he had been told it might one day.

"Beasts attacked me," Bawb said. "The claws..." He trailed off, collapsing to the floor.

"Aww, hell. Looks like a Zikik got a swipe on him," the man called Fargis said. "I hate those damn things."

His larger comrade gave him a look. "Yeah, all right. We'll help him." He turned to the housekeeper, busy cleaning at the far end of the room. "Akolia, get him cleaned up, will ya?"

"I'm working," she grumbled.

"You expect us to do it? This sort of thing falls under your job description."

"Does it, though? Really?"

"You help patch *us* up."

"But *you* work for Lathus. This is just some kid off the street."

"Akolia, c'mon," the larger man said.

The woman sighed, resigned to her task. "Fine. Dump him in the bathing chamber. I'll see to his wounds."

"Thanks, hon. I'll make it up to ya."

"Don't call me hon. And you're damn right you will," she said as strong hands picked up the injured boy, carrying him deep into the building.

Bawb watched with interest, taking in the floorplan through squinted eyes as best he could. This wasn't quite the infiltration he had planned, but he would make it work.

He had no choice.

CHAPTER TWENTY-SIX

Bawb found himself dragged off to a surprisingly clean bathing chamber. A few low benches lined one wall, and a pair of deep tubs sat steaming along the other. Clearly, the hired muscle was well taken care of here. Say what you might about their boss, but he knew how to gain loyalty from his people. Sometimes the little things meant more than coin alone.

Akolia stripped him with practiced skill, throwing his ratty clothing in a basket, but not before checking the pockets for anything of value.

"Twigs and leaves?" she said, disappointed, emptying one to the floor. "Ow!" she exclaimed, a tiny blossom of blood welling from her fingers where she jabbed herself with the exposed barbs of the power device. Angrily, she tossed the lot in the basket, turning her attention to the boy.

Bawb remained silent, waiting to see how the magic might affect her. The other barbs were still wrapped in bark, thank the gods. Perhaps a boost of magic might improve this one's mood.

No such luck.

But Akolia did continue her efforts, moving with efficiency as she scrubbed him clean and bound his wounds.

"A konus?" she said, examining the band on his wrist. "How'd a kid like you wind up with this?"

"My mother's," he said quietly, ersatz tears forming in his eyes. "She perished. Murdered. It is all I have left of her."

The ploy, while a bit heavy-handed, worked.

"Well, it's old but a pretty konus," she said, her demeanor softening slightly. "You take good care of it."

"I will. Thank you for helping me."

"It's nothing."

"It is everything. No one has shown me such kindness since her passing."

Akolia fell silent a moment. "Tell you what. I'll get you some clean clothes and something to eat."

"Really?" he said, the tears flowing freely now.

"Yes, really. Wait here."

She headed out of the chamber, leaving him alone, but for how long he had no idea. Bawb hurried to the basket. He couldn't take his barb devices, not if he wanted to remain incognito. But the divining rod twig was small. Small enough to conceal, though it would be uncomfortable.

He quickly tucked the twig between his butt cheeks, the small piece of wood nestling in quite snugly, then stepped back against the wall to wait. Akolia returned just a few minutes later.

"Here. These should fit you," she said, handing him a folded stack of clothes.

"Thank you," he said, feigning shyness, covering himself as he dressed, though the act was more to allow him to keep the twig in place as he donned the clothing.

Akolia sized him up differently now that he was clean. Clean and naked. She had felt his muscles as she washed and bandaged him, and was surprised at the extent of his musculature. He was dirty and hurt, but quite sturdily built for a youth.

"Come with me," she said, leading him from the chamber.

He followed her down the hallway to a small bedroom. A tray of food was waiting for him on the little bedside table. Nothing extravagant, but a nice selection of fresh produce and a bowl of stew of some sort.

"Eat up. I'm sure you could use it."

"I could, yes."

"I figured. You can rest here for a while," she said. "No one's using this room."

"Thank you. You are too kind," he replied, almost feeling guilty for tricking her. But she worked for Lathus, and that meant she couldn't be all good, even if she was only the housekeeper. That sort of man only hired a certain kind of person, and Akolia was surely one of them.

Nevertheless, he felt that faint pang in his gut as he tried a spoonful of the stew.

Noble, but misplaced, the konus said in his head.

Bawb ignored it. Something else had grabbed his attention. Quite firmly.

"How old are you?" Akolia asked, sitting beside him on the bed, her warm hand firmly on his thigh.

"Uh," he blurted, sputtering on his stew, his pulse rising in spite of himself.

"Old enough, I'd wager," she said with a blazing grin. "You eat up. Regain your strength. You know, you should stay the night. Get some proper rest."

"I—"

She squeezed his leg then walked to the door, flashing him a wink. "You just relax. I'll be back to check on you later."

Bawb swallowed hard as she slowly stepped out, leaving him to his own devices for a while. He felt a strange sensation. One he hadn't felt in some time. It wasn't fear, exactly, but it was definitely a surge of adrenaline and a feeling bordering on panic. Bawb realized he was actually freaking out a little. Violence, pain, and even death he could handle. But this?

You'll get there, the konus said.

"Get where?"

The display flashed before his eyes. A new icon had unblurred. It had a big zero flashing next to it.

"Sexual prowess?"

It's a zero.

"Yes, I can see that. Thank you for the reminder."

Don't take it personally.

"I think that is *quite* personal."

Yeah, okay, sure, I can see how you'd feel that way. But hey, you did level up in subterfuge skills just now.

"I did?"

You want it formal? Fine. Level up: Subterfuge. There, you happy?

"I have work to do."

Yeah, you do. And you'd better get to it. From what I can see, you might have company back here sooner than later.

Bawb reached out with his senses, trying to feel the scroll's protection on his own. No dice. But he had an ace in the hole. Or a stick in the butt, to be precise. He dug the divining rod twig from its cozy hiding place and opened the door. No one was in the corridor. What's more, the slightest of tugs now tickled his fingertips, the twig turning and pulling him to the right.

He stepped out, following its guidance, drawn to wherever the scroll was hidden. Voices gave him warning of approaching guards before he saw them. Bawb tucked into the nearest room. It was no more than a storage closet, but he squeezed in and closed the door. The voices grew louder, then faded as they passed. Unfortunately, more soon arrived. There was a lot of foot traffic, in fact. A shift change, perhaps? He had no way of knowing. Whatever the cause, he was stuck there. Stuck for hours, in fact.

When the hall finally fell truly silent, he cracked the door open. He was alone.

Bawb was in the hall in a flash, moving faster now, the press for time more urgent. More tangible. The clock was ticking, and he had to get this done sooner than later. He followed the twig's pull, his feet silent on the stone floor as he rushed ahead.

Yeah, in there, the konus confirmed as he neared a closed door.

He cracked it open. No one there. Bawb slid inside, closing it behind him.

The room he wound up in seemed to be a changing area rather than a proper office or secure facility. But this was where he had been led, and the divining rod had no reason to lie to him.

The pull drew him to a heavy table. It appeared like any other at a glance, and that was precisely what its owner intended. Bawb ran his fingers along the thick edge, feeling the slightest of seams beneath his fingertips.

"Clever," he murmured, appreciative of the design, especially having practiced crafting concealed weapons and devices for so many years. Whoever had made this was very skilled. Unfortunately for them, he was better.

Bawb applied pressure to the edge, pulling both sides at once, sliding the body of the surface free from the top. The whole thing was a hiding place, it seemed. One that contained quite a bit more than just the scroll he was to retrieve. In fact, he had to dig around a moment to find what he was looking for.

The scroll was smaller than he expected, but that was to his advantage. This he could conceal on himself far easier. He tucked it into his clothing. There were many other valuable items there, but he left them untouched. He could have hidden them on himself, but in so doing he would have made his theft more readily apparent. As it was now, odds were no one would even notice the missing scroll when there were so many other more interesting items hidden there.

He slid the table shut and sealed it just as it had been, ensuring the spell hiding it was intact. He then stepped into the hallway and backtracked. He had passed the storage space when he heard footsteps. Familiar ones.

Bawb tucked back into the room he had been given, sliding into the bed, closing his eyes and slowing his breathing. Akolia stepped inside, quietly moving to the bed. She rested her hand atop him, feeling his chest rise and fall.

"Hey," she said quietly. "Are you awake?"

"Ngh," he replied, feigning deep grogginess.

"Come on, wake up. I want to show you something."

Bawb just snuggled down deeper in the covers, like a drowsy child might. Akolia waited a moment then rose with a sigh. "I'll come back a bit later in the evening, then, when you're properly recharged," she said, smiling to herself, then left the room.

Bawb leapt to his feet a minute later, when he was sure she was gone, hurrying down the hall to the nearest chamber with a window. He peeked inside. Empty. It only took moments to make it out the window, avoiding the questions his appearance in the entry hall would have raised. Clean-clothed and well fed, he moved through the streets smoothly, forcing himself to walk slowly. He could not afford to draw attention to himself. Not now.

It was later than he had realized, eyeing the setting sun. He had been on task for nearly a full day. And he still had to make it to the rendezvous point. Fortunately, the directions the Vessels had been given were clear. Getting out would be far easier than getting in. He only had a few hours of light running to make it to where the shimmer ships were parked.

"The first to arrive," a cheerful voice said.

"Master Kopal?"

"Good to see you again, Bawb. It has been a while."

"Indeed. Are you to be my ride home?"

"It seems that way. Come, let us get moving. Your task is not complete until you step inside the training house walls."

Bawb didn't need to be told twice. He hurried aboard the ship, Kopal lifting off a moment later, jumping as soon as they cleared the atmosphere. Upon arrival at their destination Bawb exited the ship at a run. He was first, but for all he knew, someone could be close behind him. And if it was anyone, it would be Elzina. He had no intention of letting her win. Not this time.

He ran through the streets, only slowing to a casual walk around the corner from the entrance he had chosen. Once inside he felt a wave of relief wash over him. He hurried along, though he had come in first, depositing his prize in the hands of Teacher Warfin, who was waiting in the dining hall.

"Back so soon?" he asked, appearing genuinely surprised.

"I am."

"How?"

"I did not sleep."

"Oh?"

"And I ran through the night."

Warfin raised a brow slightly, impressed at the boy's drive.

"And you are now returned far earlier than expected. And successful, I see," he said, accepting the scroll. "Well done, Bawb."

"Thank you, Teacher."

"What else did you bring back?"

"Nothing."

"But there was quite a bit of booty in that location from what I understand."

"There was indeed. But to disturb it would have brought attention to the missing scroll, and that would not have served the Ghalian."

Warfin smiled. "*Very* well done. Go relax. Or train, since I know that is what you will likely do. Your time is yours until the others return. And again, a good job."

Bawb gave a little bow then headed off to take a nap. He'd been awake for longer than he cared to think about, and a bit of a recharge would do nicely.

It wasn't until the next day that the others began to trickle in. Word of what Bawb had done spread quickly, and even Elzina had to grudgingly admire his strategy, uncomfortable as it had surely been. He had employed true Ghalian tactics, doing what others were either unable or unwilling to. And that had made all the difference.

CHAPTER TWENTY-SEVEN

Dinner was a lively source of discussion that night, each of the students relating their own adventures, trials, and tribulations.

It seemed that there had been many objectives in this instance, and all of them had been sent to retrieve a different item. There was no overlap, and as such, anyone's success or failure rested entirely on their own head and not anyone else who might have beaten them to it.

Bawb was listening to Finnia's detailed description of her quest and how she had employed many of the spy skills she had learned in the real world for the first time.

"It sounds exciting," he said.

"It truly was. To practice deception and disguise here in a safe environment is one thing, but out there, it was entirely different."

"I don't know if I would call this place *safe*, exactly," Albinius joked.

"You know what I mean. It was just different. There were real consequences, and as a result, the intent behind the spells carried more weight. Did any of you notice the same? Did your spells gain in efficacy?"

"Not that I noticed," Albinius replied. "Bawb?"

"Not particularly, though I suppose the little magic I did employ did function without issue. But that could just as well be the result of our training."

"I suppose, for you that could be the case. But I'm telling you, it felt different." Finnia trailed off, her eyes shifting to the girl approaching their table.

"Mind if I sit here?" Elzina asked, sliding into the space across from Bawb before anyone could reply.

Though they all dined at the same time, Elzina never sat with this group, and the change was disquieting, though there was nothing threatening about it. Just a change in their usual pattern, which unintentionally drew their attention to the fact that they had a pattern at all. And patterns could be dangerous things to be used against you in the outside world. They would have to keep that in mind.

"Please, join us," Bawb said politely.

"So, I hear you ran into bandits," Elzina asked, jumping right to the point of her visit. "Ran all night, too."

"Yes, and yes."

She shook her head, chuckling to herself. "How you managed to get out of that mess is beyond me. I mean, there were what? Ten of them?"

"Twelve, actually."

"Twelve. Ridiculous. And yet, somehow, here you are. Unharmed no less."

Bawb shrugged. "They were working under Nixxa's orders."

That got Elzina's attention.

"Nixxa?"

"Yes."

"But she's a pirate. A *spac*e pirate."

"And her reach is far. You know she supports many villages on many worlds with her acts of charity and largess."

"Which I've never understood," Albinius chimed in.

"She is seeding the systems with coin and food to build goodwill," Elzina replied. "It is how she avoids capture. Being something of a folk hero to locals has served her well and provided her and her crews many safe harbors."

Bawb nodded his agreement. "Indeed. And in this instance, I played up my circumstances."

Albinius's eyes widened. "You told them you were a Ghalian?"

Finnia slapped his arm. "Idiot, they'd have killed him if he had."

"Or worse," Bawb agreed. "I mentioned nothing of my task, only that I was a boy alone in the wilderness. Given that I had no food or currency, it was not a difficult stretch."

"So they just let you go? Incredible," Elzina said with a sigh.

"Actually, they gave me food and a small amount of currency to acquire a hot meal when I reached the township."

"You're kidding me."

"Not at all."

"It just keeps getting more unbelievable," she grumbled. "I did not get a free meal out of my efforts. Just a side full of brambles and a scratch from a stupid Zikik. Numbed my leg with its cursed claws, and that made it a damned hard trek before the toxin wore off."

"It was a small one, then," Bawb mused. "I encountered one as well. Far larger than any we've seen in training. I did not realize they could grow to that size."

"You killed it?"

"No. I did not fashion a cutting or stabbing weapon. But I did manage to subdue it unscathed, though not without effort."

"So you ran all night, escaped bandits, fought off a Zikik, and stole your target item out from within a secured compound? All on no sleep, no food, and with no magic?"

"I did use a *little* magic," he said, then explained how his makeshift divining rod had escaped detection. He did not, however, delve into Akolia's advances. That would be one detail he would keep to himself indefinitely.

Elzina listened to Bawb's tale attentively. Yes, she would interject a snarky comment from time to time, but overall, she could not help but respect the sheer force of will that had driven him to make that frigid trek through the night. It had given him the advantage and won him the day.

If she was being honest with herself, part of her annoyance was that she hadn't thought to do it first. Making camp and securing food and weapons was just what they did. At least, in training. But Bawb had shown a flexibility of mind that served him well, and even she could not help but have grudging respect for it.

Bawb also had a different impression of his nemesis of so many years. She had made his life hell when he first arrived and hadn't really let up even as he grew more skilled. But their competition was tinged with an underlying respect. Not a personal sort, but for the undeniable skills they each possessed.

She had a much harsher mindset. Aggressive, even. But to her, it all made sense and was perfectly acceptable in her quest to remain at the top of her class and one day reach the level of Master. She was a difficult person, but he understood why she thought she was good. It might not have made the most sense, but he could not fault her for it. And her skills were undeniable.

The Vessels talked among themselves a while longer, enjoying the leisurely meal, then separated for the evening before eventually heading back to the bunkhouse. There were no classes tonight. Theirs had been an arduous quest, and a bit of recovery was in order.

"Quite the adventure," Hozark said, appearing out of nowhere.

Bawb did not jump, but he was definitely startled. The master assassin was incredibly skilled with the shimmer cloak. Bawb hoped that one day he might be even a fraction as talented.

"Master Hozark. What are you doing here?"

"I wanted to commend you on your performance, as well as your victory. Though it was the process more than the result that mattered in this task."

"And it was quite a process," Bawb joked.

"Indeed. Running through the night was inspired. And to show mercy for a beast even though it tried to make you its meal? You performed admirably."

"Thank you."

"I am sorry you had to deal with Nixxa's people, though. They can be difficult, to say the least."

"You know them, I take it."

"Not those in particular, but as you know, Nixxa and I have something of a history."

"Right. Back when she flew with Bud and Henni."

"Yes. She and I became familiar with one another through proximity initially. A rather conflicted woman, but very skilled and very dangerous. Always keep your wits about you when she and her lackeys are involved. They may appear to be many things, but they are rarely as they seem."

"Thank you. Duly noted."

"You know, you did quite well with the retrieval of the scroll. Using a twig in that fashion? Inspired use of magic and very clever. And leaving behind all of the additional treasure a lesser mind might have thought to take? Again, you were thinking like a true Ghalian."

"Again, thank you, Master Hozark."

"But the woman. Akolia. It seems there are some things you have yet to learn."

"You heard about that?"

"Oh, I did more than hear. I was watching, and I saw it all."

A slight blush darkened the teenager's cheeks. "She was somewhat perplexing, I admit."

A smile spread across the master's lips. "Perplexing? That is one way to look at it, I suppose. But you realize you will need to learn the ways of the bedroom as well as the battlefield. It is a different sort of combat, but a skill that can open many doors and pry even the most hidden secrets from unsuspecting lips."

"I-I suppose, yes. But I am still only a Vessel. No one has mentioned this sort of lesson."

Hozark put his arm around the boy and laughed. "And now someone has. Come with me."

CHAPTER TWENTY-EIGHT

This outing with Hozark was different from the previous ones Bawb had enjoyed. It felt more off the cuff. More improvisational. More spur of the moment. For one such as Hozark to go off-script was unusual. Unusual, and kind of exciting.

Bawb followed him out of one of the access doors to the training house that he had never noticed before—one that emptied them onto a quiet street. One several blocks from the training house.

"How did we—"

"It is one of the little secrets of the compound," Hozark replied. "One known only to the Masters."

"A secret entrance?"

"Of sorts. More of a secret *exit*, though we truly hope to never need to make use of it."

"But I am only a Vessel."

"In title and rank, yes. But you have proven yourself not only a resourceful student, but also willing to endure extremes in pursuit of your goal. While we do not make this knowledge available to students as a simple precaution should they find themselves compromised, I have the utmost confidence in your commitment to the order. You would not tell of this secret, would you?"

"Not even if faced with death."

"Which I hope you will not have to prove."

"But why now?"

"Let us call this impromptu training," Hozark said as they turned out onto a far busier pedestrian walkway. They walked quietly for a few streets before he spoke again. "Do you see all of these races? How they act and speak?" he asked rhetorically, nodding toward the throngs. "You will need to learn to disguise yourself as any of them. And you will need to learn to do so with or without the use of magic, depending on the task. As you know, on some occasions, even the slightest magic would be detected, and that could limit your options greatly."

"We are learning more advanced spells, as well as more creative practical means. Some of the combinations of techniques are difficult but quite effective."

"Demelza is one of the best I have ever seen. You are in good hands in this regard. Consider yourself fortunate to be training in this facility."

"Master Hozark?"

"Yes?"

"I am unsure if this is allowed to be known, but I was thinking the other day. We have a gradually diminishing class that trains for many years. By the time we reach mastery, I feel not too many of us will remain."

"Quite possible. In fact, that is a normal occurrence. What is your question, Bawb?"

"The Ghalian are spread across the galaxy, yet we are a relatively small group."

"Ah. You wonder how many other training houses and compounds exist."

"If I overstep, please tell me."

"Your curiosity is natural. And once you reach the higher levels you will have the answer to your question. For now, let us just say that while we are few compared to other orders, our reach is vast and our operatives entrenched across many realms."

"Hidden from sight."

"As we always are. Hence the focus on disguise and disinformation."

"Which is what we are out to do tonight?" the teen asked.

"Oh, no. I have something quite different in store for you. A lesson you are now old enough to learn. Not a part of the normal curriculum, but given your recent encounter, I think you are ready."

"I do not understand."

"You will," Hozark said with an almost mischievous grin teasing the corners of his lips. "And I believe you will enjoy yourself in the process."

Now Bawb was really confused. Was this to be a test? A lesson? A reward? He had no idea, but he had a rather long walk to wonder about it. They bypassed the landing sites, skipping right over ships and transports. Wherever they were going, it was not only on this world, but within this very city.

As their training had progressed, that seemed to happen less and less. More intensive activities required more distance and privacy from prying eyes, and as these were assassins in training, the less the locals saw them out as a group, the better.

But this was just the two of them on a casual outing. No one gave them a second glance, and why would they? Hozark's demeanor was relaxed and his movements almost sloppy in their casual fluidity. He walked just like any other oblivious civilian, unaware of their surroundings as they blundered through life.

Of course, that observation could not have been farther from the truth.

They walked for nearly an hour before arriving at a nondescript building on a side street around the corner from an upper-class dining establishment. This was a nicer part of the city that Bawb had not spent much time in beyond the occasional outing to practice tracking and the real-world use of some of the disguise techniques he had learned.

But here, in this part of the city, he felt a blunder would have no consequences. There were no rough and dangerous taverns here. No gritty trading markets with their fragrant stalls and under-the-table dealings. It was about as safe a part of the city as one could find themselves in, and it made Bawb wonder just what sort of lesson he could possibly be learning here.

As he watched Hozark shift course toward one green door nestled among several other entrances to the nearby building, he realized he was about to find out.

Hozark held up his hand, pausing a moment before knocking. To any observing it would be nothing, but Bawb knew he had just cast a tiny spell. A signaling one. Something to let the occupant know who was outside before his knuckles hit the wood.

It was a common Ghalian trick. One that they utilized regularly. Given their line of work, it only made sense.

"Yes? Who is it?" a raspy voice asked as the door swung open.

"It's me, Alara."

"Oh, so good to see your face," the woman said, swinging the door open wide.

Bawb, to his credit, did not stare. He kept his composure, but it was not easy. This woman was hideous. With sickly yellow eyes and stringy, greasy black hair plastered to her head, he recognized her race. A Goolaran. They were bipedal and of a roughly similar build to his own kind, but they were known for the heavy oil their skin produced and the foul smell they emitted if they neglected bathing for any period of time.

Hozark waved the boy over.

"Bawb, this is Alara. An old friend. Alara, Bawb is in need of your services."

"Of course," she said, looking the boy up and down.

"Pleased to meet you," Bawb said, politely.

"Nice to meet you too, Bawb," she said with a knowing grin, resting a warm, damp hand on his arm.

He fought back the instinctive flinch that threatened to move his limb. Hozark had brought him here for a reason, and no matter how uncomfortable this woman's flirtation might be, he would not embarrass him.

Alara took his hand in her damp one, to his distress. "Well, we should get to it then."

Bawb looked at Hozark, but the Ghalian's expression was unreadable. "I will see you in a bit, Bawb," he said, then turned and left him with the woman.

"This way," she murmured, pulling him inside.

Bawb took one look at the decor inside and realized what sort of place this was. What sort of woman Alara was. Horrified, he put on a smile all the same. He would not disappoint Hozark, no matter how distasteful this might be.

He swallowed hard as the door closed, leaving him quite alone with her. It would not be a night he would soon forget.

CHAPTER TWENTY-NINE

Alara led him into the colorful depths of her abode. Bright tapestries and fabrics were draped over the seats and hanging from the walls. The scent of musky incense clung to the air, surprisingly pleasant for a Goolaran's abode.

The lights dimmed with a wave of Alara's soggy hand as she led him down a short hallway. The door at the end was open, the large bed plainly visible. Hozark had brought him here for a reason, all right, and he was horrified at the prospect.

But whether a lesson or a test, he would do what he had to do. It was bound to happen eventually. It just seemed it would be sooner rather than later. The hideous woman smiled at him, craggy, stained teeth peering out from between her lips like half-toppled gravestones.

Bawb smiled back, controlling his expression with every bit of willpower he possessed.

"We're going to have fun, you and me," she said, shimmying side to side as she slowly undressed, exposing her oily, blotchy skin. She stepped out of the clothes piled at her feet and stepped over to the teen. "Are you ready for me?" she asked.

"Uh, yes," he replied, forcing his face into a happy expression. "You are quite lovely."

"I bet you say that to all the girls."

It was a cliché that seemed incredibly unfitting for this woman, but Bawb rolled with it, smiling brightly and playing the part. To any observing, he was thrilled for the encounter, no matter the turmoil churning inside of him.

"Are you excited?" she asked, her hand grazing his crotch.

Incredibly, he managed to force his body to react, the growing bulge quite the opposite of what his bits wanted to do.

"Oh yes," he lied. "Very excited."

Alara locked eyes with him, her expression shifting slightly. Studying him rather than seducing. She stepped back and gave an approving nod.

"Good. You did well. Far better than most."

"I don't understand. What do you mean?"

She laughed. "As a Ghalian, you may be called upon to seduce those you are not attracted to. To gain access and information using your body in a non-lethal way. It's not easy, and some just can't, shall we say, *rise* to the occasion. Sometimes visceral reactions can overpower the will despite your best interests. This disguise was a test of your resolve."

"Disguise?"

Alara pulled the thick konus from her wrist, breaking the powerful spell masking her true form. The greasy hag melted away, and in her place stood a stunning, yellow-skinned woman with long golden hair. Quite nude, and quite beautiful.

"You are an Ootaki," he marveled.

"Observant, this one," she said with a little chuckle.

"But Ootaki cannot use magic."

"And that is normally the case. However, the konus I have is *extremely* powerful, charged with a quite particular bit of magic specifically designed to alter my Ootaki appearance and mask my magical signature."

"A custom disguise konus for an Ootaki? I did not know such a thing existed."

"They don't. But this was a very special gift from your friend, crafted to allow me to live the life *I* want, not the one the rest of my kind are forced to live should they be fortunate enough to break the bonds of slavery."

"You do not wish to live with your people? In a safe colony?"

Alara laughed, her true voice bright and cheerful. "Oh, Bawb, my kind will always be at risk, even in the Ootaki enclaves. Even with Ghalian protection. The power our former captors have stored in our hair is too much of a temptation for those who would seek to use us to further their goals." She placed the heavy konus in his hand. "Do you feel the power? A Ghalian can sense it, but no other can."

"I-I do," he marveled, the slight hint of the immense magic contained in the golden band tickling his palm.

"This protects me. It allows me to live freely in a real city. To experience life among so many races, to see all the things, to taste all the foods. The life of a refugee is not the life for me."

Bawb marveled at the lengths Hozark had gone to in order to keep her safe. The coin he must have spent to create this specialized konus would have been immense. Not that the order was lacking in wealth. They had more than any could spend in a hundred lifetimes, if not more.

Something else captured Bawb's attention. Undisguised as she was, and standing before him nude and at ease, the woman's natural beauty was stunning. In spite of himself, he felt a stirring between his legs. Alara seemed quite pleased by his response.

"Ah, good," she said with a smile, her lids lowering slightly. "I see you are ready to begin."

"Wait. I thought the purpose of this visit was—"

"Oh, you excelled in that little test. But that's not ultimately what you're here for."

"I—"

Pathetic, the konus snarked in his mind. *You expect to be a great Ghalian yet something so simple as this frightens you?*

"I do not know what to do," he replied aloud.

"Oh, you will," Alara replied with a genuinely delighted laugh, unaware he was talking to his konus. She reached out and began undressing the nervous teen. "I think you'll do just fine."

CHAPTER THIRTY

It was late. Not terribly late, but still deep into the dark hours. A tall, pale man stood casually leaning against the wall next to a green door, but there was nothing exceptional or unusual about him. In fact, no one paid him much mind at all.

He remained that way, relaxed and immobile, until the door swung open and a hideous Goolaran woman escorted a young Wampeh outside. The teen was positively beaming, unable to contain the elation bubbling up within.

Had anyone known he was a Ghalian in training, the leaking of his emotions would have been even more of a notable event. In any case, the boy was walking on air.

Level up: You know what you leveled in.

Bawb glanced at the invisible icons floating before him. "This cannot be right," he silently replied to the voice in his head. "This shows the wrong level."

No, it doesn't.

"What are you saying?"

You're really going to make me say it? After everything you did these past few hours? Ugh, fine. You skipped levels.

"But how—"

Because you're damn good at it, okay? Now pay attention to them *and stop talking to* me.

Bawb calmed his mind and turned his focus to the man waiting for him. Hozark was watching him with what looked like a normal, almost disinterested gaze. But Bawb know the Master Ghalian was assessing him. A little smile grew on the man's lips. He seemed satisfied with what he saw.

"Alara, thank you for your services," he said.

"Oh, it was my pleasure. And I do mean pleasure." She glanced at Bawb, and he could have sworn she almost blushed a little. "This one? He has a special talent."

"I am pleased to hear it."

"Special indeed," she repeated, a satisfied grin on her face.

Now that Bawb had spent quite a lot of quality time with the real Alara, the hideous disguise almost didn't exist to him. He saw it, of course. The magic was far too powerful for him not to. But what he saw regardless was the beautiful golden-haired woman who had just changed his life.

"Bawb," she said, resting her hand on his arm. This time, he had no flinch impulse whatsoever. "If you happen to find yourself in this part of town again, do drop by. I would very much enjoy spending more time with you. If you are so inclined, that is."

"Thank you, Alara," he said, a slight blush rising to his cheeks.

Hozark dug in his pocket and pulled out a small sack of coin. "We have a long walk ahead of us, Bawb. There is a tavern on the way. We should get you some sustenance," he said as he extended the payment to Alara.

"Oh, this one is on me," she said, closing his fingers back around the bundle.

Hozark cocked his eyebrow, more than a little surprised. This was quite unusual. A little flush of pride flowed through him at the boy's performance. Clearly, he had made quite an impression. Hozark paused only a moment. He would never dream of insulting Alara by insisting she take the coin. He would find other ways to ensure she was without want. With a little nod he pocketed the sack, and that was the end of that.

"Alara," he said with a nod, then turned and walked away.

She stepped back into her boudoir and shut the door, pleasantly surprised at the turn the evening had taken.

Bawb and Hozark walked in silence for a while, the older Ghalian allowing the boy time to process what had just happened. He would undoubtedly be replaying it in his mind for some time to come, but never more so than while the experience was fresh.

"Master Hozark?" he finally said.

"Yes, Bawb?"

"Do all Ghalian do this?" he asked, a little uncomfortably.

Hozark noted the tone and knew it well. "Not all, no. Alara has offered to help on occasion, but she is the ultimate arbiter of her actions, and coin is in no way her master. Had you made a poor impression, believe me, you would have been shown the street before you knew what hit you."

Bawb mulled this tidbit over. She would test people's resolve with her disguise, but it seemed what had come after was an infrequent lesson only given to those she selected. It made sense, considering her choice of lifestyle. Eschewing a refugee colony for the bustle of the city. Hers was a vibrant life, and Bawb had been fortunate to have been allowed to be a part of it.

"You rescued her?" the teen asked.

"Yes."

"But this was not a favor?"

"She owes no favors. What she does, she does of her own

accord. It is not often she takes such a liking to a student. Or anyone, for that matter. She has a way of reading people. Not exactly like Henni's skill—*she* is a true reader, after all—but nevertheless, Alara has a good sense of a person's worth. And she truly likes you, Bawb."

"I like her as well. She is a remarkable woman."

"Indeed. So, you feel good?" Hozark asked, shifting course to a small alleyway.

"Better than good."

"And the lesson?"

"Most enjoyable," the boy said with a faraway look in his eye.

Hozark moved far slower than he could have, sliding his foot in front of Bawb's, tripping him. The boy stumbled but caught his balance quickly enough, only to find a strong arm around his torso pinning his arms and a cold knife at his throat. He froze. There was no escape from this. If the Master wanted him dead, there was nothing he could do about it.

Hozark released him, the blade disappearing into his clothing as invisibly as it had appeared.

"A lesson, young one. The blade of this experience can cut both ways. Enjoy your time, but know that it can render you vulnerable in such moments. Always keep your guard up, but even more so when sensations such as this might distract you. Even a Ghalian can lose their edge after such an encounter. Especially with the likes of someone like Alara."

Bawb, surprisingly, hadn't felt his adrenaline spike. He was calm. Had faced death without fear, just acceptance. A truly Ghalian reaction, he realized, and he did not think it had anything to do with the evening's activities. It was another lesson learned, but this one was much longer in coming. So much so that its arrival had come unnoted. That is, until this moment. The moment Master Hozark could have ended his life with ease.

"I am sorry, Master Hozark. I will endeavor to not let it happen again."

"Do not be sorry, Bawb. This is a safe place, and this is how we learn. And it would appear that learn you have. Something of a prodigy, apparently. Alara was quite taken with you."

"Well, it is her job."

"And yet she declined payment," Hozark replied with a warm pat on the back. "But her offer to play? You should not take her up on that, no matter how tempting it may be. You are young, and learning. She is older and living in the outside world. A very different life. It would be as dangerous for you as it would be for her. She is an emotional being, at heart, and Ootaki can be fierce in their affections. But you are a Ghalian, Bawb. You know our ways. No attachments."

"But surely further practice would be beneficial," the boy protested.

"On this I agree. But I am sure you can find one of your cohort willing to learn with you. It is not a thing that is frowned upon, so long as it is discreet. But remember, Ghalian do not bond. Not ever."

"Why not? I understand the need for added precautions, but *never*?"

A faraway look slid over Hozark's gaze as the memory of the boy's mother made an unwanted appearance. The folly of his youth and the ramifications of his actions.

"It does not end well," Hozark finally said. "And I would spare you that pain. But enough of that," he said, pushing the morose feelings away in a flash. "Let us get you some food and drink. You certainly earned it, my boy. Well done. Well done, indeed."

CHAPTER THIRTY-ONE

It was late when Bawb returned to the training house. Late enough that the others had noticed his absence even as they each enjoyed the evening's downtime. Several were relaxing in the bunkhouse, while others had chosen to train in the quiet peace of the nighttime hours.

Bawb opted for the spa portion of their bathing facilities, ready for a nice hot bath. It wasn't that he was aching—he actually felt quite invigorated—but following a day like this one a good soak and scrub would only aid the quality of his sleep.

"You were absent for some time," a voice said from the steaming communal tub, the owner submerged to her chin.

"Usalla, I did not notice you there. A new stealth technique?" he joked, his spirits still running high.

"Funny, Bawb," she replied, sliding up to a seated position. "You disappeared after dinner."

"I had something to do," he said, undressing with a casual slowness that seemed to radiate quiet confidence.

Usalla watched curiously. They had known each other since they were Nulls and had all bathed together more times than any could count. It was just what it was. Their way of life. And having developed from children into teenagers together, she had never taken particular notice of Bawb, or any other classmate for that matter.

But now there was something about him. The way he carried himself. A quiet almost glow to his demeanor, as if there were a faint smile just behind his façade, waiting to sneak out.

"Bawb? Something happened."

It was a statement, not a question.

He shrugged, stepping into the tub and submerging up to his neck. He leaned back against the side and relaxed, the warm mineral water soaking its heat into his body.

"Bawb, what happened?" Usalla persisted. "You are not telling me something."

"It was nothing. Just more training."

"You have never returned from training acting like this. Something is different. Where were you?"

Bawb hesitated. This was not something he would share with the others. It wasn't exactly a secret, but it was his business, not theirs. But Hozark's words echoed in his mind. This was also a skill they would all need to master in their trade. And Usalla was one of his dearest friends.

"I only ask that you keep this to yourself," he said.

"I will. But what is it you feel the need to keep secret?"

"Master Hozark took me for a, uh, different sort of training."

"You received private instruction?" she asked, her interest now quite piqued.

"Well, yes. But it was not from Master Hozark."

"You make no sense, Bawb. You just said it was he who took you for training. A private lesson."

"Yes. But the lesson was not given by Master Hozark."

He paused, searching for the right words. For some reason he felt strange talking about this, but he had no idea why. It was just another lesson, and the information would be valuable to his friend. But for whatever reason, it just felt odd talking about it. Perhaps it was because it was all so fresh in his mind that he hadn't fully processed the night's activities yet.

Bawb shook off his uncharacteristic reluctance.

"There is a tool of our profession. One that can be put to varying degrees of use, depending on the circumstances."

"A new sword technique? Hozark is a great master of the Vespus blade."

"Nothing so martial in nature, though it does require vigorous effort."

"Bawb, you are being cryptic."

He took a deep breath and let it out in a low sigh. "I received instruction in the bedroom arts," he said, the unease in his belly releasing now that he had said it aloud.

Usalla cocked her head slightly. "The bedroom arts? But *not* with Master Hozark."

"No, not with Master Hozark," he replied with a chuckle. "There is an expert in such things. Apparently, her services are called upon on rare occasion, and on this one, I was the fortunate recipient of her tutelage."

"And? What was it like?" she asked, curiosity clear in her eyes.

A little smile crept onto his lips in spite of himself. "It was delightful."

"You were not worried?"

"At first, yes. I did not know what was expected of me. It was all a bit overwhelming."

"So, you did not perform up to standard? It is to be expected when learning any new skill."

"Oh, no, it was not like that at all. Apparently, I have a natural talent for it, in fact. And we trained for quite some time. A most pleasant form of grappling, one could call it."

His friend stared at him with a curious gaze, as if sizing him up in an entirely new light. And in a sense, she was.

"It seems the lesson has made quite an impression on you."

"I suppose you could say that. There is so much for us to learn."

"Like the first time we were instructed in the use of a shimmer ship. Do you remember that?"

Bawb grinned. "That was an interesting experience."

"If by interesting you mean frustrating," she replied with a chuckle. "I did not realize just how hard shimmer spells were until Master Kopal let us attempt them on his craft."

"Yes, it was not a good outcome."

"And that is quite an understatement. Shimmer cloaks are hard, but to cast powerfully enough to cloak an entire ship? It is an incredibly challenging use of power."

"And yet the Masters make it seem effortless."

"Which it will be when we finally learn to do it ourselves," she noted.

"That is akin to something Master Hozark has said to me on occasion."

"Which is?"

"That when you are truly skilled, the techniques become as easy as breathing. As instinctive as walking. Not just the use of shimmer spells, but all of our skills."

"Demelza says the same. That when you ascend to mastery, you will be able to come and go with ease, using shimmers, disguises, and subterfuge with such skill that none will ever even know you were there."

"It is something to aspire to."

"And for that we must practice."

A faraway look drifted across Bawb's gaze as he recalled the evening's activities. "Oh, I intend to practice any skill of use as often as possible."

Usalla's head tilted slightly, a lone brow arched. "That is a good attitude, Bawb. I may ask for your assistance in the future."

"Of course," he replied, wondering why she was looking at him like that.

Hozark's warning about continuing his lessons with Alara rose up in his mind. How he could not form bonds, but he was more than welcome to pursue further training on his own with one who understood the Ghalian way. And with that thought present, he mused that there was something new in Usalla's gaze. A curiosity. He wasn't sure exactly what she meant by her comment, but given that look, he had an idea.

Things could get interesting in the training house, he mused. *Very* interesting. Or not. Time would tell.

CHAPTER THIRTY-TWO

Teacher Pallik paced in front of the assembled Vessels.

"Many of you have been speaking of your travels now that you are not restricted to this world. With the need to increasingly visit other systems for your training and tasks, it is now time to formally instruct you on the basics of flight and navigation spells." Pallik surveyed their faces, searching for signs of doubt. There were none.

This was vital, of course. Any concern or fear about flying would lead to improper application of the spells, the intent behind them sensing the hesitation. And where spells of this nature came into play, confidence was absolutely necessary. Even in the most stressful of situations, such as battle or difficult infiltrations, focus was key. Anything less would result in failure, capture, or death.

"You are going to learn to fly smaller craft to start, but the spells are the same. What varies is the amount of power needed to move them, as well as the additional layers of spells that are required to maintain other systems aboard the vessel. Gravity, for instance. If your Drookonus is running low on magic, you can cancel that spell in some or all of a craft to conserve your power. If it is a battlecraft in use, there is the modulation of shielding spells to better fit the situation, again, saving you power."

"Would we not have a dedicated caster for shielding and weapons on a larger craft?" Zota asked.

"Sometimes, yes. And sometimes you will be commanding a team of Drooks to power its flight rather than utilizing their stored power in a Drookonus. But not always, and often not in the manner you might prefer. There are many variations to take into consideration. If you have a caster aboard you will be able to have them dedicate power to shielding spells rather than drawing from your Drookonus. Sometimes you will be defending against magical attacks, but others could be kinetic."

"Kinetic?" Albinius asked. "But how? In space you cannot throw a spear or let loose arrows."

"No, you cannot. But a skilled caster can utilize other items at hand as projectiles. Asteroids and space rocks, for example. I have used this tactic on more than one occasion to overwhelm a lesser ship's defenses. Defending against both magical and physical attacks can drain an opponent's resources quickly. The shifting of spells required invariably leaves a small gap in the casting when a sole caster is in play. And even teams of casters often have difficulty adjusting to this form of attack. They will adapt quickly, but that brief crack in their defenses is one the Ghalian have become experts in exploiting. But there are many other tools in our arsenal."

"Like shimmers," Bawb added. "Will we learn to use shimmer cloaks?"

Pallik turned to focus her attention his way. "That is advanced magic. Beyond a Vessel's skill level. You are not yet capable with a shimmer cloak on your person, let alone anything larger. It is natural to wish to advance in this skill, and your drive is commendable, but you must master it on yourself before attempting it on so large an item as a shimmer ship."

"Shimmer spells are only used on smaller ships though, yes?" Usalla asked.

"Yes. They may be used for a larger craft for the briefest of periods, but only when stationary and in atmosphere. Temporary camouflage, essentially. As you know, shimmer ships have some difficulty being used in space, but smaller ones can successfully be employed. However, the spell works best in atmosphere."

"Is that why Ghalian shimmer ships are all so small?"

"That, and other reasons. We operate alone. It is the Ghalian way. But on occasion we will fly with others, as the use of a larger craft can be advantageous in certain situations. But larger ships, while more imposing, can actually be easier to defeat in many instances. There are almost always multiple weak points in their systems and defenses. And often their captains enjoy an ill-advised sense of confidence in the power of their ship. That cockiness can be exploited."

"Kind of how pirates sometimes use swarms of smaller ships to overwhelm a larger cargo vessel or transport ship rather than face off in a head-to-head fight with just one craft," Bawb noted. "Basically, they overwhelm their enemy's defenses with multiple angles of attack, forcing them to spread their defenses thin."

"Pirates are a different manner of beast altogether," Teacher Pallik replied. "Unpredictable and very, very skilled in their craft. Not only how they fly, but, as Bawb pointed out, also how they utilize their numbers to their advantage against larger prey. It is rather specialized knowledge, but something that will eventually become part of your training as well. One must understand all manner of threats, after all, from the military elements of the Council of Twenty's fleet to Tslavar mercenaries, to marauding bands of pirates."

"What about the pirates who work with our enemies?" Finnia asked. "I understand that some connected individuals have made arrangements with certain factions."

Pallik nodded her agreement. "This is true. Some have indeed aligned themselves with benefactors as a means to an end. They enjoy moderate protection in exchange for not attacking certain resources. Or, for that matter, for taking out their patron's competitors. It is a symbiotic relationship that serves both parties well."

"And there are those with a support network," Bawb added. "Loyal backers who have bought into their cause."

Pallik chuckled. "You clearly speak of Nixxa. And from what I understand, you have had a few run-ins with her and her followers."

"They have been interesting, to say the least."

"I am sure they were. But she is an anomaly. Most in her trade do not have so overdeveloped a sense of misplaced justice."

"Is it really misplaced, though?" Albinius asked. "As I understand it, she is a difficulty and thorn in many people's sides, but it seems her underlying purpose is to help the underrepresented. The poor."

Bawb shook his head. "Trust me, she may do good for some, but it is not solely altruistic."

Teacher Pallik nodded her approval. "You are very astute, Bawb. Go on."

"Well, Nixxa in particular has a large network of bandits and raiders spread across the systems. Those she put in place to steal from the better off, then distribute a portion of their take to the local populace. Those who do not have much, if anything. She is something of a hero to them, and as such, she is provided safe haven all across those systems."

"Exactly," their teacher agreed. "Though Nixxa is not the only one to employ this tactic. She just happens to be among the most generous with their booty. A smart woman, and one with quite an extensive network. She has been problematic for the Ghalian on occasion, but she is simply not worth the effort to bring to heel. She causes our enemies far more grief than us, and she generally steers clear of Ghalian craft."

"Foolish, attacking the Ghalian," Elzina noted.

"Yes. But oftentimes pirates make the mistake of targeting craft under our control without realizing it. That is one of the pitfalls of stealth. And sometimes we must stand down and let them, lest we blow our cover and ruin months, or even years of infiltration work. Finnia, you are on the spy track. You have studied long infiltration techniques more in depth."

"I have. And we have been forced to abandon extremely valuable craft on more than a few occasions for precisely the reason you mention. Even take injury in the process to sell the event and remain under cover."

"Yours is a different course than most others, but no less dangerous. More so, in some regards. But typically, pirates will let a crew escape. Only those more deeply invested in the slave trade, such as the Tslavars view a captured crew as a prize as valuable as the ship itself."

"So many potential enemies," Zota mused.

"Yes. But for now you will focus on the main factions you will be most likely to encounter. Mind you, the small players outside of their number can also be quite dangerous. Deadly, even. And simple bad luck against a lesser adversary has brought about the demise of far more skilled individuals on more occasions than you can imagine. It is something you must always keep in your mind. *Anything* can potentially lead to your abrupt end, even if you have taken every precaution. You simply cannot prepare for or defend against every risk. But you can at least be aware of as many as possible. Learn to recognize them when they rear their ugly heads. And with that, hopefully you will be able to lessen the blow should such an instance arise."

"Hope for the best but prepare for the worst," Bawb noted.

"Ah, Master Hozark's favorite expression. I know you have spent some time with him. It seems you have picked up one of the more useful lessons in the process."

"He is a wealth of knowledge. I am grateful for the time he has shared with me."

"As you should be. But enough about these things. I digress, and we are focusing on flight today. Yes, you will need to remain aware of, and guarded against, these, and other, threats. But first, you must learn to fly. Each of you will be assigned to a pilot and ship. Some will start on smaller craft, others on larger ones. Some will learn to control Drooks, other to use a Drookonus. Do not concern yourself with the different paths you will take. You will rotate through many types of craft in the course of your training."

She walked to the small table to her left and opened an ornate box. Bawb felt the tickle of power as soon as the lid lifted. It was a magic-masking container, and what was inside had power.

"These are minor Drookonuses," Pallik said, lifting one of the rods from the box. "Not strong enough to power a ship, but good for you to learn to activate the basic spells you will be employing, and safe with which to attempt to focus your intent. You are to take one apiece and separate to different training rooms."

"Would it not be beneficial to work as a group?" Martza asked.

"In other things, yes. But for this you will need to focus your attention fully, and a little solitude will help. Attuning with a Drookonus is tricky at first, but once you get the feel for it, it should be as simple as walking. This is the first step of many you will need to become proficient in, but once you are, you will be ready to fly. And one day, you may even have your own shimmer ship. Now, go practice. Tomorrow you will be assigned a pilot, and your practical training will begin."

CHAPTER THIRTY-THREE

Training day arrived, and the Vessels were up and ready, full of energy and excited for what the day might bring. Every day was a valuable lesson, but this was something new. This was *flying*. This would be fun. Fun, and not the sort of lesson that would result in broken limbs and bruised muscles. They would be tired from the effort, naturally, but it would be mental exhaustion rather than physical, and that was a welcome change.

Bawb had done what the others had the prior evening, namely sitting quietly and focusing on intent, connecting with the minor Drookonus he had been given to work with. But he had felt the strength of a properly powerful one up close and personal in the past. The one he had stolen from Nixxa, in fact. Compared to that, this felt like a ripple in a pond versus a tidal wave thundering and raging across the sea.

Nevertheless, it would more than suffice.

Come morning he had returned the device to its holding box and headed to the courtyard, where he had been instructed he would meet his teacher. Upon his arrival, however, he saw two men standing together, and he knew both of them.

"Master Hozark? *You* are my teacher?"

Hozark's lips creased into a little smile at the sight of the boy. "No, I am here for other reasons."

"Hey, kid. Looks like you're gonna play co-pilot today," the other man said.

"Bud? I did not know we would have non-Ghalian instructors."

"Yeah, well, they kinda make an exception for us," the pilot said with a wide grin. "Ain't that right, Hozark?"

"Clearly. Your grasp of the obvious—"

"Is exceptional. I know."

"Yes, that is what I was going to say," Hozark joked. "Now, before you head out, you were saying?"

"It's freaking Nixxa making a mess of things again. Confirmed by three sources."

"She is becoming quite problematic."

"I know. And she's making some pretty powerful friends in the process. This all seems a bit more than her usual kind of stuff. I'm actually a little worried."

Hozark's expression darkened slightly. "Does she need to be *dealt* with?"

"No, nothing like that. But your people should really keep an eye on her."

"We already are, but I will relay your information and have our agents watch her with greater focus."

"Good. Let's hope she doesn't do anything stupid. We don't want to get into that sort of mess."

"Do not worry, my friend. We will keep her in check."

"That would be pretty ideal. You know our history, and Henni and I don't really want to get into a fight with her if we can avoid it."

"Excuse me," Bawb said. "But I've also met her—"

"Yeah, we know, kid."

"Yes, well, from all everyone has said about her, yourself

included, she's protected by some fairly powerful casters on her team. With that degree of magic on her side, it does not seem you and Henni would want to get into an altercation if it could be avoided."

Bud burst out laughing at that.

"What did I say?" Bawb asked, perplexed.

Hozark's eyes crinkled slightly with amusement. "Oh, Uzabud is *quite* skilled in battle, and one of the best pilots I have had the pleasure of flying with," Hozark replied. "And Henni? She is a magnificently powerful woman. That is, if she ever learns to fully control her power."

"She is a natural magic user?"

"Yes."

"And she has *that* kind of power?" Bawb asked. "But she is so small."

"I heard that!" a voice shouted from across the courtyard, its diminutive owner stomping toward them.

"I am sure he meant no disrespect, my friend," Hozark called out with a chuckle.

"Apologies, Henni. Hozark is correct, I meant no offense." He turned back to Hozark with a questioning look.

"She possesses considerable magic of her own, yes. But unlike any you have ever encountered. I suppose we have not told you previously, but she is descended from a lost race only spoken of in ancient texts, thought to have died out long ago. A people with exceptional powers. And we are still just learning all she might be capable of."

"You are saying she casts mighty spells *without* a konus? I had no idea."

Bud wrapped his arm around his tiny partner. "She keeps it under wraps. Unless she gets *really* pissed," he joked. "But yeah, my girl's got some serious juju."

"What level of caster is she, then? An emmik? Or is she even as strong as a visla?"

A look of what could almost be described as quiet awe and respect crept onto Hozark's face. "That is difficult to answer, Bawb. Henni's power is unique, and it requires an entirely different classification. One, in fact, that we are still devising."

"So, *strong*, then?"

"Let us just say that her kind were previously rumored to possess a sort of power akin to the ancient Zomoki."

"The ones who traveled between systems?"

"The very same. And Henni has, on occasion, done exactly that."

The boy's eyes widened, focusing on the small woman. "You mean you jumped an entire ship?"

She just shrugged nonchalantly as Hozark chuckled. "Oh, that she did. And a rather large one at that. It was quite a spectacle, that."

"Yeah, no one saw that coming," Bud added.

Hozark nodded his agreement. "Indeed. But, again, Bawb, this is something we keep quiet. While some within the order are aware of her skills, it is better that outsiders remain unaware."

"Yeah, until it's too late," Henni added with a wicked grin. "But we don't need to worry about Bawb keeping his mouth shut, do we, Bawb?"

"Of course not. I will not speak a word of it."

"I know. That's why we like you, kiddo. So, you excited to be flying with Bud and me?"

"I look forward to learning to pilot your ship."

Bud and Henni glanced at Hozark. He gave a little nod. Bud put his arm around the teenager. "Kid, we're gonna do a lot more than just teach you how to fly."

"I do not understand."

"You will. You see, our buddy here has asked us to add a little, uh, *spice* to your training. Something a bit beyond the usual boring stuff. Yeah, you'll fly and take off and land and all that, but the fun bits are far more interesting."

"Fun bits?"

"Piracy and smuggling," Henni chimed in. "Jeez, Bud, just tell the kid already."

"I was about to before you interrupted me."

"Uh-huh. The point? You need to get to it quicker," she snarked at him with an affectionate gleam in her eyes.

"I thought you enjoyed my regaling and storytelling."

"This isn't a tavern, and Bawb sure as hell doesn't need to waste his day listening to you ramble. Come on, let's get a move on and get to the good stuff."

"I must admit, I am quite intrigued," the teen said.

"I bet you are," Henni said with a laugh. "Flying is fun and all, but we get to do a lot more than just that. And I think you're really gonna enjoy it."

Hozark gave them each a little bow of his head. "Thank you, my friends. I leave him in your capable hands. And, Bawb, make sure you pay close attention. While they may not always look it, these two are among the best at what they do."

"Excuse me? *Among* the best?" Bud replied. "That cuts deep, Hozark."

"I am sure you will survive," the Ghalian replied with a little grin. "As will you, Bawb. Remember your training, and all will work out for the best."

With that he left them in the courtyard alone. Bud and Henni knew the way out—at least, the one they were allowed to know—and they required no chaperone. Not after all they had risked fighting alongside the Ghalian over the years. That, and having Hozark vouch for them was all anyone would have needed.

"Well, let's go," Bud said, pulling the boy along with him. "Just a quick walk to the ship, then you get to practice your takeoff skills."

"And fly us out of the atmosphere?"

Bud chuckled. "Always eager to do more. Well, you've always paid attention when we fly, so sure, why not?"

"Thank you, Bud."

"Don't thank me. You've earned the privilege through hard work," he replied. "And now, speaking of work, we've got an eager student to teach, so let's get out of here and get this show on the road."

CHAPTER THIRTY-FOUR

Despite flying with Bud and Henni on occasion over his limited years as they shuttled him at their friend's request, Bawb had never been allowed to actually pilot their ship. He had watched, and he had learned, committing as much to memory as he possibly could, but manning the controls was not in those cards.

Nevertheless, Hozark had long ago told him to pay close attention. That Bud was an incredibly talented pilot. And having been on a few rather *interesting* flights with him, Bawb had to agree. But today was something new. He was actually at the helm, lifting the ship up and out of the atmosphere.

It was larger than any he had flown before. Hozark's shimmer ship handled differently. It was far smaller and required a fraction of the Drookonus's power to maneuver. Bud and Henni's ship, however, was quite a bit larger, but the principles were the same.

"Hey, you're doing good, kid. Now ease us out of the atmosphere. The intent's the same for a big ship as it is for a small one. You can do this," Bud encouraged.

Bawb heeded the directions and focused. He felt the magic in their Drookonus flow smoothly under his command, guiding the vessel out into space. Once free of the pull of the planet's gravity and the turbulence of the air and wind, he found he could almost pilot it without even having to concentrate.

"So, you feeling pretty confident?" Bud asked. "You seem to have the hang of it."

"This is a big ship, but yes, it feels almost intuitive, if that makes sense."

"Looks like he's got it," Henni said with a grin. "Yeah, once you really dial in and just let the magic flow you'll really connect with the ship. It'll feel almost like an extension of yourself in a way." She glanced over at Bud. He gave a little nod. "Hey, you wanna try something new?" she asked.

Bawb gave her a questioning look. "New?"

"Yeah. We have a little something planned in another system. The coordinates spells are already cast and locked in. You want to try jumping the ship this time? It's a small one, nothing crazy for now."

Bawb felt a surge of adrenaline despite his Ghalian training. This was a big step, and an exciting one. Even with Hozark allowing him to fly for a bit, he had not ever *jumped* a ship, and this one was so much larger.

"I would," he replied.

Henni grinned. "Excellent. You know what to do, right?"

"I believe I do."

Bud chuckled. "Oh, he knows. This one's been paying attention since he was little. Been waiting for this, haven't you?"

"Well–"

"Yeah, we know you have. I've seen how you watch. You always were an attentive kid."

"Thank you."

"You're the one putting in the work. Not everyone has that instinct. Getting all of that information to stick with a student can be like pulling teeth sometimes, from what Demelza says."

"She is an exceptional teacher."

"An exceptional woman in general," Henni corrected. "Now, come on. We've got cool stuff to do. More flying, less yapping."

Bud smiled wide. "As you wish," he said with a laugh. "Bawb, the ship is yours. Just feel the connection between the Drookonus's power and the ship's guidance spells. You sense them?"

Bawb quietly cast the spell powering the craft for a jump. "Yes, I sense it," he marveled. He had never been allowed to tap into this sort of power before. Not in a real-world setting. But now that he was doing so, it felt surprisingly natural.

Bud seemed pleased. He also kept a secondary control spell ready just in case he had to jump in and steer them to safety. He was confident in the boy but no fool.

"Okay. You know the spell, and the location is dialed in. Jump us to the destination."

Bawb did not hesitate. More often than not, hesitation caused far more problems than simply committing. A lesson hard learned and with more than a few bruises to show for it.

He cast the spell. The ship blinked out of existence immediately, reappearing not terribly far away, their destination system being quite close to their origin point. A safe jump. One that did not require much power and with few obstacles in the way, just in case something went awry. They didn't anticipate that happening, but the pirates knew full well that the unexpected was always a possibility.

You already know it, the konus said. *But you leveled up: Jump magic.*

He did know it. He also knew they were not alone. They had jumped into what looked like a trap.

"There appear to be other ships in our proximity," Bawb realized, raising their shielding spells without another thought.

"Wow, the kid's good," Henni said with an appreciative nod. "Relax. You don't need to worry about those. They're ours."

"Yours?"

"We kinda have a *lot* of ships, actually," Bud admitted. "Let's just say the life of smugglers often requires the rapid adjustment of plans. And that often includes switching ships mid-task."

"And the piracy thing means we sometimes wind up with extra ships," Henni added. "Not that we really do that anymore."

"No. It's mostly the other things these days. Leave the hardcore stuff for the less risk-averse."

"You mean those like Nixxa," Bawb said.

"Ugh, *her*," Henni grumbled. "No, not like her. Frikkin' pain in my ass."

"In *all* our asses," Bud agreed. "But we did have some good times."

"Sure. But were they worth it? She's a disaster waiting to happen. And she's been making some *bad* decisions."

Bud shrugged. "Point taken." He glanced at the teenager. "But that's a discussion for later. We've got things to do. Bawb, fly us toward that wrecked ship over there on your left. See it?"

"I do."

"Take us around and approach from the side. I'm going to show you how to take advantage of the gaps in the layering in defensive spells. I think Hozark's shown you some of that stuff already. But then we'll work on fun stuff. We'll practice boarding. And we'll do it with umbilical spells."

Bawb's eyes widened slightly. "We are going to practice pirate boarding maneuvers?"

"Oh yeah. Tactics, battle techniques, and, of course, a few of the little tricks we use that don't exactly follow anyone's standard rules of engagement. It's why pirates are so successful. Asymmetric assault techniques using normal people's adherence to a more rigid set of rules against them."

"I see. Leveraging their expected actions and reactions in a manner to best exploit them," Bawb mused.

"Yeah, you've got it. Same as the Ghalian in that respect. Know how everyone else fights and then do what they absolutely don't expect. Use their rules to create opportunity. Exploit every last thing we can think of. Now, first things first. Gotta get past their shield spells before anything else. Usually, we'll have layered attacks. The head-on ones are diversions, forcing the target to focus the majority of their defensive spells forward. They know this is a ploy, obviously, but the ships we deploy from the rear are *also* a diversion. All so a much smaller craft can get close enough to deploy the umbilical spell where the defenses are the weakest. Focusing so much magic against forceful attacks, an umbilical will be felt as almost benign and won't even register with most casters. They usually get tunnel vision in battle, focusing only on the aggressive ships."

"Like slowly pushing through resistance rather than hitting it hard and causing a more intense defensive reaction," Bawb said, appreciating the concept.

"Exactly. Now, get us in position, then we'll take a little walk."

"Walk?"

"You didn't think this was just going to be a lecture, did you?" Bud laughed. "Oh no, we're gonna do way more than talk."

"You'll love it," Henni added with a laugh. "Just try not to puke."

Bawb maneuvered the ship into position as instructed, feeling the weak spot in the spells reacting against the ship's gentle probing, then locked it into place with a tether spell. Bud led the way to the hatch while Henni stayed at the helm just in case anything went awry.

"Okay, now, this part is going to feel a bit weird at first," he said, then cast the umbilical spell, creating an invisible air passage linking his ship with the target's hull. "Just let go of the concept of up and down. Once we're out that door, all you need to think about is forward and back. Trying to maintain any other orientation will just confuse you and slow your progress."

"I understand."

"Good. This isn't like operating in atmosphere. Things happen in all directions. There's no up-and-down orientation in space, and that means we need to be aware of what's around us in all directions. But don't lose focus on what's in front of you. I know it can be a bit much at first, so we'll take it slow to start."

He opened the hatch, the void of space staring in at them but the air remaining safely locked inside. Bud then stepped out into the nothing, propelling himself into the almost invisible tube leading to the other ship. Up close, Bawb could see the faintest ripple where the spell separated them from space, but from any distance it would look like he was just floating in the nothingness.

"Come on," Bud urged, moving ahead.

Bawb stepped out after him. His stomach flipped at the sensation. He had been weightless aboard a ship before, but like this? This was entirely new.

"Relax your body. Go with the motion, don't fight it. Just move and learn how it feels. It's going to be weird for now, but you'll get the hang of it."

Bawb heeded his instruction, forcing the tension in his body to ease up. It was akin to being in a turbulent river. Fighting it would exhaust you, whereas letting the flow move you would allow you to conserve energy and maneuver more effectively.

This was undoubtedly a lesson the others were not getting on their flight training. Bud and Henni's friendship with Master Hozark meant that this particular Vessel was getting a little something extra today. And Bawb knew that while he would usually be working from a stable platform, be it aboard a ship or on solid land, it was inevitable that at some point he would likely have to operate outside a ship rather than inside, and this was his first taste of it.

"There ya go. You're getting the hang of it," Bud encouraged when they reached the ship's hull. "We'll do a quick breach then head back. And then it'll be *your* turn to cast the spell."

"Already?"

"No time like the present," Bud replied, not mentioning that he would have Henni cast a larger, secondary spell around them as a backup. While he trusted the boy's power and intent, he wasn't a fool.

CHAPTER THIRTY-FIVE

By the time Bud and Henni were through with the day's space pirating training, Bawb was physically and mentally drained. Much of what they were running him through was far more than mere ship flight and maneuvering. Yes, they focused a great portion of the day on that aspect, as it was the actual core point of the excursion, but with every new exercise guiding the ship, they also had their eager pupil running drills on all manner of space combat and boarding techniques.

Casting spells to adhere to the outside of a ship was second nature by the time they finished, and Bawb was getting fairly proficient at casting the robust protective air bubble spells that could withstand space as well.

His umbilical spells still needed work, as did his application of grappling and tension ones to anchor a ship into place while making the transition from one to the other, but those were things that would come with more practice. And that was something Bud and Henni offered to lend a hand with even after this particular outing.

"Happy to help, kid," Bud had told him. "You've got a knack

for it, just like Hozark. I think you'll be really good at this one day."

"Better than good," Henni corrected. "He's gonna be *great*."

"I appreciate the confidence and hope I do not disappoint you."

"Bawb, you're not gonna disappoint us," Henni said, tossing him a piece of fruit to help replenish his blood sugar. "Hell, you're already much better than most newbies we've taken on as temporary crew over the years, and those were people who had actually trained for this life. So yeah, don't worry about it, you'll be fine."

Bud rose from the pilot's seat and gestured for the teen to take over. "See that planet?"

Henni smacked him. "How can he miss it? It's huge."

"Well, yeah. But my point is, that's where we're going to land. Perfect spot to set down and rest after a long day. And the fresh air will feel great. You feel comfortable taking us down?"

"I do," Bawb replied.

"Good. There are coordinates already cast. The Drookonus knows where to go. Just guide us through the atmosphere in one piece and we'll be golden."

Bawb nodded once and slid into the seat, immediately connecting with the Drookonus powering the ship. He felt the coordinates at once, boosting the shield spell as he dropped the ship down into the atmosphere.

"Smooth. Well done," Bud commended him. "Didn't feel so much as a bump."

"As it is supposed to be," the teen noted.

"Yeah, but supposed to be and reality aren't always the same thing. Not all pilots have the feel for re-entry."

Bawb guided the ship through the clear skies, following the curvature of the planet as the sun lowered against the horizon.

Finally, he reached the designated location and dropped the ship to the surface, settling it into a low hover inches above the ground.

"Nicely done," Henni said with an appreciative grin.

"What about your other ships?"

"We'll take care of those. Don't worry about it. For now, let's get some fresh air and make a shelter."

"Why not sleep aboard the ship?"

Bud snort-laughed. "Because camping is actually fun when no one is trying to kill you. I know, not the sort of thing the Ghalian usually teach you, but sometimes ya just gotta stop and enjoy the great outdoors."

"And this way he won't smoke up the whole ship with his cooking," Henni added.

"Hey, you love my blackened Garrabeast roast."

"Blackened. Yeah. Just a fancy way of saying burned," she shot back with an adoring grin.

"You know you love it."

Bawb watched the two with amusement. They talked an epic amount of trash to one another, but the bond between them was powerful and undeniable.

"I will go make a shelter," Bawb said, heading toward the hatch.

Henni watched him go. "Great. We'll be out in a minute and set up for a cookout. There's kinda limited game around here, but we have plenty of food on the ship. Oh, and you'd better put your shelter a little bit away from here just so it doesn't get smoked out."

"I do not burn my food," Bud grumbled.

"Of course not," Henni said with a chuckle, throwing a little wink Bawb's way.

The teen stepped outside and jogged a little distance from

the ship. They had set down in a clearing amidst some tall trees with golden orange bark and speckled brown-and-green leaves. Some branches had fallen naturally, and it was from those that he crafted a basic lean-to shelter. It was a quick build and something he could break down in a hurry, blending the pieces back into the environment if he had to.

This was a friendly outing, but Ghalian habits were embedded in his mind at this point, hopefully unnecessary but also useful no matter the circumstance.

"You all good?" Bud asked when he rejoined them by the ship.

"Yes. I have made a comfortable shelter not too far from here."

"Excellent. Henni whipped us up a little spot close by too. She's just grabbing some stuff from the ship while I get started cooking dinner. You wanna help?"

"I would be glad to."

"Good. I don't know if Hozark's already told you, but cooking is a really useful skill in your line of work."

"He hadn't mentioned it, but I can see the utility of it. No one pays attention to servant staff, including those who prepare food."

"Yep. And you can slip all kinds of things into someone's meal if you need to. But ya gotta know what you're doing if you want to blend in. Gotta know your way around a kitchen. You can only get so far faking it, after all."

Bawb picked up one of the knives Bud had laid out and began deftly dicing the cleaned root vegetables sitting on the small folding table they were using to prepare dinner.

"Well, you've definitely got the hang of that," the pilot said with a chuckle, watching the teen's hands fly in a blur of activity.

"We spend a *lot* of time with knives. And a cook has access to them in locations that are otherwise locked down to any manner of bladed weapons. Something all Ghalian are trained in the use of extensively."

"Oh, I know all about that. Hell, you should see the set Henni carries around with her. She's scary good with them, in part thanks to Hozark and Demelza's mentoring."

"They are excellent instructors," Bawb said, combining ingredients and grabbing spices from Bud's selection. "Do you mind?"

"Go right ahead. I'm usually the one doing the cooking, so I'm happy to share the load. Heck, this is kind of a treat."

"I find it relaxing. I am also not bad at it," Bawb noted, his konus having leveled him up for his cooking skills on several prior occasions.

"Me too," Bud said, pulling skewered cubes of meat and vegetables from a tray and setting them aside. "And with two of us working together, we'll have dinner ready in no time."

And that they did, the three of them devouring the respectable spread well into the night, cooking and noshing until they were ready to burst.

"Okay, I'm done."

Henni flashed an amused grin. "Wimp."

"Hey, that was a lot of food. Ugh. I need to pass out before I die from overeating," Bud griped, slapping his distended belly.

"I could still eat a little more," Henni mused, wiping her plate with a piece of bread.

"Where do you put it all, woman?"

"I'm hungry, what can I say?"

Bud laughed and began gathering the plates.

"I can do that," Bawb offered.

"Nah, I got it. It'll only take a minute. You go get some rest. It's been a long day, and I'm sure you need it. We'll rise early and fly to the city in the morning."

"Is it far? I only caught a glimpse as we landed."

"Not too far. Still, it's a decent flight. But you don't need to think about that until tomorrow. Now get outta here and get some sleep."

Bawb nodded and rose from his seat, then walked off into the darkness to his cozy shelter. Bud and Henni shared a little look and began cleaning up the dishes and cooking implements. Ten minutes later it was all washed and stowed.

Bawb woke with the sun, stretching languorously in his surprisingly comfortable shelter before crawling out into the morning light. He rose and spread his arms wide, taking in a deep breath, invigorating his lungs with the cool, crisp air. Despite sleeping on the ground, he had slept quite well thanks to layers of soft leaves cushioning him from the ground and insulating his body from the cool soil.

His stomach let out a little growl. Eating so much the night before had kicked his digestive tract into overdrive. Nothing a little morning snack aboard the ship wouldn't fix. He turned and walked to Bud and Henni's vessel.

At least, to where the ship should have been.

It was gone.

A chill washed over him. He hadn't heard it take off, but then, he wouldn't have. Not with a skilled pilot and powerful Drookonus.

"They likely just flew to retrieve and relocate their training ships," he rationalized. "I am sure they will be back shortly."

Even so, that meant he was on his own for breakfast, and there was not much in the way of game in the area from what he'd seen. Regardless, he started a small fire and went for a hunt while also foraging for berries and other things he could eat.

The area, while lush, was far more scarce when it came to

edibles than one would have assumed given the overall look of the place. But his keen eyes had taken it all in and come to a logical, educated realization. Most of these plants were toxic to all but animals, and there were woefully few of those beasts to hunt. And the ones that did live in this wooded area were either too small to be worth the effort or too cautious to make an appearance and be caught for his next meal.

All day he waited for the ship to return, staying close to the landing site, searching for food while his attention regularly turned skyward. The sun set, leaving him all alone to curl up in his shelter. Alone and with the cold realization that Bud and Henni were not coming back, Bawb accepted the situation for what it was. He was on his own.

"I need to make it to civilization," he decided the following afternoon.

He had woken early and climbed a tall tree, getting a visual reference of the area to work with. It only took a moment to orient himself. If he followed the arc of the sun, he would eventually wind up at the distant city he had spotted from the air upon their arrival. He knew nothing about it, not even its name, but at least he would be in civilization there.

Bawb gathered up his few possessions and started walking. This would take time. A *lot* of it. The question was, exactly how much?

After two days his stomach was a knotted ball of agony, having only found a few edible ferns and one lone mushroom that was of the non-poisonous variety. Other than that, he had been walking on empty for days.

A stench reached his nose long before his eyes found the source. A large animal had perished some time ago and lay rotting in the tall grass of a clearing. His belly rumbling, he walked to it without hesitation. He did not have a knife on him, but he had chipped a piece of stone to fashion a primitive cutting device of sorts. With that he set to work on the disgusting remains, slicing away the most rotted parts and putting aside the few relatively sound pieces he could salvage.

Casting a small fire spell, he then set to work cooking the hell out of the foul meat until it was nearly charred all the way through, killing anything that might still be growing on it. He ate the nasty meal with gusto, forcing his tastebuds to ignore the flavor.

Level up: Survival.

"Survival? Really?"

You're doing the unsavory in order to live. Not as exciting as some of your other skill sets, but an important one all the same. To do what others are not willing to do sets you apart from them, Vessel. Remember that.

"Great. Thanks, Konus. I'll be sure to keep that in mind," he grumbled, setting off once more.

He soon came across a small marsh blocking his path. He could have probably gone around, but the question was, how long would it take to do so? Too long, he decided, making the decision to wade right across.

The water was surprisingly warm, and not entirely unpleasant. When he reached the other side, however, he noticed something rather alarming.

Leeches.

Several of them, latched onto his skin, slowly swelling in size as they sucked his blood. He peeled them off quickly, but rather than throw them back in the water, he tucked them into a small pouch fashioned of waxy plant leaves then tied it shut with a strand of flexible reed. He would cook them later, replenishing his energy from the things that had tried to do the same from him. From his blood.

His konus didn't say anything, but he could almost *feel* its satisfaction with his performance. But he wasn't doing this to level up. He was doing it to survive. To survive long enough to make it to civilization. Long enough to find a way home.

CHAPTER THIRTY-SIX

Bawb trekked for days. Hungry, tired, filthy, and alone.

He had been fortunate to come across some small game as he progressed, but the animals were almost insubstantial in the amount of nutrition they provided him. Additionally, given their size, they were woefully lacking in fat, which meant while he was getting some protein from his catch, that much-needed nutrient was lacking.

It was the sort of thing one would not think about until it was too late. A body could run on protein for some time, yes, but fats were required as well. As for carbohydrates, the scattered edible plants he had come across were nowhere near enough to quell his hunger, but they at least covered his body's basic needs in that category.

This was not at all like in training. Nothing like being stranded on a pleasant forest world as it had been on his outings with the other Vessels. In that situation, everything was relatively easy, comparatively speaking, and with plenty of game and edible berries and plants to scavenge, no one went hungry.

Here, however, it was a far more difficult task. And one that was beginning to take its toll.

Bawb knew that he was expending more energy than he was taking in, and his clothing had begun to hang looser on his body. He was well aware that he needed more sustenance than what he had been gathering, but he also knew he could survive over a month like this so long as he had water. And that, at least, he was able to find easily and in relative abundance.

He walked and walked, crossing streams, climbing hills, crossing marshes and arid stretches on his trek toward what he hoped was civilization. But traveling as far as he was, it was also foremost in his mind how just a slight deviation from his path could have him overshoot his goal, missing it entirely and never being any the wiser. Vigilance was crucial, but reduced caloric intake was making that a bit harder, regardless of his awareness of the situation.

A fire blazes, dead without embers. Storms rage, yet a feather floats, he thought as he walked, repeating it on a loop, pondering the cryptic message Hozark had given him so long ago. Something to focus on as he trudged along, keeping his mind occupied. It still didn't make sense, no matter how many years he had spent trying to decipher it, but one day it would. It had to. Hozark would not have recited it to him if he didn't think he would eventually figure it out.

Bawb was so caught up in thought that he almost walked right into the small but ferocious animal gnawing on a carcass. The creature was no taller than his waist, covered in soft fur, currently spotted with rotting gore from its feast. It reared up and hissed at him. Bawb pulled a stone from his pocket and threw it hard.

The projectile flew true, bouncing off the animal's snout with a loud thud. The beast let out a yelp and scurried away, looking back at him with an angry gaze but not wanting anything more to do with this strange bipedal creature.

Bawb felt his pockets. He still had two more smallish rocks

in them, gathered as he walked for just this sort of encounter, sparing him the danger of crouching down to find a weapon when facing whatever he might come across. As it turned out, his foresight had paid off. Best of all, he hadn't needed to spend any of his precious energy fighting an animal. He had scared it off, and that was all he needed.

His stomach growled angrily, and Bawb hurried to the remains of the kill, picking through the mess of bones and entrails. There was not much left of it, but this had been a larger animal. Likely some sort of migratory one. And more importantly, it had apparently had ample fat stored on its body. Most had gone rancid by now, but cutting away the foul exterior revealed relatively unspoiled fat and meat close to the bone.

He gathered as much as he could, bundling it up in a large leaf, then set a snare to capture whatever other game might come investigating the kill. He then trudged off to set up a camp for the night. He was tired, he was hungry, and he finally had something substantial to eat. He would cook it up to make sure he didn't get sick then would eat his fill. With his stomach shrunk from days of little food, it would not take much.

He settled down on a small rise above a little stream. The elevated position would not only keep him from the damp, cool air closer to the water, but it would also afford him a view of anything that might be coming his way. He would cast basic alarm spells as well as fashion a few tripwire alerts, but all of that would only do so much if he wasn't in a position to take advantage of any early warning.

That done, he cast a fire spell and ignited some dry wood beneath an elevated flat stone he had washed in the stream. It took all of his patience to wait for it to heat up enough to cook on, but once he put the meat and fat on it, the smell of it cooking rewarded his restraint. Best of all, the slight indentation in the stone collected the fat and juices as his meal cooked.

Bawb pulled a piece free, careful not to burn his fingers, and popped it into his mouth. It was quite possibly the most satisfying food he had ever eaten.

"Oh, yes," he muttered, stuffing more through his eager lips, licking his fingers clean after every bite.

The food hit his stomach hard, making it cramp up after so many days running on near empty. But to Bawb it was worth it. He could feel the nutrients coursing through him, his mind and body both responding almost immediately to the surge of energy his meal was providing him.

He tilted the stone to let the juice run into a cupped leaf and sipped it down as he walked to the water's edge. There he washed himself and took a long drink. His stomach a little distended from the meal, he returned to his campsite and climbed into his little shelter. It wasn't much, but it would be more than enough for the night.

Tired as he was, he was asleep in minutes.

When Bawb woke it was morning. He had barely moved.

He hurried off into the bushes to relieve himself, his stomach both happy and upset from his fatty meal, then cleaned off in the stream before readying himself for yet another day's trek. His leftover food bundled in a large waxy leaf, he headed back to check his traps. All were empty. All, that is, but one.

An animal roughly the same size as the one he had encountered the day before was snared, its leg caught up in the makeshift cordage. It did not appear to be of the fierce variety, but Bawb did not care. This was a food source, and by the look of it, one that would feed him for several days.

He killed it quickly and without hesitation, stunning it with a spell then ending it before it regained its senses. It was as clean and painless as he could make it.

Level down: Stealth, tact, survival, the konus announced.

"Down? What do you mean down? I successfully trapped game. And the kill was good. Quick and clean."

Look closer, the konus replied.

Bawb did, studying the animal's inert form.

Flip it over.

He did. Only then did he see what the konus was referring to.

"A brand?"

Yes. In your excitement, your careless trapping has removed this animal from its herd. And now its absence may go noted. And that may bring attention your way.

"I–I could—"

You can do nothing now. What's done is done. Claim your prize, but get moving. And hide the damn body and disassemble the traps. At least that may buy you some time.

Bawb could hear the frustration in the konus's tone. Yes, it was technically not alive, but the longer he knew it, the longer he had to believe there was more to it than a simple spell responding to questions and rewarding or punishing his actions.

Whatever the case, the konus was right. What was done was done.

He butchered the animal quickly, wrapping up as much as he could reasonably carry in the large leaves that grew in the area, bundling them tight and tying them to his back with makeshift cordage. He then buried the remains rather than leaving them for scavengers as was normally the Ghalian way. Yes, it was a meal that could support other animals, part of the circle of life. But at the moment, stealth was of the essence. While he wanted to find civilization, it had to be on his own terms. And being caught as a poacher was most certainly not on his agenda.

He hurried to the stream and washed the blood from his

hands then started his day's trek, frustrated with himself as he thought back to the animal's brand.

"How did I miss that?" he chided himself, then let it go. Dwelling on mistakes was not something he could afford to do. Not now. Not ever. Not if he wanted to survive.

CHAPTER THIRTY-SEVEN

Bawb stalked through the tall grass at the edge of the tree line, slowly creeping closer to the animal he had simply dubbed *food*. It was a four-legged herbivore with elongated limbs and a strangely cylindrical body shape. Its neck was thick and strong, powerful jaws grinding whatever plants it ate into a paste that soon made its way to the first of its two stomachs.

Food lived in small groups, traveling the wild from area to area, spreading out in the early hours, then gathering close come afternoon for safety in numbers. The predators of this world were not early risers, and that had led to the ingrained habit.

Bawb, however, was not of this world. And he had learned *Food*'s habits and had quickly adapted to them.

He crouched low, tufts of long grass woven into a blanket of sorts, covering him from head to toe. Dung was rubbed into the fibers, masking his scent, making him blend into the environment nearly as well as any shimmer cloak could.

It was practical camouflage, not magical, sparing his magic for when he might truly need it, however long that might be.

And that might be some time. After all, he had been stranded for weeks now.

Bawb's muscles tensed slightly. The animal hesitated just out of reach, its ears scanning for sounds of something it sensed but could not see. Hidden danger it had evolved to feel even if it didn't know where or what it was. Bawb, however, stayed perfectly still, even his breath so shallow that his grass covering did not move but for the strands' gentle swaying in the cool morning air.

The animal's body eventually relaxed, and it resumed its breakfast grazing. One step, then two, it drew closer to the hidden teen.

Bawb's short spear flashed out in a blur, piercing his target's heart, the chipped stone tip's razor edge slicing through it with ease. The animal gave a look of surprise then dropped to the soil, dead in an instant.

It was a clean kill.

The konus had stopped leveling him up after the first week or so. Bawb's skills had transitioned from tentative application in the real world to confident displays of surprising expertise. As a result, he had leveled up in multiple areas in rapid succession. It wasn't combat training, but after a few days of severe hunger and discomfort he came to appreciate just how useful these survival skills truly were.

A classroom could only teach so much. This put it all into much clearer focus.

Bawb hefted his kill and hurried from the field into the trees, leaving the area clean so as not to spook the others of the group that might wander this way for their morning repast. Safely clear of the field, he gutted and cleaned his prey, scraping the skin for later use and butchering the carcass for either smoking into jerky or cooking for the next several days' consumption.

All of it he wrapped in another skin he had lined with sturdy leaves, securing it to his back with the straps he had fashioned from hand-cured leather and woven plant fibers. His larder full enough to sustain him for several days, he then began his daily trek.

He had covered a very long distance over the weeks, crossing from regions of sparse game into this more fecund region. Not only did he discover animals to hunt, but also an abundance of edible plants, and he had done so just in time. Had resources remained limited, his energy would have been far too low to have been able to make such substantial progress.

Bawb bit into a piece of jerky as he walked, enjoying the fresh air, wondering when, not if, he would finally come across civilization. He might have been a bit upset at first when no one came looking for him, but he had resigned himself to the situation, settling into the new role of survivor. But that didn't mean he was just going to sit on his laurels and wait. The Ghalian had a saying. Many sayings, actually, but in this instance, one in particular held true.

"Assume no one is coming. Accept that you are alone. It falls to you to rescue yourself."

And that was exactly what he was doing. Whatever had happened to Bud and Henni, he was on his own. And having traveled so far from his original landing site, there was no turning back even if he wanted to.

He walked all day, maintaining a steady pace, not pushing himself too hard, his feet falling into a comfortable rhythm as he strode across dirt, stone, and grassy fields. Bawb was beginning to think about finding a suitable location to settle down for the approaching night. He still had several hours, but it was far preferable to stop early in a great location than get an extra hour or two of trekking but then be forced to sleep less comfortably as a result.

Sounds reached his ears, disrupting the quiet he had

become so accustomed to. Sounds of conversation. Somewhere close by there were people.

He felt his pulse quicken slightly, the promise of rescue from this world flooding him with relief and hope. He walked faster, still cautious but excited. His excitement quickly faded.

Tslavars he realized, his enthusiasm replaced by a feeling of dread.

The tall, deep-green-skinned race was brutal, known across the galaxy for their ways. It was the natural Tslavar proclivity for violence and aggression that made them the mercenaries of choice in many conflicts, specifically those whose principals had enough coin to bring on outside combatants for pay. And the Tslavars were more than happy to fight for the highest bidder.

They also competed with pirates and smugglers, crossing paths and weapons with them often, but also participating in things even those ruffians found distasteful. Slave trading was the one that came to mind first and foremost. It was also what put them squarely on the Ghalian shit list.

Bawb hid his homemade pack in the brush and cautiously crept closer until he could see them clearly and hear the conversations of the dark elf-looking brutes. There were a lot of them milling around their ship, the craft settled down with tables set up around it. Apparently, their captain had decided to give the crew an evening on land rather than in space, though he had to wonder if there was anything more nefarious to their presence.

But there did not appear to be any huddled slaves or wounded troops. It seemed this was simply a bit of respite for a crew likely tired of so many weeks or months out in the void. Fresh air did wonders for morale regardless of race. Bawb watched and listened, plotting the best course around them to avoid detection. Then he heard something that changed his plans quite drastically.

"I'm glad they caught her. Lalaynia is quite a prize."

"That bitch has been a thorn in our side for years. I can't count how many times she's ruined a deal."

"Pirates'll do that."

"Yeah, but Lalaynia's always been a particularly troublesome one. And her team is pretty damn formidable."

"Not now, without their leader," the other replied with a rumbling laugh that sounded like he had been gargling broken glass. "Do we know where they took her?"

"Last I heard she was on Zephin."

"Zephin? Frakkin' pirate den, that place. Odd she would be held there."

"I know. But what better place to hide her? No one would think to look for her there. And the captain said we're heading there on this run."

"I know. But after Farrahl, though, right? We gotta sell that batch of Drooks first."

"Obviously. Sooner we sell them the sooner we get back to more fun work. Playing Drook babysitters is no sort of work for us. I want a fight!"

"Soon enough, brother. Things are afoot, and we should have plenty of fun once they kick off."

The Tslavar nodded his approval. "Hey, you think they might sell her to us?"

"Who?"

"Lalaynia, of course."

"Why would you even want her?"

"Because she's quite a prize. And with all the people she's raided over the years, I bet we could get a good price for her."

"We would have to lug her around with us from system to system far too long for that. And besides, I doubt the captain wants that sort of trouble on his ship. You know she lives up to her reputation and then some."

"She won't steal our ship."

"Alone and in chains? Likely not. But is it really worth the risk?"

"Eh, not my call to make."

Bawb took careful note of the number and location of the Tslavars, as well as the access points on their ship. No shielding was up as they were safely resting on the planet's surface. They were safe, at least from just about any form of detection and attack they would usually face in orbit, and as such, their guard was down, at least somewhat.

An idea blossomed in his mind. Moving slowly, Bawb quietly crept back into the woods and gathered his stashed supplies.

I don't know about this idea, the konus said. *You know I can read your thoughts.*

"I do. And I do not care," the teen replied. "I need passage to *anywhere* out of this wilderness. Once in a proper town or city, I can acquire a ride home."

I also sense a but.

"But they know where Lalaynia is. If I can confirm that, it would be most welcome information to the order."

Except you are not a spy, have no resources to speak of, and are on your own.

"Come now, Konus. We Ghalian are always on our own." He crept back toward the parked vessel, a plan forming in his mind.

You've got to be kidding me.

"You have a better idea?"

Any idea is a better idea.

Bawb stifled a chuckle. The konus knew what he was up to and was not amused. To be fair, he wasn't exactly thrilled about the idea either, but he needed to get off this planet. And if he could make it to Zephin, he could quite possibly achieve far more than just getting home.

He pulled up the icons from his konus, surveying his levels in all manner of disguise spells and camouflage.

Your skills are not yet there, the konus said, knowing full well what he had in mind. *You might be able to pull off a disguise spell to appear as a Tslavar for perhaps a moment, but there is no way you will be able to hold the spell and blend in.*

"I am aware of that. What I need is to get on that ship in some other way."

You actually intend to sneak aboard? Looking as you do?

"You know that is my plan, unless you have a better suggestion."

The konus's silence was all he needed to hear. Bawb would have to sneak close and wait for the right moment, then hurry aboard their ship. A little diversion spell might help. Something to draw the Tslavar eyes away from the craft for a few moments. *Those* sorts of spells he had ample access to. All he had to do was pick one. One that would truly draw their attention. Making their cooking fire burst from its containment stones would likely do the trick without raising suspicions.

Bawb moved to the area on the periphery closest to the entry hatch he had determined to be the least likely to take him into a heavily traveled area of the ship and calmed his mind, taking deep breaths and preparing himself. He felt his heart slow, his senses sharpening as he slipped into action mode.

"Very well," he said, his body ready for action. "As Teacher Griggitz often says, fortune favors the bold. It is time to get to it."

CHAPTER THIRTY-EIGHT

Tucked away safely aboard the Tslavar ship, Bawb knew he had gotten lucky.

Yes, skill and tactics were involved with his ingress as well, but at the end of it all, it was pure luck that had carried the day when it came time to actually sneak aboard the Tslavar ship. There was no real planning when one was breaching an enemy vessel with no intel whatsoever. He would have to simply choose his moment and then commit, consequences be damned.

Fortunately for him, the little diversion spell he had cast on their cooking fire, causing it to flare up momentarily, had worked as intended and drawn the attention of those on the outside of the craft, allowing him a brief moment to sneak aboard unnoted, all while seeming like a natural event rather than some sort of attack or trick.

He just hoped no one was lurking directly within.

As it turned out, when he rushed from the cover of brush into the ship, he found himself in a completely empty corridor. Bawb knew where he was, having studied the basic layout of most ships at this point. The Ghalian made a point to memorize designs, capabilities, and details of the main categories and variants with special focus on those belonging to likely adversaries. As mercenaries often affiliated with the Council of Twenty, Tslavars most definitely fit that bill.

Bawb hurried ahead on stealthy feet, quickly making his way to what should be the Tslavar equipment storage locker nearest this particular airlock. There were many spread across the ship, each situated to allow them access to weapons and gear no matter where they were should they come under attack. Unless that happened, however, they would go untouched, and Bawb would be able to ride out the trip in relative peace within.

Opening the door to his would-be hiding place, he was pleased to see he was in luck.

Bawb slid inside and closed the door behind him, casting the faintest of illumination spells but not before putting a deactivation tripwire spell on the door. He couldn't have someone noting the unusual light inside if they happened upon his impromptu hiding place.

He then slipped his parcel of food from his back and stowed it securely, layering masking spells upon it to hide any smells. There was cooked meat and jerky within, along with a small assortment of edible plants, but if the flight lasted more than a few days he would have to resort to the raw meat. Cooking was simply not an option.

As it turned out, they were departing that very night after their cookout, and the flight to Farrahl went quickly, the planet only being a few short jumps away. He cracked the door open to listen to conversations of the crew as they led the Drooks off the ship and to the auction grounds. This was not a simple transfer to another vessel. This was the worst kind of slavery. The kind that would see families split apart, likely to never see one another again. It made his blood boil with an anger he thought he had finally mastered.

"Let it go," he told himself, taking a deep breath, followed by another. "Bad things happen every day, and this is not your mission."

He hated having to remind himself of that, wanting to find a way to put an end to this if he could. But he knew one man against an entire galaxy-wide systemic problem was an impossible solution. For now, at least, he would have to focus on his task at hand. And that was learning what he could about Lalaynia, followed by getting his ass back home.

Fortunately, the auction was only the following day, so the Tslavar ship was back in the air and on its way to Zephin in no time. And while Zephin was a slightly longer flight, having just topped up their coffers, the Tslavar captain was apparently willing to expend a little more magic from his ship's team of Drooks, cutting the next leg of their flight short with a few powerful jumps.

"Can't wait to get a proper drink," a gruff voice said as a large group of crew marched off the ship. "Ran out of the good stuff weeks ago."

"Yeah, tell me 'bout it. Cap says we've got a few days, so let's make the most of it!"

A raucous cheer erupted from his crewmates as they headed off to quench their thirst for alcohol or whatever other delights they might have in mind. What mattered to Bawb was that if this was a longer shore leave, that would mean only a skeleton crew would remain aboard the ship. He could most likely just walk off at his leisure. Hell, he could probably even sneak around the ship and look for useful intel if he felt truly daring. But that would be inviting disaster, and while his younger self might have tried, he was less impulsive these days, and a better Ghalian for it.

That wasn't to say he didn't still have the same drives and urges as before. Case in point, he was aboard a Tslavar ship trying to suss out details about a kidnapped pirate friend of Bud and Henni's, which was in no way a sanctioned mission. But that considered, he was being far more cautious about it than he might otherwise have been.

As it was, Bawb waited a good hour before creeping out of his hiding place, taking one small, sealed cargo box with him. While its absence might raise questions, opening a container full of someone's waste and rotting food remains would raise far more.

He hurried to the open hatch then paused, peering out, ensuring no Tslavars were stationed outside the door. Knowing this was a Tslavar ship, no one would be foolish enough to think about breaking *in*, so it had been left unattended. Bawb stood up straight and walked right off the ship as if he was supposed to be there. A few people looked his way, but only for a moment. Seeing the confident way he carried himself, it seemed obvious that, whatever he was doing, he was supposed to be there.

He quickly surveyed the transport ships and noted their listed routes and the fare for each, then strode out of the landing site, depositing the box in a waste pile. He then hurried into town, searching for some fresh water to wash himself with. Clean dirt was fine, but stench could get him captured. Unfortunately, he had no coin for clean clothes, and the vendors in this area seemed the wary sort. New clothing would be a later priority.

A public fountain caught his attention. He quickly shed his shirt, soaking it and wringing it out several times in rapid succession before putting the damp cloth back on. His trousers would have to wait. Fortunately, they were already a darker color, and the grime blended in for the most part.

The fortified building at the center of town was his next stop. The magistrate of the city was a thoroughly corrupt individual, and it was she who was supposedly holding Lalaynia somewhere in her compound. Bawb didn't know much about the woman beyond what he'd overheard the Tslavars say, and that was woefully little. But Bud and Henni's friend needed help, and he had no option but to do what he could. Gather information, or even help her break out. Whatever he could do, he would.

But first, he needed to get into that building.

He walked the perimeter, blending in with the crowd, no one paying much attention to the grubby teenager in their midst. So long as he wasn't trying to steal anything, no one really seemed to care. It took several minutes to walk all the way around. Bawb noted the windows, while unbarred, were too high to climb in without being noticed. He would have to enter through a door somehow.

The main entrance was clearly out of the question. Guards were stationed there in abundance, and he could feel powerful casters among them ready to repel any intruders. The rear entrance was much the same. The service entrances on either side, however, were far less protected. As soon as he opened one of the doors and stepped inside, he realized why.

It led not to an interior hallway, but a small courtyard. Undoubtedly it was a means to delay any unwanted intruders, keeping them from the building proper. A large beast with deep red eyes and thick orange scales looked up from where it was resting its head on the ground. It yawned, massive fangs dripping with bright-yellow drool. Bawb forced his adrenaline to stop flowing, instead locking his gaze on the massive creature.

"I mean you no harm," he said quietly, walking very slowly across the courtyard.

He noted the gouges in the stone as well as a few spatters of very old blood on the far wall. It was clear why there were no guards here. None would be needed. Not with this thing protecting the entryway. But somehow, he felt a tickle in his senses. As if the creature could almost understand him.

"That's right. I am just going to go inside over there. Nothing at all to be concerned about," he said, walking cautiously past the beast.

It rose to its feet, but slowly, turning to watch with a curious but unalarmed gaze. Bawb reached the door and gently opened it.

"Thank you, friend," he said, stepping inside.

The animal didn't react. In fact, it didn't even make a sound. Rather, it lay back down as it had been, a bored look on its face.

Level up: Empath. A new icon unblurred from his skills display.

"You mean I can communicate with animals?"

In a way. But I think you should focus on the task at hand, don't you?

Bawb didn't need to be told twice, taking off down the corridor at a jog. Amazingly, once inside, the security setup was almost laughable. After all his Ghalian training, it was child's play avoiding the roaming patrols. He simply tucked out of sight when he heard voices, discussing moving a prisoner to some planet called Boxxna. Bawb had never heard of it, but then, there were more worlds out there than he could visit in a hundred lifetimes.

He remained in place, motionless and silent, only re-emerging when they were gone.

"If I were them, where would Lalaynia be held? High above, or below ground?" he wondered, making a choice and climbing the nearest stairwell to the next level.

He dodged more guards, quickly walking the floor before climbing to the third level. He had repeated most of the pattern when a different voice caught his attention at the far end of the hallway. A woman's voice. One he recognized.

Bawb pressed himself to the wall, his eyes focused at the far end of the corridor where another passageway intersected it.

The woman walked through it, accompanied by a few of her people, as well as a pair of the magistrate's guards. It was a brief glance, but he recognized her. How could he not?

"Nixxa," he gasped.

"Hey, you there!" a voice growled from behind.

In his shock at seeing Nixxa, he had somehow missed the guards that had exited the doorway behind him. He was unarmed and outnumbered. He would have to think fast.

"I'm sorry, I think I'm lost," he said, trying to buy time.

Hard fists and heavy boots rained down on him, knocking him to the stone floor.

"How did you get in? Why are you here? Who sent you?" the largest of the guards demanded.

"I'm just—"

A hard slap cracked across his face.

"Please! I'm just hungry and trying to get something to eat."

"Then beg in the street!"

"I was told there was an emmik here. One who favors boys my age," he said on the fly. There were casters with unsavory proclivities, and perhaps this ruse might just make the guards uncomfortable enough to let him off with a warning.

"Not in this compound there aren't," the guard said, smacking him hard again.

"You have no sympathy," Bawb spat. "You are cruel, stupid men!"

The guards, already the violent sort, took exception to his words and lay into him even more, punching and kicking him as a group before unceremoniously throwing him out the nearest open third-floor window.

Bawb twisted in the air, doing his best to keep his head from hitting the ground first, his konus powering a small cushioning spell. It was a risk, but the choice of his magic being detected or his head cracking open was an easy one to make.

Bawb still hit hard, his body bouncing from the impact. It hurt, but without the spell he would have broken bones and possibly even been killed. The guards didn't even stick around to admire their handiwork.

Level up. Infiltration, improvisation, deception, and escape. But we'll discuss that later. You need to move.

"I know," he said, his ribs aching from the impact.

Bruised and bloody, the boy slowly climbed back to his feet, his smile surprising the few who had witnessed the event. But Bawb was in fantastic spirits, and with good reason. He pulled the two small pouches of coin from his pockets and hefted them in his hands. Not a bad take, all told, and more than enough to buy him clean clothes and passage home.

Best of all, the guards he had so expertly riled up wouldn't even notice they'd been pickpocketed in the scuffle until he was long gone, the planet no more than an uncomfortable memory.

Bawb hissed as he took a deep breath. Yep, those were cracked ribs all right. But he had dealt with worse. He pulled a tiny bit of power from his konus and did what he could to dampen the pain, then headed to acquire his new clothing and a ride back home.

CHAPTER THIRTY-NINE

His skin rinsed of the sweat, dirt, and blood from his ordeal, and wearing clean clothes that lacked both the stench and grittiness of the attire he had spent the last several weeks surviving in, Bawb settled down into the comfort of his seat on the transport ship and drifted into a shallow sleep.

His body wanted more, the need to mend pushing him to just let go and let all of his energy go toward that goal. But Bawb was on edge, drifting in only the lightest of sleep, aware of all around him as the craft lifted off without incident.

Finally on his way home, he let himself float a tiny bit deeper in his meditative nap but nowhere near full sleep. There would be time for that when he was in the safe walls of the compound he called home, and no sooner.

The ship he had selected was a cheap one. The sort of vessel filled with the dregs. Those who society typically didn't pay much attention to. And that was exactly what he wanted.

Several stops were required along the way, making it a much longer flight than he would have preferred. But with just a little coin remaining in his pocket, he knew it was wise to conserve his newfound resources any way he could. Anything could happen on the way home, and he would be well served maintaining what little he had as a monetary safety net.

As it turned out, he made it back without incident.

Bawb walked the familiar streets with a sense of relief washing away at least a small portion of his stress. He fought the desire to run, to hurry the last stretch home, instead moving calmly, even stopping to purchase a little snack from a street vendor. When he reached the nondescript door on an unremarkable building and stepped inside, no one paid him one iota of attention. Just as he intended.

He walked across the entry foyer and ran his hand over a seemingly ordinary section of the wall. Without so much as a click, it shifted and slid open. Bawb stepped inside, the door sealing behind him. Only then did he finally release the tension that had been present since he had first woken to find himself stranded and alone.

He trudged the corridors, heading to the dining hall, his stomach ready to restore his energy with a real meal before he sought out his teachers. Stepping inside, he realized he needn't have worried about that.

Demelza was standing there, waiting. Seated at the table behind her were Bud and Henni, the latter demolishing a plate of food that seemed far too large for one as tiny as she was. But Bawb had learned long ago, Henni burned through food as easily as a black hole sucked in matter. It was impressive, and almost disconcerting.

"We were wondering when you would make it back," Demelza said.

He looked at her with confusion. "I do not understand. They left without me."

"And?"

The realization hit him like a slap. "That was no accident. It was intentional."

"It was. And you have proven yourself. The teachers felt you possessed the requisite skills, and you excel in more controlled settings. It was simply your confidence in the real world we needed to assess, and you have done well. After all this time, you appear unharmed for the most part, though you have lost a bit of weight. And you successfully made your way back without incident."

Bud rose from the table and brought him a cool drink.

"Hey, I'm really sorry, kid, but we had orders. Glad to see you're okay."

Bawb felt no ill will. He'd been with the Ghalian too long for that by now. "It was trying at first, but then my training kicked in."

"And with great success," Demelza noted. "Eat and rest. A mission has come to us. One that will be utilized as a training exercise. We will depart in two days. That should be enough time for you to see the healer and recover, yes?"

"It will."

"Good. I will inform the other teachers of your return."

She strode out of the dining hall, leaving Bawb alone with Bud and Henni.

"Hey, for real, we hated having to do that," Henni said between bites. "But you know how it is. The Ghalian ask for a favor, you don't say no."

"Not like they'd do anything bad if we did," Bud noted. "But yeah, we kinda have an arrangement, as you know."

Henni patted the seat next to her. "C'mon, sit down and tell us all about it. We tried to drop you somewhere with plenty of water. You didn't have any problems with that, did ya?"

"Water was not an issue, no. Game was another story, but it all worked out in the end," the teen replied, sitting down with a groan.

A look of concern briefly flashed across Henni's face. "You okay?"

"It is just my ribs. I will be fine."

"What'd ya do to your ribs? Fighting off some wild animals I bet."

"No, nothing like that, though I did encounter a few. But this was sustained when I was thrown out a third-floor window. A most unpleasant experience."

Bud and Henni seemed legitimately shocked.

"Hang on," Bud said. "Someone threw you out a window? But that city's a super relaxed trading center."

"It did not happen on the world you left me on. It happened in the magistrate's compound on Zephin."

Bud's look changed to one of legitimate shock. "Wait, what? How the hell did you wind up on Zephin? That's a pretty rough place."

"And how did you get in the magistrate's place?" Henni chimed in. "Those are *not* the sort of people you want to mess with."

"I realize that," Bawb replied, gently feeling his cracked ribs.

"What were you thinking? And how did you even get there?" she asked before taking another large bite.

"I stowed away on a Tslavar slave ship."

Henni nearly spat out the food she'd just shoveled into her mouth. Bud stared in shock, and more than a little concern.

"Are you nuts? Why would you risk that? If they'd caught you—"

"But they did not."

"That's beside the point. There are plenty of other ways off that planet. But stowing away with Tslavars? And to Zephin no less? That was dumb, Bawb. I expected more from you."

The boy brushed aside the critique. He had his reasons.

"Your friend, Lalaynia. I heard them discussing her. Where

she was being held. I thought I could help. Gather information at the very least, if not help free her. Stowing away to Zephin and sneaking into the magistrate's compound was the logical path, though I did not find her. I did, however, see Nixxa there."

"Nixxa? On Zephin?"

"In the magistrate's compound, yes. Fortunately, she did not see me."

Bud's disappointed gaze had shifted to something else. Concerned, mostly.

"Listen, you're still just a kid, Bawb. A very talented one, but still a kid. What you did was reckless. You've gotta let the adults handle this sort of thing."

"I am sorry you are angry."

"I'm not angry. I admire the initiative, I really do. But Hozark would have been so upset if anything had happened to you. It's just too risky."

"We take risks constantly, and I am merely a trainee. A lowly Vessel, no less. If anything *had* happened to me, well, though I would prefer it not, nevertheless, it is simply a part of Ghalian life."

Bud bit his tongue, his eyes darting to Henni. Hozark had never come out and said it, but they both knew Bawb was his son, and they also knew that while he pushed the boy hard to succeed, there was no way he would treat his injury or demise with anything less than a quiet, vengeful rage. They'd seen it before. He was a Master Ghalian and one of the Five. As such, his emotions were always under control, at least publicly. But once wronged, he would make it his mission to exact revenge, no matter how long it took.

Fortunately, Bawb had come back in one piece, and with information that truly was useful. Bud rose from the table and crossed to the door.

"Look, I'm glad you're back safe, and I do appreciate the

effort you made. But in the future, be more careful, okay? Henni, make sure he eats something, will ya? I need to go talk with Hozark."

"Can do," she replied, sliding one of her plates to the boy. "Eat."

"But I—"

"I said *eat*."

Bawb hesitated a moment then tucked into the food, his first real, substantial meal since he'd last seen her.

Bud hustled down the corridors to where his friend would almost certainly be training. Hozark had few habits, the repetition of anything making one vulnerable to attack, but here in this safest of spaces, he did allow himself a regular practice session in the smallest of the second-level sparring rooms.

"Hozark, we need to talk," Bud said as he entered.

The assassin stopped his movements, fluidly sliding from a combative stance to a conversational one.

"What is it, Bud?"

"Bawb's back."

"I heard. Is there a problem?"

"He went to Zephin."

"Oh? How unexpected."

"Stowed away on a Tslavar ship."

Hozark's brow arched slightly, but his demeanor remained otherwise neutral. "An unusual choice of transport, but I am sure he had his reasons."

"He went looking for Lalaynia. He heard the Tslavars talking about her and stowed away. He even snuck into the magistrate's compound, if you can believe it."

"Hmm. Impressive, especially at his age."

"You're not mad?"

"Mad? I am perhaps a little concerned, but not mad, no. He has returned to us unharmed and with valuable intelligence. His training has paid off in a difficult situation. Now, however, I will need to assign a spy to verify his claim, and that will take time. I know you are worried about her, but rest assured, I will seek answers and let you know as soon as I hear anything of Lalaynia's whereabouts."

"He also said he saw Nixxa there."

A distasteful look creased Hozark's lips. "Ah, Nixxa."

"Yeah. So, what now?"

"Now? Now we let the boy continue as normal. He still has much training to do. In fact, it is fortuitous he returned when he did. There is a rather difficult lesson for the Vessels that begins in just a few days, and he will need the rest."

CHAPTER FORTY

Bawb discovered that he was not alone in his being abandoned on another planet. While most of the other Vessels were taken to train in flying skills, a few of the more advanced in their cohort had received roughly similar experiences to his. Minus the Tslavars and being forcibly thrown out a window, of course.

Usalla and Elzina had been selected, naturally, as they were both exceptionally skilled in most areas they had trained in. But Finnia had also been chosen, though for a slightly different group of qualifications and skill sets. In her case, she had been dropped on a world where her spy skills would serve her best, and she'd certainly had them put to the test.

Bawb, however, had experienced the most difficult of trials, requiring far more of him than the others. Elzina shrugged it off as his simply being less adept than she was, thus taking literal weeks longer, but Usalla knew it to be otherwise. Bawb had somehow gotten on the Masters' radar, and they pushed him harder than most. To their satisfaction, he performed admirably more often than not.

"Are you ready for this?" she asked her friend as they packed up the limited gear for their next task.

They were only allowed the clothes on their backs, their konus, a single blade, and one other item of their choosing. Beyond that they would have to improvise, barter, or steal as needed.

"We have all prepared for years," Bawb replied, tucking a metal cup into his small pack.

"Yes, but this is different. This time we are not only retrieving an item. We are to kill."

He shrugged casually, but truth be told, the task had been weighing on him since the moment they had been told what was in store for them. This was it. This was their moment to truly level up. To do what they all would eventually. They were going to kill someone.

His name was Ballazar, a go-between who had been contracted anonymously by the Ghalian to deliver a rather valuable relic they had been storing for some time. It was a channeling staff, allowing the wielder to condense and focus one spell at a time for greater effect. While it was a prized possession, the Ghalian possessed far stronger items, and the opportunity to trade it for vital information had come their way.

Only Ballazar had never made the handoff.

The Vessels were to find him on his home planet of Croxxor, a desert world, harsh, hot, and mostly barren. Life outside the cities there was rough, but that very nature of the planet also provided the residents a bit of freedom from outside interlopers. It was unpleasant, but they were left alone.

Mostly, anyway.

Very soon a group of Ghalian students would descend on the planet to compete for their prize. Reclaiming the channeling staff and eliminating the traitor. Bawb almost felt bad for Ballazar, in a way. The fool clearly had no idea who he was double-crossing. Finding out would be the last thing he learned.

The entire group of students loaded onto a single ship and

settled in for the flight. This was a difficult task and a harsh world. Unlike a more welcoming planet, where they might easily survive in the wild, their teachers would be waiting as a sort of safety net, ready to retrieve them at various rendezvous points once the mission was completed. From what they had been told, it would be quite an ordeal.

"You are to be deposited on the surface in the general area Ballazar was last seen," Teacher Warfin told them. "From there you will be on your own to devise the best manner to carry out your task."

"Do we know where he is?" Dillar asked.

"*We* do. *You* do not. You must all learn to not rely on Ghalian spies for your intelligence. Use what you have been taught and find the man. Collect what was stolen from us and complete your task. Once it has been retrieved by any member of your cohort and the man dealt with, your konuses will receive a notification to return to the nearest rendezvous point. Any other questions?"

The group remained silent.

"Very well. Prepare yourselves. This will not be easy."

The ship made several jumps until it finally arrived at Croxxor. Looking at it from space as they approached, it seemed even more inhospitable than they had been told.

The binary suns were orange and red, the two of them burning hot in the sky, far closer to the planet than they were used to back home. The heat would be a real challenge from the moment they set foot on the surface. And that surface was largely desert, by the look of it. Reddish sand and rocks as far as the eye could see. There were strange plants sparsely dotting the landscape, but nothing remotely resembling a forest, or even an oasis.

Water would be an incredibly valuable commodity here. Something to be preserved and not wasted no matter what. With pale skin, this was going to be tough for the Ghalian. Bawb realized he would need to cover up, naturally, but would also need to shift his appearance in a way that disguised his true nature. No way would a Wampeh willingly choose to reside on this world.

The ship dropped to the surface into an expanse of nothing, the waves of heat radiating off the ground in all directions but with no sign of civilization. They had seen several outposts, or perhaps townships, during their descent, but there was no telling which one might lead to their target. There were options in all directions. They would just have to choose and use their infiltration and info-gathering skills to the best of their ability.

Warfin opened the hatch, a blast of hot air filling the cabin. "Everyone out. You start now. Your konuses will guide you to the nearest retrieval point when the task is completed. Remember your training, and good luck."

The Vessels filed out of the ship, turning as a group to watch it rise then vanish in the sky, the sun already beating down on them with an intensity they were not accustomed to.

Bawb spun around, taking in the landscape. A few scrub plants clung to life, but that was all. Other than that it was sand as far as the eye could see.

The other students were doing roughly the same thing, getting their bearings and planning their course. Would they follow the suns or wait for stars? Or would they simply start walking and go from there? Each had their own plan, and a few of them overlapped.

Bawb calculated the rough distance to the towns they had flown over, figuring the time required to reach them given the harsh reality on the ground now that they had landed. Several of the others had already started trekking, heading out following the course of the suns. Bawb, however, waited. Something seemed off.

He cast an unusual spell, detecting the pull of the planet's core in relation to the twin suns' arc across the sky.

"Ah, that is interesting," he noted, shifting his course away from what seemed a logical choice to one that appeared to head into the most hostile expanse around them. But he had a reason.

It seemed the planet's core reacted one way while the suns did something else. As a result, the planet's poles were causing something of a misdirect. Most would simply follow the suns, or rely on navigational spells, but this world's very nature made those usual tools unreliable.

Level up: Navigation

Bawb took the notification in stride, saying nothing. He was too busy assessing his unlikely companion.

Elzina, it seemed, had selected the same course.

"You figured out the irregularity with the poles, I see," she said.

"As did you," he replied, trudging along calmly.

"No sense in running," she replied, recognizing this was a marathon and not a sprint. "Just know, you will lose."

"We will see about that," he replied, confident in his abilities but wondering what would happen once they actually found civilization.

They walked for nearly an hour before coming to the same conclusion. If they kept this up, they would exhaust themselves long before reaching a town. Bawb and Elzina shifted course to a small cluster of desert shrubs to use as a temporary sun shelter. They would walk again when the suns set.

Bawb dropped his small pack and pulled out the one elective item he had packed.

"A cup? You brought a cup?" Elzina mocked, drawing the short sword that she had chosen as her one additional item. "Not much use out here."

"It will serve me well."

"Taverns have cups, you fool. Once we reach town there will be cups-a-plenty."

Bawb just shrugged and began pulling leaves and small branches from the shrubs, crushing them as he did. He walked a little distance into the desert and drew his knife, digging a shallow hole in which he placed the plant matter. He paused a moment then relieved himself in the hole as well, draining his bladder fully before placing the cup atop the damp pile.

He traced a circle around the hole then carefully cast a very small but very secure sealing spell. No air got in, and none would get out. He picked up a small rock and gently placed it in the middle of the magical barrier, the weight of it causing the spell to dip slightly, creating a low point. Then he stepped back to watch.

It didn't take long. The twin suns' heat quickly began to cause the evaporation of the urine and sap from the leaves, the moisture collecting on the spell above, condensing into droplets that began to slowly run downhill to the low point, dripping into the cup one drop at a time.

It would take hours, and it would not be a lot of water, but they had nothing else to do, and there was no naturally occurring water source anywhere nearby. And with hours to go before night fell and they could start moving again, he was hopeful this little survival trick would provide him at least a few mouthfuls of water.

Bawb had practiced the technique in safer environments, but now was the time to put the skill to the test in a real-world situation. He walked back to the shrubs and settled down in the shade near Elzina to rest and wait for nightfall. He would find out soon enough if bringing a cup had been the wise choice. If his plan had worked, then clearly it had. If not? He would carry on as best he could. There was little else he could do.

CHAPTER FORTY-ONE

Even staying completely still in the meager shade, it was hot. *Miserably* hot.

Bawb and Elzina both kept to themselves, napping as they waited for night to come—not that they would have chatted much anyway. Dusk was a long time coming, however, the days on this world being long, extended by the binary suns' paths across the sky in this hemisphere.

Finally the heat began to dissipate, and the sky grew darker. The rocks and ground still radiated the stored heat from the day and likely would for some time, but at least there was no longer the feeling of a blazing fist beating down on them from above.

The two Vessels slowly crawled from their cover, standing tall and reveling in the slight breeze cooling the sweat on their bodies. Even lying still they had lost a fair amount of fluid in this heat. Getting to a town, *any* town, was imperative.

They nodded to each other, a rare moment of solidarity in their shared suffering, then parted ways. Elzina took off at a fast walk, draining her water skin as she moved, hoping to get ahead of her nearest competitor. Bawb, on the other hand, took his time, standing still as he contemplated his next steps. There was no rush. They would have all night and quite possibly another full day before civilization was reached by his estimation.

He took a tiny sip from his water skin to wash the taste of sand and dust from his mouth, then sealed it up tight. Water was too precious to waste, especially his fresh supply. Hopefully his solar still trick had done its job as well as he believed it would. If not, it would be a miserable trek indeed.

He tapped the invisible barrier over the hole he had dug, sending the remaining droplets of condensation trickling into the cup below. Bawb then removed the rock in the center and tossed it aside before releasing the spell. A whiff of pungent air rose to his nose, the smell of evaporated urine and slow-cooking desert shrubs. But that wasn't what mattered. What did was sitting in the middle of the hole.

Bawb carefully lifted his little metal cup, now brimming with warm but clean water. He took a sip. While he would have preferred cool liquid, this bonus water on top of what was in the water skin each Vessel had been given was incredibly refreshing. More than that, it would give him an advantage the others lacked. It wasn't a huge amount of water, but with all of them exerting themselves similarly in the hot environment, the extra hydration meant he could push on a little harder before dehydration would set in.

Bawb drank deep, swallowing several mouthfuls then stopping, sealing the cup with a spell and starting his trek. It was crucial to remain hydrated *before* he started to feel the thirst take hold. By then it would be too late. But with his liquid prize he could afford to indulge a bit before the true rationing began.

He pulled out his lone serving of food, the same amount each of them carried, and began eating as he walked. Getting it in his system while he had enough water to help wash it down made the most sense. Energy-wise he could afford to go weeks without a meal if he had to, but few possessed the self-control to do so.

The teachers had, of course, given them something dense in nutrients but also difficult to swallow. Dry and likely to stick in one's throat. A cruel, but calculated and quite intentional, little trick to force the students to properly assess their resources and strategize accordingly.

Bawb looked ahead in the darkening light. Elzina was making good time toward a large rocky outcropping jutting from the soil like a jagged scale from a beast's back. She took the right side. Bawb decided to take the left. While their direction was the same, at least they would not be forced to travel with one another. And who knew? Perhaps one path was easier than the other. There was no way to tell.

He glanced back at the line of his footprints leading from the other direction and made sure his course was still true. It seemed so, but nevertheless, he paused a bit longer to orient himself with the rising stars just now becoming visible as true night approached. Between the two guide points he determined his path. At least, as close as he could, given his resources.

Now it was time to walk.

This planet had no moons, and as such there was little illumination to be had. The stars and other planets in the system reflected some light, but it was paltry and not terribly helpful. Still, he could see the jutting rocks ahead of him clear enough as his eyes grew accustomed to the dark.

He avoided casting his night-vision spell, conserving his magic for whatever challenges might lie ahead of him. The trek was undoubtedly only the first of what would be many difficulties for him to overcome.

Bawb walked for nearly an hour before finally drawing close to the rocks jutting up from the ground. The formation turned out to be much larger than he had thought at first glance, the combined distance and earlier heat waves of the day having played tricks with his eyes. He found himself actually looking forward to the rocks, as the sand had become far looser as he progressed. It was exhausting, and the added effort was starting to take its toll, his muscles burning through vital energy much faster than had he been on even ground.

He almost didn't feel the strange vibrations running through his legs, assuming them to be cramps at first, but his gut told him something was wrong, a twinge of adrenaline leaking into his bloodstream, his primal survival instinct screaming at him from deep within. Something was out there, and it was getting closer.

He cast his night-vision spell at once, scanning the sand around him. Now was not the time to conserve magic. He looked everywhere but could see nothing. No beasts approaching, no threat visible on the horizon. But it was there. He sensed it.

Bawb drew his dagger and quickened his pace toward the rocks. Solid footing would be much preferred to face whatever was coming. The sand at his feet abruptly sank, his foot sinking in up to the ankle. He pulled hard, yanking it free just as a barbed tentacle shot out of the ground, wrapping around it, drawing blood as it latched on.

Bawb did not hesitate, dropping low, his blade slicing hard and fast. The tentacle spurted blood where it was severed, his leg released. The ground surged and vibrated as whatever it belonged to reacted to the unexpected pain.

Bawb turned and ran. Ran as fast as he could in the soft sand, every step a test of his endurance and strength. "*Ignius omalla grunnto*," he cast, drawing magic from his konus as he ran. The spell locked onto his very clear intent and surrounded his feet with cushioning magic, softening his footfall while also keeping him from bogging down in the sand in a manner akin to wearing snowshoes. Not exactly the original purpose of the spell, but it seemed to do the trick.

He ran faster, sinking in less, his steps easier as a result.

Level up—

"I know!"

Then run faster!

Bawb didn't need to be told twice. Nor once, for that matter. His legs churned furiously as he raced toward the rocks, the subterranean beast now recovered from its original shock and pursuing him at speed. Bawb glanced back, the faint rippling of the ground where whatever manner of creature coming for him was gaining quickly.

He pushed himself harder, using every bit of strength he possessed in an all-out sprint for the rocks. If he didn't make it, that meant he would certainly be dead, and there would be no use for whatever energy he conserved.

The beast grew closer, nearly upon his racing heels. Bawb leapt into the air as a tentacle lashed out, just missing his leg. He landed on a rock, his feet finding solid purchase. The ground was dotted with them, he realized. He wasn't at the main body of the outcropping, but this change in terrain just might protect him enough to get there.

As if it heard his thoughts, the enormous beast burst from the sand, slithering toward him at speed like an undulating serpent at least four meters long. A half dozen barbed tentacles surrounded its gaping mouth in addition to the spikes jutting from its body to help propel it underground.

It lacked eyes from what Bawb could tell in the dark, likely sensing its prey by vibrations from its movement. But now that Bawb was among the scattered rocks, it lacked the ability to surge up from below, and whatever vibrations it felt would only be sensed by a fraction of its feeler organs.

Bawb grabbed a fist-sized rock and lobbed it to the side. The impact made the creature turn and hesitate, but it did not commit to the decoy. Instead, it fell silent, holding still much as he would do in its situation, sensing the area around it as best it could, hoping to find its next meal.

Bawb looked over his shoulder. The main body of rocks was still too far. He was going to have to deal with this threat, and sooner than later. There was only one present for now, but there was no telling if they traveled in packs.

The teen crouched and gathered more projectiles then started to run. The creature surged after him, moving far faster on the surface than he would have expected. He steered right toward a boulder, throwing two more rocks just off his course behind him. It wasn't much, but the slight variance it caused the beast to take in its pursuit gave him the opening he needed.

He jumped as high as he could, his feet finding purchase on the rock. Bawb scrambled up as the animal slammed into the stone below him, its tentacles waving wildly, searching for its prey. Rather than flee, Bawb pushed off hard, flipping backward and coming down atop the beast's back, his feet narrowly missing the jutting spikes.

Bawb drove his dagger into the spot atop what he assumed was its head, slicing a large opening with its razor-sharp blade. But that wouldn't be enough to stop something this size. He needed a killing blow, and there was no time to learn this thing's physiology. He would have to make a guess.

Without hesitation he shifted his grip on the dagger, the tip pointing up now, and drove his blade downward into the wound with a tight fist as if attempting to punch all the way to the ground below. The blade parted the thing's flesh with ease, his arm driving down until he had pushed it all the way to his shoulder.

He just hoped it was far enough to hit something vital.

The tentacles lashed back at him in a quivering barrage,

then abruptly fell silent. Bawb lay still atop the beast, feeling its life ebb away from its fatal wound. He pulled his blood-soaked arm free, ready to fight, but the creature moved no more.

Bawb hopped down to get a better look at the thing. It was specialized for survival on this world, living underground while seeking prey from below and above equally. Whatever moisture there was out here, it was subterranean, and the animal had evolved to utilize it.

Bawb looked around at their battle site. A few dry shrubs sprouted up from the rocks. With the right magic, that should be enough for a small fire, allowing him to conserve most of his remaining magic.

He began working the hide with his dagger, cutting through the tougher outer layers to the tender flesh within. Bawb then set to work slicing as much meat as he could reasonably carry, laying the strips out before piling broken shrubs together and starting a fire on the rocks.

While the meat cooked, he dug deeper until he found an organ of some sort. Perhaps a stomach, he wasn't sure. Whatever it was, it was tough and strong. He cut it free, emptying it of the sludge inside, then tied one end shut and began filling it with the thing's blood. Once it was full, he tied off the other end tight. It was a bladder, but full of blood rather than water. But it contained valuable moisture, and if he had to make another solar still, having that large a quantity of fluid at his disposal would make the task magnitudes easier.

Something else caught his attention. A cluster of what looked like water-filled pouches. He sliced one free and cut it open. He dipped his finger and sniffed. As it seemed, it actually *was* water. A bit gamey smelling, but this was how the creature survived. It stored water in its body. Another boon for him, it seemed. He cut them free and ensured they were sealed then put them aside, an extra source of water to help wash down his unexpected windfall.

Bawb then wiped his hands in the sand, rubbing the blood from his fingers, and sat to eat a far larger meal than he had anticipated, the creature's flesh replacing the vital energy he had expended fighting it off. And more than that, he now had ample food for days.

He had lost over an hour to the whole ordeal, but there was nothing to be done for that. He just finished eating, packed up his supply of both cooked and raw meat in separate wraps made of the beast's tough hide, and started walking once more, invigorated and alive and more than ready for whatever might come next.

CHAPTER FORTY-TWO

Daybreak.

Bawb had made good time in the dark hours, covering a lot of ground now that he had the benefit of a belly full of nutritious food and ample water to wash it down. His injuries from the encounter with the creature were relatively minor, and the dust and sand of his walk had obliterated traces of his blood many hours ago.

He continued to pull magic from his konus, softening his footsteps as he walked, doing all he could to ensure he would not have another run-in with a subterranean beast. It was a drain he would have preferred to avoid, but not being eaten was far more important than conserving his magic. He also carried a few rocks, ready to throw them to distract any such attacker.

Fortunately, he felt no vibrations in the sand. Apparently, they did not travel in packs, nor were they common in these parts, and that was a great relief.

He felt the increase in temperature well before the twin suns began to rise, shifting his course toward a cluster of rocks rather than the sparse shrubs in the area in response. There was still time to dig in for a proper shelter from the heat before sunrise, and he would make the most of it.

Bawb laid out a great many long strips of raw meat atop a nearby rock that was relatively flat, lining them up to dry into a substantial amount of jerky in the day's heat while he slept. It wasn't a perfect system, but it would keep the food fresh enough for him to utilize for weeks with rationing if needed. Hopefully, his trek would not take that long.

That task accomplished, he set to work digging a hole in which to set up his solar still, pouring the stored blood into the indentation along with bits of plant matter he collected nearby. Sealed up and waiting for the sun to start working its evaporative magic, Bawb then scooped out a large wall of sand and rock from beneath the one section that had a little overhang, building it up to provide added protection from the heat as the suns eventually transcribed their blistering arc across the sky.

That done, he crawled into the cool cocoon, cast a few small tripwire spells just in case, and closed his eyes, his tired and aching body thrilled for the rest. He wondered how the others might be faring on their paths but soon slipped into a sound sleep, recharging his internal battery for the upcoming night's trek.

He woke at dusk, the hot air wafting into his hiding spot but not overheating him as it had when he sought shade under only sparse shrubbery. He pushed himself out, the last rays of sunlight almost painful against his body despite the thick layer of dust and dirt caked on his skin. It was a good thing too. Without that natural sunblock, he would have been forced to use even more magic to keep himself from burning.

He checked on his jerky. It was dried and ready to be packed up, as he had hoped. And with the added fluid of the blood he had used, the solar still had produced so much water it had overflowed his cup. He unsealed the spell and took a long drink, the creature's water sacs as well as his survival trick providing him enough liquid to not be forced to ration it. At least, not yet.

As a result, he felt good. Really good, in fact. The meat apparently had an extremely high nutritional value, likely as the creature he had killed needed to store as much energy as possible between meals. And that was now coursing through his body. He was hot and dirty, but, otherwise, he was ready to go.

And go he did.

It was still light out, and he would feel the lingering effects of the suns for a little while, but he knew the others were out there on the same task, and among them, Elzina was on roughly the same course as he was. He would have to push himself. He knew she would be doing the same.

He moved faster as the suns set, covering a lot of ground now that the soil had turned from sandy to a firmer texture. He ceased casting the spells on his feet, saving that precious magic for later.

It was early in the evening when the lights of a small town came into view in the distance. It wasn't a city by any stretch, but he was happy for anything. Once he reached it, the real task would begin.

He increased his pace, slipping into an easy jog in the cooler air. A few hours later he reached his destination, and right around dinnertime from what his nose told him. Bawb made a beeline for what had to be the local tavern, a squat building with thick walls and what appeared to be a false roof, the entire second level serving not as livable space, but as a buffer for the tavern itself against the heat.

Stepping inside, the relatively cool air confirmed his theory. The walls still radiated stored heat outward from the day's solar barrage, but inside it was comfortable, and the patrons all seemed at ease as they enjoyed their evening repast. Bawb quickly checked his konus, scrolling through his levels. Disguise was better but not strong enough to do what he had originally planned given the magic he had expended.

He was going to have to do this a different way.

"Excuse me," he said, walking up to the bar in his own form, his only disguise the dirt covering his body.

"You look like you've had a day of it," the hairless, nearly black-skinned man behind the bar said, sizing him up with all four of his eyes. "You want a drink?" he asked, his six arms moving in different directions as he manned the bar.

"I've got no coin," Bawb replied.

One of the man's hands stopped pouring.

"No coin, no service," he said.

"What about barter?"

"You said you had no coin."

"And I don't. But I have a lot of jerky. Good stuff too. Surely, that's worth something."

"Lemme see what you've got."

Bawb withdrew the majority of his stash and placed it on the bar. No sense hoarding it. Not when he needed to stay in this tavern to pump the patrons for intel. His belly was full enough. Now it was time to take a gamble.

The barkeep picked up a piece and sniffed it, a curious look in his eyes.

"Go ahead and try it. That one's on me," Bawb offered. "It's fresh, and it's good."

The man took a bite, surprise clear in his eyes.

"This is Boolalong jerky."

"I know," the teen bluffed.

"How in the world did you get it? This stuff's incredibly hard to come by."

"I got lucky. I was traveling with a group of traders I met when we were attacked."

"You survived a Boolalong attack? You really *are* lucky."

"I guess so. But my so-called friends robbed me blind and left me for dead when it came at us. It killed three of them before the others scattered. Really, it was blind luck that one of them must have hit something vital in the fight. When I finally came to, it was just lying there."

"Do you remember where this was?" the man asked, clearly thinking about trying to harvest the rest of the creature if possible.

"I don't. I cut it up and made as much jerky as I could carry, then I found a shady spot and hid out until night. I've been at it for days."

"Lucky thing you had the Boolalong water sacs, or you'd have died out there."

"I know. And I'm so grateful to be in an actual town with an actual tavern. I need a drink like you would not believe."

The man stroked his chin with one of his hands. "I don't know. It's tough to come by, but I don't know how demand is this time of year." He dug under the counter and produced a small pile of coin. "This is the best I can do. And I'm taking a bath on this, if I'm being honest."

Bawb knew he was not.

"That much for everything?" he asked.

"Yeah. Like I said. Best I can do."

Bawb pointed to the bottles behind him. Bottles he knew were cheap rotgut with a very high alcohol content designed more for rapid inebriation than quality of flavor. "Throw in three of those and you've got yourself a deal."

"I don't know—"

Bawb reached for the jerky.

"Okay, okay. You drive a hard bargain. It's a deal," the barkeep said, retrieving the bottles. "I'm Logus, by the way."

"Uh, I'm Binsala," the boy replied.

"Pleasure doing business with ya," Logus said, tucking away his haul beneath the counter.

Judging by his actions, Bawb had just provided him with quite a rare item, and one he was undoubtedly going to mark up significantly as soon as Bawb was gone.

"Thanks," the teen replied, then took his bottles and slid into a seat at a long table crowded with all manner of races who had for whatever reason, chosen this world as their home. Taking a closer look at them, Bawb thought it was likely because they were nefarious sorts, but he kept that opinion to himself, putting on a big smile and offering drinks to those around him.

"You're pretty generous with your coin," one fellow noted, happily accepting the drink.

"I just survived not only a Boolalong attack, but days in the desert alone. It's worth celebrating."

Bawb quietly cast the spell Hozark had taught him, hoping it would work, then downed a shot as if it were nothing. He waited, expecting the painful burn in his throat and belly, but nothing happened. The alcohol had been transported elsewhere. Hopefully, outside the building, where it would evaporate quickly.

"Hey, my seat's wet. Who did that?" someone grumbled from across the tavern.

Bawb noted his error in silence and tried to adjust the spell, laughing like a drunken fool the whole time, making himself everyone's friend. Binsala, it seemed, was popular. That may have had something to do with the drinks he was giving away, but whatever it took to quickly acquire the goodwill of these people was worth it.

"So, what brings you here?" a rather large man wearing thick hides over his deep red skin asked. "We don't see many passersby 'round here."

His interest was particularly keen, and Bawb had clocked the weapons strapped to his body and the blood dried on his knuckles as soon as he'd sat down. The blood was clearly not his.

The teen just played up his cheerful inebriation even more, his body language as unthreatening and weak as he could manage.

"I was supposed to deliver a message, can you believe it? Me, Binsala, sent to a desert world I've never been to and told to track down this guy. And you know what happened? I got robbed, that's what happened. Robbed and damn near killed! I'm just lucky I found this place when I did."

Bawb punctuated his tale with another shot. This time he saw where it materialized. Across the tavern, on top of a table. Fortunately, the patrons there were already quite drunk and had spilled enough to not notice.

"Robbed, huh?" the man said. "But you're buying drinks."

"Well, yeah. I traded most of my food with Logus over there," he replied, waving to the bartender across the room. The six-armed man waved back with three of them, bolstering his story. "I think surviving a Boolalong is worth a bit of celebration."

The man's eyes surveyed the teen. He certainly did seem to have been through it, covered in dirt head to toe. And his leg showed signs of something damaging his pants and some dried blood if he wasn't mistaken. All told, it actually did look like the kid survived a Boolalong attack. Then he noticed a glint of gold at his wrist.

"Hey, but you still have a konus. You want to trade it?"

Bawb chided himself for not covering it better. "This old thing? Nah, it's pretty much worthless. Weak and ran out of power ages ago, but it was my mom's, so I always keep it on me. Sentimental value, you know. She died when I was younger, and this is all I have left of her. You still have your mom?"

"I do."

"Then tell her you love her, man. I wish I'd done it more when mine was still alive."

The man's menacing demeanor softened a bit. It was a gamble, but Bawb had pinpointed one of the few psychological trigger points that he had hoped would help avoid a fight. He could take him, no doubt, but that was not the point of this mission. He had to blend in. More than that, he still had to find his target.

Your lies are working, the konus said inside his head.

"Shut up and let me work," Bawb silently replied, his cheerful smile not faltering for an instant.

"My mother always said I should stay close to home and not take these jobs hopping to planets I didn't even know."

"And why are you here, again? To deliver a message?"

"Yup," he said, pouring them both another drink.

"Thanks," the man said, downing it in a gulp. "Who's the message for, anyway? Maybe I know them."

"A guy named Ballazar."

Heads turned and grumbles were heard. The man drinking with him spit on the ground in disgust. "Yeah, I know him. We all do. He a friend of yours?"

"A friend? I have no idea who the hell he is. I'm just a kid trying to earn a living. I was told to deliver him a message, and that's it. And I don't get paid until I do."

"You don't want to deal with the likes of him, believe me. Plus, it's a day's trek from here, and it's not a fun one by any stretch. Tell ya what. You give me the message, and I'll pass it along for you."

"Believe me, I wish I could. But if I don't deliver it personally my employers won't use me again, and I can't afford to lose this job. Not when my grandma's at the healer."

"Your grandma?"

"She took me in when my mom died. She's the only family I

have left."

The man looked at the other rough faces in the tavern. It seemed they all had the same thought. Namely, it was not worth it to rob this kid and take the coin for completing his task, especially because it would hurt his grandma. They may have been criminals, but that was something even the worst of them would not do. At least, not under the disapproving eyes of the others in the room.

"Well, I wish ya luck," the man said. "Just follow the far exit from town in a straight line. You'll get there in a day or so. Two if the sandstorms kick up."

"Thank you so much," Bawb replied, sliding the man a full bottle. "I want you to have this."

"Thanks, friend," he replied, a bit surprised, glancing around the room now that he had come into this alcoholic windfall.

"I think I've had way too much already. It's time I get a little food in me then get some sleep."

"You staying in town?"

"I'll sleep rough. There's a cozy spot near the marketplace at the other end of town I noticed. I'll be fine." He rose to his feet, unsteady and apparently quite drunk. "Thanks again. It was great talking with you."

Bawb headed out the door, staggering into the night, knowing full well that at least one of the thugs who had been watching him would almost certainly come to rob the drunken visitor in the middle of the night.

What they didn't know was he would be long gone by then.

He made his way a few streets over then shed his inebriated demeanor, picking up his pace and heading out of town. It was time to trek, and with a destination within reach, he was going to do it as fast as he could. If he pushed hard, he might even reach his target before sunrise.

Time would tell.

CHAPTER FORTY-THREE

Bawb ran through the night, his pace steady and unrelenting, rapidly putting distance between himself and the ruffians in the town he had departed. By the time they came looking for him he would be far from their reach, a lone dot on the horizon, swallowed up by the vastness of the expansive desert.

Still, he pushed himself to move faster, putting his stamina to the test and finding it more than adequate for the task. Years of hard training was paying off even more than he had thought it would. The teachers knew what they had been doing, honing the youths into the most durable, strongest versions of themselves they could become. And tonight it was serving him well.

Bawb had also become more proficient with the minor spell cast at his feet, allowing him better traction and ease of passage on the sandy ground. He was also using far less power than previously, and his konus had leveled him up for his newfound talent and fleetness of foot.

As for finding his way, he discovered another unusual use of a spell, opting to save his power as much as he could, using not a night-vision spell, which could drain his konus at a higher rate over a long period of time, but rather a spell typically used in daylight. A contrast spell.

It was most often used to gain clarity when searching for things in the distance, the added contrast allowing greater ability to sift out items from afar. But at night, with only starlight illuminating the way, he found that, while it did not let him see like he would in the day, it did add contrast to the obstacles in his path.

Was it a perfect system? Not by a long shot. But it was enough to let him run fast without fear of tripping over anything. At least, not anything large enough to cast a slight shadow or stand out against the coloration of the sand.

Unconventional use of a spell, the konus noted. *And rather effective. Level up. You're becoming better at thinking beyond normal constraints, Vessel.*

"Thank you, Konus. But if you do not mind, I am rather busy."

Busy running in a straight line.

"And casting, as you know."

And maintaining your focus even when I speak with you. Again, an improvement.

Bawb realized the konus had gradually been shifting its tack with him, taunting and giving him grief to no end, of course, but also behaving in a manner that seemed designed to test and strengthen his abilities, though the device would never admit as much.

"Your point is noted, as it is appreciated. However, I must conserve my mental energy as well as physical, so, again, if you do not mind."

Fine. Go on, then. Run, Vessel, run, the konus said, then thankfully fell silent.

Bawb increased his pace slightly, perhaps motivated in part by the desire to bolster his point to the inanimate device. It was ridiculous, of course, but whatever it took to get him to his destination was all that mattered.

On and on he ran, pushing hard until sunrise. As the twin orbs crested the horizon, he saw the small city ahead in the distance. He was close, but not close enough, he feared. A larger formation in the rocky and barren terrain caught his eye. He would have to wait for sunset there. To push on as the heat arrived would be foolish. Fortunately, he had plenty of water to wait out the day.

His skin was burning by the time he reached the shade of the rocks. It was a larger cluster than he had thought at first glance. Several piles of jutting stone protruded from the ground at sharp angles. He didn't bother setting up his solar still, not this close to the city. Instead, he simply tucked himself into the shade and settled in for a power nap.

His senses jerked him fully awake just as a boot kicked his leg. He was on his feet in an instant, dagger in hand and defensive spells on the tip of his tongue. A moment later he relaxed his stance.

"Elzina?"

She looked like absolute hell. Sunburned with cracked lips and clearly dehydrated skin, it seemed she had pushed on through the day in an ill-advised attempt to get here first. Despite their competing against one another, she was a fellow Ghalian, and that would always come first.

He handed her his water bladder, keeping his additional stash tucked safely in his pack. She downed it greedily, coughing at first as her parched throat spasmed from the sensation. She downed half of the contents before realizing what she was doing. She forced herself to stop, offering it back to him.

"Go ahead, you need it more than I do," he said. "But slowly or you will upset your stomach, and it would be a waste to vomit it all back up."

She nodded gratefully and sat beside him, letting the water absorb into her system before taking another drink. A few minutes later her head seemed to clear, her demeanor steadying to some semblance of her usual confident self.

"Thank you."

"Of course. Here," he said, handing her a piece of jerky. "Eat slowly. It is dehydrated and will pull water from your system to digest."

She accepted the offering and chewed with relish, a visible shift in her coloring rising almost as soon as the food hit her stomach.

"Again, thank you."

Bawb merely nodded.

"So, here we are," Elzina mused, staring out at the city in the distance. "Just you and me, it seems."

"So far as I know. I assume you received directions to this location in that little town back there?"

"I did. Nasty group of people, but I managed to beat it out of one of them when one of them got inappropriate with me."

"Deep-red skin?"

"So, you met the guy."

Bawb chuckled. "Always the hard way with you."

"Or the easy. It just depends how you look at it."

"Fair enough. I take it you inquired about me as well."

"Of course."

"And heard I had already been there."

"You had a head start, but I am strong. I closed the gap."

He looked at her with an almost pitying gaze. She had indeed caught up to him, but by running well into the daylight and jeopardizing her own life in the process. A little longer and she might very well have succumbed to the heat and exertion. Bawb, however, wisely kept his mouth shut.

Elzina sized him up now that her head was clear. He seemed

in good shape. Better than her no doubt. He also seemed well rested. Reluctantly, she had to admit to herself that he was more ready for what came next than she was.

"Bawb?"

"Yes?"

"I propose a temporary truce."

"Oh?"

"Yes. It is still some distance to the city, and we both need the rest. So, let us agree to wait until the suns begin to set before resuming our quest."

"And then?"

"And then? Then, may the best Ghalian win, of course," she said, that familiar overconfident twinkle back in her eye.

It gave Bawb an idea.

"Very well. Until sunset," he agreed, then settled back down for a nap.

Elzina did the same, quickly slipping into a much-needed slumber.

The two of them ran silently together toward the city as the suns disappeared below the horizon. There was no sense in getting into a footrace. They both had to figure out where Ballazar was located once they got there, as well as devise a means to reach him and their prize. Until then, the truce, while technically over, was loosely upheld.

Once they reached the city limits, however, all bets were off. Without a word Elzina shifted course, sprinting into the city before ducking into a side street to make her approach.

"She must have received information about the whereabouts of his residence," Bawb mused, following at a distance.

Gee, ya think? the konus said with a laugh. *Get after her.*

"No. I will confirm on my own."

Even though she gets a head start?

"I have taken that into account," he replied with a knowing grin.

Bawb quietly inquired of the barkeep at one of the local dens of ill repute if he could please direct him to Ballazar's place, telling the man to keep the change. The coin he had acquired at his previous stop was far more than enough for the drink he ordered.

The address confirmed, he thanked the man, downed his beverage in a single go, then headed out. As he did, he noted the small puddle of liquid rapidly evaporating outside the tavern.

Level up, the konus informed him. *And about time. You've been practicing that spell for ages.*

"Some skills take longer than others."

Bawb moved fast but with an air of nonchalance as he made his way to Ballazar's place, his eyes scanning the area for any sign of his competition. Regular people would not notice her, but to his trained eye, the girl was relatively easy to find. She had put on a gray shawl and was making her way toward what appeared to be a side entrance to the man's building. He felt her probing spells even from down the street.

"Foolish," he muttered, knowing her overeager casting would almost certainly trigger an alarm.

Sure enough, a trio of guards rushed out of the doorway, weapons drawn. Elzina instinctively drew her short sword, her one additional item allowed, packed especially for this sort of thing, and engaged. Bawb watched, shaking his head. Had she just been stealthy, relying on subterfuge rather than aggression, things would have been quite different. Instead, she was overzealous and overconfident.

But then, Bawb had been counting on it.

He purchased clean clothes and paid for ten minutes in a public shower, then stepped back onto the street a new person.

Bawb called up the spell he had been preparing to use since his arrival on this world, gauging the magic in his konus as he did. It would not last long. He had expended far more than he had intended to just getting here. But as they said, it was what it was and there was no way around that. It was do-or-die time, knowing full well the last bit could be literal if he failed.

Quietly, he spoke the words, his intent locked in and clear. The spell took effect at once, altering his appearance not to a different race, but making him appear far younger than he was. A harmless youth, the sort often sent on menial tasks around cities like this.

He hurried to a food vendor and purchased an assortment of comestibles as well as a bottle of good liquor, then headed straight for Ballazar's building. And unlike Elzina, he went right to the front door and kicked it several times, his arms full.

"What do you want, boy? Who sent you?" a stocky man said from inside the doorway as it swung open.

"I'm supposed to deliver this to Master Ballazar."

"No deliveries are scheduled today," the man replied, starting to close the door.

Bawb stuck his foot out, stopping him, talking fast before he wound up beaten to a pulp. "Logus said I had to deliver this personally. Some sort of peace offering, or something."

The man hesitated. He knew Logus. Everyone did. He ran the best tavern in the region outside of the one just down the road. And he and Ballazar had a longstanding quarrel that had resulted in more than one conflict he and the other guards had been drawn into. Getting in the way of this delivery would surely anger his employer more than letting the kid in. And he was tiny and not a threat. The food, however, was another thing altogether.

"Hang on a sec," he said, pulling power from his konus and casting a poison-sensing spell. The man was good with the device, a skilled magic user, and Bawb knew what it was as soon as he heard the first syllable, but he played it cool, not reacting in the slightest. The food was clean. He had made sure of it.

"Okay, come on. I'll take you to him," the man said, letting the youth inside.

Bawb stepped through the door and steeled himself as it shut behind him. Now the risky part began.

He cast his spell in a flash, a powerful stun spell that dropped the guard in an instant. Had he been expecting it, he could have defended against it with ease, and with his hands full, Bawb would have had a hard time transitioning into a traditional fight. Fortunately, that was not the case, and the man hit the ground hard.

Bawb quickly set down the tray of food and hauled the slumbering victim out of the corridor. He had to move fast. There wasn't enough time to properly hide the sleeping body. Not for long, anyway. And with the expenditure of magic, the remaining time on his disguise had grown shorter by a lot.

Ballazar's study was easy to find, and fortunately, the man seemed to only have a limited guard staff, most of whom were pursuing Elzina after her ill-advised attempt. Bawb was alone with him, at least for the moment. He stepped into the room, his eyes falling upon the gray-skinned man with twin horned ridges running the length of his head.

"Master Ballazar? I have a delivery for you," he said in the most timid voice he could manage.

"Who are you? Where's Gallutz?"

"He told me to deposit this and leave. Where should I put it?"

"What is it you've got there?"

"An offering from Master Logus, I was told."

Ballazar cocked his head slightly. "Oh? Really? Bring it here."

Bawb did as he was told, his eyes casually scanning the room for the missing channeling staff. It was nowhere to be seen.

He placed the food on the man's long desk and moved to step back. Ballazar grabbed his wrist hard, leaping to his feet, pulling the boy closer.

"No way Logus would ever admit he was wrong. Who really sent you?"

Ballazar reached for the cudgel resting on his desk. Bawb realized he had no choice.

He yanked his hand free, leveraging against the weak point of the man's grip as he'd trained so often that it was simple muscle memory by now. Ballazar seemed surprised, but not scared. The boy was so young, why would he be? But he was sure as hell going to get an answer from him.

"Come here, you!" he growled, lunging for him.

Bawb dodged him, landing a series of rapid elbows and kicks to his opponent's nerve clusters, dropping him to his knees as his legs suddenly failed him. The boy moved in a flash, jumping behind the larger man, his blade drawn and pressed firmly to Ballazar's neck.

Ballazar, wisely, held very still.

"You're quick for a kid."

"Thank you."

"Why are you *really* here?"

"You were tasked with delivering an item. A channeling staff. You failed in your task. I am here to retrieve it."

"That? Well, it seems you're out of luck."

"How so?"

"I sold it, that's how so," he replied with a tiny shrug. "You've come all this way for nothing, I'm afraid."

Bawb's mind raced. This was not how it was supposed to go. "You had a contract for delivery."

"Yeah? Well, someone paid better."

"Better?"

"You heard me."

Bawb felt his anger begin to slip past his calm façade. For once, he decided to let it.

"Better, you say?" he repeated, moving in front of the man, staring him in the eye as his disguise faded away and his fangs slid into place. "Better than the Wampeh Ghalian?"

Ballazar paled, a patch of dampness appearing in the crotch of his trousers as he realized his mistake. Whom he had unintentionally double-crossed.

"I didn't know."

"That does not forgive your actions."

"I know where it is. I sold it to Voralius."

Bawb stared at him hard and cold, his unsettling gaze unblinking, just as he'd been taught. "Where is this Voralius?"

"He's on Boxxna. He lives in the capital. I can tell you how to get into his compound."

Bawb hesitated. This wasn't the plan, but perhaps he could still salvage the recovery. A flicker of movement at the doorway caught his eye. Elzina peered around the threshold just as Ballazar drew a blade hidden beneath his tunic. Bawb sensed the movement and reacted, avoiding the weapon and parrying it aside. Ballazar lunged again, throwing everything he had behind the attack. Bawb sidestepped and spun in a flash. His dagger hit hard and slit the man's throat so hard and fast it nearly took his head off.

He released the body, letting it fall to the ground. His first real kill.

Level up, Vessel. Well done.

Bawb felt almost disappointed. It had been so easy. Too easy.

"Where is it?" Elzina asked, looking for the staff.

"He sold it," Bawb replied, staring at the fallen body and the blood on his hands.

"And you believe him?"

"I do," he said quietly.

"Well, shit. I guess the mission is not over after all," she grumbled. "Come on, we need to get out of here. I ditched the guards, but they'll be back soon, and we do not want to be here when they do."

Bawb nodded once, pushing his emotions down safely, then followed her out of the building and out of the city, his mind racing faster than his feet as he absorbed all that had just happened.

CHAPTER FORTY-FOUR

Elzina's competitive streak was put aside for the time being as she and Bawb ran through the desert on the long trek to the rendezvous point closest to their location. The other Vessels would be doing the same, their konuses letting them know the task had been completed by another, just as Elzina's had done.

Fortunately, their teachers were well aware of just how dangerous simply existing on this planet could be, and as such, they had established multiple locations from which they would retrieve the students. They would face incredible hardships on the way to complete their task, but once it was done, a relatively quick extraction made the most sense.

Even so, it was nearly a full day's trek to the empty spot in the middle of nowhere that the duo's konuses were directing them to. Visitors and strangers were afforded a great deal of scrutiny around these parts, and seeing as Ballazar had just been slain in his own home, the less new faces were shown in the area, the better. Especially once the alarm had been raised.

Bawb was generous with his supplies, freely sharing both his food and water with his companion as they moved on through the night. There was no sense in rationing, at least not to an extreme. What he held in reserve was simply enough to hold them over should something go wrong and they be forced to spend an additional day out in the wild.

They slept during the day when sunrise intruded on their journey, then they rose with the dark, continuing at a steady pace into the vast nothing of the desert. They made good time, the silent comfort of a familiar companion helping each of them maintain their stride.

"This is it," Bawb said when they reached an empty expanse of dirt and rock that looked just like every other bit they had seen over the past days.

Elzina checked her konus for confirmation. "It seems we are either early or late."

"Whatever the case, they will pass by here shortly."

"Unless the teachers are employing a shimmer ship without telling us."

Bawb took a swig of water and handed her the remainder. "I doubt it. There is no sense bringing extra vessels all the way out here. Not for a training mission such as this. Likely, they are simply picking up the others and will arrive here soon enough."

"Let us hope they do so before the sun rises," she said, scanning the still-dark horizon. "There is little in the way of shelter here."

It was an unusual feeling, having a normal conversation with his nemesis. Elzina had been on his ass for so many years, always badgering him and subtly undermining him at every turn in her quest to be number one, that Bawb almost didn't know how to talk to her like just another classmate. Now that the competitive energy she pretty much always radiated was gone, at least for the time being, he found he was actually enjoying their time together.

They waited there for hours, discussing their disparate paths taken to their ultimate goal. Elzina had pushed herself hard, he had to admit, and if not for his both fortunate, and unfortunate, encounter with the Boolalong, he might not have managed to come out ahead. But luck favored him on this occasion, and he was not about to look that gift Boolalong in the mouth. At least, not until he had slayed it and stripped it of its meat and water sacs.

Just before sunrise the transport craft approached, flying low across the desert floor, staying well out of sight of any who were not right below it. As there were no real obstacles or threats here, the flight was safe enough, and a generally safe tactic they had been taught since their first flying lessons.

The ship silently settled into a low hover, its hatch sliding open and the spell sealing the opening retracting. Bawb and Elzina stepped aboard, the cool, fresh air of the interior feeling like a welcome hug from an old friend after their time in the desert.

"Welcome back, Vessels," Teacher Warfin said, handing them each a flask of cool water. Surprisingly, the pair did not down them immediately. In fact, they looked quite fresh given their ordeal. Ever so slightly, he nodded his approval, then gestured for them to go take a seat with the others.

All of their cohort had already been retrieved, it seemed, and by the look of them, they had all had quite a hard time of it. Some were nursing injuries, bloodied and bruised. Others were sunburned and peeling. And then there were the dehydrated ones with the faraway stares, their lips cracked and their skin loose from the loss of fluids.

Bawb and Elzina shared a look. It was clear why they had been picked up last. The others needed retrieval far more urgently than they had, and the teachers seemed to always keep track of their whereabouts. That brought up one question, though. The question of how much of their trials the Ghalian teachers and spies had actually observed.

"Where is the staff?" Warfin asked the pair, sizing them up and finding them in good shape but lacking the object of their mission.

"It was sold," Bawb informed him.

"Sold?"

"Voralius is the name of the one who acquired it. Apparently, he is located on Boxxna in the capital city."

Warfin stroked his chin as he pondered this news. "How certain of this are you?"

"I have no reason to doubt Ballazar's words."

"Hm. An unexpected development. This Voralius must have employed a fair amount of power to have made the transfer off world without our spies being aware."

Bawb's mind turned to the problem. To what might come next. "So what do we do now? The mission is technically not complete."

Warfin sighed. "Now? Now we go after it." He strode to the command chamber and leaned in the door to instruct the pilot of their new destination.

The ship lurched into the air, now heading to Boxxna rather than home. The most exhausted of their cohort had some trouble keeping their displeasure to themselves, but somehow, they managed to keep their groans internal rather than aloud.

"You did well, Bawb. Ballazar is dead, and though the channeling staff was not recovered, you did acquire its location."

"He hesitated," Elzina said.

Bawb glanced at her, but only a tiny bit surprised she had slipped back into her old ways as soon as they were safely retrieved, and especially as a new task, and therefore a new opportunity for advancement, was before them.

Warfin raised a brow at Bawb. "Did you, Vessel Bawb?"

"Yes, I did," he replied.

"A Ghalian does not hesitate," the teacher said, perhaps a bit concerned about the boy's resolve. He knew his history and reluctance to kill as a youth. Perhaps it had returned. Or perhaps it was something else. "Were you afraid?"

"No."

"I saw it," Elzina interjected. "He froze."

"I was not afraid, and I did not freeze. I sensed he was going to attack me long before he did. I just wished to finally test my worth against an opponent in real combat."

"Foolish," Warfin growled.

"I apologize, Teacher."

Warfin sighed. "Do not apologize. Your instincts were good, and you performed admirably. And while it would be ill-advised to try such a thing against a truly skilled opponent, Ballazar was the sort even a Vessel is well-equipped to deal with. And you showed a desire to push yourself. To increase your skills, even if not in the wisest of manner. You have drive, Bawb. And that could take you far one day. Now, go rest. The flight to Boxxna is a short one, and you will have work to do once we arrive."

CHAPTER FORTY-FIVE

Bawb felt quite good as they flew to Boxxna. The name had been rattling around in his head for some time, familiar, though he had never been there. Only now that he was resting comfortably among his peers and able to let his guard down did his mind wander to where he had heard it before.

It had been mentioned in the compound on Zephin. The one where Lalaynia was being held.

Coincidence? He wasn't so sure about that. In his life, it seemed that things were quite often anything but.

Whatever the case, there was nothing he could do but regain his energy in preparation for the next leg of their journey. The one where they would all be sent out on another task. One that had not been planned.

Warfin gave a little speech to the assembled Vessels, making it quite clear that while they were tired, this was how their lives would often be. Plans changed on the fly, and a Ghalian would have to adjust and adapt accordingly. And that meant they would sometimes remain on task for days, or even weeks, longer than anticipated, and often without the benefit of rest.

At least on this occasion they had time to recover their strength a bit as they flew.

Tired as the others were, there was no chatter among them. Rather, everyone was sitting quietly, either absorbing the much-needed food and drink they had wolfed down upon retrieval, or napping, their taxed systems and psyches rebooting for the challenge ahead.

Bawb closed his eyes and breathed deeply, settling into a shallow meditative state. He did not need sleep, but he had learned his mind would benefit from purging extraneous thoughts and concerns before a task. In his case, that meant thinking about them before putting them aside.

He thought about the way his mission had gone. How he had improvised and come out better for it. Replaying his encounters and actions, he felt he had done just about everything as well as he could have all things considered. Some good fortune had gone his way, but the vast majority had been of his making, not mere blind luck. His training had served him well, as had his instincts, and he had been victorious in this challenge.

More than that, he had made his first true kill. And not sneaking around, quietly executing some nefarious sort in their sleep. He had faced his foe, extracted information, and defeated him in single combat. A warm feeling began to fill his chest, and he let it. For the moment, at least. He was *good* at this. Not just in the classroom, but in the real world. The confirmation only served to boost his feeling of contentment, and with it, a calm sort of confidence flowed over his body.

Bawb was a Ghalian now. Sure, he was still a Vessel, but with this kill, he was essentially an Adept. All that remained was to further develop his own fighting style to the satisfaction of his teachers. From there it would be several hard years before he ascended to the level of Mavin, but once he had achieved that, he knew it would only be a matter of time before he became a Ghalian Master.

He opened his eyes a moment, looking at the boys and girls of his cohort, wondering how they might fare. Some he knew for certain would excel. Others he was still unsure of. A few he had to wonder if they were truly cut out for Ghalian life at all. He closed his eyes again and slid back into his meditative calm. The question, however, remained.

It was something he had pondered for himself on more than one occasion. What about a different sort of life? One where romance and even love could be a part of it. He was a dedicated student, no one could argue that, but he had recently finally been with a woman and had experienced the joy of physical connection. It was pleasant on a purely primal level, no doubt, but it had also awakened an urge for emotional bonds, the feeling quite unexpectedly dredged up from the orphan's youth.

Is there more for me out there than this life? he silently wondered to himself.

The ship lurched slightly as it hit atmosphere. Apparently, it had jumped and arrived at Boxxna without his notice, so skilled were those piloting the craft. One day, he hoped he too would wield his flying magic with such impressive technique. For now, he had other things to consider.

Bawb looked out at the world they were descending toward. It was unlike any he had ever seen, and it was beautiful.

The ground was nowhere to be seen. All that was visible, proving there actually was land down below, were tall peaks rising up from the fluffy cloudcover that stretched out as far as the eye could see. It didn't appear to be a simple weather pattern of the day. This looked like a planet-wide state of being, with cities and estates nestled at the tops of the jutting land masses, absorbing the golden sunlight that was blocked to the realms below.

Just how far down it was to the surface below the clouds was anyone's guess.

"I see you studying the land. Or what you can see of it," Teacher Warfin said, not just to Bawb but the entire group. "Boxxna is an unusual world, but this is where Voralius lives, and this is where our channeling staff is being kept."

"Is the entire planet like this?" Albinius asked.

"It is. Some of the cities and towns are atop isolated peaks, but the capital, where we are headed, is part of a large chain of them, a linked network forming a ring atop the dormant remains of a large volcano."

"Is there a risk of eruption?" Martza asked, looking sunburned, dehydrated, and far worse for wear than the others.

"No. There are robust spells not only monitoring the volcano but also layered over centuries, ready to suppress it should the unexpected occur. See down there? The largest city is our destination. We will, however, be landing to the right on the smaller peak. That is a less-visited area, and one where our arrival will go unnoted."

"Could we use a shimmer ship and just drop into the main city?" Finnia asked.

"The clouds make that difficult. While the shimmer cloak hides the vessel from sight, it does not keep it from affecting the clouds around it. Motion would be noted, and this particular city is, shall we say, a bit on edge."

"Why is that?" she wondered.

"Because Voralius is known to be quite the collector, and a very connected one at that. City resources are redirected to help protect their facilities. No, we must make the approach the long way, traveling from peak to peak."

"We will trek through the clouds?" Zota asked.

"We will do better. On this world, Malooki are native and

commonly used. We will acquire them upon landing and *ride* to the capital."

The Vessels were a little abuzz. Malooki were impressive beasts of burden they had only heard about in their studies. Tall, sturdy animals, they were empathic in nature, their hair changing color with their emotions. For that reason, they were excellent guardian animals, used not only for transport but also warning of danger before it might be seen.

In most cases, that meant lurking beasts hoping to strike. In this one, it meant the Ghalian youths would have to keep their feelings and thoughts in check lest the creatures pick up on them. Fortunately, as tired as they were, it would be relatively easy to just settle in for the ride. They would be able to worry about the task before them once they arrived in the capital. For the time being, they could just relax and enjoy their journey.

"We are on a family outing," Warfin announced as they landed. "You are all cousins, and I am your uncle taking you on a family adventure. A Malooki ride. Act accordingly. You are young enough that none will question this story if you seem properly enthusiastic."

The Vessels nodded their understanding. They were teenagers but still of an age that could be used to their advantage in this sort of situation. And that was exactly what they would be doing.

Warfin strode from the ship with a cheerful smile on his face, his demeanor magnitudes more relaxed than when in his teaching role. Here he was fitting in. Adopting a disguise. And he was damn good at it.

He approached one of the farmhands standing by the Malooki corrals, his arms gesticulating in big movements, his tone one of jovial friendship. The woman tending the animals greeted him with a broad smile, one that only grew brighter as he handed her a sack of coin.

"Come on, you lot! We've got an adventure ahead of us!" he called out to the group of teenagers streaming out of the ship. "This is going to be great!"

The Vessels all put on cheerful faces, even the most exhausted of them who had been given a bit of extra magic in their konuses to allow them to cast disguise spells to cover their sunburns and generally ragged appearance. It was only enough to get them out of the landing site and down into the clouds as they followed the trail to the next peak. The unexpected bit of magical help would not give them an advantage once they arrived at their destination.

Bawb approached a Malooki, gently reaching out to stroke its translucent hair, astonished at the beauty of the beast. The animal's colors shifted, a rippling rainbow running over its body. None of the other Vessels' animals were having that reaction, he realized, suddenly very self-conscious.

"How unusual," the woman said. "Chuffy is usually a bit standoffish. A good Malooki mind you, but not exactly friendly. But he seems to really like you."

Bawb felt his momentary alarm diminish. He also realized he could almost sense some sort of connection with the Malooki, as if they had clicked, empath to empath. He knew he could sometimes reach out to an animal, though he still didn't know exactly how it worked. But apparently, facing an animal that was extremely sensitive to that sort of thing just enhanced the reaction.

The students mounted their rides and followed their teacher, Warfin laughing and joking all the way to the trail leading into the mist. Once they dropped down into it, however, his jokes ceased. It was quiet, the sounds around them muted by the natural phenomenon. Each Malooki's hair shifted, as if they had gone into alert mode. And, as it turned out, they had.

"Things lurk in the mist," Warfin told them. "Dangerous

things. Not likely to bother a group of us this high up, and especially not with all of these Malooki. But should you find yourself separated and at a lower point for any reason, you will need to be at your most alert. Now, stay close. We ride to the capital. Once there you will be on your own to complete the task. Find the channeling staff, retrieve it, and make your way back to the ship. I do not need to tell you the importance of doing this without being detected."

With that he turned his attention back to the trail and led them into the mist and onward to adventure.

CHAPTER FORTY-SIX

The ride was uneventful, something they all were grateful for. The sounds of whatever it was lurking in the mist below them made one thing abundantly clear. While it was a beautiful, sunny world above, whatever was relegated to living within the clouds was a dark threat they would do well to avoid if at all possible.

The Malooki seemed at ease despite the distant noises. They knew the path and clearly felt comfortable in numbers, their shifting hair color remaining in the calm and relaxed spectrum, moving to downright happy as they emerged from the mist upon their ascent into the capital city.

The beasts of burden walked right to the stables, clearly glad to be in the company of more of their friends as the "tourists" slid down from their backs and they were released into the large corral.

Warfin, the jovial uncle persona glued to his face, thanked the young man working the stables profusely, tipping him well for such a wonderful ride. Bawb knew what he was actually doing, of course. He was making sure that their rides back would be readily available when it was time to leave, the little extra coin in this situation not appearing whatsoever like a bribe but merely a tip. A large one, but not so much as to draw unwanted attention. The sort of tip, nevertheless, that would motivate a worker to perhaps put a little extra zip in their efforts when the generous patron came back for their return ride.

And if they succeeded in their task, they would want to leave in a hurry indeed.

Emergency extraction was a mere skree call away if it came down to it, ready to fly in and snatch them up for a hasty, and likely dangerous, egress if things went wrong. But these were Vessels, students with enough skill to *hopefully* not require such a drastic measure.

Warfin led his ersatz family into the city, pointing things out with the wide-eyed fascination of a tourist. The teenagers did the same, oohing and aahing at the architecture of the unusual structures.

Being built atop the craggy rim of a volcano, there had been adjustments made in the construction process, and as a result, the buildings were not uniform in shape and design, but rather, built to conform to the environment, using it to reinforce the structure rather than them knocking it all down to make a perfectly flat building surface.

And among the most robustly constructed of them would be Voralius's keep. Gaining access would make for an interesting experience, no doubt, and a difficult one at that.

"You know the task. Go," Warfin said through his grinning teeth. The students scattered, laughing as if they were on a fun outing, not a deadly mission. "Don't run too far!" he called after them merrily. "And don't get lost!"

He was fully confident the assassins-in-training would not do anything of the sort.

Warfin wandered the streets, looking around, playing the part of a tourist while the Vessels fanned out, exploring the city, looking to any who might observe them as no more than curious youths.

It didn't take long for them to learn which building was the one they sought. Knowing it would be a difficult one to breach and undoubtedly more robustly constructed than most others gave them something to look for. More importantly, it also gave the supposed tourists a reason to simply ask who owned such an imposing building without raising any suspicion.

As it turned out, the tall structure built right into the volcanic rock at its base was the one belonging to Voralius. The upper levels were normal enough, though much of them had been constructed with volcanic stone hewn from the surrounding fields, shaped to give structure while also presenting an appearance that looked almost as if the building itself had been forced up by volcanic upheaval.

Bawb kept his distance, weaving through the streets as he made his way around the structure. He saw the others doing the same thing, a bunch of teenagers just out exploring a new city, their tourist stares not drawing any unwanted attention. He finished his circuit around the building and stopped at a food vendor for a snack. One that allowed him a vantage point from which to study the building as he slowly ate.

There was good news and bad news. The good was the building had two very clear doorways hewn into the jagged stone base. One was a large, formidable-looking entryway with a massive, tall set of double doors. There were no guards outside, but it was a given there would be one or more directly inside.

The other was a small servants' entrance around the side. He noted Elzina acting casual as she looked at the front doors and opted to walk around the far side toward the lesser entryway. A few of the other students could be seen in the crowded streets doing the same.

The windows only began above the second level, and while

the structure appeared easy enough to climb, Bawb noticed the gaps between handholds were just far enough to leave someone stuck if they attempted to scale them.

"Clever," he mused, admiring the trap that wasn't obvious to any but the most aware.

Bawb walked toward the building, heading the opposite way from his peers. Something had caught his eye as he made his first pass. Something on the opposite wall from where his classmates were heading.

The jagged stone seemed like everywhere else on the building, but there was something in the shadows. A sense of shape to them, as if someone had formed them that way. In fact, if he unfocused his eyes a little, the outline of what looked like a door presented itself, but only just.

"What's this?" he wondered as he drew closer.

It was a series of glyphs formed by the stone itself. If you weren't focusing right at them, you'd walk right by. But Bawb's sharp eyes were already hard at work, deciphering them as he had been taught. This was an entrance, and the stone was a mere spell masking it. He just had to decode the spell required for access.

It was written in an ancient script, one that none of the locals would have ever seen. A clever way to hide it in plain sight. And fortunately for Bawb, it was one of the many languages he had studied in his runes and puzzles classes. A small grin creased his lips. The others had taken the bait and headed to a decoy entrance. While it might lead into the building, it would likely be partitioned from the main structure. They were on a wild goose chase.

He squinted his eyes, making sure he got every accent correct as he read it over and over, working on the phrasing, ensuring he had it just right before making his attempt. He was certain that on *this* door, a failed entry attempt would surely trigger all sorts of alarms.

"And here we go."

He quietly spoke the words, his intent firm and the words spoken with confidence and clarity. To the outside nothing had changed. The stone wall looked the same. But to Bawb, who had spoken the unlocking spell, the illusion had faded. He and he alone had access. He stepped inside immediately, unsure of how long he would be able to do so. To any who would have been watching, it would have just seemed he had walked away, though they wouldn't be able to recall exactly where he might be.

A clever entrance indeed, and one that had employed a fair amount of magic to achieve such an effect.

Now that he was inside, Bawb's momentary feeling of elation immediately evaporated. He could *sense* the danger looming all around him. This was definitely where valuable items were stored. No one would have layered traps and tripwire spells like this if not. He was going to have to move slowly and carefully. Speed was simply not an option.

Fortunately, this sort of thing was Bawb's forte. More than any other Vessel, he had a knack for detecting precisely these sorts of hidden hazards. And now he would put that skill to use in the most real of settings. He just had to move slowly, taking care and note of every last detail.

The tripwires, both magical and mechanical, were easy to spot. The fine wires and pressure-sensitive magic were readily apparent to one of his degree of skill. Several of the other spells and mechanisms, however, required quite a bit more attention. He was doing more than just deactivating and bypassing them. Bawb was also leaving them fully intact and ready to reactivate when he released the tiny bits of magic he had cast to block them.

The building was not going to be an easy one to get out of, and odds were he would need to make a hasty egress the way he came. But more than that, when he had done so, he had to leave no trace that he had ever passed that way. He would move through the building as if a ghost.

At least, that was the plan. Whether he could pull it off or not was yet to be seen.

It was slow going, but at long last, and after much mental exertion, Bawb finally made it to the end of the deadly corridor. The rest of the way, he saw, was actually rather straightforward. A strong pull of magic directed him to his left, where he sensed a sizable cache of valuable and powerful items. The door was warded, but Bawb nullified the magic with a few carefully placed spells then stepped inside, closing it gently behind him.

The chamber was massive, with high, arched ceilings and three other doors on each of the walls. It wasn't just a storeroom; it was more like a small warehouse. And somewhere inside was the channeling staff. Bawb reached out with his senses, straining to discern the staff's power among so many other enchanted and magical items.

A massively powerful blocking spell caught his attention not far away. A locked box far too small to contain the staff. But whatever was inside had to be of great value given the amount of magic applied to the container. Bawb hesitated. He was there for the staff, but he was still a teenager, and ultimately, his curiosity got the better of him.

"It will only take a minute or two," he reasoned, quietly applying both lockpicks and disarming spells to the box, his nimble fingers working their magic, unlatching the catches and safeties while his words shaped the magic in the air to do his bidding, rearranging the wards on the box without breaking them, allowing him undetected access.

The final tumbler emitted a satisfying click. A little grin on his lips, Bawb opened the box.

A wave of nausea washed over him as soon as he did, but he realized it was not a trap. It was whatever was inside. He looked closely. All that was there was a small vial nestled in the velvety cushioning. Bawb felt a visceral need to get away from it. One that ran all the way to his core. He had never seen it in person, but he immediately realized what the liquid inside had to be.

"Balamar water," he marveled, carefully picking up the vial and wrapping it in several layers of padding before applying a trio of robust sealing spells and tucking it inside his tunic.

It was the deadliest thing in the galaxy where Ghalian were concerned. For others it healed all wounds, and for some it even enhanced their powers when applied topically. But his kind? Instant death. Immolation, no less, burned to a crisp in seconds. Not a pleasant way to go. Not at all.

Bawb felt the dampness of a faint sheen of sweat form on his brow as he continued his search. Carrying certain death on his body was enough to unsettle even a Ghalian. He forced himself to focus, pushing the nagging worry from his mind and resuming his task. The channeling staff had a very particular power signature, and he could feel it nearby. It was definitely in this chamber, somewhere near the far-left wall.

Bawb began to move that way, careful to avoid tripwire spells that dotted the floor as he did. The staff's magic abruptly moved. Bawb froze, his senses on fire. Something was wrong. The hair on his neck stood up. He dove aside just as a stun spell flashed through the air. It was not cast by a trap, however. This was aimed at him by a caster across the room.

He pulled up his own magic, layering defensive spells, ready for a fight. Movement caught his eye. There was more than one of them. Three casters by his count, and several others working behind them. He cast a spread of minor, tightly focused attack spells, hoping to distract them and buy himself time to escape.

They blocked them and cast their own attacks, but they seemed to be as restrained as he was, not wanting to trigger any of the chamber's defensive or alarm spells. Bawb looked closer at their attire and realized why. They weren't Voralius's guards. They were bandits. Pirates, to be exact, and a familiar face locked eyes with him from behind her defensive team. A glimmer of recognition flashed through Nixxa's eyes.

"Looking for this?" she taunted, waving the channeling staff in the air. She studied him a moment, then turned and ran for the far door, her minions protecting her retreat, their arms loaded with looted treasure.

Bawb hurried back the way he came, wondering why she didn't trip the alarms on the way out and give him away. Professional courtesy, perhaps? He realized the silliness of that idea. More likely, she was just giving herself as much time as possible before her own theft was noticed. Whatever the case, she had the staff, and there was no way he would be taking it from her.

Bawb hurried down the corridor he had so carefully arrived in, re-arming the spells and tripwires as he passed before sliding out into the fresh air and re-sealing the door's masking spell. He looked around. No one was reacting. It seemed that however Nixxa had managed to make her escape, she, too, had gone unnoticed. At least, so far.

Bawb put on a relaxed air and walked back to the rendezvous area, acting as casual as he could, taking in the sights like any other tourist might. But other tourists wouldn't burst into flames if someone bumped them too hard and broke the vial concealed in his clothing. With great care, he increased his pace, more than ready to get off this world.

CHAPTER FORTY-SEVEN

Bawb found Teacher Warfin relaxing in a shady spot near the stables, his demeanor that of a man utterly at peace and enjoying a quiet day. Bawb knew that beneath his façade that was anything but the case.

"Back so soon?" Warfin commented, noting Bawb's empty hands.

"It was a fun outing, Uncle," he replied, a big grin on his face. "Unfortunately, the thing I was looking for was already gone."

"Gone? You're sure?"

"Yep. I was disappointed, but that's life, right? Anyway, I figured I was ready to go home if the others aren't having too much fun."

Warfin gave a little nod and quietly cast a silent notification spell. Each of the other students' konuses would inform them to regroup at once. Bawb took the opportunity to purchase a sweet from one of the local vendors. That done, he sat down in the shade to wait.

The other Vessels were quick to return, some of them arriving together, laughing and seemingly completely at ease. Warfin gathered them up and led them to the stables, where the young man he had dealt with earlier had already begun gathering their rides when he saw them approaching.

"Thank you so much, my friend. It's been a fantastic outing, but now it's time to get these youngsters back home to their parents," he said, slipping the fellow another sizable tip.

"Come back and visit again. There is still quite a lot to see. And if you ever need a guide to the other peaks—"

"I know who to ask for. Thank you, my friend. Now, all of you mount up and follow me. Remember to stay close. We wouldn't want anyone getting lost in the mist."

Warfin mounted his Malooki awkwardly, which, for an expert rider with decades of experience, must have been quite difficult, and led the students back to the trail and into the clouds. The sounds of the city faded at once when they entered the murky mists, but no alarm had been raised. So far, they were in the clear.

Warfin increased the pace, but only a little, not wishing the animals to appear as though they had been ridden hard. That would raise suspicions, and that was certainly not the plan. In short order the foggy air brightened, and moments later, they emerged at the trailhead near the Malooki stables. With peals of laughter and merriment in the air, they returned the animals and thanked the stable hands, then headed back toward their ship.

Bawb looked up at the sky, a familiar craft lifting off from another nearby peak and streaking into the upper atmosphere. Nixxa's ship. There was nothing to be done for it now. All he could do was get aboard their own ship and relay what had happened. Beyond that, it was out of his hands.

Warfin waved and called out his thanks and goodbyes then sealed the hatch. The moment they were safely ensconced in the ship's protective walls, the cheerful expression dropped from his face.

"Bawb, I believe you have something to tell me," he said as the ship lifted off into the air.

"Yes, Teacher. The channeling staff was taken before I could reach it."

"I did not see you enter the door with the rest of us," Elzina interjected. "How could you have known such a thing?"

Warfin cast the boy a questioning look "Bawb? Is this true?"

"It is."

"Then how are you so certain? We scrapped this mission on your word. Your word as a Ghalian."

"And it still holds." Bawb turned to his nemesis, back to her old ways, it seemed. "Elzina, you and the others went in a decoy entrance."

"And how do you know that?"

"Because I found the real one."

"You went in the main entry? That seems highly unlikely."

"I did not say the main one. That was far too heavily guarded. But there was a hidden doorway on the opposite side, concealed in the volcanic rock itself."

"I did not see any such entrance," the girl challenged.

Bawb allowed himself a rare smirk. She deserved it. "Obviously. If you had, you would not have wasted your time elsewhere. But that is beside the point. There may be a problem with retrieving the staff. I was not alone in Voralius's treasure chamber. There were others there. Pirates."

He could almost hear the silent groan that threatened to escape the teacher's lips. "Let me guess. Nixxa?"

"Yes, Teacher. She was there with several strong casters as well as a small team, looting what they could, then hurrying out. She had the channeling staff, and she seemed to know what it was. In fact, she taunted me with it before making her escape."

"And you didn't follow her?" Elzina asked pointedly.

Warfin shook his head. "He did the right thing. A lone

Vessel against those odds? Even for a full-fledged Ghalian it would be challenging, and that is not even taking into account the alarm spells. Well done avoiding them, by the way."

"Thank you," Bawb replied. "I am sorry, though."

"It was not your fault. Not by a long shot," Warfin said, a serious look in his eye. "Nixxa is becoming something of a problem, and to steal an item she is apparently aware belongs to the Ghalian? Well, that is not an innocent mistake. It is too much, too far, even for the likes of her. I may have to deal with her myself. Quite an unfortunate turn of events. Unfortunate, indeed."

Warfin left the students to relax and discuss the blown mission, heading to the small galley space in the rear of the ship to get a drink and take a moment to ponder how utterly wrong this day had gone.

"Teacher?" Bawb asked, leaning through the door.

"Yes? Come in, Bawb."

"Thank you."

"What is on your mind? You know you did no wrong."

"I do. It is just there was something else. Something I thought I should show you in private."

Warfin sat up straighter, his curiosity piqued. "Oh? And what would that be?"

Bawb reached into his tunic and carefully removed the bundled vial, gently releasing the spells he had placed on top of its wrapping then handing it to his teacher. Warfin felt the power immediately, his eyes actually widening in a rare display of shock and emotion. With the utmost caution he unwrapped the vial, holding it up to the light.

It seemed so benign. Just a small container of water. Hardly any, really. Yet this little vial was worth more coin than some entire towns would earn in a lifetime.

"Balamar water," Warfin said with quiet appreciation. "I assume you found this in Voralius's keep?"

"I did."

"Out in the open?"

"Well, it did take a few minutes to pick the locks and release the spells protecting it. Time I should have been spending looking for the channeling staff. If I hadn't delayed, perhaps I would have beaten Nixxa to it."

"No, you did right. The staff has power, but this? This is *true* power, and far more rare."

"That was why I took it. I know you said we were not to take anything else so as to not raise any suspicions, but we have also been told the Ghalian try to acquire and control as much of the remaining Balamar water as possible, not for the value, but to prevent its use against us."

"And you would be correct," Warfin said, then cast a series of incredibly strong sealing spells on the vial before tucking it away in his pocket. "Tell no one you have found Balamar water. Not now. Not ever. Outside of your Ghalian brothers and sisters, you must deny even knowing of the existence of the whereabouts of any small quantity of it no matter how trusted your company. It is the only way to keep our hidden stores of the waters safe. Do you understand?"

It all made perfect sense to Bawb. He knew the stuff was priceless, and the Ghalian had been accumulating the remaining traces whenever they could, even if, and especially because, it was utterly deadly to them. And the amount they now possessed, locked away safely, was quite substantial. Enough to wipe out the entire order, and then some, with ease.

"I do," he said. "If anyone knew for certain we possessed any, let alone a significant amount, many would risk life and limb to steal it."

"And that would lead to all manner of problems."

"I am sure it would. I swear to you, I shall never speak of it."

His teacher nodded, satisfied with the boy's understanding of the seriousness of the situation. "You have done particularly well on this outing, Bawb. Far better than your classmates. While many of them have been lacking, you have excelled of late. I hope it is a sign of things to come with you."

"I will do my best."

"I am sure you will. Go rest and spend some time with your friends. Relax for the flight. You have certainly earned it."

Level up, the konus quietly reminded him, but Bawb put those thoughts out of his mind, his attention fixed on what had gone right and what had gone wrong. Everything was a learning experience, and Nixxa and her goons had gotten the drop on him. He would do all he could to ensure it did not happen again.

CHAPTER FORTY-EIGHT

The Vessels were given a full day to themselves in the training house to recover after their ordeal. Recover, and think about what had gone right as well as wrong. There had been little of the former and plenty of the latter in most of their cases, something they quietly discussed amongst themselves as they replenished their energy and had their injuries tended to by the healers.

The following day they were afforded no such leisure. Roused at their usual early hour, the Vessels were told to gear up with their standard lightweight kit and gather food and water in preparation for a long trek. The students did so in quick order, their resilient bodies rested enough and ready for the day's challenge. When they reached the designated gathering point, however, they were in for a surprise.

All of their teachers were present, standing silently in a rather intimidating line, each of them watching the teens' arrival without expression. It was Teacher Demelza who stepped forward to address them.

"Recent events have made the Masters call into question some of your dedication to your training and your abilities in certain adverse settings. You are Vessels. You are expected to perform at a higher standard, and any who cannot fully commit and adapt to the Ghalian ways will be weeded out."

The students stood still, but a tension could be felt as her words set in.

"Yes, you heard me correctly. You are to be tested. Assessed. And should you prove unworthy, removed from the order. Is that understood?"

"Yes, Teacher," the students replied in unison.

"Good. You will follow Teacher Warfin. He will lead you to your destination. You will all need to apply disguises, as this is a trek on this very world, but outside the compound walls. None may travel as a Wampeh. Teacher Warfin, they are all yours."

Demelza and the others strode out of the chamber, leaving the lone teacher standing before the youths, a disappointed look in his eye.

"All right, then. Apply your disguises and follow me. We have a long walk ahead of us."

Warfin turned and headed into the corridor, not waiting, assuming the students would be quick to follow, all of them applying their disguise spells as they moved. Even this was as much a test of their skills as was whatever the teachers had waiting for them at the end of their trek.

Warfin surprised them by taking a tunnel to an exit far from the actual training house compound. This one deposited them closer to the outskirts of town in a more sparsely traveled area.

"Do not bunch up. Exit a few at a time. Follow and be discreet. We will be heading out of the city shortly but maintain your disguises for the duration of the journey."

Warfin stepped out first and kept moving. Shortly after, the first of the students followed until, eventually, they were all out in the open, walking so spread out that they did not seem to be connected in any way other than happening to be heading the same direction.

They remained that way until they were a fair distance outside the city limits. Only when they were far out into the wilderness did Teacher Warfin pause to allow them to gather in a group. He then continued on, leading them into a stretch of land they had never visited before in all their years.

The stinking muck and mire might have had something to do with it, a vast stretch of foul, brackish water and sludge that stank horribly, keeping even the most foolhardy away. Warfin raised his hand and cast a release spell, the magic falling away and exposing a thin walkway into the marsh.

Bawb noticed the swarming bugs and feeling of dread the area produced ceased as well. It was a Ghalian barrier spell, or more like several of them layered atop one another, all designed to make any would-be intruder decide there were far more pleasant places to explore.

"Clever," he said, admiring the trick of magic.

"What was that, Vessel Bawb?"

"I said it is a clever use of spells, Teacher."

"That it is. And a lesson you should all learn. Sometimes you do not need walls, guards, and beasts to keep people out. Sometimes, you can do so with seemingly nothing at all."

Warfin stepped onto the walkway and headed deeper into the marsh, the students following in a row like deadly, magic-wielding ducklings. Once all were on the walkway, the spells behind them slid back into place, leaving them invisible to the outside world once more.

They walked for a bit until they reached a large expanse of dry land in the middle of the swampy muck. Tall trees and fallen logs littered the area, and hills and depressions in the soil gave the whole area an unsettling feel. Teacher Demelza was also there, waiting for them, a few teachers visible tucked into the landscape behind her.

"I see you made it here in reasonable time, Warfin."

"They moved quickly and did not require rest," he replied.

"Good. Perhaps there is hope for them yet." She walked to the line of students, slowly pacing in front of them almost like a general giving her soldiers a motivational speech. And, in some regards, she was. The speech part, anyway. Whether one could call it motivational was another story altogether.

"Welcome to the Oxxnid proving grounds. It is here you will be assessed and your worth weighed. Victory is not the only thing that matters here. All of your actions, all of your decisions, everything you do will count toward your final score."

"Teacher Demelza? Is victory not our ultimate goal?" Elzina asked.

"Of course this is your concern, Elzina. Always looking to come out on top. Admirable, but a trait that can be leveraged against you." Demelza slid her gaze across all the assembled Vessels. "Every one of you has a characteristic that can be taken advantage of. You would do well to look inward and assess yourselves with bare, brutal honesty. You will be a better Ghalian for it." She turned to the stretch of land behind her. "Out there, somewhere, is a banner. Plainly visible and not hidden. Your task is to retrieve it and bring it back to this starting point. If you do so, you will have won."

"Capture the flag?" Elzina asked, clearly excited by the idea. It was a game she excelled at.

"Yes. But not as you have played in the past. Counter to our normal ways, you will be working in teams." She saw the looks of confusion in the students' eyes. "Yes, you are all older now and accustomed to acting on your own, but sometimes circumstances will require you to work with others. Even those you do not particularly like. But these things happen, and you must adapt and put the mission above all else, do you understand?"

"Yes, Teacher," Elzina replied.

"Good. Now, we realize this is a particularly difficult task, and as such, should any member of a team succeed in retrieving the banner and reaching this safe zone, each of the teammates will be considered victorious and receive their first shimmer cloak. While your skills are not yet developed enough to fully take advantage of its uses, these are, nevertheless, extremely valued items in any Ghalian's arsenal, and this will give the winners ample opportunity to advance their abilities."

Elzina's mood had perked up significantly. "And all we have to do is retrieve the flag?"

"Yes. But you should know, none have succeeded in this for many, many years."

"But it is just capture the flag."

"It is. But it will be the teachers defending it."

The students kept their cool, but a general feeling of "*oh shit*" was clearly flowing through the group. Demelza grinned.

"Yes, now you understand the nature of the task before you. You will all be competing against each other, but against the defending teachers as well. There will be three attempts, each spaced out with a day between for you to consider your lessons from your prior efforts. Choose your tactics wisely, and learn from the mistakes you and your cohort will surely make. Learn from them, adapt, improvise. Overcome and prevail, if you can. Teacher Warfin will assign your partners. Your first attempt will begin as soon as you are all partnered. Good luck. You will need it."

Demelza turned and walked away, passing behind a tree and vanishing before their eyes. Even without a shimmer cloak, she was damn good. And any minute now they were going to be facing her. Her, and all the other teachers.

Warfin quickly paired off the students, each being partnered with the one they would be the least likely to choose if they were given a say in the matter. Naturally, Bawb and Elzina wound up together. Elzina asserted herself from the first moment, taking charge, as she was wont to do.

"We cover each other on the approach. Defensive spells overlapped," she said. "We will let the others engage the teachers first to create a gap. We will then exploit it and make for the banner."

Bawb shook his head. "No one has succeeded at this in ages. You heard what she said."

"And?"

"And clearly you are not the first to think of this tactic."

"Do you have a better idea?" she shot back.

"At this time? No. But I do believe we should approach this attempt with a different goal in mind."

"What's that?"

"We will undoubtedly fail on the first try. We have no intelligence on the location of either the banner, nor the forces defending it. Nor do we know the terrain and any pitfalls that may add to the task."

"Your point is?"

"That we should use this to gather as much information as possible before we begin the *real* attempts."

"*Every* attempt is a real one, Bawb. You know what we could win. Shimmer cloaks!"

"Do not let an emotional need for victory cloud your judgment. Sometimes you have to first lose in order to win."

"You may feel that way, but I do not," she said as Warfin announced they were to begin at once. "And we *will* win."

CHAPTER FORTY-NINE

The other teams charged ahead, each employing different tactics as they rushed into the unknown dangers facing them. Some raced for the gullies and trenches, opting for an attempt at a stealthy approach via a lower position. Others headed for the denser areas of foliage and trees. And then there were those who made a straight shot through the open land, hoping the defenses were all focused on those who would try to circumvent the easy path and make a sneak approach.

The stink of the swampy water bordering the area made it impossible to sniff out any telltale smells from body odor or remnants of a last meal eaten. Given that their opponents were all Ghalian Masters, it was highly unlikely such a simple mistake would have been made anyway.

No defenders were visible as the pairs made their approaches. But just because they weren't able to see them, that didn't mean they weren't there. Of that there was no doubt.

Albinius let out a muffled cry as he fell into a pitfall, his leg snapping on the rocks at the bottom of the pit. He had been partnered with Martza, who noted his predicament and carried on without hesitation. There was nothing to be done for him, and they had a goal to reach. Besides, the healers would fix him up once they got him back home at the end of the day.

Bawb watched from the rear with Elzina, each of them knowing what was coming next. Martza had fallen for the trick. Her partner hurt, she seized the moment to hurry her advance, running right into the shimmer-cloaked teacher in front of her. Teacher Griggitz uncloaked as he drove his dagger into her shoulder. It was not a fatal wound, but it was painful, no doubt, and would serve to make sure she remembered this lesson. Always be alert. And never assume.

Griggitz nodded to the other students then vanished, hidden by his cloak once more. Bawb stared hard at the ground at his feet, but the teacher was so skilled hardly a trace of his footfall showed. There was, however, a slight indentation where he had been standing still, he noted. Interesting, but of no use to them right now. Now they had other things to deal with.

One by one the others fell to an assortment of traps and barriers as well as teachers hiding with various forms of camouflage. It seemed Griggitz was the only one using a shimmer cloak, at least so far, but Bawb knew full well that could change at any time.

Elzina led them forward, sticking to the easy cover of the trees. "There," she whispered, pointing to a distant bit of movement far ahead atop a small rise.

It was the banner, plain to see once you knew where it was. At least they had that going for them now. This angle allowed them to spot it while those taking the central route had their view blocked by trees and bushes, not to mention blocking spells and traps.

Bawb looked at the path ahead of them and shook his head. "Too many ambush points."

"It is the best way. Look, they are occupied with the others," Elzina countered, noting the other students falling to the teachers on the other side of the area. Apparently, a few of the teams had decided to make a push forward as a larger group, hoping strength in numbers would overwhelm the defenders.

Several now either hung from a leg, snared in a trap, or lay pinned under a log or heavy rock, also having triggered a defensive spell. The teachers were moving more now, visible for a moment as they stepped from their hiding spots to take down the students as they passed.

It was a mess. A mess Elzina sought to take advantage of.

"We must go *now*. This is as clear a shot as we are going to get," she said, rushing forward in a crouching run.

"Wait!" Bawb called after her, but it was too late.

Elzina had been so focused on the teachers being occupied that she had neglected to do a proper scan of the ground ahead of her. The pit she fell into would have been easy enough to detect if she had just held back and been cautious, the covering spell masking the hole not quite perfect along the edges, allowing an astute eye to spot the trap. Unfortunately, Elzina had been too aggressive. Too confident. And it had been her downfall. Or pitfall, as the case happened to be.

Bawb ran around the edge of the pit, realizing that as the others fell that would mean more adversaries able to focus on him and him alone. He saw the basic pattern the teachers were employing. A staggered defensive positioning that allowed them to cover both sides and the center, each stepping out in any direction if a student managed to pass one of the others.

It was an elegant solution to the problem of a potential horde of attackers, allowing a small number to protect a larger area. It also gave Bawb a brief opening. Elzina was right in one regard. This was the most occupied the defenders would be. Once the others had been eliminated, they would all be focused on one thing. Namely, him.

Bawb hurried toward the banner. If he could claim it, at least he might stand a chance making his way back at a full run. It would all depend on how fast the teachers could react. But he had to move fast.

He raced ahead, his goal in sight, when his feet abruptly slowed. He looked at the ground. It seemed normal enough, but he realized it was dense, sucking mud with a layer of dry dirt and leaves atop it, and he was now ankle-deep in it.

Bawb pulled hard, yanking one foot out, only to have it sink in with his next step. He pressed on as fast as he could, expending a great amount of energy in the process. But it looked like this trap was only a few steps across. Enough to trap the unsuspecting but also small enough not to hinder the defenders. Defenders who uncloaked and stepped from their hiding places, Demelza and Rovos walking casually toward him from either side of the flag.

Bawb drew his dagger, ready to fight, but found himself quickly disarmed. Unable to pivot or run, and with far less magic than either of them individually, let alone combined, he knew he was finished. The teachers did as well, but unlike the others, no painful blow was landed on him. In fact, he could have sworn Demelza almost smiled as she helped him from the mud.

"You are the last man standing," she informed him. "And you made it farther than most on a first attempt. Not bad, Vessel Bawb."

"Thank you, Teacher."

"Do not thank me. You failed nevertheless. Now, get back to the gathering point to join the others."

Bawb gave a slight bow and headed back the way he came. He stopped to reach down and help Elzina from the pit and found he was actually glad she had not been hurt in the fall. It would have made her healing take longer and undoubtedly inspired her to push even harder in two days' time when they made their next attempt. This way, however, he hoped she would at least be open to discussion about their next try. He would find out soon enough.

"Failures, all of you," Warfin said, shaking his head as he looked at the bloodied and beaten youths. "Many of you fell victim to traps even an Aspirant would have seen. You developed tunnel vision, so focused on what was ahead that you failed to note what was right below your feet." He stared at them, hard, displeasure clear in his eyes. "Get back home and have your wounds tended. You train tomorrow. The day after, you try again. I hope you learn from your mistakes."

CHAPTER FIFTY

Albinius was walking fine on his newly mended leg the following day, but the shame he felt at being the first to fall victim to one of the many traps on the flag course hung over him like a dark rain cloud. The others left him alone to work through it on his own. In fact, all of them were given the entire day to themselves.

They were told they could train however they desired now that they had endured the challenge for the first time. Whatever lessons they may have learned from their group failure, this was the time to practice the skills they believed might serve them well on the next outing. They had one full day to work on them, then they would make the trek to the swampy marsh once more.

Usalla spent her time focusing on her sensing spells, realizing the many traps would always play a part in just how far and fast they could advance. The quicker she was at detecting them, the more prepared she would be to defend against the teachers' attacks. Partnered with Dillar, she would lead the way, clearing them a path while her less skilled counterpart would cast the minor diversionary spells he was practicing.

Finnia spent her time working on stealth and disguise.

While she could not yet make herself appear as one of the teachers, she could possibly blend into the surroundings enough to allow for a shot at the banner. That is, if her movements could be restrained enough to not draw attention.

Elzina simply ran through the many mazes and obstacle courses at their disposal, casting attacks and defensive spells on the fly as she did. Her plan was the same as before. Let the others clear a path, then make a charge for the flag. And this time she would not be so overzealous that she would fall into another pit.

All of the students were working hard in preparation. All, it seemed, but Bawb.

Unlike the others, Bawb was seemingly doing nothing. Nothing but sitting and thinking, leading his classmates to wonder what it was that bothered him so much to keep him from training. He simply ignored them, lost in thought.

The following morning the students donned their gear, cast their disguise spells, and filtered out into the city to make their way to the Oxxnid proving grounds. This time they had come on their own, Teacher Warfin having left to join the other teachers to prepare well before the students. By the time they arrived, only Demelza was standing in the open.

"Ten minutes, then you begin," was all she said before turning and walking into the trees.

"You heard her. Ten minutes," Zota said. "We need to work together on this."

"We are," Martza replied. "We are in teams of two, and that is more than enough."

"But if we join forces, we can overwhelm them. Not let them split us up and pick us off."

She shook her head. "You truly believe that would work? I don't. I believe spreading out and moving fast is the best course of action. Cause them to thin out. If we avoid the traps we can penetrate deep into the course in short order."

Albinius looked at the others, not so sure about that plan. "Elzina?" he asked. "What do you think?"

Elzina was fuming, her eyes darting around, looking for a partner who was not there. "What do I think? I think that when I find Bawb I am going to thrash him within an inch of his life. That's what I think."

The others hadn't been paying attention to who was there, assuming that all were present, as was expected of them. But now that she brought it up, it was readily apparent that one of their number was missing. Bawb was not there.

"He seemed troubled yesterday," Usalla noted. "He said he just wished to be left alone to think."

"Is he okay?" Zota asked.

"I assumed he was. But it is not like him to miss a test, especially not one as crucial to his standing as this."

"Whatever his reasons, he's left me to do this alone," Elzina growled. "But to hell with him. I will win without him."

No one voiced their opinions on the matter. She was pissed, Bawb was missing, and they had a test at hand. One that could determine their very futures within the Ghalian order.

The Vessels set their minds to their last-minute preparation. This was it. The second of three attempts. If they failed here they would only have one more chance.

The ten-minute mark arrived and the group set out, stepping into the active playing field en masse. Within five steps Albinius had fallen victim to another trap, a snare this time, the rope around his ankle dragging him across the muck before hoisting him up into the air.

Martza shook her head but kept moving. They all did. New traps had been laid while they were practicing, it seemed. The teachers had altered the course, and now they would have to be extra careful on their approach.

Elzina, now operating entirely on her own, stayed close to the others, moving behind them, allowing them to act as meat shields for any attacks that might come their way. When one of her cohort was engaged, she switched to following another, leapfrogging her classmates and using their efforts to further her progress.

It was actually a somewhat sound strategy, and to her pleasure, it was working. She was making good time as the others fought, ran, and eventually fell to the skills of the teachers lying in wait.

Elzina spotted the flag, sitting precisely where it had been the prior attempt. That, at least, had remained constant. The approach, however, would likely have changed, and teachers were sure to be staged nearby.

She moved fast, staying low and using the bushes and fallen logs to hide her advance. A cold blade on the back of her neck froze her in place.

"You are done, Vessel Elzina," Teacher Pallik's deceptively cheerful voice informed her.

She thought about trying to fight. To spin and disarm the kind-faced killer. But she had seen Pallik demonstrating her skills in the past and knew there was simply no way she would succeed. And the pain she would endure for so foolish an attempt would likely be significant.

Elzina raised her hands in surrender.

"You did better this time," the teacher said. "Now, go join the others. You have a lot of preparation to do."

No one had made it past the teachers, though their injuries, overall, were less severe this time. Even Albinius, despite the violence with which he had been yanked off his feet, had not suffered any serious damage.

The Vessels made their way back home and had their wounds tended then ate well and settled in for the night. After a good night's sleep they would train even harder. They had to. There was only one more attempt left.

Bawb, however, remained nowhere to be seen.

He had not only skipped the test but was now missing from the training house entirely.

"He likely realized he would not succeed and ran," Elzina snorted. "But to abandon the house entirely? I am surprised even he would be that cowardly."

"Bawb is not a coward," Usalla objected. "He may have faults, but so do we all. Let us not stoop so low as to call him a coward."

"Whatever you wish to believe, Usalla," Elzina said with a smirk. "The facts are quite clear."

"We will see. I am sure he will turn up soon enough."

Usalla was taken aback when Bawb failed to show up anywhere to train on their next recovery day, and he remained missing as the others disguised themselves and made the trek to their final attempt on the Oxxnid proving grounds. Much as she hated to admit it, it appeared, incredible as it might seem, that Elzina was correct.

Bawb was gone.

CHAPTER FIFTY-ONE

The assembled students paired up into their respective teams, quietly waiting for their instructions for the day of their last try. They doubted they would be any different. Get the banner, return it to the starting point, and do so without being taken out by either a trap or teacher. There wasn't much the teachers could do to make it any more difficult.

"What do you think they have changed?" Zota wondered.

"Traps, no doubt. Pitfalls and snares," Usalla hypothesized. "Perhaps a few other things as well. We will find out soon enough."

"The trick will be keeping them from getting the drop on us so easily," Albinius added. "I think I will be able to avoid them this time."

"Oh, do you?" a familiar voice said out of thin air.

The students looked around, scanning for their teacher, but saw nothing. Nothing until Demelza uncloaked right in front of them, dropping her shimmer spell with disconcerting silence.

"This is your third and final attempt," she continued. "Some of you appear to be learning from your mistakes. This is good. We all slip up in our lives. The key is to recognize that fact without ego and adjust accordingly. Pride has no place in our line of work, and it can get you killed or worse."

"Worse than being killed?" Albinius asked.

"Capture by the right people would make you wish you had merely died," she replied. "But if you take your lessons to heart, and make sure that never happens to you, you will have nothing to worry about."

It was not exactly a pep talk. Not by any stretch of the imagination.

"Five minutes," she said, then vanished before their eyes.

The Vessels spread out into their respective pairs and set their sights on their chosen courses. Beyond that, there was little they could do until the exercise began.

On the other side of the equation, the teachers all sat nestled into their positions, staggered and spread out to cover every possible angle of attack. There was a good reason none had successfully completed this task in longer than any could remember. It was essentially impossible. But that was the point, though the students did not know it.

The five-minute mark arrived and the test began. The teachers settled into position, a few of them opting to employ shimmer cloaks in addition to the natural camouflage. The poor students didn't stand a chance.

Teacher Donnik felt a blade press against his neck. He was the rearmost guard, yet somehow, someone had taken him by surprise despite his shimmer cloak. He lowered the spell and raised his hands in a silent sign of defeat as he turned around.

Filthy, covered in muck and mud from head to toe, he almost didn't recognize his attacker at first, the boy carrying the banner taken from behind him approaching silently without his noticing. But he knew who this was. Bawb's eyes shone bright through the grime smeared across his face. He gave a satisfied little nod, acknowledging his surrender.

The student silently stripped him of his shimmer cloak and moved on, casting a mediocre shimmer spell as he moved. It was nowhere near what he would need to properly use the cloak, but at a glance, it might hide his form somewhat and be just enough to buy him some time.

Donnik watched in awe as the teenager hurried ahead, avoiding all the traps with ease, leapfrogging the hidden teachers one by one, submitting them in the same manner he had been taken. Even the shimmer-cloaked ones didn't stand a chance. Bawb knew their positions, taking them out before the onslaught of approaching students even reached them.

Bawb shifted course, heading right toward the densest group of students. The teachers ahead of him reacted as he expected them to, focusing entirely on what was approaching them from the front, never expecting that the hunters were now the hunted.

Only when a streak of the partially shimmer-cloaked teen flashed past them running the other direction did they begin to realize something was amiss. The students drew their weapons, preparing for a fight with the cloaked intruder, but Bawb did not slow his pace, shifting his course and avoiding their attacks as well. The teachers now pursuing him were not as fortunate.

They took down the students quickly enough, but Bawb had used them as living shields to buy him precious time. All of the remaining teachers immediately flew into action, converging on the boy's location as fast as they could, forced to avoid their own traps along the way.

Bawb pushed hard, sprinting as fast as his feet would carry him. The other students turned to watch, confused as to what was unfolding behind them. Whatever it was, this was definitely not what the teachers had planned.

Stun spells flew hard and fast, but Bawb had been prepared, layering defensive spells behind him, embedding them in the shimmer cloak itself. He shed it as he ran, casting a minor lifting spell to keep it aloft behind him, seeming for an instant as though its occupant had been stunned. The teachers ran faster, closing the gap when the cloak fell to the ground, empty.

"I believe you are looking for me," Bawb said, standing atop the finishing point, the banner held aloft.

The teachers immediately slowed to a walk, looks of both surprise and approval on their faces. The students soon followed, making their way back to find out what exactly had just happened.

"Bawb?" Usalla blurted, seeing his filthy shape standing before them.

"Where is he? I have words for that—" Elzina fell silent at the sight of the banner in his hands. "You did it?"

"Yes."

"You actually did it?"

"I did."

Demelza walked to the front of the group to take the banner from him, the corners of her eyes crinkling with pride in spite of her best efforts.

"*How* did you do this, Bawb?" she asked. "There is no way you passed your classmates to the banner's location. We would have seen you."

Bawb shrugged. "You are right, there was no way for that to occur. But that was not what happened."

"Oh?"

"Per the rules, we had three attempts to reach the flag, located within the confines of the proving grounds. There was no restriction, however, on *when* we could visit the area, only when the contest itself would be active."

The teachers nodded their approval, his unconventional ploy clear to them. The students, however, were not in on the feat.

"So, you gamed the system. You came here early," Demelza said, enlightening the students.

"I did, yes."

"And you hid."

"In the marsh."

"For three days. Without moving or sleeping."

"That is correct."

"And you told no one. Not even your teammate."

"It would have defeated the purpose. I needed them to make the attempt as they normally would. It was the only way."

"Using them to distract the teachers."

"Exactly."

Demelza couldn't help but chuckle. "And from your hiding place you watched us place the new traps on the day. That is how you were able to sprint through them unscathed so easily."

"Of course."

"Clever, clever boy. And in our overconfidence, we teachers allowed ourselves to fall into precisely the habit we teach you to be wary of. An attack from behind was never even an option, so we did not think to prepare for one."

"I was hoping that would be the case."

"And you were rewarded for your efforts."

Elzina followed the discussion, but one thing still confused her. "They were using shimmer cloaks. How did you get around them?"

"I did not. I engaged them from behind."

"But how?"

Bawb shrugged once again. "I was watching when they took their positions. None thought to cast their shimmer spells before they arrived, as they came far in advance of our class, so all I had to do was remember where they were."

Teacher Donnik clapped his hands, grinning at the boy. "And as soon as the contest began you retrieved the banner, as the rules dictated, then began your return across the playing field. And we were so busy stopping your cohort that we did not see you coming."

"Exactly."

"You used our staggered defense against us. Very well done, Vessel Bawb. You did not attempt to engage those not directly in your path, allowing your classmates to draw their attention until it was too late to react in time to stop you."

"That was the plan, yes. I assumed I would have lost otherwise. Fast and direct seemed the best option. Running through the others was a risk I had to take, but I felt confident I could avoid any serious blows as they would all be in a defensive posture, expecting a teacher, not a fellow student."

"And you were right," Demelza said. "You suffered great discomfort and took quite a risk, but it paid off. And now, to you and your partner go the spoils of victory."

"After I bathe?" he asked with a wry grin.

"I think that would be best," she agreed with a laugh.

The group made fairly quick time back to the training house. Bawb stopped at a stream along the way to wash off at least some of the muck and grime, and by the time they entered the city limits he seemed like any other somewhat dirty teenager back from a day of frolicking in the hills.

His first stop once safely inside the compound walls was the bathing chamber. The others headed there as well, eager to clean off the stink and sweat of the day. Usalla took a spot close to her friend, peppering him with questions about his brazen attempt. Questions he was happy to answer. It wasn't every day someone outsmarted a teacher, let alone all of them.

"This is going to be talked about for *years*," she said, giddy with the thought. "You surprised them, Bawb. You surprised *all* of them."

"It is rather exciting, isn't it?"

"An understatement, I think."

"In this case, perhaps I agree with you on that," he said, grinning wide.

"Hey, Bawb. Demelza wants to see us when you are done," Elzina called out from the entryway.

"I will be right there," he replied, rinsing off and stepping to the drying area. A few minutes later he joined his partner in Demelza's small office area. She rarely used it, but each teacher had such a space to plan the day's activities and have quiet meetings if needed. Today, however, it was being used for a different purpose. The two students sat quietly, waiting for their teacher to speak.

"I hope you both realize what this means," Demelza finally said, handing them each a brand-new shimmer cloak from her storage trunk. "To have a shimmer cloak at your age? It is unheard of. I expect you both to study extra hard on your shimmer spells. You have a lot of expectations to live up to now, and your cohort will be looking to you for leadership. You may still be Vessels in name, but to the teachers, you have proven yourselves worthy as Adepts even if you have not leveled up to that rank yet. But soon, I expect that of both of you."

"We understand, Teacher," Bawb replied.

Demelza tossed a small pouch to Bawb, the coin inside jingling as he caught it. He opened it and poured out half, handing it to Elzina.

"No, you earned that," she objected.

"I would not have succeeded without both of us playing our parts. You deserve it as much as I," he replied.

Elzina shrugged and pocketed the coin. Demelza watched the exchange with a look of neutral amusement. Forcing rivals to work together had really paid off in this case. Far better than even Hozark had expected when he suggested the pairing.

"You did well today," she said. "Both of you. A clever ploy, and expert use of diversion. Well done. Now, take your spoils and go join your friends. I am sure you wish to celebrate. And it is well deserved."

Bawb and Elzina rose, gave a little bow, and stepped out, closing the door behind them. It wasn't until they were a full level away that Elzina spoke.

"You should have told me."

"I know you would have liked that, but I needed your genuine anger to distract them from looking for me. It had to be real."

Elzina gave a reluctant nod. "This doesn't mean we are friends, you know."

"I know."

"I will still rank ahead of you."

"And I will still do my best to prove you wrong," he replied. "But that does not mean we cannot work together when needed."

Elzina gave him her best version of his casual shrug. "We'll see," she said. "Come on. The others are waiting. I believe you have a long night of storytelling ahead of you."

CHAPTER FIFTY-TWO

The students enjoyed their evening, the excitement and buzz over what Bawb had done being the subject on everyone's lips.

Elzina watched and even participated in the conversation, intimating that she had known what her partner was up to and had simply been playing a part, acting angry while she was actually in on the plan. Bawb heard but did not correct her statements. There was no point. They had won, they had each acquired a shimmer cloak, and most importantly, Demelza and the other teachers knew what had truly happened. In this one instance, it felt good to reveal that not-so-little secret.

In any case, Bawb was something of a celebrity among his peers, at least for the day. What he had done was far more significant than merely winning a difficult challenge. In stepping outside the *perceived* rules while technically remaining within them, he had shown them all a new way of thinking.

They had all been trained extensively to think outside the box, but this? This made them realize they had merely stepped out of one box and into another. It may have been a larger one, but it constrained them all the same. But now they had seen firsthand what *truly* radical thinking could achieve, and it had inspired them.

The masters and teachers had gathered to discuss the boy's actions, all of them expressing appreciation of his drive and creative thinking. They would be keeping a closer eye on him moving forward. It was this sort of initiative that could fast-track him for advancement, and if he continued to grow into his unusual way of achieving his goals, he could move quite high indeed. Hozark even wondered if the boy might one day take a place beside him as one of the Five.

Time would tell.

For now, however, it was training, training, and more training. Training that would grow in difficulty. On top of that, the students would be sent on more real-world missions moving forward, and soon enough they would do so truly on their own without the benefit of teachers nearby to extract them. They would advance and become Adepts, well on their way to Mavens and eventually Masters.

One bit of uncertainty still hung in the air, however. The singular reason they had been forced to face their entire teaching staff in such a difficult test of skill and resolve. Some of them had not been living up to the Ghalian standards, and it was possible the new day would bring with it a smaller class. More than one of them slept uneasy as a result.

When they woke and gathered for breakfast before their first training session of the day, everything had gone back to normal, it seemed. Bawb was treated like he normally was, the brief bit of excitement induced by his actions overshadowed by the uncertainty hanging over the rest of the class. *He* was secure in his position. The rest of them were not so certain.

The students felt Elzina, Usalla, and Finnia were undoubtedly in the clear as they were consistently top performers in their cohort. A few of the others were well aware of their lower standing. Albinius especially was concerned. He was something of a joker among the group, and that was a very non-Ghalian trait. He also asked a lot of questions. To the point, at times, of making the others wonder if the saying there were no stupid questions really held true.

"Fall in at the sparring chamber," Teacher Griggitz commanded when he entered the dining hall before class. "Level three."

This was unusual but not unheard of. Sometimes meals were interrupted, as they would be in the real world. One could not always rely on a full belly to carry them through the day.

"Martza, with Elzina. Zota, with Finnia. Albinius, with Dillar," Griggitz commanded as soon as the students arrived.

Albinius hesitated. "Teacher? Does this mean I am not being kicked out?"

Griggitz softened his expression the tiniest bit. It was a blink-and-you'll-miss-it moment, but Bawb had seen it. From the look on her face, he was pretty sure Usalla had as well.

"You are not being kicked out, Vessel," the teacher replied. He spun slowly, sizing up each and every one of them. "None of you are. You all performed admirably these last days. Even you, Albinius. Despite injury you returned to the task with not just the same gusto, but even more. And yes, you were hurt again, but you did not give up. All of you showed that sort of drive and commitment. Now, it is upon your shoulders to maintain that level moving forward. There will be no further assessment opportunities. If you fail out from this point forward, you are done. Does that answer your question, Albinius?"

"It does. Thank you, Teacher."

"Do not thank me. It was you who did the hard work."

"I—"

"And now it is time for more. The rest of you, pair up. Sparring. Freestyle. No magic or weapons allowed. Begin!"

The students launched into combat at once. There was no warming up. No stretching or calisthenics beforehand. They had to be ready to act on a moment's notice at all times.

Bawb found himself paired with Moralla. The girl's high-kicking style was always a pleasure to watch but also quite a pain to face. Today, however, he squared off against her with an ease of body and mind that surprised him. It was almost as if he had unlocked some secret part of himself that had been holding him back. Her attacks, still smooth and fast as ever, were just more apparent to him as she moved. Almost easy to see coming.

Bawb parried and blocked, landing hard punches then sweeping her lead leg, sending her off-balance. She recovered quickly but flashed him a curious look. Bawb had never used that technique on her before. He was adapting. Changing his style. Suddenly, things had gotten interesting.

The two sparred for several more minutes before Griggitz had everyone rotate. And then with new partners, they all set to work again. And once more, Bawb found himself having an easier time of it. He was blending techniques fluidly, finding unlikely combinations from the myriad styles he had studied and applying them with great efficiency.

His teacher watched, nodding his head approvingly. Bawb, it seemed, had settled into the beginning of what might very well become his own fighting style, and from what he could see, it would be an effective one indeed.

For hours they carried on, rotating and sparring, only taking the briefest of breaks for water then setting to it again. The prior days might have been an arduous challenge, but that was behind them, and as the instructors loved to remind their hard-laboring students, the only easy day was yesterday.

"Bawb," Usalla said with a little bow as she faced her friend for the third time this session.

"Usalla," he replied, then launched into a relentless attack.

She was good. Better than most, and she had fought him on so many occasions that even his new variations on his techniques only gave her pause for a moment. She landed a hard kick to his ribs. Bawb in turn caught her leg, his own foot flying high toward her head. She caught it, but only just, the momentum sending them both tumbling to the ground, transitioning to grappling without hesitation.

"Bawb, may I ask you a favor?" she said as she evaded an arm bar.

"Of course," he replied with a grunt, shifting his hips and sliding across her in an attempt to lock in a different submission hold. "What is it?"

Usalla pivoted beneath him, leveraging herself free of the attack and moving in for one of her own. "You have learned skills that others have not."

"A few," he agreed, pulling his arm clear just before she got a proper hold on it. "What did you have in mind?"

She spun underneath him, shifting her angle yet again. "Will you teach me to sex?"

Bawb felt her leg wrap around his head as she pulled his arm, trying to lock in a choke.

"They do not say it like that," he replied, shaking off the surprise, barely escaping her powerful legs.

Usalla reacted at once, going for an arm bar instead.

"However it is said, this is a skill I must learn. Will you share what you have been taught?"

"I am not a teacher."

"Yet any of us can practice skills outside of class. Just as with swordplay or hand-to-hand combat. I wish to learn this new technique."

"It is not just one technique," he said, feeling a strange twinge in his gut as they fought.

"Then teach me all of them."

He fell silent a moment, sweating as he lay grappling with his friend, the two of them well matched in the ways of combat. Finally, he came to a decision.

"Very well. We will schedule a time."

"Why not today? After dinner, perhaps? We have free time then."

"Switch!" Teacher Griggitz called out.

The two rose to their feet, sweaty and out of breath.

"Very well," Bawb said. "After dinner. Eat light. You would not want an upset stomach."

"Thank you," she said as they moved on to their next partner. "You are a good friend."

Bawb nodded then turned his attention to his new sparring partner, a little distracted, pondering what he had just gotten himself into. A fist to the ribs snapped his attention back to the challenge at hand. There would be time to think about his liaison with Usalla later. For now, he had to fight.

CHAPTER FIFTY-THREE

The next morning the Vessels noticed there was something different about Usalla, though no one could put their finger on it. She seemed to be silently laughing at a joke that only she was hearing, a little grin turning up the corners of her lips throughout their entire breakfast. She was carrying herself differently as well, moving with a slightly more confident feel to her movements.

When Bawb joined her for their morning meal, her new demeanor seemed even more heightened by his presence. The others thought it was odd, but then, they were all Ghalian, and a lot of their daily lives were precisely that.

After they had dined and attended their first class of the day, a refresher on certain spells particularly useful to the Ghalian, Teacher Rovos instructed them to assemble at their usual gathering point at the landing site. Today, they were going to have an outing, and one that, while difficult, would also be quite interesting and even enjoyable.

The students were abuzz with excitement. Something new. Something unknown. This could be fun. They made their way to the landing site, split up in their approach so as not to raise attention, though Bawb and Usalla had chosen to walk together.

"This way," Rovos called to the students, directing most of them aboard a small but nice transport ship while Bawb, Usalla, and Finnia crammed into a shimmer ship piloted by a familiar face.

"Master Kopal," Bawb exclaimed as he and Usalla boarded. "It is good to see you."

"And you, Bawb. I hear today is going to be a fun one."

"Oh? Teacher Rovos hasn't told us where we are going yet."

"You will love it. We are to fly to the Askarian Menagerie."

Usalla's eyes widened with excitement. "I have heard of it. The site of an amazing collection of creatures from across the realms."

"And then some," Kopal agreed. "It is an impressive sight. You will get to see beasts that you would normally only encounter in the most dire of situations. But at the menagerie you can study them quite safely. In fact, it has been arranged for you to have a behind-the-scenes visit while you are there to learn some of the more arcane taming techniques and spells."

"This is fantastic! We are quite fortunate, indeed."

Kopal chuckled. "Oh, there is more."

"More?" she asked, her interest quite piqued.

"There is also a marvelous obstacle course not far from where we will be landing. One that even the most skilled among you will find challenging. I have run it many times myself, and it is always as invigorating as it is difficult."

Usalla was sold on the outing. "Marvelous. Just marvelous."

"And you say there are creatures of the deadlier sort there?" Bawb asked.

"Always. And I hear there may even be a mature Zomoki present, though that has not been confirmed. You know how difficult it can be capturing an adult specimen."

"I have heard."

"So, how do you feel about piloting us through the jump?" Kopal asked. "I hear Hozark has been giving you lessons."

Bawb suppressed a blush. "He is generous with his time."

"He would not do it if he did not see potential in you. Come, we have several jumps ahead of us. You can each try your hand at it. Bawb, would you like to go first?"

The teen nodded, suppressing his excitement. Jumping a regular vessel was something they had only recently learned, but jumping a shimmer ship was above his level. Above all their levels. But Kopal would not let them try if he did not feel they were capable. Bawb slid into the pilot's seat and reached out for the control spells, the Drookonus connecting with him with ease.

"You can do this. The coordinates are already set. Just relax and do as you've practiced."

Bawb cast the spell without hesitation or doubt. One had to be decisive in any craft, and even more so with a shimmer ship. The vessel flashed out of existence, reappearing some distance away.

"Well done," Kopal said, noting the transport ship appearing nearby a few moments later. "Usalla? Finnia? Which of you would like to try next?"

They took turns, each jumping successfully to a distant location. By the third time around, their confidence was growing geometrically. At long last, their jump took them quite close to their target system.

It was then the world went to shit.

"Who is that?" Finnia blurted as the nearby transport came under attack. Its defenses flared bright, stopping a barrage of vicious magic, but only just. Had anyone less skilled been at the controls they would have been taken for sure.

"Pirates," Kopal growled. "Up. Out of the chair."

Usalla scurried clear and the Master Ghalian slid into place, powering up shield spells and weapons in a flash. It was amazing watching him work in a real situation rather than practice. He was good. Fast. Confident. Now he had to find a way to stop the attackers.

Bawb realized it was a small swarm of ships, none of them particularly large, the bulk of them attempting to distract the transport captain while a pair of small craft tried to lock onto its hull to board it. In other words, a typical pirate ploy, as Bud and Henni had taught him.

Little did the attackers know who they had targeted. If they had, they likely would have thought twice about the ill-advised attempt.

One of their craft managed to latch on to the transport, its crew quickly casting an air umbilical spell as they breached the hull and streamed into the craft. Bawb knew they would refrain from using magic now. The risk of depressurizing the ship was too great. It would be a traditional boarding, carried out with blood, sweat, and aggression.

"We need to help them," Bawb urged.

"When the moment is right," Kopal replied. "We must wait for their ships to be in the optimal position. Do not fear, Teacher Rovos is a *very* skilled fighter, and the crew of that transport have all had extensive training."

"Is that normal?" Usalla asked.

"Let us just say that an anonymous donor provided them with lessons after they survived an attack several years ago. They are one of the Ghalian's favorite ships of choice when traveling incognito, and it serves us well to ensure those we fly with can protect themselves. It saves us having to break cover, though I assure you Rovos will not hesitate if it comes down to it."

Bawb watched as another craft latched onto the hull. This

one's breaching spell caused a bit more damage than they had intended, but the result was the same.

Access.

Bawb watched as the men and women streamed into the targeted craft and realized he recognized their garb. "These are Nixxa's people," he said.

That got Kopal's attention. "Are you sure?"

"Certain. I have had a few run-ins with them."

"This is not good. They will go for the Drookonus first to immobilize the ship. And if Nixxa is directly involved, her flagship will be only a short distance away. Heavily armed and heavily shielded, invulnerable to most attacks. We need to act at once. There is no time to wait for the prime moment. Sit and buckle in. I am directing all spells to shielding and weapons. We will lose gravity momentarily."

Kopal dove into the fray immediately, the passengers suddenly weightless and tossed this way and that by his violent maneuvers. He let loose with a barrage of spells, all designed to shock the pirates but not cause any real damage. If they took losses they might decide they had no choice but to fight to the end, but a wise man knows to leave his enemy a path of escape.

The pirates saw the ship and recognized the unusual spells as Ghalian. This was *not* what they had planned. Still, they had people aboard the target ship, and it would make no sense to make a retreat without taking whatever they could. The transport ship lurched then went dead in space, drifting toward the nearby planet's gravitational pull.

"They lost their Drookonus," Finnia gasped.

Kopal let loose a barrage of spells, driving away a few of the ships. "I see that," he growled, concentrating on his targets, trying his best to avoid breaking the umbilical spells and voiding the transport of its precious air.

"Rovos, do you hear me?" he called into his ship's skree.

"Pirates have taken the command chamber," the teacher replied. "The crew fought them off and sealed themselves in a forward compartment, but we are without power."

"I will drive them off. Have the students cast sealing spells. There are two breaches in the hull."

"On it. Thank you, Kopal."

"Of course, my friend."

The shimmer ship spun again, forcing two of the support ships away from the transport. From what it seemed, only a few of the pirates had returned to their tethered ships.

"Can the others take them?" Finnia asked. "If the crew is locked in another compartment, they would not see that they are Ghalian."

Kopal shook his head. "They are but students. Vessels, and quite talented, yes, but this is where pirates thrive. Never face a foe where they have the inherent advantage if you can avoid it."

"He is right," Bawb agreed. "This is their element. Our friends would be at a terrible disadvantage."

They all shifted their attention as a flurry of motion appeared in the umbilicals attaching the ships to the transport. Their crews were scurrying aboard with great haste. Apparently, having a Ghalian ship targeting them was more than they wanted to deal with today. And besides, they had gathered a significant amount of booty from their attempt.

The two craft released their spells and broke free, leaving the powerless ship adrift, falling into the planet's gravity.

"Do they have a spare Drookonus?" Bawb wondered.

"No. It is too valuable an item to afford extras for off-books transports. We often have a spare aboard our own ships, but at their rate of fall, even if we did, we could not board their ship to provide it to them. At least they have blocked the ship from losing air."

Bawb was more than a little alarmed. "They will burn up any minute."

"No, their combined spells should keep the ship intact into the atmosphere. It is what comes next that worries me."

Finnia shifted in her seat as she watched her friends drop closer to their deaths. "What are we going to do?"

"The only one thing I can," Kopal replied, activating his skree. "Rovos, I am going to latch onto your ship and guide you down as best I can. Have the students prepare. It is going to be a rough landing."

"Heard. I will prepare a cushioning spell for the impact."

"Good luck. I will see you on the ground, and in one piece."

"I hope you are right about that. Rovos out."

Kopal dove his ship to the transport and cast a powerful tether spell, linking his small ship to the much larger one, guiding it into the atmosphere as smoothly as he could. The spell held, but only just, the heat and vibrations threatening to shake the larger ship free.

Aboard the transport, the students put aside any personal drama and worked as a team, overlapping their spells, most sealing the breaches in the hull, while a few cast cooling spells to lessen the intense heat of their atmospheric entry. It was all or nothing. Survival or death.

With a jolt, the ship rumbled through the exosphere and into the planet's bubble of air. Once safely out of the vacuum of space, their flight smoothed out considerably.

"How long can we keep them aloft?" Finnia asked.

"They are far too heavy to sustain this for long. This ship was not designed to carry such a load. I must bring them to the surface as quickly as possible."

Kopal's shimmer ship began to shake and shudder from the strain as if to punctuate his words. "Hang on, this will be rough."

The surface was closing in far too fast for anyone's liking, but this was how it had to be. Kopal and Rovos were both saving their most powerful spells for the last possible moment. And as the ground rushed up to greet them, the pair cast together.

Both ships lurched hard, the passengers pressed down forcefully in their seats as the deceleration threatened to make them black out. In fact, a few of the students and crew of the transport did just that, all the blood forced from their brains as the ship screeched to a halt.

Kopal released his tether spell at the last second, separating from the transport, allowing it to hit the ground hard, but intact. His shimmer ship rebounded like a slingshot then settled into a steady hover. He quickly landed beside the smoking transport ship, his own smaller craft damaged from the effort.

Kopal and his passengers stepped out into the air. It was breathable, and the planet seemed fairly lush. But where they were, exactly, was another question altogether.

CHAPTER FIFTY-FOUR

"There is a fair amount of structural damage from the stress, but it will fly," Master Kopal said upon finishing his careful inspection walk around his ship. He had circled it three times to be extra certain. "It will have to travel light, and I fear jumps may be hindered. It appears the transport, however, is in better shape."

"A sturdy craft," Rovos agreed. "But one not intended to fly with holes in its hull, and certainly not without a Drookonus. It may have survived the landing, but we are stuck here for the time being."

"If we are where I think we are, this is the planet Dirrix. It would be one of only two inhabitable worlds in the system in which we were adjusting course before our final jump destination."

"I think that is likely. We will be able to tell for certain once in orbit. Your shimmer ship's navigation spells are functional?"

"Yes, the system is undamaged. But my craft can only carry one in its present condition."

"Not to worry. I believe that while unplanned, this may prove a good outing for the Vessels to practice their skills. The transport's crew is recovering in their quarters, and the ship will keep them safe from the environment. I will have the students set up a campsite while we await your return."

Kopal turned for his ship. "Very well. I will be back as soon as I am able. Use the long-range skree aboard the transport to communicate if need be."

He lifted off, tested his maneuverability spells, then headed up into space.

"Well, it would seem we have an impromptu camping session come upon us," Rovos said. "Build shelter and source your food and water. We will be spending the night here, so make yourselves comfortable."

Rovos turned to leave.

"Where are you going, Teacher?" Martza asked.

"I am going to run to the top of that nearby mountain to better ascertain our location. One must always be aware of their circumstances, after all."

With that he set off at a steady jog. It would take him hours to reach the summit, but Teacher Rovos was in remarkable shape, as were all of their teachers.

The students split into groups, some tasked with fashioning shelter while others were to gather food and find fresh water. There was plenty aboard the downed transport, but this was a good opportunity to practice their survival skills.

It was still early in the afternoon when the shelters were completed. Large lean-tos where multiple students could sleep comfortably together, conserving heat and saving time otherwise spent fashioning multiple smaller ones.

The scavenging and hunting teams returned soon after, arms loaded with wood, small game, and an assortment of edible plants. There was a fair variety available, but not enough of any one thing to make a meal. Moralla volunteered to cook, gathering a container from the transport in which she could prepare a stew. In this way, she reasoned, they would each have ample servings rather than a few bites of each item.

"Is the perimeter secure?" Elzina asked as Usalla and Bawb returned from a somewhat long time out in the woods setting warning spells. Their cheeks were flushed, she noted. The terrain must have been tougher than it appeared.

"All is prepared," Usalla replied with a contented grin. "We will be safe from intrusion tonight."

"And Teacher Rovos? What about when he returns?"

"We made the spells readily apparent to a skilled caster. Only animals and bandits would stumble right into them," Bawb noted.

"Excellent. Moralla is cooking up a stew. We should be eating within the hour."

Usalla seemed surprised. "Moralla?"

Elzina shrugged, looking over at the girl tasting the stew as she cooked, adding what few seasonings she had as the makeshift pot bubbled enticingly. "She is actually a decent cook, at least back home."

"It is a little different out in the wild," Bawb pointed out. "Fewer herbs and spices, for starters."

"Do you want to do it? I am sure she would gladly step aside if—"

"No, I am happy to let her cook. I was merely making an observation. I am looking forward to seeing what she comes up with."

The students set about making a comfortable campsite, each of them working together as they had when they were children. It was a nice change of pace, despite the circumstances. This was not a competition, and they felt good simply relaxing without pressure for once.

"Dinner is ready," Moralla said after nearly two hours of cooking, tasting, and adjusting. She scooped out heaping portions for each of her classmates, the bowls taken from the transport's galley.

While they were eating in the wild, the students did not think Rovos would mind this indulgence. Besides, if they were at any other crash site, they would naturally think to salvage what they could from the ship.

"Make sure to save plenty for Rovos," Finnia said. "He is going to be hungry after such a long run."

"There is plenty to go around," Moralla replied, piling the girl's bowl high. "Eat up, and enjoy."

The students tucked into the meal with gusto, each of them surprised at how good it was.

"Really tasty, Moralla," Zota said. "An interesting flavor combination. What did you season it with?"

"Whatever we had available. I think it came out pretty good, actually."

"It really is. Thank you."

"I am happy to have been able to provide for my friends," she said with a warm smile, relaxing and enjoying the outing as best she could.

The sun was setting a few hours later, and as it dropped in the sky, the students lay doubled over in pain. Some were vomiting, others simply lay shivering on the ground, drenched in sweat. All of them were in distress, and it was getting worse.

"We need to figure out what happened," Elzina said, managing to rise to her feet.

Bawb somehow made it to his feet as well and shambled over to the food prep area. Elzina was already there, digging through everything looking for a clue, though she was hunched over from the agony. There had to be something to explain why they were all so ill, but there was not much to look at.

Bawb's gaze darted across the sparse remains of the ingredients, his head pounding painfully. Nothing caught his eye. His tongue, however, was tingling. Bawb's eyes widened, then he turned and ran. Ran from the area as fast as his legs would take him.

"Come back, you coward!" she yelled after him, dropping to the ground from the exertion.

Bawb ignored her, running as fast as he could, his body feeling like it was on fire, his muscles cramping hard. He forced them to heed his will, drawing from his konus in a way he didn't know he could, instinct taking over, channeling power into his limbs, keeping him moving when he otherwise would have stumbled and fallen.

The konus sounded an alarm. One that only he could hear.

Life force approaching critical, it informed him.

Bawb ignored it, his eyes blurring in the dimming light. "There!" he gasped, heading for a cluster of bushes, the footprints of his fellow students apparent in the soil. He somehow managed to cast an illumination spell, its minimal light just enough to help his search.

"Where is it? Where the hell is it?"

His shaking hands worked fast, searching through the plants growing in the area. He saw a patch of Slipp nearby, which meant Grazz was close. "Yes!" he blurted, spotting it and yanking up all of the plants he could, gathering them in his tight fists.

Bawb turned back toward their camp, pulling leaves and crushing them as he ran, stuffing them under his tongue. The burning sensation was agony, as if acid was eating away his mouth. He blocked out the pain and kept going, his konus's warnings quieting as he reached the campsite.

Bawb shoved crushed leaves into the mouths of each of his classmates. Some fought, shrieking in pain, others barely moved, twitching but nothing more. When he finally finished with the last of them, his body could simply take no more, his legs failing him as he tumbled to the ground.

Bawb sensed something through the ground. A vibration, his aching head and ears picking up on the rapidly approaching footsteps despite his condition. Teacher Rovos burst into the clearing, uncharacteristic alarm in his eyes. He raced to the transport ship, returning a minute later, the crew in tow.

They arranged the teens for immediate evacuation, lining them up beside the craft. Rovos crouched down beside the more coherent of the group, her mouth burning from the crushed leaves.

"Elzina, what happened?"

She weakly lifted her arm and pointed at Bawb. Rovos looked at the boy, anger in his eyes. This was not how the trip was supposed to go. Not at all. A boom sounded above, then another. Two ships jumped into the edge of the atmosphere, their hulls glowing hot as they dove toward the surface.

Inside the ships, their Drookonuses were smoking, burned out from the massive drain placed upon them. When the long-range skree distress call reached the nearest Ghalian ships they had spared no effort in reaching them as fast as possible. The craft each had a backup Drookonus, fortunately, and the ruined devices would be pulled free and discarded, then replaced for the trip to the nearest healing house. The Ghalian supply of the powerful devices would come in extremely handy in this time of crisis.

"Get them aboard the ships the moment they land!" Rovos commanded. The transport crew snapped into action, teams of two lifting each student as the ships nearly slammed into the surface before coming to an abrupt halt.

Bawb felt like his entire face was melting off, the burning sensation worse than anything he had ever endured. He watched through watering eyes as his friends were hurried into the ships with great urgency. All but one.

Rovos crouched over Moralla a moment, then pulled the konus from her wrist. Bawb saw her unseeing eyes staring at the sky, her skin already cool to the touch. Moralla was dead, and as he slid into unconsciousness, his last thought was wondering if he would be joining her.

CHAPTER FIFTY-FIVE

Bawb woke to find himself in a soft bed, wrapped in blankets, immobile. His body ached like it had never ached before, and his mouth felt as though he had gargled molten metal. He raised his hand, his arm weak, and touched his face.

His heart sped at the sensation. Pieces of his lips and cheek felt as though they were missing, a slimy substance smeared across his face and even inside his mouth. He moved what was left of his tongue, the pain not as bad as he'd feared it would be. Nevertheless, he could feel pieces were missing there as well.

He seemed to be alone in the room, a quiet, tranquil space with soothing light from a gentle healing spell that pulsed down upon him continuously. Bawb tried to sit up, but his body had other ideas.

"He is awake," a familiar voice said.

Bawb turned his head slowly. Master Hozark and Teacher Rovos were both beside his bed, standing silently, watching, their faces grim.

"Bawb, is it true you did this?" Hozark asked.

Despite his training, a flash of shame and fear flooded the teen's body. He had screwed up. He had let them down.

"I failed. How bad are they?" he asked, sounding as if he had a mouth full of cotton balls.

"The others will survive," Hozark replied, his expression softening.

"And it was all because of you," Rovos added, resting his hand on the boy's arm. "You performed admirably, Bawb."

"I did? You're not mad?"

Hozark let out a pained laugh. "Mad? We could not be further from mad."

"But the burns. The others–"

"Elzina told us what happened. And yes, the injuries to their mouths were your doing, but your instincts were right. You were the only one who realized Moralla had mistakenly put stems and leaves of Slipp in your food. A deadly mistake, and one that cost her her life."

Bawb felt his stomach sink. "But the others?"

"Alive. You got the Grazz leaves in their systems in time. It was quick thinking. You saved nearly all of them, Bawb."

"Nearly?"

"As we said, Moralla was too far gone for the antidote to work. Elzina informed us that it was she who had prepared the meal, and she was tasting it as she cooked. The poison had been in her system far longer than the rest of you. There was nothing more you could have done."

Bawb fell silent. He had known Moralla for a long time. They weren't close, but she was one of his cohort, and they had trained together on countless occasions. And now, because of one stupid mistake, she was gone. It drove home the reality of what was to be his life. That it could be extinguished in an instant. All anyone could do was prepare to meet their fate as best they could.

"I want to train," he finally said, a flare of emotion welling up inside of him.

Hozark shook his head. "There will be a very difficult challenge set up to get your class's heads back into the game. Wait for that. It will be extremely grueling. You need to rest."

"How much longer? I want to train *now*," he repeated, a fierce determination in his eyes. Stubborn and not likely to take no for an answer. A look that reminded Hozark of the boy's mother.

Hozark hesitated, a tug at his heartstrings, urging him to go against his better judgment. "The mending balms are the most comfortable means to restoring you, and that is the best way," he said, glancing at Rovos. "But we can have the healer speed the process, if you truly wish."

"I wish."

"It will hurt if you proceed in that manner, Bawb," Rovos chimed in. "A *lot*."

"I am already in pain. Do it."

The two Master Ghalian shared a look.

"Very well," Hozark replied. "But you may come to regret this decision."

Hozark and Rovos stepped outside, leaving the boy to rest before the grueling healing process was implemented.

"He is a tough one," Rovos said with an approving nod. "Far tougher than the rest of his class. Frankly, I am amazed at what he managed to accomplish."

Hozark nodded his agreement, a pensive look on his face. "As am I, my friend. As am I."

"He pushed aside the pain like one years more advanced. Even as the Grazz juice ate into his flesh, he persisted."

"I know. But that is not what stands out to me the most."

"Oh?"

"He managed something else. Something only a Master

should be able to do, and even then, only a few are capable of such a feat."

"What did he do, Hozark?"

"I connected with his konus, seeking any information I could about the event, and discovered quite the surprise. He tapped into it, Rovos. He actually drew magic from his konus to power his own body. To keep him going."

"That is impossible, especially at his age."

"It should be, but the konus does not lie. Its magic was drawn down and funneled into him."

Rovos was shell-shocked. This was so far beyond what even most masters could do, and Bawb was only a Vessel.

"He could become quite the Ghalian," the teacher finally said.

"I agree," Hozark replied. "And I think if he endures this healing well, it will be time to push him even harder. To help him achieve his true potential. It will be an interesting process, to say the least, and one I look forward to undertaking."

CHAPTER FIFTY-SIX

After a day of agonizing treatment forcing his flesh to regrow, Bawb was healed. While most would take at least an additional day to allow their body to recover from the strain of the ordeal, Bawb felt a newfound fire burning inside of him. One that demanded tribute in the form of hard training.

Hozark came and gathered him from his bunk house. Normally, a Master would try to avoid the students' one bit of personal space, but the others would still be out until their healing was completed.

"Are you ready?" he asked the boy.

"*You* are taking me to train?"

"I am. Again, are you ready?"

"Yes," he replied with stubborn resolution.

"Then follow me."

Hozark led the way through the familiar halls of the training house, leading the lone student deeper and deeper beneath its many levels until they reached what Bawb had thought was the lowest of them. Hozark walked down the corridor at the bottom of the stairs until he reached the small weapons' locker at the end of the hall.

He opened the door and stepped in. It was a small room, no more than a closet, really, but he gestured for Bawb to follow him inside. Without hesitation the teen did as he was told. Hozark closed the door behind him, casting a minor illumination spell as he did.

"You are about to become privy to something, and I need you to keep it to yourself. Can you do that?"

"You know I can."

Hozark nodded his approval. "That I do." He held up his hand and pressed it to the wall, then uttered the words "*Sorsha valmora*." The hidden door swung open, revealing a staircase leading even deeper beneath the compound.

"This way. You know the caverns and tunnels run far and wide, but there are also areas that go deep. So deep that the rock shields even the most sensitive above from feeling the use of power," he explained, leading the way down the dark stairs, the door sealing behind them. "It is ideal for practicing undisturbed."

"Why you?" Bawb asked. "I mean, why one of the Five?"

Hozark shrugged. "I am between contracts, and as you have been showing great promise of late, I wished to see your progress personally. You have come a long way, my boy, and I feel you may have an exciting life ahead of you."

Bawb walked in silence as they continued down the stairs, the weight of the stone above feeling as though it was pressing down upon them as they traveled farther and farther under the compound. Finally, they arrived at a simple door, deep beneath the training house. Hozark opened it and stepped through, no unlocking spell required. If anyone had made it this far, they were intended to be here.

The chamber illuminated at once, its layers of magic activating at the presence of a Master Ghalian.

Bawb looked around, less in awe, as he would have been in

his younger days, and more with the critical eye of a Ghalian, taking in everything and filing that information away in his mind, committing the layout to memory.

There were racks of weapons, as was common in pretty much any training area, but there was also a fascinating obstacle course taking up nearly half of the sizable chamber. The ceiling was smooth and domed, clearly formed by magic rather than the natural churning of the planet's core. A dizzying array of ropes, poles, beams, and swinging obstacles hung all over the place, some with fingerholds so tiny they were almost invisible to the naked eye.

At ground level there were poles and pits, shifting sands and breakaway flooring, the latter evidenced by the faint difference in sand around the seams between the stones. Hozark watched with pride as his son studied the chamber. This was as close to quality time as they would ever get. No one could ever know who Bawb was—besides the three who were with him through it all when he discovered his existence, that is. But Bud, Henni, and Demelza would take his secret to the grave if needed.

"Well?" he called out to the eager pupil. "I can see your interest. Go try it out."

Bawb flashed a bright grin and raced toward the obstacles, his mended body anxious for movement and strain, reveling in the exertion as he used his abilities as easily as breathing.

Bawb deftly crossed the loose sand, using his newfound skill with a certain spell to spread his weight wide and mask his footprints. When he reached the breakaway flooring, he easily leapt from safe stone to safe stone, his keen eyes and amped-up senses telling him where to tread. Then it was a quick scramble up a series of poles and a climbing wall that shifted and tilted as soon as he took hold.

Rather than fall, however, he pivoted, adjusting his center of balance with ease as he moved to new hand and foot holds.

Hozark couldn't help but grin. The boy was excelling beyond his expectations.

Bawb scrambled high, leaping without hesitation to grab a pair of ropes, each of them counterbalancing each other. He figured out the mechanics of the obstacle on the fly, swinging from pair to pair, launching himself through space with a sharp kick of his legs, his hands slapping home on the nearest dangling handhold.

Across the course he sped, his momentum carrying him over some of the sections where any delay would have meant slow and cautious progress. In this case, speed was his ally, allowing him to launch himself over some obstacles in ways few would have thought. He cleared the final rope, leaping to an angled pole and sliding it down to the ground, where he dove into an easy roll, springing to his feet, a good sweat on his forehead and a happy grin on his face.

Hozark threw something at him. Something long and blue. Bawb reached up instinctively and snatched it out of the air, his fingers wrapping around the hilt of the Vespus blade. The sword flashed bright, crackling with magic in his hands for several seconds before slowly fading to its normal inert appearance.

"What was that?" he asked, shocked.

"That was you connecting with my Vespus blade, Bawb. An incredibly powerful weapon, capable of storing vast quantities of magic from which one can draw upon as needed. A most potent weapon in the hands of any skilled swordsman, but one whose magic can only be wielded by a Master Ghalian."

"But it reacted to me."

"That it did. You clearly have the gift, even at your young age. Demelza did as well, though she was a bit older when—well, that is a story for another time."

Hozark picked up a sword from the rack and walked closer, then, without warning, unsheathed it in a flash, the blade arcing toward the boy's head. Bawb's arm reacted at once, years of muscle memory kicking in, but only barely. The metal rang out in a loud clang but the blue blade remained dark.

"Without proper training in its use, it will remain no more than a sword," Hozark said, lunging into a series of attacks, driving Bawb back against the onslaught. "A Ghalian must feel the power. Embrace it. Take it as your own and let it flow through you," he said, unrelenting in his assault.

Bawb spun aside, shifting the course of the attacks, buying himself a little space. Hozark immediately peppered him with small spells, simple ones designed to hurt but not kill. Bawb cast his defenses fast and furious, blocking most, but not all. Hozark pressed his attack as a spell landed, driving Bawb back on his heels, the magical blade flickering slightly as he desperately defended himself.

Oh, the konus said softly. *Oh my.*

Hozark unleashed an even more powerful spell, the force of it more than enough to throw the student clear across the chamber. Bawb felt it coming, his senses tingling as he cast the most powerful defense he knew, willing the spell to press out hard and stop the attack.

The Vespus blade flared bright, its light almost blinding as its magic raced into Bawb, powering his spell like never before. Hozark took the force of it full-on, flung violently across the room, tumbling along the floor but quickly rolling to his feet, a slight trickle of blood dripping from his nose.

A whole new series of skills flashed and abruptly unblurred on his konus display, but Bawb was too shocked to look at them, forcing them to minimize, lowering the sword in an instant. "I am so sorry. I-I don't know what happened."

"You do, Bawb," Hozark said, walking back toward him.

"Did *I* do that?"

Hozark's smile spread wide, bright with pride. On instinct,

he wrapped the boy in a hug, slapping him firmly on the back before catching himself showing emotion and releasing his embrace. "That you did, Bawb. I am very pleased with your performance. I thought you might be able to, but I had to push you hard to be sure. I am glad I was not mistaken."

Bawb looked at the sword in his hands, a feeling of serene confidence flowing through him. Hozark knew that look. He had the same one on his own face when he had first learned to wield the blade.

"Now, just imagine what you will be capable of once properly trained."

Bawb swung the Vespus blade a few times, then offered it back to his teacher. Hozark accepted it and sheathed the sword.

Level up: Vespus blade, advanced casting, defensive channeling–I could go on, but you will see in your display. That was actually amazing, Vessel. Far beyond your age and abilities. You're punching way above your weight here. You shouldn't have been able to do that for several more years, at the very least.

"Well, I guess you are not always right," he replied with a chuckle.

"What was that?" Hozark asked, a knowing gleam in his eye.

"Oh, nothing."

"Of course," he said, letting it go at that. "Well, I think you have more than proven yourself, Bawb. Let me teach you a few new spells. Far more advanced than any you know, but I have a feeling you are up for the challenge. But you will have to keep them to yourself, and only practice them down here where your magic will not be detected."

"I will. I am ready, Master Hozark, and I will not say a word to anyone."

"I know you won't. Now, I think we should start with a spell that is both challenging and fun, and I have just the thing."

CHAPTER FIFTY-SEVEN

It wasn't until three days later that all of Bawb's classmates were fully healed, and they were afforded a fourth to prepare themselves both mentally and physically for what lay ahead. Hozark had not been overstating when he said they would be given an extreme challenge to get their minds back in training mode, putting this incident behind them. It was going to be quite possibly their hardest yet.

"You are all to venture forth on a recovery mission," Demelza informed the gathered students. "This is not simply a quest to recover an item, though it is that at its heart. This is a test of your minds, of your will and fortitude as well. You will be tasked with reaching a specific location undetected, claiming a powerful tablet, a sacred item the Ghalian wish to acquire. Once you claim it, you will make your approach to the safety of the evacuation craft however you see fit."

"That is all?" Elzina asked.

"It will not be so simple. This will take days, possibly weeks. And you will be hunted."

The Vessels glanced at one another.

"Yes, I said hunted. Once you land, your presence will be

known. The people protecting the riches hidden in the area are fierce, and they will undoubtedly be pursuing you. They have been known to protect their treasures with great ingenuity. You will receive a head start if you keep quiet and do not immediately draw their attention, but nothing more. You will search out the correct location of the tablet and attempt to evade capture. Know this. You may not succeed. You may be taken, and if so, you will be tortured, possibly killed. It will not be easy on you. You must be willing to endure no matter what. The Order depends on your silence. Be smart, be silent, and keep your wits. Your transport awaits you at the closest landing site. Teacher Griggitz will greet you there. You leave at once."

The students left immediately, spreading out to use different exits as was their habit, never presenting the sight of so many young Wampeh leaving through a single doorway at once. In no time they wound their way through the streets and alleys, arriving one by one at the waiting ship where their teacher ushered them aboard.

"You are in for quite the adventure," he said with no sign of mirth or humor as they took their seats. "This is the sort of challenge all Vessels must undertake. I have gone through this. Teacher Demelza has. All of us faced some version of this ordeal. Having just recovered from your unfortunate incident, it has been decided to put you through this a bit sooner than normal. I expect each and every one of you to rise to the occasion. You are talented and strong. You would not have made it this far in your training if you were not. This is a brief on your destination. It is missing some information, but it will be enough to give you a basic idea of the landscape and your target. The rest is on you."

He cast an image spell, projecting the relevant information for them on the ship's wall, then left them to study the details. They would be in the thick of it soon enough.

They landed a short time later, having neither jumped nor even left the atmosphere. This quest, it seemed, would be carried out close to home. But that did not mean it would be easy.

"This swamp goes on forever," Albinius griped soon after they were left on their own to start the long wade through the muck and grime.

"Quiet. They will surely be after us sooner than later if we are detected," Elzina hushed him.

The group fanned out wide, working alone but also close enough that they would be able to notice if one of them was attacked. On and on they moved, the hours ticking by in the hot, swampy marsh. This was a part of the planet they had not visited previously. Remote, seismic, and wild. It was no wonder it had been selected as their proving ground. Even crossing it without being stalked would be quite a challenge.

They moved silently, not a word spoken as they sloshed ahead, but amazingly, they did not fall under attack. The students knew better than to let a sense of confidence make them careless. The protectors of this realm were out there somewhere, and they could be coming for them at any time.

The path that lay ahead was easy enough to follow. Even through the moss-draped canopy above them the students could see the sun's path, and with it their direction was relatively clear. Unfortunately, there was simply no way around the vast expanse of murky water. On the bright side, the foul nature of it kept all but the hardiest of creatures at bay, but the Vessels couldn't wait to be out of it.

At long last their prayers were answered when the trees parted and dry land presented itself, a broad swath of sand separating the swamps from the freshwater lake that bordered it. The lake was not terribly far across, but it was quite wide, making a traverse around it unreasonably dangerous. To be out in the open for any length of time was to court discovery and capture.

Zota hurried to the water's edge, rushing in and washing himself clean. He was a strong swimmer, and the crossing would be relatively easy, even pleasant after the long slog in the muck.

"Zota! Look out!" Usalla called to him as quietly but urgently as she could.

He saw the serpentine outline of the massive lake eel rushing toward him, the creature twice as big as he was, if not larger. He was waist-deep and knew there was no way he would make it out of the water in time. Not before the eel reached him. Instead of fleeing, he pulled his dagger, ready for a fight. But this fight was one he would not be having alone.

Bawb, Usalla, and the others rushed to his aid in the shallows, all of them striking the deadly beast as it attempted to attack. The flurry of blades made quick work of it, and the enormous creature floated dead before it knew what hit it.

The students rinsed the rest of the muck off quickly then hurried back to the safety of the shore.

"Thank you," Zota said, sheathing his blade.

"You would have done the same for us," Usalla replied. "And you have uncovered a surprising obstacle. We cannot swim across, even in a group."

Bawb turned and scanned the area, his eyes settling on the treeline where many fallen branches and trunks lay.

"No, but if we work together, we can build a raft of sorts."

"We are to work alone," Elzina protested.

"You are welcome to. But the sooner we cross this water, the more likely we are to avoid being observed. And this is the most expeditious way."

She hated to admit it, but she knew he was right.

"Fine. But we should make several smaller ones. They will be constructed faster, and we will have better odds."

Bawb shrugged, perfectly fine with the suggestion. "Agreed. Let us begin. There is no time to waste."

The students quickly lashed together fallen branches as best they could, using the long vines from the edge of the swamp to bind them. Elzina's suggestion turned out to be a good one as the plant material wasn't strong enough to hold together a raft of any significant size. In the end, only two to a raft was possible, the group making several of them in record time, each pair setting out to cross the lake as soon as theirs was completed.

The students paddled quickly, eyes scanning the water for any signs of predators. Fortunately, they reached the shore unscathed. At least, so it seemed, though a few of their number who had reached the shore first were already gone, likely hurrying ahead the moment they landed.

"You are on your own now," Elzina said, splitting off from the group and rushing toward the long stretch of open ground separating them from the trees.

The others followed suit, discarding their rafts and fanning out as they hurried toward the cover of the tree line. Unfortunately for them, it was not so simple as that. The mud at the shore was thick and tough, sucking at their feet and slowing their progress. It was misery, every step requiring far more effort than any cared to exert lest they need it later.

Bawb pulled his foot free, studying the obstacle in his path. This was going to be an arduous process. The others were trudging along, but it was slow going. He looked around and realized a few more of their cohort were no longer with them, hopefully simply taking a different path. He couldn't worry about that now, though. He had a task to complete.

Bawb put it out of his mind and turned back to the largest of the rafts, his knife in hand. He made quick work of the biggest log, splitting its bark the whole length then peeling it from the core. That done, he cut it into two large pieces, which he strapped to his feet. It wasn't perfect by any stretch, but it would be good enough. At least he hoped so.

He strode out onto the muddy soil, his weight spread out across the increased surface area. The makeshift mud shoes did as he had hoped, keeping him from sinking in. A slight grin on his face, Bawb carefully walked ahead, soon catching up to, and passing, his classmates as they struggled in the shin-deep mud.

He untied the bark from his feet when he reached the tree line, washing himself off in one of the puddles of water that lingered beneath the canopy. The other students soon joined him, each doing the same, rinsing the mud from themselves then preparing for the next part of the trek. If the intel on the area was to be trusted, it was going to be a difficult one.

Bawb felt the heat long before he reached the field of volcanic rocks. This was an active zone, the smell of sulfur and lava nearby acrid in his nose. His clothing steamed dry as he stood examining the expanse. This was going to suck.

Elzina was the first to venture out into the blistering expanse, her protective spells keeping the heat at bay, but only just. One by one the others followed. All but Bawb. He hesitated, then turned back the way they had come.

"Coward," Elzina scoffed, her clothing scorching on the edges where her spell was weakest. "He'll be caught in no time."

The others weren't so sure, but they had committed to the crossing, and nothing more was to be done for it. Concentration was paramount. Any failure in their magic could prove quite fatal, and no one wanted to cook to death. Not today. Not ever.

The students were scattered, spread across the lava field, each of them moving as fast as they could to reach the safety of the far side. And they were all suffering the heat of the ordeal. Some were simply reddened by the heat, while others found their skin burned, their protective spells lacking enough power to fully block them from harm. They moved quickly to the far side, dropping to the safety of the shady ground, releasing their spells and letting their roasting bodies cool from the effort.

"What is that?" Albinius wondered.

They turned to look at the brown form racing through the lava field, seemingly impervious to its heat. It was Wampeh-shaped, and as it grew closer, they realized what, or more precisely, *who* it was.

"Bawb?" the boy marveled.

Indeed, it was his friend, covered head to toe in mud from the vast field they had just traversed. He had applied a thick coating to his entire body, the mud turning to clay as he raced through the relentless volcanic heat. Bawb stopped in front of the others, the clay on his body steaming from the heat. He shook it free, peeling off large sections with ease as if they were giant shards of some massive pottery.

Underneath, he was sweaty but unharmed.

"Clever," Elzina grudgingly admitted.

Bawb looked at his classmates, spread out and recovering from their passage. "Where is Usalla? Where is Finnia?"

The others looked around, surprised. The two girls were gone, and they had been there just a minute ago.

"Gone ahead?" Zota wondered.

"Or taken," Elzina replied.

Bawb started moving for the trees at once. "Whatever the case, to remain stationary is to be a target. I, for one, do not intend to be captured."

CHAPTER FIFTY-EIGHT

The remaining members of the group split up after the volcanic crossing, spreading out wide in hopes they would thin their pursuers, giving at least one of them a chance at reaching the goal. Who that might be was anyone's guess and entirely up to the fates. Bawb intended it to be him, whatever it might take.

He crept silently for some time, his ears straining for any sound of a potential enemy. Bawb was without a shimmer cloak, but he had no doubt their adversaries, if skilled enough, could very well be using them. He would have to look for signs of passage, a crushed leaf here, an indentation in the soil there, and use that to postulate the most likely of paths to lead him safely to the tablet. From there, it should only be a short run to the finishing zone, though he was certain it would be anything but easy.

Amazingly, if he had memorized the topographical information they had been shown correctly, he was rapidly approaching the area where the tablet was to be found. Naturally, it was also quite close to what the intel had described as some sort of local prison camp. The sort of place captured students would have been taken to. The closer to the sacred tablet, the faster you could wind up in a cage or worse, it seemed.

Bawb pressed on, the cries of the captured students as they endured all manner of indignity echoing out through the evening air. They were all hardened to discomfort at this point, and they had all suffered more than their share of pain and injury. For their captors to be able to elicit such a response, the torment must have been something special, indeed.

"No!" one pained voice rang out in particular, clear in his ears.

Usalla.

Bawb's stomach clenched, his instincts telling him to run to her aid. But his mind was stronger, willing him ahead, onward to complete his mission.

Protection trap, his konus noted as they drew close to a small clearing.

"I sense it," he silently replied. The tablet was near, but apparently there was something Demelza had conveniently forgotten to mention. It was booby-trapped.

Of course it was.

Bawb stopped in his tracks, every sense on alert, sniffing the air for even the slightest whiff of sweat, his ears listening for anything out of the ordinary. A faint rustling sound reached him on the breeze, as did something else. A pungent, meaty stench. This wasn't one of the local adversaries. This was something else. Not part of the challenge, exactly, but it was getting closer.

Bawb wove through the trees silently, muffling his footsteps as best he could as he reached the edge of a small clearing. The tablet was there, dangling from a vine only a few feet off the ground above a decorative sand painting. A holy relic, but something else. He was sure there was more than just magic protecting it. There was some additional sort of trap in play as well.

He picked up a pair of small rocks, one flat and sharp, the other round like a marble. He chose the round one and tossed it toward the tablet. The faint ping of magic redirected it. The rock was too small to trigger the spell fully, but it confirmed his concerns in an instant. He tucked the other rock into his pocket and studied the problem carefully.

An idea began to form in his mind. The tablet was smaller than he had expected. Small enough to fit in his pocket if he really tried. His plan crystalizing, he turned and headed back into the wooded area, heading right toward whatever beast was drawing near. The clearing was directly behind him, a clear shot at a dead run with only a few trees in the way. Easy enough to weave through, but sturdy enough to slow any animal that might be pursuing him. And that was exactly what he intended to happen.

The inky-black spines on the Barzooki's back raised as it sniffed the air, the cow-sized creature anything but a docile herbivore. Its long claws dug into the soft soil as it padded closer on enormous paws, its golden eyes gleaming in the dim light. The Barzooki's irises sharpened into focus, locking on the young Ghalian.

"Yes, here I am," Bawb said, opening his trousers and releasing a spray of urine. Now that he knew what was stalking him, he knew what would upset it most. And a territory-marking display like that was sure to do the trick.

The beast let out a roar and charged without hesitation, but Bawb was already running. Running back toward the clearing, the animal chasing close behind, just as he'd expected. The Barzooki's enormous mouth snapped at him, but the trees forced it to alter course, narrowly missing his back. It was just enough distance for what he had in mind. At least, he hoped it was. If not, this mission would be coming to a much more abrupt ending than he intended.

Bawb burst into the clearing, sprinting right for the hanging tablet, the Barzooki close behind. He glanced over his shoulder. It was right upon him, gaining fast, its mouth open for the kill. Without warning, Bawb cast a force spell against his own back, forcing himself to the ground face down, hitting hard as he came to an abrupt stop.

The Barzooki had already committed to the attack, unable to stop itself. Its trajectory carried it forward. Forward into the dangling tablet, the protected item going right into its gaping mouth. The trap released at once, a large log swinging down from above, slamming into the creature. But Barzooki were tough beasts, and while the impact would have surely broken a few ribs, if not more, on a Ghalian teen, the Barzooki stood and shook it off with barely a scratch.

It spun to face Bawb, anger in its eyes. He climbed back to his feet, his dagger seemingly tiny against so large a foe. The Barzooki crouched, ready to pounce, but it froze in place, its body shaking violently. A moment later it fell to the ground, dead.

The corpse shook again several times as the tablet's defenses deployed over and over until the magic had finally run out. Only then did Bawb approach the dead animal, quickly pressing his blade into its belly and slicing it wide open. He dug around in its stomach, the partially digested remains of other animals sliding under his fingers, until he felt it. The tell-tale shape of the tablet. He pulled it free, its protective magic safely dispersed.

Bawb wiped it on the beast's lower hide where the spines were not present, then stuffed it in his pocket. Other animals were approaching now. He could smell them as well as hear them draw near. Smaller than the Barzooki, it was a group of what seemed to be foraging creatures. Powerful jaws, but bodies not built for the hunt. These were scavengers, evolved to eat whatever they could find.

Odds were, they did not want a fight. And to be fair, neither did he.

Bawb slowly stepped away from the fallen animal, maintaining eye contact with the approaching pack. "It is all yours," he quietly said. "I mean you no harm. Go ahead. It is still fresh and warm. A good meal for you and your family."

Amazingly, the animals shifted course, heading toward their free meal, though maintaining a wary eye on the two-legged animal slowly moving away from them. Bawb had to wonder if they somehow actually understood him.

Level up: empathic connection, the konus said.

Apparently so.

A pained cry rang out in the air. Again, Usalla. Whatever they were doing to her, it had to be bad. Bawb's fingers traced the outline of the tablet in his pocket, his mind urging him to find the escape vessel and run straight for it. But his gut pulled him in the other direction. His friend was in need. She was hurt.

Bawb turned from his path, heading instead into the woods, right toward the sounds of torture. He was going to help his friends. And if he timed it right, it would be something their captors would never see coming.

CHAPTER FIFTY-NINE

"This is foolish," Bawb silently chided himself as he crept in the direction of the cries of distress. "I should be heading for the recovery vessel."

Yes, you should, the konus agreed.

"I was not asking you."

Yet here we are. You know this is the wrong decision.

"Quiet. I must concentrate. And I need power."

Your disguise? Don't worry, you'll have more than enough for what you have in mind.

"How do you—stop reading my mind."

You mean like right now? Because you can talk out loud if you want, but I think you'll find yourself captured rather quickly.

Bawb ignored the konus, its observations hitting disturbingly close to home. He called up the device's power and cast the disguise spell he had decided on, opting for a simple skin and hair coloration change. Nothing drastic, nothing that would require too much magic, but enough to make him appear anything but a Wampeh. He had already buried the tablet, hiding it for quick retrieval, allowing himself to move faster without the cumbersome item stuffed in his pocket.

Sounds of beating grew clearer, the sharp crack of what appeared to be a whip or flog ringing out in his ears. Bawb stopped in his tracks. A tripwire spell lay hidden in the leaves before him. Clever. Whoever these people were, they were clearly skilled in the ways of defenses. He shifted his course accordingly, heading deeper into the brush, steering clear of anything resembling a footpath.

A lone figure sat resting against a tree, an empty bottle in his hand, slumbering soundly, it seemed. But Bawb knew better than to trust his eyes, no matter what the teachers may have told him prior. He quietly cast a detect disguises spell at the figure. The drunken man's green skin and red hair, however, remained unchanged. He really was an enemy hostile. At least this one was not much of a threat, but the others? That remained to be seen. Bawb snuck closer still.

Structures became visible through the foliage. Single level, built with wood and mud. The most basic of compounds, consisting of a few shack-like structures and a series of open-sided cages, the thick branches serving as bars more than adequate to contain the prisoners inside. The cells had plain dirt floors, devoid of so much as a twig. Nothing the prisoners could use to effect an escape. A wise choice on their part, as the Ghalian youth could use just about anything to break free, given enough time.

And Ghalian they contained, Bawb confirmed as he saw the telltale pale skin of his classmates. Most of them. A few were not present, but judging by the sounds coming from within the structures, their location was pretty obvious. They had all been stripped of their equipment, their blades and konuses missing. They had, however, been allowed to keep their clothing, so there was that at least.

He pressed forward through the brush, scanning for any

more spells. He didn't detect any, but a lone twig snapped in a manner that made his body tense.

"Oh no," he thought just as the hidden vine yanked tight around his legs, pulling him up into the air.

He reached for his knife but stopped. Footsteps were rapidly approaching. There was no way he would get free in time. Bawb quickly pulled off his konus, barely keeping the disguise spell active as he did, tucking it in his trousers as fast as he could. Nestled in place, the konus was still connected to him and as such, it fed the disguise spell its steady flow of magic.

You put me—

Bawb ignored the indignant device, his fingers searching his clothes for the small stone he had casually pocketed. He felt the sharp edge and took it from his pocket, tucking it between his cheek and teeth. It was just small enough to fit without being obvious. He hoped they would not punch him in the face. Not before he had been brought to a cage, at least.

"Got another one," a gruff voice called out.

A pair of thickly muscled brutes with deep green skin and brick-red hair approached, laughing at the teen snared in their trap. They stripped him of his dagger then bound his hands while he dangled there before cutting him down. Bawb hit the ground with a thud.

"This way," the smaller of the two said, nudging him forward with the tip of his own blade. "Move."

Bawb did as he was told. He was shoved into a cage, falling to the dirt as the gate shut and magically locked behind him. He spat out the rock, concealing it in the dirt as fast as he could. It turned out to be a good thing as a different brute came to retrieve him a minute later.

"Who are you? Where are you from? Who sent you?" he demanded.

Bawb remained in character, feigning innocence as best he could.

"I was lost. I don't know how I got here. Please can you—"

A sharp slap cracked against his face.

"Don't lie to me, boy! Who sent you?"

"I told you, I—"

Again, the meaty hand laid him out on the ground.

"Take him," the irritated man growled.

The pair that had captured him originally emerged from one of the huts, dragging the unconscious form of Finnia between them. They tossed her into a cell and locked it, then came for Bawb. This was going to be worse than he thought.

Bawb was beaten, flogged, then beaten again, but he maintained his story of innocence. Just as importantly, his konus remained undetected, tucked away in his trousers, and with it, he managed to maintain his disguise. Fortunately, he had cast a long-lasting spell. One that maintained even when he lost consciousness. Something that happened more than once during his initial interrogation.

It was clear that these were not just some rugged beastly primitives. Their use of magic made as much clear, and Bawb felt certain that had he tried to use his konus for anything externally focused they would have detected it and taken it from him in short order. He could use it to maintain his disguise, but nothing else.

Bawb was conscious when they tossed him back in his cell, but his body was aching from the ordeal. He looked at the others in their nearby enclosures. They'd clearly had it even worse.

Usalla was close, lying on the ground, resting as best she could. Zota and Elzina were nearby as well, similarly exhausted. Finnia had regained her senses in the time Bawb had been tortured. Interestingly, she seemed better off than the others. But then, she was on the spy path, and she had spent a great deal of additional time learning to endure this sort of thing. More than her assassin kin, she was likely to face interrogation at some point in her life. Possibly multiple times.

Bawb lay still, surveying his enclosure. As he had observed from the outside, it was indeed fashioned of sturdy branches bound with strong, dried vines. These, unlike the variety they had used to lash their makeshift rafts together, appeared to be quite durable. And their captors had not skimped on the construction.

Bawb felt the spell holding the gate shut. There was no way he was breaking it. Not even if he did risk using his konus for it. And as close as the huts were, their captors would be upon them in no time.

He crawled toward the far side of the cage, the most distant from both the gate and their captors' huts, his fingers stealthily retrieving the small rock from the dirt. He felt the edge. It was sharp, but the rock was so small. He began rubbing it against the bindings closest to the ground, masking his movements as best he could. The rock barely made a dent. This would take time. Unfortunately, it seemed that was something they would all have a lot of.

Days of torment passed, the time moving so slowly as they endured all manner of torture. Impact, heat, wet, and cold, their captors weren't holding back any tricks as they tried to extract any information they could from their prisoners. Bawb held fast, his resolve only strengthened by their brutal behavior. Others, however, were starting to crack.

Albinius was nearly in tears when they dragged him away to one of the structures at the far end of the compound after yet another torture session. The man in charge of his interrogation stepped out of the torture hut and waved over one of his minions.

"Bring him a hot meal and a blanket. All the water he wants as well."

"At once," the man replied, gathering a heaping bowl of the most wonderful-smelling stew, walking it slowly past the caged prisoners, each of them having survived on cold scraps and a few sips of water a day.

Bawb watched his friend with a fierce gaze, furious that he would dare betray his oath. His friends. But Albinius was gone before any words could be uttered, led to comfortable lodging and a warm meal.

The lead interrogator spun slowly, looking at each of them in turn. "Your cooperation will be rewarded. Each of you can be treated the same as your friend. Just tell us who sent you and you can sleep in a real bed. Eat hot food. You have been abandoned here. Why protect those who discard you so easily?"

Bawb stared daggers at the man, his resolve only strengthened by his words. He looked at the others and was pleased to see similar reactions. Usalla was holding strong, and he felt a sense of pride in her stoicism. He would get her out. He just had to keep doing what he was doing. Patience would reward him. It would just take time.

It was well over a week of captivity when he finally felt the last strands of vine part beneath the pressure of the tiny shard of rock in his fingers. He had worn the little fragment down to barely a nub in the hours and days he had surreptitiously filed down the bindings. But now he had finally done it. Bawb waited until it was late, then carefully pushed the freed branch, giving himself just enough space to squeeze out to freedom.

He froze, listening for any reaction, any alarm. There was none. He saw Usalla watching him with curiosity but nothing more. He was just another prisoner, after all. But now he let his disguise slip, revealing himself to her for the first time.

Her eyes widened but she remained silent. Bawb held up a

finger, as if to say he would be back in a minute. He then turned and quietly snuck out of the compound, careful for *all* manner of snares and alarms as he did.

Bawb gathered up the buried tablet. It was right where he'd left it. Satisfied that at least that had gone right, he stuffed it in his pocket then found a larger rock. He took the konus from his pants and slipped it back onto his wrist, casting the muting spell he had practiced for so long as best he could. He took another rock and struck the two together, holding still and listening. There was no commotion anywhere. No reaction. The spell must have worked. He struck it again, chipping away until a wicked edge had formed. This he could use. *This* could cut much, much faster.

What are you doing? You have the tablet. Get out of here, already!

"One last thing," he replied.

Are you an idiot? No! Finish the mission.

"I said one last thing."

Bawb hurried back the way he came, careful to step exactly where he had on the way out until he was back in the compound. He moved silently to Usalla's cage and began whacking away at the bindings holding the bars in place.

"What are you doing? Get out of here," she said.

"I am going to get you out."

"It is too risky. You must flee."

"Not without you. They are all asleep, and I've cast a muting spell. No one can hear us."

"*I* can hear you," she replied. "I have heard you this whole time."

Bawb felt a sudden sinking feeling in his gut. If she had heard him, that meant—

The stun spell from behind knocked him unconscious before he could finish the thought.

CHAPTER SIXTY

Bawb woke from the stun spell slowly, his head still a bit foggy from the powerful magic that had blasted him unconscious. He lay still, gathering his thoughts, assessing his body. He had been working to break Usalla free when something had happened.

It all flooded back. His muting spell. It had failed, yet again, and his captors had allowed him to think it worked, lulling him into a sense of security and luring him back to camp. With the stolen tablet, no less.

He had failed. Miserably, at that. And yet, as he surveyed his injuries, something odd stood out. His wounds appeared to be healed, the bruises and aches gone. And was that a mattress he was lying on rather than hard dirt?

Bawb forced his eyes to open slowly, careful not to draw attention to himself as he took in the situation. He was in a large hut, and all of his classmates were there as well. Healed, cleaned up to a degree, and eating big bowls of warm porridge.

"He is awake," Usalla said, Bawb realizing she was sitting beside him this whole time.

"Ah, good," a familiar voice replied. "He has been out for a while now."

"Teacher Donnik?" he said, sitting upright.

The Ghalian was wearing the garb of their captors, he noted. In fact, there were a few other familiar faces, Masters he had seen in passing, all of them similarly clothed.

"It was all fake," he realized.

"No. It was real, but also a test. We simply removed the real guardians of the tablet for now. Heavy sleep spells that will keep them out for days yet. We did see you utilize your disguise detection spell on the decoy we left in plain view. A wise course of action, though you did not think to apply it again after that."

"But why—"

"You had all faced a situation recently that could have caused any one of you to doubt your calling. It was your closest brush with death, and one of your number succumbed. We felt it was appropriate to throw you back in the deep end, so to speak. What you have endured is standard evasion and escape training. We simply combined it with an actual mission."

"And the torture? The attempts to get us to betray the order?"

"Merely part of the process. All of you would eventually be captured, though *you* did give us a good run of it for a time. You nearly completed the task, much to all of our surprise."

"But I failed."

"Yes, but because of your propensity toward emotional responses. You care too much, Bawb, and it could cost you one day. Now, you fared better than the others, I give you that. But you allowed your feelings to get the better of you. Twice, in fact."

"I have no feelings. I am a Ghalian," he protested, but only half-heartedly.

"It is not wrong to care, Bawb. Even the Masters have feelings. But we keep our emotions under control. Hidden. Locked away where they can do us no harm. I would only remind you that while we are not entirely cold, you must nevertheless be aware of your actions, and just as importantly, your visceral reactions."

Bawb had no defense for the accusation. He knew it was true. Had he simply focused on the task and left Usalla behind, he would very possibly have completed it. But his concern for his friend made him make an illogical choice. A mistake.

"I understand you and Usalla have been spending much time together."

"I...we—" He looked at his friend. She held his gaze, but her cheeks flushed slightly despite her best efforts.

Donnik simply nodded. No judgment, just acknowledging the situation. "She is your friend, Bawb, and friendship is always a worthy bond. But do not let it cost you your life. Or, worse yet, cost *both* of you. You may face similar challenges one day. Ones where you are deployed and come across another Ghalian, even a friend, in a dire situation. And it is possible you will simply be unable to help. Always remember, it is not enough to simply complete your task. You must also live to continue your work. Ghalian are few, and much effort goes into molding you into your final form. We are not mercenaries or simple killers for hire. We are the elite of the elite, and not disposable pieces to be played and lost carelessly in some foolish endeavor."

"I understand, Teacher. Thank you."

"Good."

"But what of the promise of comfort? Of freedom? I see Albinius is with us, yet he betrayed the order."

At that Donnik actually chuckled. "Oh, he remained true to the order. What you saw was merely a ploy. A means to get students to fracture alliances and pit them against one another. And we are pleased that you all passed the test."

"He did not betray the order?"

"Hardly. He was simply chosen as the most probable to elicit a response from the rest of you if he was to be seen as a turncoat."

Bawb felt something unusual in his gut. Shame. He had assumed his friend had turned on them and would have possibly killed him had he been given the chance. But it was all a ruse. A play on all of their emotions. And after falling for the trick in such a visceral fashion, it was a lesson that would stick with Bawb for the rest of his days. Things were not always as they seemed, and he would do well to use that knowledge not only to avoid being deceived, but to fool others himself. One more tool in his arsenal of tricks on the path to becoming a full-fledged Ghalian.

"You will have plenty of time to revisit this experience and discuss it with your peers. That, too, is part of the process. Sharing and learning from one another. Someone else's experience and insight may help you one day." Donnik turned to the other Masters. "I will take them home while you return this camp's rightful occupants to their places."

"Won't they realize what happened?" Bawb asked.

"They will wake in a day or so with headaches, surrounded by empty bottles of overly fermented local liquor. Providing them with an easier, though unlikely, reason gives them a simple out when it comes to explaining what happened. A shared mishap that they will likely not speak of again. Now, come along. Let us get all of you home. You have had a long go of it, and I am sure you would like to sleep in your own beds."

The students rallied at those words, excited for the end of this grueling test. Some of them had fared quite well, while others had come close to breaking, and they had all gone through it together. It was the sort of experience that would strengthen their bonds moving ahead and stay with them the rest of their lives.

The flight back was short, as they were still on their own

planet. No lengthy jumps, no exiting and entering the atmosphere. Just a calm, quiet flight across the planet.

The transport ship set down at one of the more distant landing sites, affording the Vessels a long walk in familiar territory as a sort of psychological palate cleanser. They disembarked with a spring in their step, the smells of home filling their noses. But something was unusual. Master Hozark was there, waiting.

"To what do we owe the honor?" Donnik asked, not calling the Master by his title or name with so many bystanders around.

"I require Bawb," was the reply. Simple, to the point, and with no further explanation.

Hozark was one of the Five. None was needed.

"He is yours," Donnik replied with a little bow, gesturing for the boy to join them then turning his attention back to the other students.

"Follow me," Hozark said, nothing more.

Bawb knew better than to question, falling in behind him, quickly crossing the landing area. He saw their destination almost immediately. A familiar one at that. Bud and Henni's ship. Apparently, he was not going home after all.

CHAPTER SIXTY-ONE

"There he is," Bud greeted the teen as soon as he stepped aboard. "Been waiting on ya."

"I was away on a training assignment."

"Oh, we know all about that," Henni chimed in, joining them at the hatch.

Hozark stepped aboard and sealed it behind him, casting the locking spell to ensure no air would escape. "Shall we?"

"Yeah," Bud agreed. "Come on, Bawb. Up to command we go."

The foursome walked straight to the command module and slid into their respective seats. Bud at the helm, Henni at his side. Hozark and his young protégé took up positions nearby in the padded seats.

"Okay, hang onto your bootstraps. We're gonna fly!" Bud said with a laugh, the ship pulling up hard, pushing for the edge of the atmosphere.

A moment later the buffering spells kicked in and all returned to normal. All but the lack of explanation for their hasty departure.

"What is going on?" the boy asked, more than a little confused.

Hozark turned to face him. "Your intelligence has proven accurate. Lalaynia was indeed being held on Zephin and was later moved to Boxxna. To the very same keep you managed to enter on your retrieval mission while your classmates all failed."

"She is being held in Voralius's compound?"

"It would seem so."

This was news to Bawb, but not exactly unexpected. "Why the rush?"

Henni spun her chair around to face him. "We've gotta get her before she's moved again and we lose track of her. This might be our best shot at getting her out."

"Okay, but I do not see why this required my presence."

Hozark's expression grew serious. "Because the spy we sent to confirm your reporting was discovered and nearly captured. She only just managed to escape, but only having verified Lalaynia's presence there. She did not have the opportunity to delve further into the keep. We need you, Bawb. We are going to get her out, and you are coming with."

"Me?"

"You may not feel you are ready, but I have seen you perform well beyond your years. Believe me when I tell you, you have the skills."

"All right, but why wait for me to get back if it was so urgent?"

"Because you have been inside, and we require firsthand knowledge of the layout."

"I only got in that one time."

"One more than anyone else."

"And Nixxa and her goons stopped me from venturing farther."

"I am aware. But your experience with disarming and

avoiding the defensive system is vital. We will not have the time to spare in order to be slow and methodical in our entry. We will rely on your knowledge to allow a rapid ingress. Once inside you will fall back behind us and cover the rear. Simple enough, yes?"

"I suppose. But what do we do if someone trips an alarm once we are in?"

Henni's lips curved upward into a rather frightening grin. "Oh, if that happens, *then* we kick some serious ass. No holds barred. They took our friend, and that aggression will not stand."

The ship popped out of the atmosphere into space, powering ahead at top speed, hurtling through the void on the run to their ultimate destination. Bawb's mind was racing, taking in all the details he had just had dumped on him at once.

"So, it really was Nixxa after all," Bawb mused. "I thought it was odd, her being involved in that sort of thing, being a pirate herself."

Hozark shook his head. "No, it was not Nixxa, though she has been present in a few situations where it would make it appear that was the case. But I questioned her at length about her affairs in this matter and am satisfied she is not involved."

"Wait, you spoke with her?"

"Yes. Aboard her ship, in fact."

"But she has casters protecting her. Guards. How did you manage that?"

Bud and Henni both laughed out loud.

"Oh, kid, this is your man Hozark we're talking about," Bud said through his mirth. "Believe me, with him coming for you, no ship is as secure as anyone might think."

"Yeah, but I bet that changed the minute he left," Henni added. "Probably has a whole bunch of new spells on her hull just to prevent it from happening again."

"Her hull?" Bawb wondered.

Her eyes twinkled with amusement. "You didn't notice it when you boarded, but Hozark's shimmer ship is latched onto ours as we speak. Cloaked, tethered, and completely undetectable."

"The point is, she is not responsible," Hozark continued. "And as such, she is no longer my concern. Yes, she is quite a pest at times, but it seems kidnapping a fellow pirate is below even her ever-shifting standards."

"Damn well better be," Henni noted. "Because if she goes and crosses *that* line, she's gonna wind up in a world of hurt, and fast. Everyone pretty much puts up with her shit because she does a lotta good for a bunch of oppressed people in the process. But even that leeway has limits."

"Yeah, and Lalaynia has saved a *lot* of people's asses over the years," Bud added. "People owe her all over the galaxy. Big time. Speaking of which, we really should get going."

"But we are going," Bawb said, confused. "It will only be a few jumps to get there, if I am not mistaken."

Henni laughed, her eyes sparkling far more than usual. "Oh, we'll be there much sooner than that."

Bawb felt a strange sensation building around her. Something he had never felt before. He had always been told she possessed great power, but he had never felt it until today. Not like this.

Henni threw him a wink. "And away we go!"

She flexed her power hard. A split second later the ship jumped, flashing out of existence in its leap across the stars. It was a jump, all right, and it was unlike any Bawb had ever experienced.

They arrived a little distance from Boxxna, Henni's massive power carrying them the length of multiple jumps in a single trip. Bawb's jaw nearly dropped at the incredible display of magical force, and he couldn't help but wonder what else this tiny, fierce woman could do.

"We're still a few planets out," Bud announced. "Nice one, babe. Right on the money."

"Of course it was."

"I will never doubt you."

Bawb looked at the tiny speck of Boxxna so far away from them. "Why this distant? Are we not in a hurry?"

"Yeah, but we can't risk anything resembling a hasty approach. Hozark, you wanna explain it?"

The Ghalian took over for his friend. "You see, we will split into two landing teams. Bud and Henni will arrive at the main landing field within the capital. This will draw attention and scrutiny, as does any arrival, but they will play it cool, defusing any suspicion. We will arrive on my shimmer ship a short while later, approaching very slowly so as to not disturb any lingering mists before depositing it atop a building I have selected. Far enough from Voralius's keep to avoid triggering alarms, but close enough for rapid egress if needed."

"Two escape options if that winds up being required," Bawb realized. "Clever."

"Indeed. And once both ships are in place, we will make our ingress."

"And let's remember one very important thing," Henni added. "Today the Ghalian are *not* working alone. It's Lalaynia we're talking about here."

Hozark caught Bud's warning glance, but he already knew better than to argue.

"I would not have it any other way," he said. "Now, let us prepare. This is undoubtedly going to get bloody."

CHAPTER SIXTY-TWO

Bud and Henni's trademark jovial ease was nowhere to be found when Bawb and Hozark departed for his shimmer ship. It was that more than anything that told Bawb just how serious this really was.

He and Hozark boarded the cloaked craft and unlatched, drifting free as the smugglers sped away, dropping into the atmosphere of Boxxna and heading straight for the landing site. The one right near Voralius's stronghold.

Hozark followed a little while later, carefully entering the atmosphere far from the region they would be landing at. The shimmer magic did not work well in space typically, though Hozark was one of the few who could make it function nearly as well there as in atmosphere. But the real challenge was reentry. Most would have to decloak to enter the atmosphere. With Bawb assisting, however, Hozark had other plans.

"Take the helm," he instructed the boy as he slid from his seat. "I am going to focus on maintaining our shimmer cloak."

"Me?"

"You know you are capable. Do not think, Bawb. Just do."

Bawb took his words to heart. He knew this wasn't the time

for uncertainty or debate. It was time for action, nothing less. He climbed into the pilot's seat and began their descent as he had practiced, flying the shimmer ship with an ease that surprised him. Hozark was right. He just needed to stop second-guessing himself.

The ship barely shuddered as it reached atmosphere, the cool air on the hull allowing the shimmer spell to hold with far less effort and power.

"You did well," Hozark said, reclaiming his seat. "And now the tricky part."

"That was not it?"

"No. Many of the buildings in the area are owned by other wealthy residents. This is a rather paranoid lot, and a good portion of the structures here are protected by warding spells. We will have to make a very careful approach and select our landing site wisely."

Hozark flew a slow and cautious circuit of the city atop the volcanic peak. Fortunately, the mists were low on the mountain today, making their approach easier. Now that he knew what to look for, Bawb also felt the telltale hints of warding magic surrounding most of the rooftops. It seemed these people were more than a little wary of uninvited intruders.

"There. That one," Hozark decided, quietly setting down the ship into a low hover atop a two-story structure with stout stone walls and a thick rooftop.

He triple-checked the shimmer spell, then led the way out of the hatch, crouching low as he and the Vessel scurried to the far end of the roof, climbing down to the empty alleyway without anyone being the wiser.

They walked casually from that point, blending in as easily as breathing. There was a small outdoor food and drink vendor near their destination, and it was there they would rendezvous with Bud and Henni.

Bawb saw them from a distance. He had trained with them a lot, but he'd never seen Henni in this particular outfit. And from what he could tell of the subtle bulges under her clothing, she was carrying a lot of blades on her. As daggers were her weapon of choice, it didn't surprise him. The utterly serious look in her eyes, however, did.

The two smuggler pirates were usually jovial and fun, but now they were all business. And from their demeanor, it would likely be the bloody kind.

Hozark walked past them, heading on a roundabout path to Voralius's thick-walled keep. Bud and Henni paid for their snacks then took a parallel street, joining with them a few blocks later.

"There is an animal tied up near the area Bawb said houses the entrance," Bud noted. "I can take it, but it might raise an alarm."

"Unfortunate," Hozark said with a sigh. "Yet we cannot avoid the unexpected."

"Wait. Let me try," Bawb urged.

The others looked at one another and shrugged. "Very well," Hozark agreed. "Let us see what you can do."

Bawb took the lead, walking ahead of the others by a fair distance as they closed in on the hidden entryway. There was little foot traffic in the area, but Bawb smelled the more pressing concern before he even saw it.

The creature was chained to a volcanic rock a mere stone's throw from their destination. It seemed, however, to be completely random, not some sort of response to his prior incursion. If what they said about Voralius was true, this was one of several repositories of wealth, and it was highly unlikely anyone had even noted the break-in. Nixxa had gotten away clean, as had Bawb. Unless someone else had made an attempt and failed, they could very likely get in the exact same way he had previously.

If he could get around the beast crouched by the doorway, that is.

Bawb held up one hand, focusing entirely on the animal. It was several times larger than he was, resting comfortably on muscular haunches, its black, velvety fur seeming to absorb the sun's energy, radiant in its healthy glow. Bawb wondered if it was in some way related to the Malooki they had ridden on the prior visit. Its morphology was completely different, but maybe this was reactive hair rather than fur.

He would need to get closer to find out. And that was exactly what he planned to do.

Bawb walked closer, his eyes locked with the beast's. "Hey there, friend. I mean you no harm. You sense that, right? No need to raise an alarm. I am just going to walk over here past you. Nothing to worry about."

The animal shifted slightly, but it remained calm, watching him with more curiosity than aggression. Bawb reached out and carefully placed his hand on its flank, allowing a reassuring flow of calming energy to emit from his konus and into the creature. The beast flinched slightly, then leaned into it, enjoying the pleasurable contact.

"Yes, there we go. We are all friends here."

Bud's jaw nearly hit the ground at the sight. "Well, I'll be damned. He actually did it. Come on!"

He hurried ahead, the others following close. Bawb saw his advance and sensed the animal tense at the movement, but there was no way to warn the others off. Yelling would just spook it further. He had to make a snap decision.

The animal jumped up to its feet, baring its massive teeth, then abruptly fell to the ground in a heap. Bawb slowly took his hand from its side.

Bud pulled up short at the sight. "What was that?"

"You alarmed her. You should have moved slower."

"Jeez, sorry, kid. I didn't know we had time to spare. But what did you do to it? I don't see any blood."

"I simply overloaded her with power. I sensed her physiology was receptive to magic, and I hypothesized a sizable intake would trigger a refractory period while she absorbed it. Much like a post-meal nap. And with as much magic as I fed into her, she should be out for a while."

"Wait, you *talked* to it?"

"Not exactly. But sometimes animals listen to me. Sort of, anyway."

"Hozark, did you know he could do this?"

"I did not, but given the boy's skills, I am not surprised," he said, a glimmer of pride in his eyes. "We can discuss this later. Bawb, lead the way. We must make our entrance quickly."

"Right over here," he replied, carefully intoning the words to bring them inside the illusion hiding the doorway.

Bud stared at the suddenly visible entrance. It had been a stone wall just moments before. "Damn, kid, that's impressive. Now what?"

"Now he leads us inside," Hozark answered for him. "I will follow close behind. Bud, Henni, you take up the rear. And do not touch anything. I feel this will be a delicate incursion, so no sudden movements."

"Ya don't have to worry about us," Henni chimed in. "Slow and steady is our middle name, right?"

"Yeah, that's us," Bud replied, his spirits, at least temporarily, returning to their usual state of levity. "Okay, Bawb, lead the way."

The teen did just that, moving through the traps, wards, and tripwire spells much faster than the first time. Hozark was right, nothing new had been added, but even so, it required all of his attention to keep the magical defenses intact while creating a safe path for them to pass. Once the alarms went off, all hell would break loose, so they would avoid that if at all possible.

They reached the corridor at the end of the series of traps, each breathing a little sigh of relief. But the mission had only just begun. Hozark stepped out in front of the group.

"I will lead. Bawb, follow close behind me. Bud, Henni, you know what to do."

"Kill anyone who comes at us from behind," the little spitfire of a woman said, wrath in her eyes.

Bawb was fascinated that Hozark actually seemed amused at her reply. "Just make it fast, and do not fall behind," the master assassin said, moving ahead, his ornately handled enchanted dagger firmly in hand.

Bawb had never seen him use it. Not for real. But from all the tales he had heard, be it Vespus blade or dagger, Hozark was one of the deadliest ever to wield an edged weapon.

They made it through the treasure storage chamber, where Bawb had found the Balamar water, only to find it had been untouched since his visit. Apparently, the rumors were correct. Voralius had not even noted the theft. And that meant they had precious time on their side to find his newest valuable possession. The two-legged pirate kind.

"Which way, Bawb?" Hozark asked. "There are three other doors."

"Not that one. That is where Nixxa and her people made their escape. Odds are it leads outside. It would have to be one of the other two."

"Very well, we try the one on the right," Hozark decided, not wasting a moment on uncertainty. It was a fifty-fifty bet either way. There was no sense expending brain power on the unknowable. "Wait for me."

Hozark opened the door quietly and stepped through. A

moment later he dragged the sleeping body of a guard back into the room.

"Only the one. This is a good sign we are on the right path. Be ready. Others may not be so easily dealt with."

He led them ahead into the corridor, his Ghalian skills sensing guards before they were present, allowing the intruders to tuck away as they passed. This was not an indiscriminate killing mission despite Henni's feelings on her friend's capture. They needed to get as far as possible without being seen. There were only four of them, and one was still just a student. Against an entire compound of guards, the odds were not in their favor even with one of the Five leading the charge.

"This way," Hozark said, leading them up a staircase.

Bawb thought about the decision. Now that he knew more of the city's defenses, it made sense. Keep the pirate in a higher location, as the rooftops were mostly heavily protected. There would be no aerial rescues from this facility.

Up and up they went, Hozark reaching out with his magic, sensing for the slightest trace of their target. On the fourth floor landing he stopped, all of them silent in the stairwell. He cracked the door open, peered through, then closed it once more.

"This is it," he said quietly, then cast the most powerful muting spell he could muster.

Bawb felt the magic behind it in awe. *This* was how you cast a muting spell. He would take note, for future use. That is, provided he had a future. While the spell would deaden the sound of the inevitable carnage when they passed through that door, one thing was for certain. It was going to be a fight, and a tough one at that.

Hozark drew the blue blade from his back then turned to the teen. "Take this," he said, handing him his enchanted dagger. "It will cut deep and true. Use it well, and remember your training."

Bawb took a deep breath and steadied himself. He'd faced a lone enemy and prevailed, but this was something completely different. He would be punching way above his weight, fighting in his first true melee. He set his jaw tight with resolve, the dagger ready in his grip. He would do more than succeed. He would excel. It was his calling. Now he just had to prove it.

CHAPTER SIXTY-THREE

The first guards fell before they knew what hit them. Hozark showed why he had achieved the highest level within the Ghalian in the first seconds out of the door. This was a fortified level, and not only housed the standing detachment of guards on active duty, but also their barracks and mess hall. Fortunately, most were on duty elsewhere at this hour, so that left only a few dozen for the intruders to deal with.

A few dozen armed, trained, expert guards, that is.

Bawb flew into action, dodging the swords and daggers swinging his way, his muscle memory kicking in so hard and fast that he had made his first kill without realizing it. Bud and Henni were following behind, but not before rushing the opposite direction, taking down a trio attempting to sound an alarm.

Henni's knives were a blur of gleaming death as she lay into them. Bud, on the other hand, was far more collected, moving with the skill and accuracy of an already talented pirate who had been fortunate enough to be further trained by one of the deadliest assassins in the galaxy. It paid to have friends in high, and low, places.

The small rear contingent dealt with, they closed the gap quickly, spreading out to handle any guards who might exit a room behind Hozark and Bawb as they passed.

The floors, surprisingly, did not grow slick with blood. Not yet, anyway. The Ghalian duo leading the way were striking with speed and accuracy, their foes dropping dead at their feet, their hearts no longer pumping, leaving their precious blood to trickle out rather than spurt.

Noise was a concern, but Bawb glanced back and saw no one was rushing them from the closed rooms they had passed. Hozark's muting spell was keeping the sounds of battle contained to this corridor and this corridor alone. It would delay reinforcements, at the very least, but if they were lucky, they might even make it through their advance without the other guards in the barracks being any the wiser. If fortune was truly on their side, their enemies would open their doors to find piles of the dead with no explanation.

And oh, what a way that would be to find out they had missed a battle. Their employer would be most displeased, indeed.

"Which way, Bawb?" Hozark called back to the teen.

He had no idea. He'd never been in this part of the building. But Hozark knew that. He was asking him because he already knew the answer. He also knew Bawb had the training under his belt to discern it himself.

Bawb parried a sword and drove the dagger into the chest of his attacker, taking in the sights, sounds, and even smells despite being in the middle of combat. Just as he had been taught to do. The noise around them was still overwhelming, the clashing of metal and grunts of the dying. As for visual cues, the corridor split into three directions at the intersection ahead. But there was something. Something telling.

Bawb sniffed the air again. Yes, there was the stench of sweat, feces, and a hint of fear.

"Left," he replied, certain prisoners were being held in that direction.

Hozark nodded his approval and shifted course. Bud and Henni hurried to catch up, staying in place a moment to ensure no one was following through the converging corridors before hurrying along.

A blast of magic unexpectedly flowed down the corridor. Hozark's Vespus blade flashed bright as it defended against the attack. Casters had joined the fight, Bawb realized. Now it was going to get *really* interesting.

"On me," Hozark called back to the teen, then pressed ahead, racing toward the three casters who had come to the aid of their comrades. "They will sound an alarm. My spell will not deter all of them. We must move fast."

The guards down this corridor were better armed and ready for the attack. Someone must have seen them arrive and gone ahead to warn them. A good twenty men and women were stacked and ready, bristling with swords and knives. No spears, however. The fighting space was too crowded for that, and their comrades were being forced back toward them. Shorter weapons were called for, and all had prepared accordingly.

Attack spells flew fast and furious, but Hozark batted them aside with ease, drawing from his Vespus blade's deep well of power. Bawb felt the enchanted dagger in his hands thrum with excitement, anxious for battle now that magic was being used. It seemed the weapon almost enjoyed the challenge. Considering who it belonged to, that actually wasn't very surprising.

Hozark's blade sliced through the defenses, blood spraying as the magical tool parted arms and head from bodies with ease. Bawb felt himself slammed backward by a fierce spell. One that nearly overcame his defenses. This caster was fairly powerful, and they had tried a killing spell on him. Fortunately, it was Ghalian training to cast defenses against just such an attack the moment they entered battle. The spell would need refreshing as time wore on, but even diminished it should at least keep him alive, though possibly hurt.

Bawb rushed ahead, slipping past Hozark for a moment, driving his legs off the wall, diving in a flip over a line of guards expecting him to attack like a normal person would.

They should have known better.

Bawb landed atop the caster they were shielding, knocking him hard and interrupting his continuous chanting of spells. With one caster momentarily out, the other two would have a much harder time overlapping their attacks while the other took a breath.

Bawb's instincts kicked in immediately, his fangs springing out and sinking into the caster's neck. He felt a rush of strong magic flood his body, his every sense tingling and alive as he stole every drop of their power.

"Bawb, enough!" Hozark shouted.

Bawb snapped from his daze, rolling aside and casting a brutal force spell, crushing the two guards almost atop him into the wall with such force he could hear bones break. He looked at his konus, shocked.

It wasn't me. That was all you, the konus said, forcing the jackpot-bright display of unlocked levels and skills to minimize without Bawb saying a word. This was not the time. *Keep your head, Vessel.*

Bawb did just that, lunging back into the fight, hacking, stabbing, and casting beside the Master Ghalian. He had just used the power he'd taken, and it was a heady feeling. It flowed through him, powering his spells with so much more force than his restricted konus ever had. Now he was feeling *true* power, and it was power without a limiter holding him back.

Bud and Henni closed the gap, the four of them now forming a deadly bubble of blades and magic. They felt the magical bombardment lessen. Hozark had just eliminated another of the casters. Only one remained. But this was not the time for premature celebration. They still had to find their friend. Then, they would have to fight their way out.

More guards streamed toward them from the rear, clogging the corridor with bright blades and angry eyes.

"Any time now," Bud called out. "Where is she?"

Henni stepped behind him, allowing him to act as a shield while she reached out, trying to sense her friend. She was a reader. Always had been. And while she had politely not used her skills on her friends once she learned to control them, now was as good a time as any to let it flow free.

Her eyes sparkled as she sensed a presence masked by magic. But with the casters falling, that magic had weakened.

"She's in the second chamber on the left," she called out just as another wave of attackers reached them from the rear. Bud was having a hard time of it, their numbers simply too many for one man. But now Henni was back in the fight, and they flowed and moved together as if they shared one mind, their years together forging a sort of violent shorthand that only they spoke.

Bawb glanced back, astounded that he had never seen them fighting at full-tilt capacity. It was impressive to say the least, and to one in the order, their Ghalian tutor's training was plain to see.

Hozark cast a powerful force spell, driving the guards, and even the caster back down the hallway. They were a tough bunch, but they thought these intruders were trying to fight their way past them to reach one of the chambers holding valuable treasure. They were wrong, and it would be their demise.

The cell door was unguarded, the fallen back guards not

worrying about just another prisoner. Hozark kicked it open, directing a powerful spell to his foot, shattering the locking mechanism. It was an expenditure he'd rather not have made, but if he could get to that last caster, he could more than make up for it by taking their power.

Most importantly, though, by leaving the door unguarded, the prisoner had been set free. They had no idea who they were really holding, or her skill in battle. They would realize their mistake in short order.

Henni rushed into the cell. Lalaynia stood close, ready to fight but her hands were bound by chains, a slender control collar on her neck.

"Henni?" she blurted as a shock from the collar dropped her to her knees.

"God damn it!" Henni growled. "Cover me."

She sheathed her daggers and grabbed the collar with her bare hands, the magical restraint glowing under her grip. The metal grew hot, but Lalaynia ignored the pain, as did her friend.

"Come on!" Henni shouted, pulling hard, channeling her magic hard through her clenched fists. The band let off a burst of stored magic, then fell silent, the metal snapping apart in her hands.

She dropped the defunct restraint to the ground and wrapped her arms around her friend.

"Glad to see me?"

"You know I am," Lalaynia replied, raising her bound hands. "But do you think you could do something about these?"

"Allow me," Hozark chimed in, his glowing Vespus blade flashing through the air, separating the chains as if they were butter. "We will remove the cuffs later."

"Good enough for me," the pirate said, moving her arms freely for the first time in far too long.

"We've gotta make a break for it," Henni said. "Can you walk?"

"Walk? Give me a sword, and I'll do a lot more than walk," Lalaynia replied, still fierce as ever despite months of being beaten and tormented. "Payback's a bitch. And that bitch is me."

Bud pulled a blade from a dead man's hands and tossed it to her. Lalaynia snatched it out of the air, wincing from her injured shoulder but shaking it off, spinning the sword with glee and the promise of a most violent payback.

Henni grinned wide, her face full of cheer and violence. "Come on. This is gonna be fun!"

Bawb wasn't so sure that was the word he would use for the difficult escape they would be forced to make, but they could call it whatever they liked so long as they managed to get free of the fortified keep.

"The way back is too difficult. We must find another egress," Hozark called out.

"There are stairs to the right. They will take us to the main gate," Lalaynia shouted as she drove her sword clean through two guards foolish enough to line up and give her the opportunity. "I memorized the way when they took me in."

"You weren't hooded?" Bud asked, fighting to help drive them forward.

"I was. But we've been doing this a very long time."

"Are you calling us old?" Henni retorted with a snorting laugh. Her demeanor now that her friend was free, if not entirely safe, had shifted to one of glee. Still vicious, but of a most happy sort of violence.

"We *are* getting older, you silly hag."

"Don't you dare call me that."

"Ladies, please," Bud chided. "Can you please fight *after* the battle?"

The two friends just laughed and pressed on, killing any

foolish enough to stand in their way with brutal skill. Bawb was impressed. Even in a diminished capacity, Lalaynia was a force of nature. So much so that seeing her in action, he was amazed someone had actually managed to capture her.

"That way," she called out as the stairwell came into view.

Hozark hurried ahead, his blade drenched in blood, his chest rising fast, breathing hard from the exertion. It had been an all-out fight for far too long. Fit as they all were, they needed to get out, and now.

"Hold them back," he said, then rushed the guards protecting the last caster. His Vespus glowed bright, the caster layering multiple magical defenses to stop it. The plain, unmagical dagger that embedded in his chest shocked him, his spells collapsing as he fell to his knees.

Hozark made quick work of the guards, hacking through them with a burst of magic and energy he would ordinarily not have expended. But he had a plan.

He crouched and pulled the caster close. The man knew he was dying, but a small grin nevertheless creased his lips. "You tricked me," he said quietly. "After all that, just an ordinary blade. What a clever attack."

Hozark didn't wait for a conversation, driving his fangs into the man's neck and taking what was left of his power. Seconds later he dropped the body, devoid of magic, all of it now flowing in the reinvigorated Ghalian.

"Behind me," he commanded, stepping into the stairwell. There were guards waiting, but no casters. "*Azokta!*" he bellowed, the killing spell greatly amplified by the magic he had just stolen, further increased as it was contained within the stone stairwell, blasting downward, laying waste to those in its path. "Quickly," Hozark said, briefly wobbly on his feet from the expenditure. "Before more arrive."

The others followed fast and close, all impressed by his spell, but none so much as Bawb. He had learned the words and knew the intent, but he had never seen a killing spell used, much less with this sort of magnitude. Hozark really was that much better. It was even clearer now why he was one of the Five. And it inspired Bawb even more.

They barreled down the corridor as soon as they hit ground level, using their unexpected arrival, having taken down all resistance in the stairwell faster than anyone would have imagined, to their advantage.

"The front gate is that way," Lalaynia shouted, retracing her steps in her mind as they ran. "There's a beast out front."

"Bawb!" Hozark called out.

"On it!"

Bawb rushed ahead, shifting his mind from killing to connecting, trying to make contact with the animal before they even saw it. But something was off. He couldn't sense it at all.

"I do not understand. It is gone."

"We will find out the reason soon enough," Hozark replied, bringing up a powerful shield spell and taking the lead once more.

They burst through the gate into the fresh air. The beast was there, but it lay on the ground, dead. An alarm spell sounded loud as they exited the compound but rather than trigger a new wave of attacks, something unexpected happened.

"Look!" Bud shouted, pointing to the sky.

It was an aerial assault, a dozen or more small ships bombarding the keep's defensive spells, latching to the stone walls and burrowing their way inside.

"It's Nixxa," Henni realized immediately.

Lalaynia cast an annoyed look upward. "That bitch *knew* I was being held here!"

"And she was waiting for a rescue attempt. And now that we

softened them up, she's taking advantage of it to bust in and pillage the keep," Henni added.

"Let her have it," Lalaynia said with a resigned sigh, resting her hand on her friend's shoulder. "It's sneaky as hell, and I'm pissed, but I have to admire the gumption."

"Yeah," Bud agreed. "And it will buy us time to get clear while everyone is focused on them. And speaking of which, we need to move."

"True words, my friend," Hozark said with an approving nod. "Bawb, with me. You three get your ship and get into space. We will rendezvous at the designated location."

No one needed to be told twice, the two groups rushing to their respective ships and lifting off without notice. As Bud had posited, all eyes were on the brazen assault now underway on Voralius's keep, and the bloody trio boarding their craft and departing the city hadn't caught anyone's eye. As for the shimmer ship, the two Ghalian scrambled up to its hiding space and climbed aboard without incident, making a quick ascent into space.

Hozark jumped at once, taking them to the far end of the system in a flash rather than flying conventionally. After what they'd been through it was well worth the expenditure.

Bud did the same, using their ship's Drookonus to execute the jump. Henni could do it and was still amped up from the fight, but he knew her well. After a day like today she would crash soon enough, and she'd need to conserve the energy she still had.

Both ships arrived safely, alone in the dark of space. They had fought incredible odds but had done it. Lalaynia was safe.

CHAPTER SIXTY-FOUR

Shimmer cloaked and securely mounted to the hull of Bud and Henni's ship, Hozark's craft lay quiet and still, much like the larger vessel it was riding atop. No one had pursued them, and the victorious were savoring their success, starting with a good shower to scrub out all the dried blood, sweat, and gore from their encounter, following it up with a hearty meal.

Bud, Bawb, and Hozark were eating what would be considered normal portions for men of their size and recent physical exertion. They'd burned through a lot of energy on the rescue, and their plates were piled high as a result.

As for Henni and Lalaynia, the former was eating what appeared to be her entire bodyweight, something that fascinated Bud and Hozark as much now as when they first came across her, scavenging in the streets. Lalaynia was likewise ravenous, but more from the effects of her lengthy incarceration. Her stomach, however, was not as large as her eyes in this case, having shrunk considerably during her time in bondage.

"You gonna eat that?" Henni asked, spearing a chunk of food from her friend's plate without even waiting for a reply.

"Help yourself," Lalaynia replied with a relaxed laugh. She

seemed at ease. Happy, even. And with good reason. If she hadn't been rescued when she had, who knew what gods-forsaken pit they'd have taken her to next.

"Hey, I wanted to thank you again," she said, downing a big quaff of strong ale. "You really saved my ass back there."

"You'd do it for us," Henni replied through her stuffed mouth.

"Manners!" Bud grumbled.

"What?"

"At least *try* to swallow before talking. That's gross."

"You just gutted countless people, bathing in their blood and entrails, and you want to talk about my eating habits?"

Hozark laughed and slapped Bud on the back. "Let it go, my friend. This is not a battle you can win."

"Yeah, listen to yer buddy there, Buster. I eat how I wanna eat."

"As we are all very well aware," her partner said with an amused but resigned sigh.

Lalaynia put down her drink, her face turning serious, at least for the moment. "I really mean it, you know. It was no small feat butchering that many to get me out."

"Yeah, well, we had considerable help," Bud said, glancing at Hozark.

Lalaynia locked eyes with him, giving a little nod. He returned the gesture, then resumed his meal. Bawb watched the whole exchange—or lack of one—with fascination. Here was this legendary pirate badass Valkyrie of a woman, but where Hozark was concerned, she actually seemed almost scared, even if he was on her side.

"Hey, kid, c'mere," Henni urged. "Laynia, this is Bawb. One of Hozark's protégé students. Bawb, I'd like to properly introduce Lalaynia, one of my dearest friends in the whole wide galaxy."

"A pleasure to meet you, Bawb," she said, shaking his hand with a rock-solid grasp. "I appreciate your help in springing me."

"Oh, he did more than that. He's the one who found out where you were being held in the first place."

"For real?"

"Yeah. Hell, he even went and tried to infiltrate on his own. Crazy little bastard."

"I was merely attempting to verify the intelligence, and, if it proved correct, perhaps achieve a quick resolution to the issue."

"And you're damn lucky you weren't killed in the process," Bud noted. "But no one can deny it. The kid's got some serious skills, even at this age."

"Like another young friend of yours, eh?" Lalaynia joked. "Speaking of which, how is young Happizano these days?"

Bud shrugged. "Not young anymore, for starters. Hozark? How's Hap doing these days? He still training with Master Turong?"

"Off and on. He cycles between schools, always working to improve himself," the Ghalian replied. "Quite a change from when we first encountered him."

"I'll say," Bud agreed, turning to the teen. "Hap was a handful, let me tell you. But he came around."

"I know him," Bawb informed him. "We actually met when I visited Master Turong myself."

"Oh, hell no," Henni laughed. "Hozark, you getting Bawb and Hap together? There's gonna be a world of mischief if those two ever—"

"Happizano was merely tending to his studies," the Ghalian replied. "But yes, the pair would make a formidable duo, if ever the need arose. But he will be more cautious in the future, yes?"

"I am sorry, Master Hozark. I know I was reckless pursuing the lead like that."

Lalaynia turned to face him fully. "Hey, I wouldn't be here

without you, so whatever you think you may have done wrong, you're *always* going to be good with me. Ya got it?"

"I do."

"I owe you a big one, Bawb. If you *ever* need my help, you will have it."

"Thank you," was all he replied.

The question had been lingering in his mind. If this woman was so fearsome, backed up by scores of loyal men and women, how was it she had been captured in the first place? As if reading his mind, Bud asked the somewhat indelicate question.

"Hey, Laynia, now that you've had a chance to enjoy the sweet taste of freedom, I was meaning to ask you—"

"How I was captured."

"Well, I—"

"It's an obvious question, and one with a really unimpressive, and frankly embarrassing answer. Long and short of it, we were out drinking on Gravlax. You know the place. Kinda damp, smokey, smells like fish, but the taverns serve strong drinks and are always welcoming to our kind. Well, there I was, safe and cozy in the company of my crew, when some kid delivered a bottle and a message. Said it was from an old friend staying in town. Well, you know me and free drinks. I checked the bottle for poisons or spells, like I always do, but in my haste, I didn't check the glass the little bastard so casually put in front of me."

"They drugged the glass, not the bottle," Bawb realized.

"Yep. All the others drank from the same bottle without a problem, so I thought nothing of it when my head felt a little fuzzy. Sometimes I do get carried away, you know."

"Do we ever," Henni chuckled.

"So I stumble out of there, heading for my ship, when next thing I know, I'm on the ground. A couple of pirates said they'd help me to the ship, but they weren't my crew."

"Disguised as your people?" Hozark asked, curious how they had managed to take her without a fight.

"Yep. And with my vision blurring, all I saw were their outfits. Honestly, I was glad they were helping me back to the ship. My head was absolutely spinning. When I saw they'd led me to a different ship, it was too late. They slipped a control collar on me and hit me with a massive stun spell. When I woke up we were already in flight."

"But who took you? And why?" Henni asked.

"Funny thing, that," she said, turning her gaze back toward the Ghalian Master in their midst. "It seemed they were looking for information about *you*."

"Me?" Hozark marveled. "How odd a manner to do so."

"I thought so too. But I heard one of 'em talking. Talking about stuff we all did years ago. I mean, we've all made enemies along the way, but this sounded like it stemmed from a time when we were *all* fighting the same battle."

They all knew when she was talking about, but that was ages ago, and their unsuspected enemy was long, long dead. Hozark had made quite sure of it.

"Well, it would seem I have a little investigating to do," Hozark mused, not worried, but rather curious. It would not be the first time someone had sought him out. As a rule, it did not go well for those who succeeded.

A proximity alarm sounded, jarring them all from the story. Bud quickly activated defense spells, but a moment later the skree crackled to life.

"Captain? You there?" a gruff voice asked.

Lalaynia activated the skree. "Yeah, it's me, Duggan. Glad to hear your voice."

"And I yours, Cap. You okay? Who do we need to kill?"

"The answer is yes to the first question, and I'm not sure yet about the second. But we'll hash all of that out later. For now, we're having a little shindig. Why don't you and the crew pull up and join us? Then we'll be on our way and let our friends get back to whatever mischief they have planned."

"Sounds like a plan, Cap. Bud? Henni? See you two misfits shortly."

"Can't wait," Bud replied with a cheerful laugh.

"Who was that?" Bawb asked, more than a little out of the loop.

"Take a look," the pilot replied, pointing to the nearest window.

Bawb rose from the table and went to the window to take a look. It was dark out there, and the ships were not running any exterior illumination, but their outlines against the stars were clear. This was Lalaynia's fleet. An armada, really. And they had *all* come running when word got out she had been rescued. It seemed she really was that connected, and Bawb was very glad she was on his side. One day he might actually call on her for assistance, but he sincerely hoped that would be a long time coming. Longer, if he was lucky.

And as Bawb grew older, one thing held true. Luck was, more often than not, definitely on his side.

CHAPTER SIXTY-FIVE

Bawb arrived back at the training house late the following day, Hozark having allowed him a long, restful sleep on the flight back. The boy had done far more than hold his own in his first true test by combat, and if ever there was a time, he had certainly earned it now. Training would commence again once he was back with his classmates, though he clearly outstripped them in more ways than one.

Finally, they touched down at the landing field nearest the Ghalian compound. There was no need to take a long walk to decompress and reacclimate to life this time around. The festivities aboard Bud and Henni's ship and the new friendships forged in the process had done more than enough in that regard.

Bawb felt, for the first time in his life, like he was truly a part of something, and more than just being part of a class. This was like he really belonged. Before, he had been striving to reach a goal, hoping to one day reach the heights he aspired to. But that wasn't the same as bonding by blood and violence. And lessons learned and perfected in class would never be the same as those applied in the real world.

"You carry yourself like a man," Hozark said with an appreciative glance as Bawb gathered up his few possessions.

"I feel different."

"You are. You have proven yourself not only to me, but to my most trusted of friends outside our order. While pride is something we Ghalian eschew, perhaps, just for a moment, you should feel free to indulge."

"Thank you, Master Hozark," he replied, unwrapping a small towel. In it was Hozark's enchanted dagger. He handed it back to its owner with a little bow. "I scrubbed out all of the blood that had dried on it. I also took the liberty to hone and polish the blade. It suffered a few small nicks during the conflict."

Hozark pulled the blade free, holding it up to the light, admiring the work Bawb had done. "It is pristine," he noted, resheathing the weapon. "You have done a fine job with it."

"Thank you. And thank you for the privilege of allowing me to wield it. I have seen you carry it for years, but to actually use it in combat was, well, a joy, for lack of a better word."

"Oh, I understand completely. This dagger has seen much use over the years, and it has rarely met its match in close combat. I am glad it helped keep you safe. That, and your rather impressive use of your combative training, not only with the blade, but also magic."

"It all just seemed to make sense."

"As it is supposed to. Once you internalize your lessons and they become a part of your natural reactions rather than something you must consciously think to perform, then, and only then, are you truly ready to rise to higher levels. And you, my boy, are most certainly ready."

He reached out, clasping Bawb's wrist, his hands encompassing the konus resting warmly on his flesh. Bawb felt a strange tingle, the metal band heating for a moment, flashing bright then settling back to its normal patina.

"What just happened?"

Hozark released his grip, locking eyes with the teen. "I have just added to, and unlocked, additional power in your konus. A significant amount, in fact."

He's right. He just poured a lot *of magic into me*, the konus confirmed.

"I do not understand."

"You have earned this, Bawb. You took a natural caster's power and wielded it with great skill and precision. You did not get lost in the rush, nor did you squander it foolishly. You are ready for this, and you now have more power at your disposal. But remember, you must not tap into it unless you absolutely have to. You are not meant to have this much magic available to you at so young an age."

"I will be careful."

"I trust you will, and I am confident you will use it wisely and with all the skill and judgment you showed in battle. But for now, at least, you are still a Vessel. A trainee. And favoritism is frowned upon, so do keep this between you and me."

"I will not let you down," he replied, standing tall and feeling like he could take on the world. "I will make you proud."

Hozark reached out and ruffled his hair, a proud look on his face. Something uncharacteristic of a stoic Master Ghalian, let alone one of the Five. "You already have, my boy," Hozark said. "You already have."

Bawb walked back to the compound alone, Hozark leaving the planet at once to investigate what Lalaynia had revealed to them. Bawb would have liked nothing more than to have gone with, but Hozark was right. He was still a student, and no matter what adventures he had been on, his training was still far from complete.

Whatever they had in store for him next, whatever torturous lessons he would have to endure, Bawb found himself actually looking forward to it.

"You were gone after the last trial!" Usalla blurted when Bawb strode into the bunkhouse. "What happened to you? I was worried."

She quickly got ahold of herself, calming her demeanor to a more appropriate level.

"I mean to say, *we* were all wondering what had happened to you."

Bawb's lips creased slightly, as if he knew something that no one else did. And in fact, he did. But this was just one more part of Ghalian life he would have to get used to. Keeping secrets.

"It was nothing," he lied. "Just a training exercise."

"But you were taken by Master Hozark."

"This was not the first time."

"True, but it is interesting one of the Five would spend so much time with a student."

"Perhaps he just sees potential in me," Bawb said with a wry grin.

"Perhaps," she replied, a smile spreading across her lips as well. "Quite a bit of potential, indeed."

She looked around at the other students, all of them relaxing at the end of a long day. They were done with classes until the following morning, the remainder of the evening now their own free time.

"So, it was a training exercise, you say?"

"Yes, a training exercise."

A sparkle flashed in Usalla's eye. "I am in need of training as well. Are you available?" she asked, her intention clear as day.

Bawb felt a warmth growing in his belly. “Indeed,” he replied as calmly as possible. “The usual place?”

“I will see you there,” she said, walking out of the bunkhouse, a spring in her step.

Bawb watched her leave, musing over his life. How he had started and where he was now. This existence of trials and adventure, with death and intrigue around every corner. He headed for the door and his rendezvous with Usalla.

It was quite the life, indeed, this Ghalian way, and he wouldn’t have it any other way.

PREVIEW—ASSASSIN: RISE OF THE GEIST

The tapestries were ornate, hanging to the ground. Almost tasteful yet crossing the line to overly opulent and clearly quite costly, as were all of the things belonging to the lady of the house. In fact, the overall feel of the expansive compound was one of wealth, power, and order, and everything within her walls was always in its place.

That is, except for the two guards who now lay quite dead, their bodies hidden out of view beneath a large ornamental table in the main entertaining hall. Master Kopal, the assassin responsible for their unexpected demise, had been fortunate the oversized tablecloth hung all the way to the ground rather than partway. The stronghold's owner having a penchant for opulence and overkill rather than understated good taste helped him in that regard.

He had spent days infiltrating the series of connected buildings, carefully maintaining his disguise as he slowly worked his way through the layers of internal security his target had set in place over the years.

Emmik Forbin was her name, and she was a low-level player in the Council of Twenty. But what she lacked in power of her own, she made up for in connections. Connections and information. And now it seemed someone wanted her removed from the equation, the likely result of blackmail gone wrong.

Whatever the case, the contract was good, the money held safely in escrow by a trusted intermediary. All that remained was the completion of the task. And with Kopal on the job, it was as good as done.

His shimmer ship was so close he could throw a stone from the compound's rooftop and hit it, but no one was any the wiser, the cloaking spell holding strong and true. The ship safely hovered inches above the roof of a nearby structure, ready for his departure. All that remained was one thing.

Kill Emmik Forbin.

It was a straightforward mission, simple and to the point. But even so, his infiltration was slow and steady. The Ghalian took no chances. That was what kept them alive.

On the fifth day inside the emmik's walls, he finally took the identity of Markis, one of her closest assistants, hiding the slumbering body of the man beneath the clean linen in a nearby supply closet. If he had timed it right, no one would be changing the sheets for at least another day. That gave him ample time to complete his task and make his silent escape.

There were a series of interconnected chambers in the emmik's personal quarters, but few guards, if any. She felt safe here, deep within the layers she had protecting her every waking and slumbering hour. It was that overconfidence he would use to his advantage.

The two guards had been a surprise. No one was supposed to be patrolling the receiving area. But he was a Ghalian Master, and he had learned long ago that plans changed on the fly quite often. He would simply adapt and carry on. Once he dealt with them, of course.

"You there! You are not supposed to be in here!"

"It's me, Markis. You know me."

"Then what's the pass phrase?"

Master Kopal hadn't heard anything about any pass phrase.

"Don't be ridiculous," he said, a broad grin on his face as he drew closer to the two guards. "I don't use a pass phrase," he continued, hoping his bluff would work. "Come on, now. You know that."

The guard nearest seemed to relax, his shoulders lowering slightly. "Just had to check. You know the new rules."

"Yes, of course. And a good thing you did."

Kopal felt the other guard drawing his sword before he saw it, his senses honed to a razor's edge. He spun at once, driving his concealed dagger into the man's throat, silencing him in an instant. The blade flew into the eye of the other guard a moment later, ending their game as soon as it had begun.

This was unexpected. Something had changed. But there was no time for leisurely investigation. He had planned on no extraneous casualties on this contract, but with these two dead, he was now on a ticking clock. It would only be so long before their absence was noted. Kopal dragged the bodies beneath the table and wiped up their blood with their clothing before stuffing the soiled rags into their wounds. It wasn't much, but it would at least keep them from leaking out everywhere and revealing their location.

He rose to his feet and continued on, faster now, well aware of his new time constraints. He reached the hallway connecting several anterooms to the emmik's main suite. Kopal straightened his clothing and walked calmly ahead, his disguise in place, acting as normally and calm as the real Markis would have.

He reached the end of the hall and stopped. The emmik's door was ajar. It seemed fortune was favoring him after all. This would only serve to speed his completion of the contract. He pushed the door open and stepped inside.

"Emmik Forbin?" he called out. "It is Markis. I have a message I've been tasked with delivering to you."

The emmik walked through the far door leading from her bed chamber.

"Markis? Yes, what is it?"

"A message. Shall I share it with you?" he asked, walking closer.

The emmik's lips curled in a wicked grin. "Oh, you will not be coming any closer, Assassin."

She cast a fierce series of spells, both offensive and defensive, sending Kopal diving aside before he could launch an attack of his own. It seemed they had some additional pass phrase he was unaware of. There was little to do now but fight and kill the woman before she could raise an alarm.

As the other doors burst open, he realized it was much too late for that.

Scores of guards rushed through, along with additional casters, all of them targeting the lone intruder. Kopal was hit hard, the magic cracking his defensive spells, spears and thrown blades penetrating his projectile-obstructing spells. Enchanted blades, he realized, as he felt hot blood seeping into his tunic.

This wasn't an assassination gone wrong. This was a trap.

He shifted his plan at once, the plan for his assassination a thing of the past. All that mattered now was getting out in one piece. That meant *everyone* was a target now. Drawing both his concealed blades, he flew into battle, laying waste to the onslaught of guards as best he could. But he was tremendously outnumbered. Whoever had planned this knew the skills of a Ghalian, as well as their limitations. And with multiple casters safely behind layers of defenses, they could bombard him with magic with impunity, wearing him down until, eventually, one of the blows he took would prove to be fatal.

Kopal, a great warrior if ever there was one, turned and ran.

There was no shame in it. In fact, he was a staunch supporter of flight when warranted. And it had never been more so than right now.

Spells and spears impacted with his defenses, the magic at his back barely stopping the onslaught. This was overkill. The number of forces committed to stopping this one man would have been ridiculous for anyone, even a Ghalian Master. More wounds opened, and precious blood seeped out as attacks landed. There was simply no way he could block all of them, and likewise, the odds were so stacked against him, he could not hope to take on so many opponents.

The routes to all three exits he had planned to use were now choked with guards, bristling with weapons and ill intent. He was trapped. There was no way out.

Kopal felt himself growing weaker. He drew deep from his konus and healed the most severe wounds as best he could, slowing the bleeding if he couldn't stop it entirely. On the run, there was only so much he could do. His head pivoted, searching for something, anything that might aid him in his time of need. Only one thing presented itself.

And it was going to suck.

He barely dodged a slicing sword, disemboweling its owner as he dove aside. But he didn't stop to retrieve the fallen weapon. He ran full speed ahead, casting the most powerful force spell he knew. He just hoped it was enough to break the spell holding the window shut.

Kopal burst out into the nothingness of open air, tumbling rapidly toward the street below. He cast a protective spell as best he was able, doing all he could to cushion the impact, but even with the magic softening the blow, he felt bones break and organs tear from the hard landing. Ignoring the pain, he forced himself to his feet at once, managing an awkward run until he ducked into a low building. Guards were already on his trail, hurrying in after him moments later.

A burst of wind greeted them when they reached the roof, the shimmer-cloaked ship blasting invisibly into the sky with great speed and force. The guards called for aerial support but knew it was too late. The assassin had managed to escape. But the emmik was safe, and her attacker would likely not survive their flight to wherever it was they were fleeing.

Master Kopal managed to activate the Drookonus in his ship long enough to jump the vessel clear of the planet. He then sent a distress skree on the secret Ghalian wavelength, calling for help and giving his position before finally slipping into unconsciousness.

AFTERWORD

For all y'all who have been with me over all these years and all these books, thank you from the bottom of my heart. For those of you new to these characters, welcome to the madness.

Now, as for the business of indie author life. I don't want to be redundant, but I've got to reiterate how your ratings and reviews are so crucial to a book's success.

Your feedback not only helps stoke the creative fires and keep the stories coming, but it allows me the freedom to keep writing them. So, I'm asking pretty-please, if you can spare a moment, please leave an honest rating/review.

See you on Bawb's next adventure!

~ Scott Baron ~

ALSO BY SCOTT BARON

Standalone Novels

Living the Good Death

Vigor Mortis

The Clockwork Chimera Series

Daisy's Run

Pushing Daisy

Daisy's Gambit

Chasing Daisy

Daisy's War

The Dragon Mage Series

Bad Luck Charlie

Space Pirate Charlie

Dragon King Charlie

Magic Man Charlie

Star Fighter Charlie

Portal Thief Charlie

Rebel Mage Charlie

Warp Speed Charlie

Checkmate Charlie

Castaway Charlie

Wild Card Charlie

End Game Charlie

The Space Assassins Series

The Interstellar Slayer

The Vespus Blade

The Ghalian Code

Death From the Shadows

Hozark's Revenge

The Book of Bawb Series

Assassins' Academy

Assassin's Apprentice

Assassin: Rise of the Geist

Assassin and the Dragon Mage

The Warp Riders Series

Deep Space Boogie

Belly of the Beast

Rise of the Forgotten

Pandora's Menagerie

Engines of Chaos

Seeds of Damocles

Odd and Unusual Short Stories:

The Best Laid Plans of Mice: An Anthology

Snow White's Walk of Shame

The Tin Foil Hat Club

Lawyers vs. Demons

The Queen of the Nutters

Lost & Found

ABOUT THE AUTHOR

A native Californian, Scott Baron was born in Hollywood, which he claims may be the reason for his rather off-kilter sense of humor.

Before taking up residence in Venice Beach, Scott first spent a few years abroad in Florence, Italy before returning home to Los Angeles and settling into the film and television industry, where he has worked as an on-set medic for many years.

Aside from mending boo-boos and owies, and penning books and screenplays, Scott is also involved in indie film and theater scene both in the U.S. and abroad.

Made in United States
North Haven, CT
26 January 2025